TRACY M. JOYCE

RADA

TALES OF ALTAICA

A COMPANION SERIES TO
THE CHRONICLES OF ALTAICA

Published by Cassilis and Co in 2022

A Cataloguing-in-Publication entry is available from the National Library of Australia

ISBN: 978-0-9924619-6-6 (pbk) ISBN: 978-0-9924619-7-3(ebook)

Cover design by Karri Klawiter (www.artbykarri.com)

Map of Altaica by Misty Beee

CONTENT WARNING

Rada is a darker novel than my earlier ones – Altaica and Asena Blessed.

Since it deals with the Zaragarian Empire, whose invading army Isaura ran from, it was only natural that the content became more grim.

As such I'd like to post the follow content warning.

Sensitive issues dealt with include:

Rape (Implied / off page)
Genocide
Torture
Derogatory language

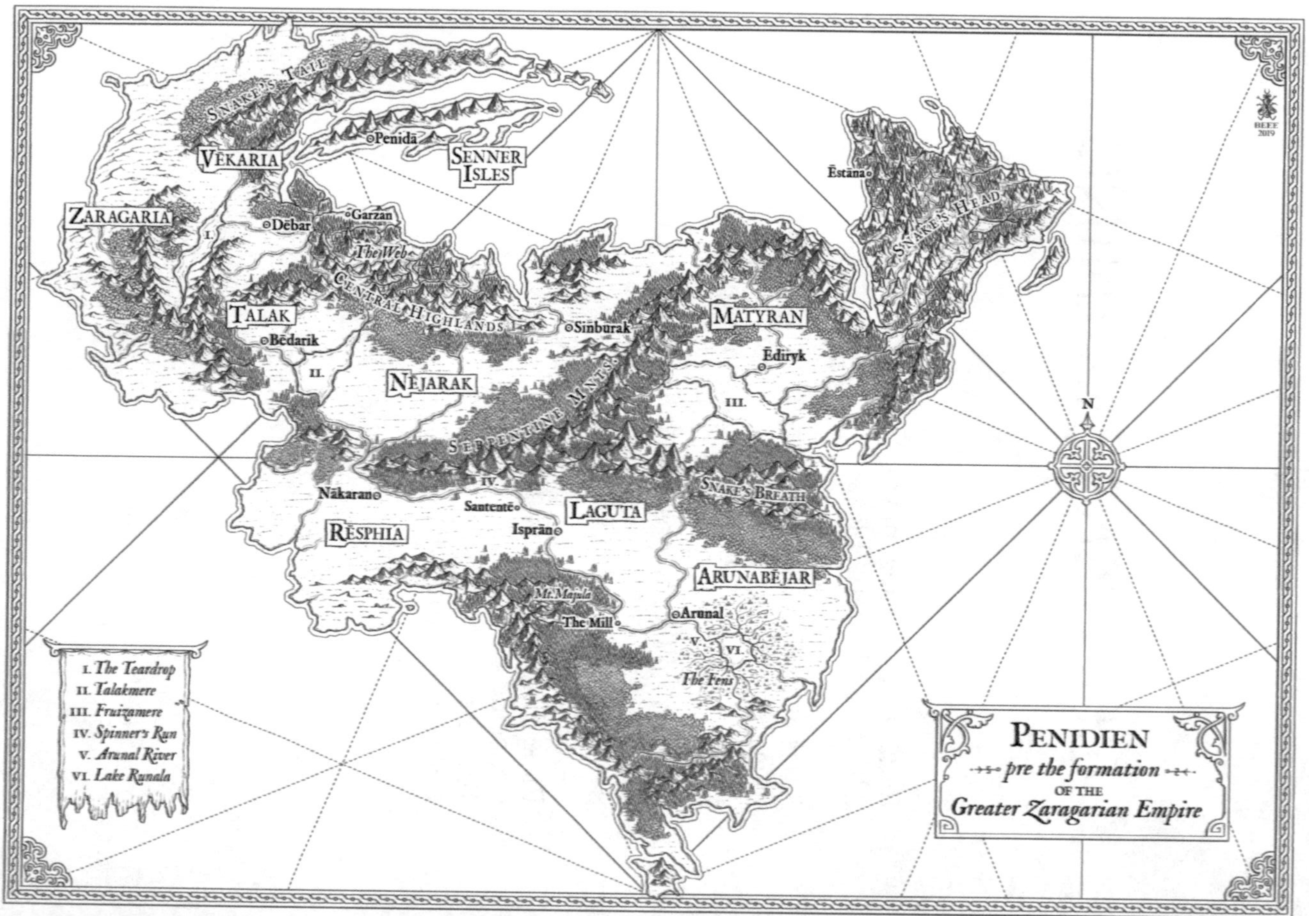

SNAKE'S TAIL
Penida
VEKARIA
SENNER ISLES
Ēstāna
SNAKE'S HEAD
ZARAGARIA
Garzan
Dēbar
The Web
MATYRAN
CENTRAL HIGHLANDS
Sinburak
TALAK
Ēdiryk
Bēdarik
NEJARAK
III.
II.
SERPENTINE MNTS.
IV.
Nākaran
SNAKE'S BREATH
Santentē
LAGUTA
Isprān
RESPHIA
ARUNABĒJAR
Mt. Mepula
Arunal
The Mill
V.
VI.
The Fens
N
I. The Teardrop
II. Talakmere
III. Fruizamere
IV. Spinner's Run
V. Arunal River
VI. Lake Renala
PENIDIEN
pre the formation
OF THE
Greater Zaragarian Empire
BEEE 2019

For Katie and Katy

CHAPTER 1

"I HATE DRESSES!" RADA tugged at the dress in horror. "But the emperor's coming and I have to look pretty. Yuk!" She screwed her face up in disgust. "And they did my hair funny! 'Stay here, Mistress Rada, so we can find you. And stay clean.'" Rada rolled her eyes. "The emperor's a grumpy old fart." She kicked a shoe under her bed. "Mami didn't come this morning," Rada said to her bear Grokky. "She always comes in the morning. We have breakfast together. She didn't come. They won't let me see her 'cause the baby's coming." Rada crossed her arms and stamped a foot.

"What's that, Grokky? What did you say?" She picked him up, cocking her head. "Good idea, Grokky. You always have the best ideas." Rada put the bear reverently back on her bed, grabbed her hemp sling, threw a small bag over her shoulder, and raced to the door.

She poked her head around the corner. All clear. Rada ran to the central garden and stared up at her mother's open bedroom window. Clambering onto the base of a portico support, she stood on tiptoe and strained to hear.

Nothing.

"Evika," she muttered, jumping down and kicking the grass. Pouting, she twiddled her sling and stared dejectedly around the garden. A small smile crept onto her face. With one hand, Rada slipped the loop at the end of the fine rope sling over her middle finger and held the other knotted end between her thumb and index finger. She fished a pebble from her bag and placed it into the woven cradle halfway along the rope. Rada prowled the garden, took aim and cast her sling, sending the stone rocketing forward and shooting a rose off its stalk.

Crouching, she stalked her enemies. Flick. Fall. One by one, the rose buds tumbled until only one remained, tucked at the back of the last bush. "You can't hide!" She loosed another stone. "Die! Bullseye!" She cheered as the flower fell to the ground in a shower of white petals. Her laughter echoed around the garden. Rada clamped her hand over her mouth and spun to check if anyone had heard. She spied two slaves climbing the stairs from the kitchen carrying trays laden with pastries. An evil grin lit her face. She wrapped her scarf around the bottom half of her face, loaded her sling, and dashed across to the portico. Hiding behind a column, she listened as the footsteps drew closer.

Rada pounced and landed in front of the two startled slaves. "I'm a bandit! Your pastries or your life!"

"A bandit!" The older slave suppressed a grin. "Oh my!"

The younger slave squeaked. "You're robbing us!"

"There's a toll on the emperor's road! I demand tribute." Rada aimed the sling's loaded cradle at the slaves. With a sly grin, she swung it casually, sizing up the best place to strike them. The younger slave's eyes widened in fear. A manic giggle escaped Rada before she clamped her lips tightly shut and narrowed her eyes.

"We've no choice. We've got to pay tribute," the older one said.

"But the food is for the emperor's banquet."

"Can't you see how dangerous this bandit is? She's famed in all of Talak for her ruthlessness."

Rada nodded enthusiastically before she remembered to scowl and growl.

The older woman nudged the younger. "Just hand over that silver plate on the side. The one with lemon and berry tarts. It's the tribute plate."

Rada stood on tiptoes, peering at the platters. "Apple cakes?"

"There's no apple cakes! But please don't hurt us! We pray these fresh-baked tarts will do."

Canting her head, Rada screwed up her nose. "Throw in one of those honey rolls and I'll let you go... this time. Put the tray on the ground. You've got 'til I count to ten."

The young slave put the plate down and the other one hauled her along. "Come on, quick!"

"One... two... three... four." The slaves almost jogged with their platters. "Five... six..." They were not quite at the door into the building. "Seven, eight, nine."

"Run!" A squeal escaped the young slave.

"Ten!" Rada roared with laughter as they bolted through the doors. "Mmm, treaties!" She took the plate and sat on the grass where she could watch her mother's window.

"Babies are slow." Sighing, she lined up the large flower head of an agapanthus. She missed. "Evika!" Rada ran over, sized up the long, thick stalk, ran her hand down it and tried to snap it off. It didn't break. "Stupid plant." On her hands and knees in the soil, she worked on the stem, twisting and pulling at it. Grunting with effort, she broke it off and landed on her backside in the dirt. She stood, snapped off the flower head, wiped her hands on her dress that left green stains in their wake. "Ta da!" She brandished the frond like a sword, slashing and spinning her way around the garden.

A cry came from her mother's room. Rada whirled about and stared. *What's happening?* The midwife came to the window and looked down at a bundle in her arms. *She doesn't look happy. She looks kind of scared.* Rada bit her lip. *Something's wrong. Mami?*

She raced into the house, through the hallways and up the stairs until she was outside her mother's rooms. "Let me in!"

Two burly guards barred her way. "Mistress Rada, we cannot. The midwife is still within."

"But I saw her at the window! With the baby."

"Mistress Rada, you must wait. Once she's gone, we'll let you in and not before."

Rada stomped a short distance away and sat on the floor, staring morosely at the guards. She toyed with her sling. "No one listens."

⟶

The harsh, summer sun of mid-afternoon reached through the open window and the faint splash of water from the courtyard fountain drifted into the room. Exhausted from her labour, Jadzia was dimly aware of Rada in the lush garden below. Her high, energetic voice as she swash-buckled her way through Neeren's roses and robbed the slaves was scant balm as she tried to visualise the little bandit.

Lady Jadzia watched the midwife examining the baby in the light by the window. The midwife's lips moved in prayer. "What are you muttering, woman?"

The midwife stared at the bawling bundle in horror, refusing to meet Jadzia's eyes.

"What's wrong?" Jadzia demanded. She jerked her head away as a handmaiden moved to wipe the sweat from her brow. *Damn midwife shouldn't be here. I've had enough babes; my women know enough.*

The midwife shook her head, bent over the baby and wrapped it hastily.

Katya, Jadzia's prime handmaiden, moved silently behind the woman. Two other female slaves blocked the door.

The midwife turned, bumping into Katya, gasped and gripped the baby. It shuddered and its tiny red brow creased in outrage as it drew in a lungful of air and screamed.

"Katya, take it from that woman now!" Jadzia ordered.

The midwife backed away, clutching the baby like a shield. Drawing herself up, stiffly indignant, she said. "I must take it to my Lord Bashtan. I have my orders."

Jadzia pushed herself upright on her bed. "You will give it to me."

"But Lord Bashtan's orders were—"

"My husband can inspect it in here."

The midwife's voice shook. "If I don't... he'll be furious..."

Katya drew a dagger.

Jadzia's voice was near a growl. "Be more worried about the danger in here, woman."

Katya herded the woman to Jadzia's bed. The midwife's hands shook as she handed the baby over.

Gently, Jadzia placed the baby on the bed beside her and uncovered it. Her mouth opened in silent surprise. "Don't let that woman leave. It's a girl, Katya. Her foot... She has a club foot; so badly it appears as if her leg is twisted too. And there's a purple birth mark spiralling down the left side of her neck from behind her ear to her collarbone."

"Doubly damned," whispered Katya.

"Katya, remember who you are! We're not ignorant Talaks! I refuse to allow their superstitions to take my child."

Katya hung her head. "Madam, forgive me. I thought only of the future, of what will lie in store for her. Shall I fetch your guards, my lady?"

"No. They're chosen by Bashtan and in his pay. We must ensure her future." Jadzia placed the child on her breast, smiling as her daughter suckled.

The midwife gasped. "Madam, what are you doing? It—?"

"Enough! She is no longer 'it'. Now she's tasted of this world her spirit is anchoring to me and no longer utterly untethered. Once she's named, The Weaver will start her thread in The Great Web and bind her soul there."

Katya pressed her dagger to the midwife's back. A pinpoint of blood soaked through the woman's blouse. "Shall I kill her?"

Jadzia hesitated. "No. It will solve nothing. Keep her a moment longer, then she can report to my husband." Exhaustion dragged at Jadzia, and she struggled to order her thoughts. "My husband's guards are still outside the door, yes?"

"Indeed, my lady."

She sighed in relief. "We've some time then, little one," Jadzia said to the now quiet babe. "All of you, remember I am of the First Circle; pure Zaragarian. She is of my blood, not his, and not cursed. Now get me out of this bed and dressed in my finest clothes."

"Careful, Madam, you've bled a lot this time."

Tight lines pinched her face and her golden-tanned skin was pale. "Yes, but one way or another, this time will be the last." To the midwife, she said, "Did you bring any stodan root with you?"

"Yes, my lady. A tincture, you'll need only a small spoonful twice a day. Any more will be harmful to..." She closed her eyes, grimacing. "To... the... child."

Jadzia swaddled the babe, tucked tiny clenched hands under the soft blanket, and placed the girl nearby on the bed. "Ladies, I must be on my feet by the time Bashtan gets here." As her women quickly cleaned her, Jadzia eyed the garments her other maids drew from her wardrobe. "No, not that. It will be months before I can wear it. The soft silk tunic from the Senner Isles – the one that ties at the side, and the deep blue Vēkarian culottes. Loose but elegant. Yes, and those gold-embroidered, black-suede boots." Jadzia winced as she stood on unsteady legs. Her vision blurred and dizziness almost overwhelmed her. Bent double, she clutched the nearest of her women for support before half collapsing on the edge of the bed. *Gods, give me strength. I can barely stand.*

Jadzia drew a deep breath, rose unsteadily once more and stood gripping the tall bedpost for support while her women managed to dress her. Finally, they placed a red and black silk brocade coat with wide sleeves upon their mistress. Embroidered on the back of the garment in gold was her family's coat-of-arms: a shield bearing a huge snarling lynx encircled by a viper. The symbol surrounded by the emperor's own – subjugated yet protected. Loyalty and security – one easily given, the other hard won. A jewelled leather belt completed the outfit.

"Let her go, Katya." Barely sparing the midwife a glance, Jadzia said, "Do your duty, woman, and never let me lay eyes upon you again."

Jadzia gathered her Vēkarian kadag dagger from the bedside table. The simple wooden grip was shaped for her hand and a notch was cut into the blade near the hilt. A fuller ran along its flat back and the blade curved shallowly, broadened, then tapered to a flat point. She admired its elegant, wicked beauty.

"Let him remember my rank," she said as she slid the dagger into its sheath at her waist.

The door of the room flew open. Jadzia snatched the babe to her and her women moved to stand between their mistress and the entrance, each with daggers drawn.

Red-faced and breathless, Rada stood before them. Her jaw dropped when she saw the women arrayed for battle.

"Shut the door," Jadzia said quickly. "What is it, daughter?" The child still stood, mouth agape. "Speak!"

"I... I saw the midwife leave and I wanted to see," her gaze darted to the bundle Jadzia clutched so tightly, "and ..." She looked at them in dismay.

"And?"

"The emperor is arriving. I heard the slaves saying he's passed through the town."

Jadzia stifled a sob, swallowed it painfully back, and broke into a shattered grin. "Thanks be to Hokati." She beckoned Rada to her and hugged her. "Now we've hope. Rada, you must get to him before anyone else. Before Neeren assumes my role and welcomes him. After that, you'll have no chance."

Rada gasped. "She'll be angry if she knows I saw the emperor before her."

"She'll not touch you, Rada. That, I promise you."

"I wish Abaya were here."

"Your sister is married and gone. Even if she were here, she wouldn't do as I ask. She believes as your father does, but you know better." Jadzia sank to the bed and revealed the babe. "Rada, this is your sister."

The girl ran her finger across the babe's face. "She's tiny." Rada's nose wrinkled. "She's a bit icky and kind of red. Will she stay like that?"

Jadzia reined in her impatience. Every delay meant the midwife drew closer to her husband. If the emperor was close,

Bashtan might be torn between greeting him and dealing with her. If not, once that damn midwife spoke, he'd be here to make sure his shame was never witnessed by the emperor. *I should've killed the woman.* Jadzia forced her hand not to tremble and cupped Rada's cheek. "My little love, you must listen to me very carefully. I don't care how you do it, just get to the emperor before Neeren and the welcoming ceremony. Say..." *Gods, what can she say? She's only six. She shouldn't have to do this.*

Jadzia struggled to think what to tell her. "Rada, listen carefully. You must give the emperor this brooch and say Mami begs that he understand I honour our alliance at this time above all else. Do you understand? You must tell him exactly this. Repeat it back."

"Mami understands... Mami says she honours our alliance and begs him."

"No, try again... Mami begs that he understand..."

"She... honours the alliance..." Rada shook her head, fisting her hands. "I can't do this, Mami! Why do I have to?"

"Rada, you must. Lives depend on you getting that message to the emperor. Your sister's leg is twisted and will stay that way. Your father will see her as a punishment from the gods; worse, a curse. You know what that will mean."

Rada nodded. "Papi will take her and..." Her gaze fell, she swallowed nervously and murmured, "She'll never come back. Just like Lady Shinta's baby." Rada met her mother's intense gaze, saying in a rush, "Can't I just tell the emperor that Papi will take her and he must help?"

"No. That will cause a different storm. One you'll not weather so well. The emperor will understand your message. You're of my blood, you're strong; you can do this. Try again."

"Mami... begs... you understand that she..." Rada faltered.

"Honours our alliance at this time above all else," Jadzia said.

Rada nodded, straightened, and drew a deep breath. "Got it. Mami begs that you understand that she... honours the alliance..." Rada bit her lip, concentrating. "At this time above all else."

"Good. First give him the brooch, then..."

"I got it. First the brooch, then the Mami says bit."

"Don't forget. Now go, quick as you can."

"Yes, Mami." Rada clenched the brooch in her fist and ran from the room.

Jadzia laid the babe in her crib. "Lock and barricade both the bedroom door and that of the sitting room. Quietly. They won't hold for long. Ladies, you'll need courage. I thank you for your service. Should we live, you'll be free to choose your own path. Katya, open the chest by the window; give me my bow." She took one last look at her babe and kissed her brow. "One way or another, this child they think is cursed will be our freedom."

⟶

Rada ran down the corridor, the brooch clutched tightly in her hand. The delicate patter of her leather sandals on the mosaic floor was soon drowned out.

A solid metallic clink on the tiles rang down the hall.

Tap. Tap.

Rada spun around and gasped. She ran on, small arms pumping.

Tap. Tap.

Heavy brisk footfalls chased her — a drumming counterpoint to the *tap, tap* which drew ever closer.

A cross junction of halls lay ahead, with the villa entrance at the end of a corridor on her right. She couldn't go that way.

Tap. Tap. Tap.

All the wives would be there waiting for the emperor.

Tap. Tap. Tap.

Neeren would be there.

Rada chewed her lip, and glanced over her shoulder as she ran. Her eyes widened; she drew a deep breath ready to speed up.

Slam!

She was pushed roughly and landed sprawled on her back on the cold, hard tiles. The brooch fell from her hand and slid across the floor. Frightened, she tracked its path until it collided with a stone column.

"Watch where you're going, girl!"

Rada stared up into the deep brown eyes of Neeren, second wife of her father. Beside her, grinning smugly, stood Neeren's eldest daughter, Sasha, and her youngest, Anfisa, who peeked from behind her sister's skirts.

Tap. Tap.

The air behind Rada stirred, sending chills across her bare arms.

Tap. Tap.

She looked anxiously over her shoulder.

"Rada! Look at me!" Rada's stomach knotted and her mouth went dry at the predatory gleam in Neeren's eyes.

Tap. Tap.

"Rada!" Neeren stamped her foot.

She towered above Rada in full court garb – a high-collared, ornately embroidered, tightly fitted dress covered by a gossamer, flowing cape. Her braided black hair snaked through a delicate silver, floral headpiece embedded with rubies – a dark, glimmering halo. Her fine face was powdered white, her eyes lined with kohl and her lips painted red. Rada thought she looked like a one of the porcelain figurines in the villa morning room, beautiful and cold.

"Rada, what are you doing racing down the halls like some hoyden? You haven't got that sling with you again, have you?"

Tap. Tap.

Before Rada could answer, the cold black tip of a metal staff plunged to the floor between her and Neeren, narrowly missing Rada's fingers. She snatched her hand back. The solid thump of a large footstep landed next to her and the hem of a black robe brushed over her leg, concealing the foot that stood on the hem of her dress, pinning her.

Rada let out a squeak.

"Madam, is there a problem?" a deep voice said.

Neeren stared at the figure behind Rada with disdain.

Rada's every muscle was tense as she sat trapped between her two nemeses: Neeren, and the tall, gaunt-faced castellan of the villa. Slowly, she tried to edge away from them toward the brooch.

"Stay still, girl. I'm not done with you."

Rada froze.

Neeren directed her attention back to the figure robed in black. "Nothing here need concern you, Castellan. I'm more than capable of dealing with this child."

"Of course, Madam... but..."

Neeren's jaw clenched each time he uttered the word madam. "Well, Castellan?"

"Madam, since you now have precedence at the welcome ceremony, it's my duty to inform you of preparations in case you wish to alter anything. I took the liberty of sending some slaves to the stable block with refreshments."

"What did you send?" Neeren drew herself up imperiously. "The emperor does not drink alcohol."

"Chilled lemon water, Madam, for him, and the finest Vēkarian wine from our Lady Jadzia's northern vineyards for the other lords. Also, scented water and wash bowls to help shed the dust and weariness of their journey."

Neeren smoothed her hands over her dress, delaying her grudging praise. "It was well conceived, Castellan."

"It was only what my Lady Jadzia would have ordered."

Neeren's face reddened. "Naturally, Lady Jadzia knows best. Leave us. Young Mistress Rada needs reminding as to the correct decorum of daughters of Lord Bashtan. Since her mother is indisposed, it's my duty to remind her. Rada, you should be more like Anfisa."

Anfisa remained partially hidden behind her sister, head bowed. Rada struggled to keep her eyes on Neeren; her every instinct was to snatch the brooch and run. Neeren watched her like a cat with a mouse, saw her distraction and spied the brooch.

The castellan cleared his throat. "The other wives jostle for precedence in your absence, Madam. They require your guidance." He bowed, long and low. Her hand clenched and unclenched and her daughter, Sasha, stood very still beside her.

"Mother," Sasha said. "Rada can wait. The emperor must be drawing near." She tugged Neeren's arm tentatively. "Mother!" she hissed. "This is our chance."

Neeren ignored her. Her brows knit as she stared first at Rada, the brooch, and then back at the castellan. "Rada, what...?"

A chorus of laughter travelled down the corridor from outside. "Those imbeciles. I swear you'd think they were barely out of the nursery." Still, she hesitated.

"Madam, without your guidance they may embarrass this fine house before the emperor."

"I'll have words with you later, Rada," Neeren said as she swept toward the front entrance.

Rada's hands fisted at her sides.

The castellan bent down and peered at her from under bushy brows. "Shouldn't you be somewhere else, Mistress Rada?"

Rada crimsoned and scrabbled for the brooch.

Large hands slipped around her waist and the castellan hauled her into his embrace. "Come, miss, through the kitchens will be the quickest and my legs can move much faster than yours."

CHAPTER 2

RADA GRIPPED THE CASTELLAN'S fine black robe, her small hand creasing its dark embroidery as he carried her.

The castellan strode through the hall and the faint scent of beeswax wafted to Rada as they passed the formal dining room. The entire villa occupied a broad hilltop that rose at one end to a rocky knoll; around it, the estate lands encompassed a large tract of undulating grasslands. In the distance lay the Talak capital of Bēdarik. He and Rada exited one wing of the building and the hall transformed into a broad portico that bordered the large central garden, around which the building sprawled.

Rada's brow puckered as she searched his face.

"Don't look surprised. I am, at heart, your mother's man not your father's. You must learn to recognise who in this house are your allies and who your enemies, young miss."

"But you're always mad at me."

"You've a habit of being where you ought not to be."

Rada bit her lip and changed the topic. "Neeren hates being called madam."

"And yet it is her title. We can pride ourselves, miss, that we have done nothing wrong in using it."

"I hope we never have to call her Lady," she muttered.

"It would be a dark day should she take your mother's place and ascend to first wife."

"Neeren's an enemy."

"Yes. When I saw the midwife run out of Lady Jadzia's chamber, the look on her face was enough for me to know trouble was brewing. I sent her in the wrong direction to find your father, though it won't delay her long. Your mother told me the rest."

They descended stone steps and delicate aromas wafted up from the kitchens. The lower basement of the house, excavated into the hillside, occupied the kitchens, storerooms, larder and some house slaves' quarters. Workers scurried around under the wrathful eyes of the cooks. Rada craned her neck as they passed, staring at the platters of fruits, cheeses, sweet and savoury pastries, ham and roasted duck that covered the benches.

A wide-eyed slave girl ran in from outside. "The emperor's nearly here!" She squealed in delight. "He's young and handsome. Better than having that lecherous old coot in charge."

"And what makes you think he'll be any less lecherous than the last one," the cook said as she slammed a clever through a hunk of meat. "Stupid girl."

"He won't be after the likes of you anyway," another slave called out from across the kitchen. "We'll be lucky if either of us even gets a glimpse of him."

"Well, I'll tell you something you won't know, things are amiss with them upstairs. The midwife—"

"Enough, girl!" The cook shook her head, flicking her wary gaze at the castellan and Rada before shooing the slave away. "Has Mistress Rada hurt herself, Castellan?"

The castellan ignored the cook. "You, girl, never let me hear you gossiping again!"

"I... Yes, Castellan."

"Have all the refreshments been laid out?"

"Almost."

"Then get back to work," he ordered.

He stepped outside and the afternoon sun beat down on the top of their heads. To their left, steps led down into the kitchen gardens terraced into the slope. To their right lay a broad cobbled path that ran the length of the villa.

Once past the kitchen windows, the castellan readjusted his hold on Rada and said, "Hold on." He ran along the path, all dignity gone; his robes billowing about him. They reached the end of the building and a dense hedge that hid the rear villa garden from the much-used servant's path.

The castellan stepped into the darkness of the hedge tunnel; he loosened his grip on Rada and she slid down his body to the ground. He frowned down at her. "Rada, if you're to meet the emperor, then you must neaten up your attire. You're like a ragged tomboy."

"Not a hoyden?" Rada grumbled as she straightened her dress and smoothed its fabric.

"That too." The castellan hid his smile. "Your hair is..." He waved his hand around her head as if afraid to touch it. "Messy. And the rest of you..." He shook his head.

Rada rolled her eyes and shrugged at the dirt and grass stains on her dress. "I'm six. Mami says to be messy and have fun while I can." She ran her fingers through her curly hair, leaving it no better than before. "Better now?" she asked with disgust.

"You'll do," he said, grinning.

Hand-in-hand, they stole through the archway. Their eyes barely adjusted to the sudden darkness before they were blinking at the stark sunlight which shone through from the other end where beyond lay a low stone wall and the stable complex. The soft sounds of nickering horses and the jingle of tack flitted across the air to them. They paused, hiding in the hedge tunnel, spying on the stable forecourt. Rada leaned forward, gripping the castellan's robe to balance herself on tiptoes in order to see over the wall.

Lord Bashtan stood in a long coat of deep green emblazoned with rich gold embroidery and lined at the cuffs and neck with fur. Her father's irritated gaze brushed by their hiding place, and Rada's breath hitched.

"My Lord Bashtan," the midwife said, breathless. "I've found you at last."

Rada gasped and prepared to charge forward. The castellan thrust out his arm, stopping her and pressing her against the prickly hedge beside him.

"We have to stop her telling father!" Rada whispered.

"It's too late for that," the castellan hissed. "You have a different mission. Remember it."

"But the emperor isn't here yet. Mami is on her own."

"She has her women. They'll defend her. Now shh."

"Well," Bashtan demanded. "What news? Is it a boy?"

The midwife would not meet his eyes. "My lord, Lady Jadzia has given birth to a girl."

His smile dimmed; he shrugged. "Another girl, a little more work, but in time she'll benefit the House of Ortakli."

The midwife licked her lips nervously and wrung her hands.

Bashtan grew wary. "What else? Speak."

She shook as she raised her head and held her hands out before her as if to ward him off. "My lord, it... The babe... I mean it... That is..." The midwife drew a deep breath; her words spilled forth, and she took a step back. "It's deformed. There's a large birthmark upon its neck; it has a clubfoot and a twisted leg."

Bashtan reared back from her as if she had slapped him. Quickly, he regained his composure. "Why didn't you bring it straight to me?"

"The Lady Jadzia wouldn't relinquish it," the midwife said. Bashtan narrowed his eyes. "She would've killed me had I attempted to leave with it."

"Evika!" Bashtan yelled.

Rada's eyes widened; she stepped closer to the castellan, half hiding behind his robes.

Seeing her fear, he said, winking, "Don't repeat that word, will you? It's a—"

"Grown-up word. I know," she whispered. He rubbed her trembling hands while watching the scene before him.

"Who else knows?" Bashtan asked.

"Only Lady Jadzia and her handmaidens. I told no one and came straight to find you."

Bashtan studied her, weighing the honesty of her words. "Good. That's just as it should be. You've done well." He passed the midwife a small bag of coins. "For your silence."

Testing the weight of it in her hands, she smiled.

Her father turned toward the stable block and beckoned a soldier forward. "One of my guard will make sure you reach home safely."

Her smile wavered. "My lord, I'm most grateful, but I need no escort."

"Rest assured, I'll call upon your services again for the next birthing. Go."

"I... Thank you, my Lord." She curtsied, and hurried away. As the guard turned to follow, Bashtan snagged his arm and whispered to him before releasing him to accompany the midwife.

From the privacy of the tunnel, Rada watched her departing back; certain the woman who'd delivered all the household's children wouldn't live out the day.

"You," Lord Bashtan said to one of his guards, "find the castellan. He should be here supervising this. You lot, come with me." They strode toward the villa.

Rada's voice faltered. "Mami."

The castellan paled. "Rada, I must go." She tightened her hand upon his. "I'll not be far, just out there ensuring all is prepared for the emperor. I'm worth more to your mother if your father doesn't suspect I've had a hand in this. This next part you must do on your own. Wait here and come forth when the emperor arrives. Remember who your mother is – she is a daughter of the First Circle. Her name, her title, carries worth. You are her daughter – don't forget it."

Rada stared at him in dismay. "But..."

Gravel crunched on the footpath behind them. Frightened, Rada yanked her hand from the castellan's grip. "I knew you wouldn't help. Coward!" She ran into the sunshine, darted along the side of the stable building, and disappeared behind it.

The castellan watched her go and cursed, just as a troop of female slaves carrying gilded bowls of scented water and soft cloths, entered the tunnel.

"Everything should already have been in place!" The castellan glared at them. "Get a move on now! Or you'll feel the back of my hand." He clapped his hands together. "Hurry!"

They scuttled past him to a colourful pavilion set up on the lawns under the spreading branches of a tree.

With one last glance after Rada, he shook his head and followed the slave girls.

Rada ran to the rear of the stables and leaned against the cool of the stone wall, panting and trying to stifle her sobs. The harsh clang of the smithy's hammer rang out behind her, followed by the stamp of a horse waiting nearby. She spun around, wiping her eyes. *Never let them see your tears;* her mother's words rang in her mind. *Mami!* She put her hand over her mouth, stifling her cry. An empty hay wain stood next to the stable and its team of great, shaggy-footed horses dozed, yet the ladder to the loft above the stalls sat in place. The slaves were absent. *They'll be back soon.*

Before her lay the smithy's forge; inside the smith roared at his apprentice, too busy to notice one small girl. Opposite, was a second stable block and the barracks; beyond these more outbuildings and slave quarters. The villa and surrounds were like a small town, usually always busy, but for the moment none were here to see. *Bless'd be Hokati. She watches over me.*

Rada crept to the open stable door and peered inside. *No one.* The nearest stall contained fresh straw and water. *They've finished.* She glimpsed an ostler waiting near the front door. Unsure, she dawdled in the rear entrance in full view of the barracks.

The barrack's door opened a crack, a burst of raucous laughter followed. Rada gasped, slipped into the stables, and peeked out at her father's guards as they left the barracks. Their green cloaks swirled as they walked and when they moved into the light, the red fox emblem of her family on their enamelled brooches and embroidered surcoats seemed to glow. She ducked back and hid in one of the middle stalls, silently closing the half door behind her.

Shaking, she crouched in the stall's corner, hugged her knees to her chest, listened and waited. Several sets of running feet pounded down the paved road between the buildings. The voices at the front of the building grew louder.

"Enough! Quiet!" The castellan's cry rang out.

The hoof beats of many horses drew closer. Rada's stomach knotted; her throat felt dry. She let out a soft mewl and clamped her hand over her mouth in panic.

"Your Imperial Majesty," the castellan began. "My apologies. My Lord Bashtan was called away to the villa. We have made all ready for you to refresh yourself a little before the formal greeting at the house entrance."

Silence save for the jingle of tack and the slap of boots hitting the stone forecourt.

"Away? Now?" Disdain laced the abrupt words.

Uncle? Is that Uncle? Her heart leapt, but tucked in her corner she couldn't be sure.

Other voices murmured, "Insult," but fell quiet.

More booted feet hit the stones.

The castellan stammered. "He will be with us momentarily and begs your indulgence."

Silence. Rada could swear the world had stopped.

"Take this to Master Pavel at the Temple of Mstislav. Do not deviate. It's from the Grand Master." A rider left at a canter.

Rada rocked back and forth, biting her fist. Hope warring with terror. *I think it's uncle, but the emperor will be there and he's mean! Wait! Soon the old goat will be and stuffing his face at the pavilion.*

Edged with irritation, the voice said, "So, Bashtan is *momentarily* delayed."

"Your majesty... My Emperor... please... Lord Bashtan..." The castellan's voice became muffled. "The Lady Jadzia has just given birth."

"Ah." The tone grew lighter. "So, Lord Bashtan has abandoned me to greet his newest arrival."

"Your Majesty, he expected to be back before your arrival. Our watchers reported—"

"I was weary of the road. I chose not to linger in Bēdarik, so we made good time. At least *you, Castellan,* are in readiness for our arrival."

"Ye-yes, Your Majesty. Please allow our ostlers to tend to your horses."

"No. We'll tend our own horses. They're worth more than your slaves. I may be emperor, but neither I nor my men will forget we are soldiers. I'll not grow soft like my father. Send your stable master to me."

Heavy booted feet and the chink of chain mail echoed between the stables. Stall doors opened and closed. Each footstep, each hoof beat, each close of the door, each slide of the bolt drew closer to Rada. *Get up! Deliver the message!* Bone deep fear anchored her. *Papi isn't there! The emperor won't come in here. Do it, now!* Sweat broke out on her brow and she clutched her belly as a wave of nausea hit her. She curled up, gripping her arms so her nails dug into her skin, bowed her head and scrunched her eyes closed.

"Out now!" A rough hand seized her, hauled her to her feet, and dragged her out of the stall. "You shouldn't be here!"

"No! Let me go!" She struggled, twisted, and tried to kick her captor as he hoisted her off the ground. Rada cried out as her foot connected with a metal grieve.

Laughter erupted around Rada. "Look out! Darcov's found an assassin hiding in the straw!"

Rada looked up into a tanned, bearded face. His nose was twisted and his eyes, slightly oval. Pockmarks dotted his cheeks and his long, dark hair was braided back and clipped together in a silver band. Kicking and screaming, she yelled, "I'm no assassin!"

Her captor dumped her on her backside outside the stall. "Get back where you belong before you get a beating."

Rada stared at his departing back in disbelief and increasing fury. Fear now gone, she pushed herself up, ran at him, and shoved him from behind with all her might. "You will not beat me! I am no slave! I am Rada Lujza Ortakli. Daughter of Lord

Bashtan Ortakli and Lady Jadzia Zora Maklova of the First Circle and I want to see the emperor! Now!"

Darcov spun and loomed over her. "Is that so?"

Wild-eyed, she stood trembling in the stable breezeway.

"Darcov, that's enough." A man with close-cropped dark hair and beard, both peppered with grey, approached her. "Hello, Rada." She sagged in relief. His brown eyes crinkled as he laughed, and she ran to him.

"Uncle Tikhon!" She threw herself into his embrace.

"Mistress Rada Lujza Ortakli, good afternoon. And what, my dear one, were you doing hiding in the stables?"

"Uncle Tikhon, I need to see the emperor. Can you help?"

"You're already seeing him, Rada," Tikhon said.

Bewildered, Rada shook her head.

"Yes, Rada. I'm the emperor — the new one."

"But the emperor's an old man. And he's grumpy. Not like you."

"Rada, it's true. I'm now the emperor."

She canted her head, leaned back and scrutinising him carefully. "True?" He nodded. "Well then, Mami told me what I should say, but you're Uncle Tikhon and you're not scary."

"Don't tell anyone else that." He winked at her.

Rada drew a deep breath. "I, Rada Lujza Ortakli, greet you in the name of my mother, Lady Jadzia Zora Maklova. She told me to give you this brooch and tell you... No! I got it wrong!" Her bottom lip trembled. "Please still help! I had to say..." She screwed her face up with a groan, before gasping and blurting, "She said to give you the brooch as a token of welcome." Tikhon's eyes widened as Rada opened her hand to reveal the ruby brooch. "... and to beg you to understand she honours our alliance at this time above all else... Please don't let Papi take the baby away."

The smile fell from Tikhon's face. "Rada, what's wrong with the baby?"

"Her leg's all twisted, and that means Papi won't want her. Mami... they're going to fight... a big fight, worse than... Mami said their lives depended on my message."

"Castellan, did you know of this?" The castellan crimsoned and spluttered. "And yet it was not the first thing to pass your lips upon my arrival. I'll deal with you later. Darcov, bring a dozen men and follow me. Castellan, you'll take us to the Lady Jadzia by the quickest way and, if we can, avoid that mindless gaggle at the front entrance." He put Rada down. "Rada, you stay here with the rest of my men." He looked at the nearest of them. "The child is in your care until I return." Gently, he pushed Rada in the soldier's direction.

"This way!" The castellan said as he raced back along the servant's path.

Rada edged closer to the soldier as she watched them disappear. She looked up at the man, tugging on his surcoat.

"What happened to the old emperor?"

"He had an accident with a sword."

"That was careless. Mami says you have to be *careful* with swords... and daggers..." She paused. "Anything sharp, really."

"He was *very* careless... It cut off his head."

CHAPTER 3

Bashtan's guards jogged to catch up with him as he hurried toward the villa.

His commander said, "My lord, the emperor... It's a serious breach of protocol..."

"We've time. I must see Lady Jadzia." Bashtan wanted to smash something. How could this happen to him? The disgrace if it became known. He snarled. "Aren't you going to congratulate me on the birth?"

The younger guard opened his mouth to speak. Hastily, the commander cut him off. "You have my sympathies."

Bashtan snorted. "I don't need your damn sympathy. We should have time to deal with this before the emperor arrives. If we take it now, then I can say it was stillborn. Only a few will know the truth and none will tell."

The younger guard paled and looked away; the commander remained carefully impassive. "Perhaps it's not so bad, my lord. You've not yet seen—"

"I've heard enough. I don't *want* to see it. Before the emperor arrives, I want it gone."

"But the Lady Jadzia... the emperor..."

Bashtan spun, fist raised. "What?"

"All I mean is that the Zaragarians do not share our..."

Shaking in fury, Bashtan forced himself to lower his hand, resting it on the commander's shoulder. His men did not deserve his ire. "You've served me loyally and long, but I'll not be told what I can and cannot do in my home. Restrict your advice to military matters."

Bashtan's eyes strayed to the villa's main entrance. Lined up primped, preening and giggling nervously, stood his other three wives and children. His children – his healthy, beautiful children. *It's but a babe.* Bashtan closed his eyes, breathing deeply. Slowly, he raised his head and his gaze came to rest on his children again. *No, it's not like them.* "The law is on my side. This contamination will not remain in my bloodline. I pray there's time. Come."

Neeren, at the forefront of the assembled wives, stepped forward, smiling, reaching out to stop him. Bashtan swept past her without a word. The tittering of the others ceased at the sight of his grim face as, jaw clenched, he barely spared them a glance.

Bashtan halted outside the double doors to Jadzia's suite. The two guards stationed there stiffened to attention. "Has anyone left?"

"Only the midwife and Mistress Rada."

"Rada?"

"We saw no harm in letting her in, my lord. She was most excited."

Bashtan sagged slightly. "I'm sure she was. Open the doors."

The guards pushed upon the doors to no avail. They tried again, grunting with effort. Bashtan tapped his foot impatiently. "They're locked, my lord."

"I can see that. Get them open!" Bashtan's guards threw all their weight against the doors, budging them only a little. "Again!"

The guards hurled themselves against the unyielding door.

"It's the new locks Lady Jadzia had put in."

"She does value her privacy," he ground out. *She couldn't keep me out last time and she won't this time.* "Get me an axe."

"My lord, that'll bring a lot of attention."

"I think that standing in the corridor in my own house trying to break into my own wife's rooms has already alerted the entire house that something is amiss! Get me a damn axe!" Both guards bolted, veering in different directions at the corridor junction. Bashtan drummed his fingers on the door. *She has no right. She should've learnt last time. There'll be no locked doors between us again!*

Both men returned, one with a short, plain axe. "From the kitchens..." he panted.

The other bore a ceremonial axe, which Bashtan recognised as being from his study. He seized it and the guards fell back.

"I hope this does more than look pretty." Bashtan swung the axe, striking the timber next to the lock. Its blade was dull and the force of the blow only cracked the wood a little. "Evika!" he tossed it aside and grabbed the axe from the kitchen. "At least this'll be sharp." He hacked into the door. Shards of timber exploded in all directions. With each stroke, Bashtan's face reddened, and the veins on his neck stood out. *How dare she! No more!* A sharp crack rent the air. Breathless, he stepped back, nodding at his men. They hurled themselves into the timber. The lock gave way, but the doors moved only a little thanks to the furniture shored against them.

"Hurry." Bashtan waited, fighting against his rage, as his men shouldered the door. Success came with the harsh scraping of wood on the tiles as they inched the furniture stack forward, gaining enough room for the two guards to slip in and clear the way. Bashtan passed them the axe. "Remember where you are. This isn't a battlefield. Her, you can't kill."

The guards headed for the second set of doors that led into Jadzia's bedroom.

"Wait, there has to be an easier way." He walked between them and pounded on the doors. "Jadzia, open up!" He waited. "Open the damn doors now, or we'll break our way in."

Bashtan rested his forehead against the timber, continuing more quietly. "Jadzia, this is madness. It's not the way."

Silence.

"Jadzia, I grow tired of this. You've one last chance."

Nothing.

"Get them open," Bashtan said flatly.

The axe cleaved through the timber. The men crashed into the doors, which buckled inward before thumping into furniture braced against them. A small spark of admiration flared in him at her sheer gall when she knew she couldn't win. He tamped it down. Her challenges should have long since lost their allure.

"Once more, gentlemen, and we'll be in. Remember, this is my wife. I don't care about her women, but do not harm her."

The two men braced themselves and slammed into the wood. A door gave; the guards staggered into the room. One fell with an arrow through his chest. Jadzia stood on the other side of the room before the cradle, armed with her Vēkarian longbow; another arrow already nocked. More upended furniture acted as a barricade. Behind this stood her handmaidens, poised with short swords. The remaining guard scrambled up; his hand closed around his sword then fell limp. He stared in horror at the arrow embedded in his torso and collapsed. His fall pushed the door partially closed. Both bodies now helped block the way into the room.

"I've plenty more arrows, husband."

"And yet you'll not win, Jadzia. No matter what! The law is on my side."

"Screw your law!" Jadzia said. "Be ready," she told her women. "Stand firm."

"Jadzia, this is foolishness." Bashtan poked his head around the door and she loosed an arrow at him. It slammed into the timber by his head. "Evika! Woman, you nearly killed me."

"Killing you is not politically expedient," Jadzia muttered. "Not yet, anyway."

She cocked her head as the sound of heavy footsteps pounding down the hall. Jadzia looked at each of her women. "This is it."

Bashtan's men shoved with all their might on one door, pushing the dead bodies enough to slip into the room. Jadzia's first arrow bounced off their shields. She targeted their legs but got no clear shot with her barricades serving as their protection and, while one guard shielded the other, they tried to clear a path. Three of her women attacked as a team. Unarmoured, they stood little chance, yet while one sacrificed herself, the others struck. They launched themselves at a guard and drove a blade into his neck, felling him. One of ladies picked up his shield and threw it to Katya before being hacked down. As she fell, a gap opened and Jadzia loosed an arrow, downing another guard. More of Bashtan's men entered, shields ready, and they finished clearing a path.

Jadzia snarled. Katya and one handmaiden remained. Her women closed ranks around her, and Jadzia dropped her bow and drew her kadag.

Bashtan entered the room, shielded by two more of his men. He pushed them aside, stood a safe distance from her and raised his hands placatingly. "Enough, Jadzia. You can't win and you cannot keep it. What kind of life would it have?"

"Not *it*, husband, but *her*. She has suckled. She's bound to this world – to me. What does your law say now?"

Bashtan paled and shook his head. "Woman, you only make this harder on yourself. She," he spat the word as if it tasted vile, "is a sign from the gods of your sin. Never has my line produced such a child. I'll not have my name and lineage tainted by the presence of such a thing."

"How can this possibly be harder for me?" Jadzia said. "I carried her inside me! She's my *child*. Bashtan, I've given you six children – three sons and three daughters. Two of your sons fight with the emperor. Your eldest daughter has already made a marriage that has furthered your alliances. Rada will undoubtedly do so too. This child is *mine*. I'm owed this much!"

"Her existence will see an end to any acceptable match for Rada. Who would want to align with this house through Rada when she could produce offspring like her sister? The taint of one will reflect upon the other. It's better for all if she dies now. We can say she was stillborn or died within hours of birth. None will know."

"No."

"I will not have that child in my sight or bearing my name!"

"She'll bear my family name."

He threw his hands in the air. "Do you think that helps?" He sneered. "Wake up! The child is evidence of your infidelity. Never has such an abomination been born in my family."

"Not that you've let live," Jadzia said.

"I'll cast you out if you do not hand her over."

"Really?" Hope flared in her eyes. "You'll cast me out? That will affect you more than me. I'm a member of the First Circle. You are not. And how do you think the emperor will feel about it?"

"He's not here, Jadzia. You're out of time."

Jadzia looked at the surrounding carnage and her two remaining women. She smiled sadly at them, drew into a fighting stance, and said, "Any actual power you have now is because of my family, my connections, and the favour I hold with the emperor. How long do you think you can hold all of that without my family's support?"

Bashtan shook his head. "You're deluding yourself. Like all women, your real value is between your legs and what can be bred from you. The old emperor traded you like a prize heifer. Your family may have power, but even they couldn't stop him." He smiled cruelly, "And I doubt his son even tried. Years have passed, Jadzia. Years in which I've been busy, my influence has grown, my name carries weight and my friends are many and powerful. This display? This is pathetic. Look at what you have wrought. For what? A mongrel cripple." Bashtan shook his head. "Take it from her."

➤——————→

"Hold!" Tikhon's voice boomed from the doorway. He took in the chaotic, bloody scene, and the air cracked with the cold fury of his next words. "Disarm them... all of them," he commanded his soldiers.

At the sight of the emperor, Bashtan's men stepped away from their master, surrendered their arms and dropped to the floor, abasing themselves.

Darcov approached Bashtan and held out his hand. "Lord Bashtan, your weapons." Bashtan glowered at him. Darcov clicked his fingers. "Now, Lord Bashtan."

Reluctantly, the man unbuckled his sword and dagger handed them over.

Jadzia's grip relaxed on her dagger and a pent-up breath escaped her. "Stilnaat Darcov," she said, handing him her weapon. "It's yours, mind you, for a short time only. Such a fine weapon must be sure to find its way home, should it not?"

Darcov gave a small bow before stepping away with a wry grin. "Indeed, Stilnassa Jadzia, I shall keep it with me until the emperor deems it safe to return it to you."

Tikhon's gaze never left Jadzia's face. "Clear the room, except for the Stilnassa and Bashtan. Darcov, ensure Bashtan's guards return to barracks and they remain there."

Jadzia prostrated herself before him. Bashtan watched, hands fisted by his sides. Tikhon canted his head and quirked his brow. Bashtan still stared, fixated, between Jadzia and the cradle.

Tikhon slapped him. "Kneel! Know your place!"

Bashtan staggered back then dropped to his knees.

"Though the crown sits newly upon my head and despite your self-importance, Bashtan, I am still emperor and you will fall before your betters."

"Forgive me, Your Majesty," he said, abasing himself. "I was distracted... I didn't wish you to witness my shame."

A soft mewl emitted from the cradle. Tikhon nudged both out of his way with his foot as he passed to the cradle. He picked up the babe in her tight swaddling and carried her to the bed, where he sat as if it were his own, laid her down and unwrapped her. A tuft of black hair stood straight up on her head and her eyes were oval, more so than her sister's. He ran his finger along her cheek; instinctively she turned her head toward his hand. Tikhon uncurled her fist and she gripped his finger. A chuckle escaped his lips. His gaze dropped to her legs, and a frown creased his brow as he traced the line of right leg to her foot. The ankle twisted, so the foot nearly sat at a right angle to the rest of the leg, which was shorter than the other. Tikhon shook his head, placing her back in her cradle and tossing the blankets over her form.

"Rise, both of you." Tikhon helped Jadzia rise. Her skin was pale and a faint sheen of sweat dampened her brow. He released her only once she clung to the bedpost for support.

Tikhon's lips drew into a tight line, his eyes narrowed and his gaze lingered on each of them.

Jadzia opened her mouth to speak, but Tikhon held up his hand, forestalling her.

"Have you actually seen the babe, Bashtan?" Tikhon said.

Bashtan paused. "No, Your Majesty."

"Perhaps you should. Step closer."

Bashtan stood beside the cradle as Tikhon tossed back the blanket, exposing the babe to view.

"Speak, Bashtan."

The man blanched. "I've seen enough. It's deformed. No amount of looking will change that. What kind of life would it have? Even if it's not witless, as so many are, its activities will be severely restricted and it will be reliant upon others all its life. Most will shun it, curse it. Friendless and without hope... it's no life at all."

"She'll have her mother's love." Jadzia was adamant. "My family and her sister will love her."

"Really? Can you guarantee this? I can guarantee the shame to my name and my family. I can guarantee the shame to you when it's known I've disowned it and cast you out." Bashtan's jaw clenched; he pivoted away. "It cannot be mine. It looks nothing like my other children and its deformity is a sign of corruption of the mother."

"Of course," Tikhon said. "Such a thing could never be a sign of corruption in the father. So your intent was then to take the child as per your traditions and abandon it to die in the hills, yes?"

"Naturally, Your Majesty. I sought to do so before you arrived. I didn't want you embroiled in this small family drama."

Tikhon gestured to the overturned furniture and the blood-stained floor. "Small family drama?" He turned his back on them and stared out of the window. "You've the most beautiful gardens." He stood with a serene smile, lost in thought. "I've always loved the view from this window in particular." Bashtan gasped. Tikhon turned, to see his furious, suspicious; eyes dart to Jadzia. The baby mewled; Jadzia moved to go to her. "Leave her be, Jadzia."

Jadzia's jaw dropped; her face creased with worry as she leaned against the bedpost, shaking. "It's not always the way amongst us to end the lives of such children," she pleaded. "My Emperor, you know this. Your grandmother was such a one... Who is to say this little one's life will not be as auspicious as hers?"

"You dare make such a comparison? You have lofty ambitions for her, then."

"Forgive me, Your Majesty, I cannot help but have such desires for all my children. I meant no offence. My duty..." She drew a shuddering breath. "Vlas and Kiril are bringing honour to this family serving in your army. My eldest daughter Abaya has extended alliances which serve this family and the empire. Rada is a true Zaragarian – she'll make us proud. Peyta and Osip perished as babes. I'll not lose another!" A sob escaped her. "After all this time, surely my duty is done."

Tikhon turned from her plea. "My grandmother's life was a hard one, one I don't think I'd wish upon another. Bashtan, your words have worth. Leave us."

Bashtan cast a smug glance at Jadzia, backed away, bowing before exiting the room.

CHAPTER 4

BASHTAN THRUST OPEN THE double doors of the villa. *I've no say in my own home! His men march mine off like they're prisoners. And my men? They just gave up!*

The tiled veranda, curtained by the lush green of a grapevine, usually gave him a sense of calm and peace, as if it insulated him from the outside world, from interference. Yet peace eluded him. Jadzia had been a marriage forced on him. After Aitor II had killed the Talak King at the Vēkarian border, several high-ranking nobles were forced into marriages to create an alliance and incorporate Talak peacefully into the Zaragarian Empire rather than via total conquest.

It had bought him and the others power – places on the new ruling council, wealth, influence... but at what price? Married to a Zaragarian bitch. Although he seemed to have the worst of the lot. She was not biddable like a trained Talak noble woman. She barely conformed to notions of acceptable behaviour. At first it was novel, interesting, exciting. Now? She'd done her duty – they both had – with six children, none could deny that and neither of them could claim it was all duty. The last time? She'd fought hard. Disgust and excitement warred within him at the memory. Maybe the babe was his punishment, but neither of them were free from guilt nor were they the same people who'd first married. Some doors should never be opened; some lines should not be crossed.

The glare beyond the wide veranda was broken by a dark silhouette. "My lord?" Neeren's worried voice broke his reverie. "What's amiss?" She moved in front of him and took his hand in her smaller one, gently uncurling his fisted fingers. Neeren scrutinised his face; her free hand cradled his cheek. "Bashtan, what's happened? We've not seen the emperor, yet his men escorted your guard from the house?"

"The emperor didn't enter the villa this way?"

"No."

"Then someone showed him the other way in?"

"Jadzia? What happened to her?" Neeren's worried brow belied the edge of excitement in her voice.

"She lives. *It* is disfigured. There was a scuffle, but the emperor intervened before I could take it. How did he even know? Someone in this house must have got word to him?"

Neeren stiffened, her nails dug into his hand. "I don't believe it... Rada. Rada must have done it."

"Rada?" The guards let her into Jadzia's suit, but she's just a child."

"Exactly, a child who loves her mother and would do anything to help her. Bashtan, I saw her in the corridor, she was in a rush and carrying Jadzia's brooch."

"Neeren, I understand you dislike Jadzia, but to implicate Rada in this is too much. I'll not hear it."

"Sasha and Anfisa were with me, and the castellan saw her too. He'll vouch for me. I left them to come out here and organise the ladies."

"How did she get to the emperor first?" Bashtan pulled his hand from hers and leaned his forehead against the cool stone wall. "The stables. Rada must have met him there." He shook his head with a reluctant, slight smile. "Clever little moppet."

Neeren remained by his side. Her hands fisted. "Clever? She turned on you! And Jadzia! How can a mother use her child so?"

He grunted, turned and rested against the wall, rubbing his face tiredly.

"She put her child in the middle of this mess." Neeren grabbed his forearms, pulling his hands from his face, forcing him to look at her. "Jadzia pitted her against you. Bashtan, this is unforgivable."

"Yes," he replied flatly.

"Bashtan, I'm sorry. This is not how this day should have gone. You should be revelling in greeting the new emperor. We..." His gaze hardened and his lips drew into a taut line. "We..." She let go of his arms, stepping away and lowering her gaze. "I'm sorry, my lord. If I was able to take the pain of this day away, if I could change its course, I would."

"Neeren, of course you would." He gathered her to him. "You've always been the one who understood me." He planted a kiss on her forehead.

"I'll disperse everyone." Neeren paced and spoke quickly. "While there'll be no official greeting now, we can shift our plans and direct them into tonight's festivities." She squeezed his arm and grinned. "Trust me, Bashtan, all will be well. Together, tonight we'll smooth this over – if not before. Where is the emperor now?"

"With Jadzia." Bashtan snorted. "In fact, he ordered me out of the suite. Out! In my home! Treated my men and I like the enemy."

"While she's bedridden, it falls to me to assume her duties and when he's finished with her, I shall ensure the emperor has everything he could possibly want."

"I need to talk to my men. You should find the castellan. It's his job to enact your instructions now you're in charge."

Neeren smiled radiantly. "The castellan is by the stables. I'll send someone to fetch him, but I think it would be better for me to see the emperor to escort him to his suites personally. After being embroiled in our family drama, he'll appreciate the gesture and it will remind him he is a guest."

"Neeren, he is emperor. We do not *remind* him of anything. He does as he pleases, even here."

"You know what I mean. Our hospitality will be legendary enough to make him well disposed toward you. Remember his father? He can't have fallen that far from the tree. What is his preference in women? There are two new indentured slaves we fished out of debtors' prison... He doesn't prefer men, does he?"

Bashtan laughed. "No, by all accounts, he does not!"

"Good. Go do what you must. Leave this to me," Neeren said. "The new girls should appeal to him. They are darker skinned like Jadzia."

Bashtan headed to the barracks. He broke stride momentarily. *Like Jadzia?* He shook his head before continuing.

Neeren smiled slyly as she watched him leave.

Jadzia clung to the bedpost, pale and shaking.

"Jadzia, sit down before you fall down." Tikhon drew her toward the bed. "How on earth are you still upright?"

She sat stiffly upon the mattress. Her arms braced as she clung to the bedding to remain upright. "In truth, I'd like to rest for a week, but I couldn't show him my weakness or the babe would be gone already."

Tikhon sat beside her and put his arm about her. She sagged against him, rested her head upon his shoulder, let out a sigh and wiped her eyes.

"This is not like you."

"I've just given birth and had to rise to my feet to defend my babe! Most of my women are dead. We all may have died. I think I'm entitled to be a little emotional!"

"I'm sorry."

She pulled away from him, feigning astonishment. "Did the emperor just apologise?"

"No. The emperor doesn't apologise, but Tikhon does and he's still in here somewhere."

The baby cried. Tikhon picked her up and handed her to Jadzia, who rocked her.

"She's beautiful," Jadzia whispered.

"You'd feel she was beautiful if she had two heads. I got a more accurate account of her from Rada – red, wrinkly and a bit ugly, I believe she said."

"Rada is six." Her mouth quirked in a brief, exhausted smile.

"But honest." Tikhon traced a finger over the baby's brow and along her cheek. "What a mess you two made. Bashtan is right about some things." Jadzia stiffened. "They'll shun her."

"Our kind won't."

He shook his head. "They will unless she can prove herself."

"I'll educate her as one of us, not them." Desperation tainted her words. "Her horizons will be broader. Not just confined to some gilded cage and raised to think only of dancing, jewels and fashion." She shuddered. "Despite my efforts, Abaya is consumed with such things. I drummed what I could into her of strategy and managing court politics. At least that stuck. She knows how to watch, listen, learn and wheedle, but..."

"But?"

"She's too like Bashtan. The tutors he chose..." Jadzia shook her head in disgust.

His voice sharpened. "Abaya's loyal?"

"Yes, but she'd agree to kill the baby."

"I'm not sure I disagree with them. My grandmother..."

"Was allowed to live!" Jadzia said.

"I suspect her mother was not unlike you," he said, tucking a strand of hair behind her ear. "My father would have sided with Bashtan. The laws are on his side."

"Talak laws, not the Zaragarian ones. Laws for the hideously deformed. She's not that, and you're not your father. You've always known your own mind. Tikhon, I've given so much... I've lost so much. I, better than any, understand there are many ways to serve."

Tikhon cradled her face. "Has life with Bashtan been so bad then?"

"He was ever the grasping, preening fool but he's come to believe in his own importance. He's forgotten who made him."

"It can't always have been so distasteful. You've had six children, including this babe." His hand fell from her cheek and he hesitated. "And Bashtan seems certain he's the father." Softly, he added, "Whose child is she?"

"Does she look like a Talak? You need not be jealous," Jadzia snapped. "Bashtan and I had not lain together for six years and then only out of necessity; as well you know, since we discussed it at length." She emitted an angry growl. "Whether Bashtan suspects or resents my power... I know not, nor does it matter. All that counts is he felt the need to reassert his rights. My consent was not required."

Tikhon shot to his feet. "Rape!" His hands fisted and he paced the before her. "I should strangle that bastard."

A sharp, bitter laugh escaped her. "There's no rape in marriage; not under Talak law," Jadzia said. "I hate him, but now she's another child that can be passed off as his... Unless you'll acknowledge her?" A plea tainted her words.

He ignored the plea in her words.

Jadzia swallowed the bile that rose in her throat, barely containing her anger. He was lover and friend, but still emperor; juggling them all required finesse she couldn't muster. "I want my freedom."

"You want more than that."

"This land is yours, is it not? You're emperor. You have absolute power here. Tikhon, you can do what you want. You said you wanted to bring their laws into line with ours."

"I will and more. Their ruling council will be abolished and most of them arrested, a Zaragarian governor installed, tax commissioner, standardisation of weights, measures..."

"And a Dibāt court." She smiled hopefully at him and snatched his hand before he turned from her. "Think of all the women in my position. Women here have no recourse from an awful marriage. They're trapped too. Under our laws, they would have had a marriage contract and could have left when it was up. A Dibāt court can order the end of a marriage before time; they could seek redress. You would win the hearts of every woman here."

"But lose all the men." He shook his head, pulling from her grasp. "I've more important things to do than this! Mstislav, help me!" He sighed, taking her face in his hands. "My father did you and the others a disservice marrying you off to seal an alliance, but you ask the one thing I cannot give you now. Be patient. Bashtan will not touch you again. You've my word on that."

"Be patient! How long?" He turned and headed to the door. "Tikhon?" A wild look filled her eyes. "The babe? At least tell me you'll back me."

He paused at her plea but would not face her. Impassive, he said, "You are not permitted to leave your chambers. I'll send Katya to you and more slaves to have this room set to rights." He turned on his heel and left.

Jadzia's face crumpled, and she rocked both herself and the baby, all the while shaking as silent tears ran down her face.

CHAPTER 5

THE STABLE BLOCK BUSTLED with workers as the imperial guards led their washed mounts into stalls. Rada stood on a small stepladder next to a tall bay horse and vigorously brushed its mane while Akim, one of the emperor's guard, rubbed the animal down.

"Just remember, the most important thing is to stay relaxed around the horses even if you're scared," he said. "If you do, then you'll help them be calm."

Rada gave a loud snort. "This one's not scary. So, it doesn't matter."

"Sounds as if you've got two horses in there, Akim," the guard in the next stall said.

Rada pouted. "Hey! I didn't sound like a horse!"

"Oh yes, you did! And not very regal for a Stilniat and the daughter of Stilnassa Jadzia Zora Maklova," the other guard said.

Akim gave a lopsided grin. "Mmm, definitely sounded like a horse. Are you finished, little Stilniat?"

"I'm not little," Rada said, eyeballing him.

"I stand corrected, Stilniat Rada." Akim gave her a half bow.

Rada nibbled her lip, unsure whether she was being mocked. At last, she nodded regally, accepting his deference. "Stilniat? What does it mean, Akim?"

"You've never heard it?" Rada shook her head. "Well, you should have. It's Zaragarian... like mistress that you use here...

only more – which is as it should be. It shows your rank and your youth. When you come of age, it will become Stilnassa; if you were a man, it would be Stilnaat."

"If I was a boy?"

"Young boys and girls are all Stilniat."

"So, you're Stilnaat Akim?"

"No, just Akim. Darcov has the rank of Stilnaat, not me. I'm from humbler stock."

Rada stopped brushing and stared at him. "But you're in the emperor's guard."

"Yes."

"You were poor... a peasant?"

Akim paused the grooming of his horse. "Does that matter, Stilniat?"

Several times, Rada opened her mouth to speak and closed it. Akim waited as she wrestled with the issue. She whispered, "Papi says, yes, it matters... but..."

"But what do you think?"

Rada glanced about the stables before hunching forward and whispering, "Uncle Tikhon... I mean the emperor... he made you his guard. If he did, then maybe it can't matter."

Akim smiled. "It still matters to many, but he can see beyond my birth rank."

"Then that must be good." Rada fiddled with the brush; her face crumpled. "Do you think Uncle fixed things?"

"I think he'll try."

"He will." She closed her eyes; murmured a prayer. "He'll make it right. I know it. Akim, will my new sister be a Stilniat?"

Akim lifted her from the stepladder, folded it up, and carried it outside the stall. "Why would she not?"

"Her legs are wrong."

His smile faltered. "Come, we've got more work to do."

"Akim?" Rada asked plaintively.

"Mistress Rada!" The castellan dashed into the building. "I've found you."

Rada's spun and glowered at him. As he reached to snag her arm, she jumped backward. "I hate you," Rada said. "You left me. I was scared and you left. You're not my friend."

The castellan bent to eye level with her. "Rada, I'm sorry, but I had to appear to do Lord Bashtan's work. If he'd seen me with you, then—"

"Then he'd know you picked sides, but you didn't pick sides, you chose yourself. I'm going to tell Mami."

The castellan threw his hands up, turning from her. "I had no choice. You're just a little girl, you don't understand."

Rada stamped her foot. "Yes, I do! And I'm not little!"

Bashtan came into view as he walked up the slight rise toward the stables. With each step, his appearance grew stonier.

Rada paled at the sight of his grim visage; her voice trembled. "He's really mad."

"Who, Rada?" Glancing over his shoulder, the castellan stiffened. He half turned toward her. "Rada, you must be careful what you say. Rada?"

She retreated, ready to bolt but Akim caught her and held her before him. Rada squirmed in his grasp yet couldn't break free. "Will running make it better or worse?" he asked.

Defeated, she hung her head. "Worse. Always."

"Then stay." Akim's hand rested protectively on her. Thumb in her mouth, she bit at her nail. As her father approached, a tremble ran through her, and Akim squeezed her shoulder.

Bashtan halted before the castellan, barely acknowledging his bow. His fists unclenched and he fixed a tight smile upon his face. "Rada, I wondered where you were. You weren't with the others waiting for the emperor. Just as well. Look at the state of you." Rada crossed her arms and gazed at the ground. "Rada, pay attention. Do good Talakian young ladies dress like this? I expected better from you. You can't meet the emperor like this. You certainly can't go to your mother like that."

Rada eyed him from under a tangle of loose hair. *See Mami? What about Bubba?* Her insides flipped and nausea hit her. *What happened? Was Uncle in time?*

"Greetings, Lord Bashtan," Akim said. The other guards murmured their own greetings, with cursory nods in his direction. None bowed.

Her father tapped his foot, looking at each of them, waiting, but they continued their work. A vein pulsed in Bashtan's temple. He turned his attention to his daughter. "Rada," he snapped. "I asked you a question. Do you believe it's acceptable to traipse around in such a state?"

"No, Papi."

"And what do you think our visitors will make of you like this?"

"They don't seem to mind," she mumbled, emboldened by Akim's proximity.

"What did you say?" he bit out.

Rada's chin jutted out. "They don't seem to mind."

His brow rose and his lips formed into a thin line.

She lowered her gaze and ground a piece of straw under her sandal.

"You know better than that. I'll deal with you later. At least the emperor hasn't seen you."

Rada fisted the hem of her dress, twisting the material.

Bashtan homed in on her hand as it tortured the fabric. Suspicion laced his words. "Rada, have you been to visit your mother this morning?"

She stopped scuffing the dirt, put her hands behind her back and crossed her fingers.

"No, Papi."

"Oh? Are you sure?"

"Yes, Papi." Rada's mind raced. "I wanted to... the guards let me in, but Katya sent me away."

"Really?"

"Yes, Papi. I heard her. Mami was hurting and yelling, it..."

He grimaced. "Yes, yes... so you didn't see her?"

Rada looked directly at him, saying earnestly. "No, Papi."

Bashtan changed tack. "Castellan, you've been conspicuous in your absence."

"I was merely seeing that all is in readiness for our imperial visitors, my lord."

"Really? Surely that hasn't occupied you all morning? You saw Rada in the corridors before the emperor arrived, did you not?"

"Yes, Lord Bashtan. She lay sprawled on the floor, having collided with Mistress Neeren."

"Was she carrying a brooch that belongs to the Lady Jadzia?"

Rada rocked back on her feet, watching the castellan like a hawk.

"I didn't notice, Lord Bashtan. I was intent only on soliciting Lady Neeren's aid in organising your other wives for the greeting ceremony. They were becoming... unsettled. I knew they needed her guiding hand."

Bashtan quirked his brow. "Didn't notice? You, who knows every little thing that happens in this house? Well, Neeren noticed."

"Mistress Neeren is particularly observant where young Rada is concerned, my lord."

"Meaning?" Bashtan snapped.

"Their temperaments are not ideally suited for a harmonious relationship, my lord," the castellan bowed.

Bashtan snorted. "So, who to believe? Are you saying *Lady* Neeren is a liar?"

The castellan paled.

Silence.

Rada stared at her father. *Lady Neeren? Mami is 'Lady', not Neeren.* Worry gnawed at her.

"I trust Stilnassa Jadzia is in good health?" Akim said.

Her father's composure slipped; he clenched his jaw and tight lines stood out around his eyes. "*Lady* Jadzia is... indomitable... as ever."

Indomitable? What's that? What's happened? Rada's breath hitched. *I didn't do good enough.*

"So, she recovers well? And the babe?" Akim asked.

Bashtan reddened. "That's of no concern to you or anyone else!"

"What about my sister? What about Mami? What did you do?" Rada yelled. She ran forward, shoved her father, and pummelled him with her fists. "You took my sister away!"

Bashtan grabbed her arms, lifting her. Rada swung in the air and kicked him in the shins. "Ow! Rada!" He shook her until she stopped, spun her around, and landed a slap on her backside.

The imperial guard ceased their work and stood arrayed around Bashtan. His lip twitched, hinting at a snarl, yet he released Rada. Bashtan's face twisted as he struggled for control and, irate, whispered, "Never do that again." Rada let out a sob as she rubbed her wrists. "Don't cry, or I'll give you something to cry about!"

She pressed her palms to her eyes and her chest heaved. With each breath her sobs subsided, until, sniffling, she stared at the floor.

"Look at me, Rada. So, you've seen your sister then?" Bashtan asked.

She nodded.

"Speak!"

"Yes."

"Yes, what?"

"Yes, Father," she murmured.

His voice was icy. "You lied... Do not look away!"

"Yes, Father."

"Never lie to me again!" he yelled. "Do you understand me? Or you'll not be able to sit for a week! And you went to the emperor, didn't you?" Bashtan spun and kicked a stable door.

Rada jumped back, crying, "I was only doing what Mami wanted! Papi, don't take the baby like they did to Lady Shinta!"

"Lady Shinta? How did...?"

"Everyone thinks I don't see or hear things, but I do! They took her baby because it wasn't right, and now she's always sad when we visit." Rada hastily wiped away her welling tears. "They said she's so sad, she hurt herself on purpose. I don't want Mami sad like her."

Bashtan's shoulders sagged, and he rubbed his temple. "Enough, Rada."

"And the baby's so small still, maybe it will grow better later... I can help take care of her. I'll be good. I'll make her strong. I promise I'll be good."

"Enough," he murmured, and crouched. "Your mother is stronger than Lady Shinta, so do not fear for her." He held out his hand to her. "I'm not really angry at you."

Rada hesitated; her stomach roiled. *Is he tricking? No more yelling?*

He clicked his fingers, beckoning her.

Better go, he'll get mad. Rada trotted forward with a too bright smile and he encircled her in his arms.

"I'll not harm the babe. Its fate will be in the lap of the gods. I should take it to the stone cradle in the hills high above Bēdarik and leave it there overnight. The next day, I'll see what the gods decided." Rada twisted, keeping one eye on Akim. Silent, thoughtful, she traced the lines on her father's palm; turning his hand over, she played with the jewelled ring on his finger.

"She won't come back though, will she?"

"Probably not."

"Why do the gods let the poor ones live?"

"Poor ones?"

"The ones on the streets in Bēdarik."

"On the streets?" His voice rose. Rada flinched and wriggled out of his grasp. "*Where* does Jadzia take you? *Where* do you see...?" Bashtan took in the imperial guard standing watch around him; he reigned in his temper. "No one understands the will of the gods. Perhaps they do it to remind us how lucky we are because we're not afflicted."

What if their families don't take them? Rada thought. "My sister can be lucky too. I'll help her."

"You can't help her forever. Someday you'll be married and gone, as is your duty, and then she'll have no one."

Doggedly Rada continued, "Mami will still be here, and Katya, and we have slaves."

"Rada!" Bashtan stood, towering over her. "Enough! It's not for you to decide!" With each word, he jabbed his finger toward her and stepped closer.

Rada darted back, stopping only when she bumped into Akim's boots. She cringed. *Mami!* "Uncle Tikhon will help!"

"Enough, girl! He's not your uncle! This is not his home!" Spittle flew from her father's mouth. "It's not his place to interfere with my household! It's mine, and you are mine."

Akim tugged Rada behind him.

Bashtan's chest heaved, he was scarlet and his hands flexed in the air as if to strangle something. His gaze darted to Akim, whose hand rested upon his sword.

Her father expelled several slow, deep breaths. "Rada, we should return to the house. You need to be made presentable."

Shaking, Rada whimpered.

"Come."

"I'm afraid, Bashtan, that *our* Stilniat Rada won't be coming with you." Akim scooped Rada up. "The emperor has charged us with her care until he returns. And until he tells me otherwise, she will stay here with us."

Bashtan's eyes bulged. The guard closed around him, cutting him off from Rada. "I'm sure you have important matters to attend to, my lord. Rest assured, Stilniat Rada will be completely safe with us." Akim dismissed him with a flick of his fingers. The guard parted; with hatred in his eyes, Bashtan turned and marched to his villa.

The rear door of the stable darkened as Tikhon entered. His men drew themselves up to attention, placing their fists over their hearts in salute. "Stand easy."

"Uncle Tikhon!" Rada cried. "Mami? The baby?"

"Your mother is safe," Tikhon said. "The babe is still with her... for now." Rada reached for him, but he turned away and beckoned two of his men. Her arms fell and she clutched Akim's uniform. "You two, return Rada to her mother. She is to remain with her. Only the slaves are permitted entry to Stilnassa Jadzia's room."

Rada clung to Akim.

"Akim cannot come. I have need of him here."

A guard reached for her and she buried her face in Akim's shoulder. Tikhon reached out, gently turning her head and cupped her cheek. "Rada, you've been a lioness. I'm proud. After everything you've done, this is the easy part. Go and visit your mami," he urged.

Akim lowered her to the ground and nudged her toward the men, nodding his reassurance. She looked toward the villa with a face twisted by longing and fear.

"Walk tall, Stilniat Rada," Akim said.

Rada nodded. Lip trembling, she squared her shoulders and marched off flanked by the guards.

Tikhon stood staring thoughtfully after them, his index finger drumming on his thigh.

"How much did you hear, Your Majesty?" Akim asked.

"Enough."

"That child is scared of him."

Tikhon grunted. "Did he strike her?"

"Not really, just a slap on the behind," a guard said.

"Many's a child who's had their behind tanned and it did them no harm," Tikhon said.

"There's more than one way to instil fear," Akim said quietly.

CHAPTER 6

RADA SLOWED AS THEY neared the villa entrance; she bit her thumbnail and stopped to stare up at one of the guards.

"Do you want to be carried, Stilniat Rada?"

Rada's gaze travelled to the villa and back to the stables. Her lip trembled.

"The emperor called you his young lioness. What do you think a lioness would do?"

Rada frowned then drew herself up and let out a long, shaky breath. "I'm ready. I'll show you the way to Mami."

She marched in front, head held high, the two soldiers shadowing her – a small queen and her guard. They passed through the main entrance into the semi-dark hallway. She fisted her trembling hands, squeezing them until her nails dug into her palms.

Her father and Neeren stood together, heads bowed, deep in conversation. Bashtan took a step toward her, but on seeing the imperial troops, scowled, grabbed Neeren by the arm and disappeared into his study.

The small queen crumpled, spun and ran along the corridor to her mother's rooms with the guards jogging to catch up. As she neared her mother's suite, the emperor's guards threw open one of the double doors and she careened into the room.

"Mami!" Rada slid to a halt on the tiled floor. Wide eyed, she stared in horror as a slave wrung out a blood-soaked rag into a bucket of red, frothy water.

"It's over now, Rada. Come here." Her mother lay propped up by a mound of soft pillows in her bed. She was pale, sweaty and dark circles hung under her eyes. *Mami looks sick! Where's Bubba?*

Jadzia clicked her fingers, attempting to grab Rada's attention. "Rada! Sweetness, it's done. Come." Jadzia held her arms open and Rada ran to her, launching herself across the bed and hugging her tightly. "You've done so well. My brave girl, thank you."

"Uncle Tikhon fixed things?"

"Yes."

Eyes red rimmed, Rada gazed up at her with a faint, hopeful smile. "For good?"

Jadzia hesitated. "I hope so." Rada's smile faltered. "Do you want to see your sister?" Rada gasped and bounced on the bed, nodding rapidly. "Well then," her mother said with a smile. "Go and get her."

She dashed to the cradle and took one look at the small, sleeping bundle and whispered, "What if she breaks?"

Her mother laughed. "She won't break. Just pick her up carefully and make sure you support her head." Rada backed away from the crib. "Rada Lujza, you have faced down my enemies this day; I trust you to do this. Pick up your little sister."

Worry twisted Rada's face as she returned to the cradle and leaned over, tilting the crib toward her to pick up her sister. She wrapped her arms around the newborn and clutched her to her chest with one hand behind her head. The baby grizzled; Rada froze. Eyes wide, she stared in panic at her mother.

"You'll be fine. Just soothe her and come here."

Rada tiptoed across the thick rug. "Shh, Bubba, shh. Rada will fix it. See? We're nearly with Mami." She placed the baby on the bed and, as her mother drew the babe closer to her, Rada climbed up and sat next to them.

"Now, you can meet your sister properly."

Rada gingerly unwrapped the blankets around the baby and peered at her small body. "What will we call her?"

"We must take care with the choice of a name. Names have great importance and influence when The Weaver starts a new pattern in the Great Web. Your forename, Rada, means filled with care, and Lujza means a fighter of renown. My name, Jadzia, means one who fights a battle, and my middle name, Zora, means new dawn. When we choose a name, it weighs with The Weaver in her plans and patterns."

Rada ran her fingers along the baby's belly. "We have names for fighters…" She paused and lay beside her sister, peering at the babe's legs. Rada's hand gently cupped her crooked foot. "Will she get a name for a fighter?"

"Do you think she'll need it?"

"I'll fight for her, but I think she should have one anyway, like us. Then no one will mess with her."

⇒

Emperor Tikhon lay on a marble plinth with his head resting upon a folded cloth. His eyes were closed and his arms relaxed by his sides as he inhaled the soothing scent of salibar that wafted around the room. Tikhon groaned as the masseur worked on the taut muscles along an old scar that spiralled down his back.

"My apologies, My Emperor," the masseur said.

"Don't, you're helping. You've been trained well. Lord Bashtan is most fortunate in you. I'm tempted to buy you."

"I'm a free man, My Emperor, and now master of my trade."

"Yet you're still here."

"Yes, My Emperor, though I do not reside here. I have a business within Bēdarik, one that flourishes thanks to Lady Jadzia."

"Thanks to Lady Jadzia?" The masseur said nothing. Tikhon chuckled. "I see. I must quiz her for more answers. And yet to hold the title of master you are no mere masseur but an olanteer. You're wasted here. I doubt Bashtan ever strains a muscle, whereas my soldiers could use the skills of another olanteer to work alongside my physicians."

The masseur remained silent.

"So, I must begin the bargaining," Tikhon said with a wry twist of his lips.

Darcov wandered in naked and lay on an opposite plinth. "Bargaining? What are you up to?"

Tikhon grinned. "Stealing Bashtan's staff."

"Well, that should make him so much happier." Darcov eyed the olanteer up and down. "He's a bit old. Is there a younger, more good looking one they could throw into the bargain?"

"Darcov, he is not a slave and therefore has a say in this."

"I can be perfectly charming you know."

"Sadly, Stilnaat Darcov, your charms are wasted on me," the olanteer said as he ground his fingers into Tikhon's muscles, making him wince. "Don't annoy him, Darcov, else he may break my back."

Darcov sighed melodramatically. "You're no fun, you know."

The masseur stopped and drew a harsh breath.

"Darcov, now look what you've done."

"Not me."

Tikhon cracked open an eye.

Two young women stood in the doorway wearing diaphanous shifts. They abased themselves before him while the slave overseer bowed behind them. "Your Imperial Majesty. I have a gift from Mistress Neeren. She hopes they suit your tastes."

Darcov groaned. "Not even close."

The olanteer stood stock still with his hands clenched.

Tikhon's mouth turned down, and in a granite voice, he said, "You're a fool to bring these now and if your mistress insisted, then she's a fool too. I said I did not want to be disturbed. I wish for peace and quiet. Should I require women later, then I'll choose them."

The overseer paled and bowed low. "Yes, Your Imperial Majesty. Forgive me, Your Imperial Majesty. I did not know." He poked the still prostrate women with his foot. "Up, up."

As they rose, he seized them by their arms and dragged them from the room.

"I understand the insult done to you by their presence while you work," the emperor said to the olanteer. "Clearly, Neeren does not. Please continue."

"Thank you, Your Imperial Majesty."

"My Emperor or Emperor Tikhon will do. Imperial Majesty sounds too much like my father." Tikhon sighed as the massage resumed.

Darcov raised his head. "Is there another to tend to me?"

The olanteer smiled. "Now I know your proclivities, Stilnaat Darcov, I will summon my daughter. She is my apprentice and waiting for me in the kitchens. If you will excuse me, My Emperor."

As he moved to leave, Tikhon snagged his arm. "Your daughter would have been safe regardless of Darcov's preferences." The olanteer bowed and left.

Darcov grunted. "So, he's worried about her safety in this house?"

"Darcov, that could be said of more than half the houses in the empire. Though his deal with Jadzia needs closer inspection."

"If you're going to investigate all her deals, then we'll be here a long time. You set her a task which she undertook at great risk while your father ruled, and she'll now have more irons in the fire on your behalf than we can ever imagine."

"Will they all be on my behalf?"

Darcov stared at him and shook his head. "Don't let all the game-playing and subterfuge of the last year rattle your mind. The one thing you can't doubt is Jadzia..." He smirked. "and me... of course."

Tikhon snorted in amusement. "Of course." He grew serious. "We should've invaded here. Not made a polite take-over via a marriage and an alliance."

Darcov grunted in assent. "They think they're our equals."

"Which is exactly why we face problems with Generals Rodan and Cēdar."

"Thanks to Jadzia, you know most of their associates — they'll get no help there. You'll likely catch their wives and children before they make the border. Surely, they'll talk."

"If they know anything."

"At the least they'll be leverage. The Order is behind you; between them and your network of spies, we'll find the generals. We've already begun rounding up their associates, the rest will be too scared to do anything. All that will be left is two rebel generals and a handful of troops."

Tikhon shook his head. "Maybe, but they're not stupid. I suspect we'll have to run them to ground. I sent word to Pavel to send members of the Order here out to track down our leads. One way or another we'll find them. These Talaks need straightening out. I'm going to abolish the Talak council. They'll be rounded up for questioning. They must've known about this."

"Bashtan?"

"Bashtan resigned last year, remember? Bastard has been playing both sides but making sure his hands don't get dirty. I wish they were, it'd make Jadzia's problem much simpler. I will put a Zaragarian governor and administration in place, as should have happened from the start. My father grew lazy, fat and indulgent after victory in Vēkaria," Tikhon said. "He knew the Talaks would fold, so he took the easy way."

"True." Darcov cleared his throat before continuing. "Jadzia paid the price though. This is not the marriage or life she should have had."

"Enough, Darcov!" Tikhon snapped. "There is no going back."

CHAPTER 7

JADZIA SAT IN AN armchair, fanning herself. The encroaching darkness made little difference to the heat, and the shrill noise of the cicadas outside scraped against her nerves. Katya stood at the ready and Rada sprawled on the floor cushions. Muffled voices sounded in the hall outside. Jadzia gripped the silk fan, snapping one of its light wooden fins. "Damn." She hurled it away and nodded at Katya, who moved to guard the baby's crib. Rada darted up and stood next to her mother, staring at the door, a worried crease to her brow and her hands fisted by her side.

Blocked by imperial guards, Bashtan stood in the corridor outside Jadzia's suite, lip curled and tapping his foot on the tiled floor.

"This is my house!" he yelled. "Jadzia cannot keep me out. She should've learnt that, at least, by now."

Neeren tugged his arm, quelling his next words. Bashtan spun and came face to face with the emperor. Tikhon sighed and squeezed the bridge of his nose. "Mistress Neeren, are these guards wearing imperial garb?"

"Yes, Your Majesty."

"Good. I thought my eyes were playing tricks on me. It must be Bashtan who has eye trouble."

Alarmed, Neeren took a step away from the two men.

"Bashtan, can you see their livery?"

"Yes, Your Majesty."

"If your vision is not impaired, then are you mentally defective?" Bashtan reddened, spluttering. Tikhon thew his hands up. "By all that's holy, you imbecile, if you can see their livery, then you must realise they bar your entry under my orders!"

Bashtan and Neeren bowed quickly and deeply, neither daring to rise. His gaze cold, Tikhon made them hold the position for several minutes. "Rise. Mistress Neeren, I regret the welcome ceremony was ruined. No doubt your husband has likewise told you of his regrets at this too."

Neeren paled. "Yes, of course he has, Your Imperial Majesty. We both apologise that this minor family drama has marred your visit."

"Minor family drama?" Tikhon shook his head. "Why are you here, Mistress Neeren? What we will discuss in this room is between Lord Bashtan and Stilnassa Jadzia. If Lord Bashtan informs you of the outcome, then that's his decision, but your presence now is neither helpful nor desired."

"My Emperor, young Rada is within and I've come only to offer to take her into my suites to play with my daughter. Her direct siblings are absent and I believe most of Lady Jadzia's women are no longer with us. No child should witness the acrimony that will occur and there is none better to shelter her. If she comes with me, she'll be safe and distracted, that's all," Neeren said, dropping her gaze.

Tikhon hesitated. "Well thought out, Mistress." He turned to the guards. "Open the door." He swept into the room, trailed by the others.

Jadzia struggled from the chair with a suspicious glance at Neeren before prostrating herself. Rada beamed at Tikhon. He raised his brow and motioned downward with his hand. Rada mouthed 'Oh' and threw herself on the floor with a flourish. Tikhon's lips twitched and his eyes creased at the corners as he suppressed a smile.

"Oh, dear gods," muttered Neeren. "She has no shame."

"Rise, both of you." He helped Jadzia to her feet and ushered her back to a chair. "Rada, go with Mistress Neeren."

"Katya can go with her," Jadzia said quickly.

"No, Katya can wait outside while we talk and then fetch Rada when we're done." He flicked his hand at Katya, dismissing her.

Rada moved closer to her mother, planted her feet apart, folded her arms, clenched her jaw, and her chin jutted out. Tikhon mimicked her glare for glare. He arched his brow at her and she lowered her gaze. "Good girl. Go."

Jadzia rested her hand upon Rada's head, leaned close to her and whispered, "Go with her, Rada. All will be well." She continued more loudly, "I'm sure Mistress Neeren will take good care of you."

Neeren nodded stiffly, but her voice stayed cheery. "Rada, Anfisa will show you her dolls and their beautiful clothes. She keeps them away from others, but today she'll let you play with them. We'll get cook to send up your favourite little apple cakes from the kitchen. I asked her to bake some in case you were to visit with us."

"How do you know they're my favourite?"

Neeren gave a high, trilling laugh as false as it was intense. "Because you leave none for the rest of us."

Rada hesitated, looking to her mother for approval.

Jadzia gently pushed her forward. "Go on. I'll see you soon."

Rada ignored Neeren's proffered hand. She eyed her father and bit her lip.

"Do as you're told," he ordered. Rada cast him a pleading look. "Go!"

Neeren stepped forward. "Come, Rada," she murmured. "This isn't the place for you."

Rada skirted around her father and clutched Neeren's hand as she led her from the room. Outside, she remained watching her mother and as the doors closed, she broke from Neeren's grasp, rushing forward to keep her mother in sight until the last moment. She winced as the latch clicked into place and rested her head against the timber.

Uncertainty and sympathy flickered across Neeren's face. She gave Rada's shoulder a gentle squeeze. Rada shrugged her off and ran to Katya, wrapping her arms about the guard's legs. Katya picked her up and rubbed Rada's back as the child rested her head on her shoulder. Neeren's hand clenched as she struggled to quell a flash of anger and school her features. *Breathe, she's just a child caught between two monsters. Nothing comes easily... Be patient.*

Katya rocked Rada and regarded Neeren with a stony face. Neeren reached out, her hand shaking. "Katya, wait here, as the emperor commanded. Rada, come with me. You can play with Anfisa. She has some new dolls."

Rada clung to Katya and refused to face Neeren. "Anfisa won't play with me. She doesn't like me very much."

"I'm sure if you promise not to cut her doll's hair again, she will." Rada half turned to Neeren. "It's true. I promise."

Neeren took a step closer to Rada and held out her arms. "Come, you'll see."

With one last, lingering glance at Katya, Rada slipped across into Neeren's arms.

Neeren carried Rada down the hallway to the suites. "Don't worry, Rada, your father loves you very much and he doesn't blame you for all the goings-on today."

"He's so angry... All the time."

"Things will settle, I promise you. It'll all work out."

"Really?" Rada said dubiously.

"Yes. Come now, smile."

She set Rada down outside a set of honey-coloured double doors inlaid with a gilt rose. "You should walk in beside me; not be carried. You don't want them to think you're a baby. You're a strong Talak."

"Mami says I'm Zaragarian. Akim said I'm Stilniat Rada. Stilniat is like mistress, only more..." Rada stopped, wide-eyed and stared at Neeren. "I'm sorry... I didn't mean..."

"That's very interesting and I understand you didn't mean to be rude, but here mistress means more than Akim thought."

Rada swallowed nervously as they entered. "Yes, Mistress Neeren." She gaped at the luxurious room. Bright tapestries and painted silks hung from the walls; soft rugs covered the tiled floor and enormous cushions lay scattered around a low octagonal timber table inlaid with mother-of-pearl.

"It's so pretty," Rada whispered.

"It's very different to your mother's suite." Rada's head shot up, a frown creased her brow.

"Your mother's room is pretty too. They're just different."

Rada remained fixated on the colours and textures around her. "You don't have a sitting room?" She reached out to run her hand over one cushion, but realised she'd blundered and looked at Neeren warily, eyes wide.

Neeren's eyes narrowed, but her tone remained light. "No, only the first wife has that privilege. It's all right, those are the rules. You may touch it, any of it, just be careful not to break anything."

Rada ran her hands over the cushion and sat on the floor, rubbing the soft nap of the cloth against her cheek.

"Fetch, Anfisa," Neeren said to a slave. "Tell her I want her to bring several of her dolls to play with Rada." To another slave, she said, "Go to the kitchens and fetch a large tray of sweets and cakes with apple tea for us. Go."

Rada's face lit up. "Cake? Apple cakes?" Neeren smiled as Rada took the bait. "Yes, if they're baked yet, but—"

"Or cherry cake. Did cook make cherry cake?"

"Rada, I do not frequent the kitchens." Rada's face dropped. "Wait," she commanded the slave. Grinning, she added, "If there is cherry cake as well, then bring it too and be quick."

"Thank you, Mistress Neeren," Rada said.

"So, you do have manners, Rada."

Rada looked sheepish. "Mami says she thinks I'm in too much of a rush to remember most of the time."

"Never a truer word was spoken." Neeren laughed. Rada's jaw dropped and she stared at her. "What? I'm not always grumpy, Rada. We've just often got off on the wrong foot." Rada remained dumbstruck. Neeren smiled, reached over, delicately put her finger under Rada's jaw and pushed her mouth closed. "Close your mouth. It's true."

A girl, slightly older than Rada, stood in the doorway, holding three dolls. She eyed Rada with distrust. "Anfisa, I want you to play with Rada and share your dolls."

"Do I have to?"

"Yes," Neeren said, clipped and cold.

Anfisa narrowed her eyes and passed Rada a doll with short, cropped hair.

Rada took it but refused to look Anfisa in the eye. "Thank you."

"I don't want her now."

"I said I was sorry," Rada mumbled. "And I promised I wouldn't do it again."

"Yes, you did," Neeren said. "And as I recall, you were punished. So, it's time to move on and make friends. Anfisa?"

Hesitantly, the two girls sat down together. The slave returned with two trays loaded down with several cakes and a pot of sweet apple tea.

"Oh!" they said simultaneously. Both reaching for the cherry cake and knocking each other's hand.

Rada pulled her hand away. "Please, you first." Anfisa gave a haughty sniff and reached for some cake. Rada whispered to her. "I think cherry cake is the best."

Her half-sister gave an uncertain smile. "Pear tart is my favourite. Don't you have your own dolls?"

Rada nodded. "But they're injured." Neeren and Anfisa stared at her. "Well, I've just started my riding lessons."

"You took your doll riding?" Anfisa put her nose in the air and crossed her arms. "I wasn't allowed."

"Sela wanted to go – she's called Sela, my doll. But I got caught going into the stables."

"We're not meant to go into the stables alone," Anfisa said. "It's unsafe when you're little."

Rada rolled her eyes. "I know, but I'm not little and it's not always unsafe and anyway, if I'd been able to, it all would've been fine... I'm sure. I had to go for something smaller and easier to get to... So, I made a slave hold a hound still and I tied Sela to its back. But it got scared, bit us, ran away with Sela hanging off it and raced straight through milking goats going into dairy. They went everywhere, but the hound ran up the hill. He didn't come back for a week." Anfisa's eyes grew wide. Rada leaned in conspiratorially. "The dairy hand said that the goats would give curdled milk for a week." She looked wistful. "I didn't get to see that, but I couldn't sit down for a week and

Sela's head fell off." She shrugged. "Mami said no more dolls until I can look after them."

"Didn't you have another one?" Anfisa asked.

"Well... she went fishing..."

"Really?" Anfisa leaned closer, eye bright and interested.

"I think we can guess what happened," Neeren interrupted.

A soft knock sounded on the door.

"Enter," Neeren said and Sasha, her eldest daughter, entered the room.

With Neeren's attention diverted, Anfisa leaned forward, whispering to Rada, "Tell me about the fishing later."

Rada grinned enthusiastically. "Yes, but I can do better than that..." She broke off as Neeren's refocussed her attention on them.

Sasha stopped in her tracks at the sight of Rada and Anfisa playing and sat down beside her mother with a bemused expression. Neeren held a finger to her lips, silencing her questions. "Anfisa, I'm sure your dolls should wear better outfits for such a grand tea party. Perhaps you can fetch a selection of their best dresses?"

"Can Rada come?"

"If she would like."

Rada leapt to her feet. "Thank you, Mistress Neeren."

"Rada, you know I'm not fond of being called Mistress. How about you call me Auntie Neeren?"

The child stood frowning. "Auntie Neeren? Is that... allowed?" Neeren nodded, saccharin smile flashing. "Thanks... Auntie Neeren." Both girls ran out of the room. Neeren flicked her hand at the nearest slave. "Follow them, make sure they come straight back here and that Rada doesn't lead Anfisa astray on the way."

Sasha put her hand on her mother's brow. "You're not feverish."

Neeren batted her hand away. "Of course not!"

"Then what are you doing? You've never let the pair of them play together."

"There's more than one way to win a war, Sasha."

→

Jadzia watched Bashtan with distrust as he sauntered into her suite.

Bashtan surveyed the room. "No one would believe you sacrificed so many lives in here for that." He flicked his head toward the crib. "What a waste."

Jadzia trembled with the effort to remain standing and her face twisted in anger, but before she could retaliate, Tikhon intervened.

"Enough!" he barked. "I've more important matters to deal with than this."

"My Emperor..." Bashtan began.

"*You* will address me as Your Imperial Majesty, Bashtan."

Bashtan bowed his head. "Yes, Your Imperial Majesty. I'm aware that this... situation is the last thing you have time for and, in reality, should not be within your sphere of influence..." Tikhon's brows rose. "It is beneath your notice."

"I. Am. Emperor." Tikhon jabbed him in the chest with each word. "Everything in this realm falls within my *sphere* of influence and is subject to my will should I choose. Your marriage was a political alliance orchestrated by my father. You both want freedom from it. Stilnassa Jadzia claims I should release her because of our custom of marriage contracts, but they've never applied to those of the ruling class. I suspect she also thinks she has served enough of her *sentence.*"

"*Sentence!* Under Talak laws, I may cast her out due to infidelity and disown the child."

"No," Tikhon said. "You will do no such thing."

Bashtan raised his chin. "I've already made it known I disown it. It's not mine. It cannot be."

"Why? Because you believe the child is a sign of corruption? Only the corruption is yours, isn't it? Not Jadzia's."

Bashtan blanched. "No stain lies with me. My rights as a husband—"

"You would do well to remember that your continued power lies at my discretion. You have had neither time nor opportunity to publicly renounce the child, and you will not. Here is my judgement. This marriage remains in place. This is not a suggestion, not advice. It is an order. You'll continue to host official functions together. Bashtan, you will continue to work for the benefit of the empire. You'll not renounce Stilnassa Jadzia. Though you'll be married in name only."

Jadzia's mouth turned down in distaste. "If I have to endure this, then there are things I would ask you grant me, My Emperor. I want control of my money."

"What! You cannot!" Bashtan said.

"Oh, don't worry, Bashtan. I don't want the money I brought to the marriage. You've already spent that. I want control of my money from my estate in Vēkaria and my share of my family estates. No longer will I pay for your indulgences."

"Why? Do I not provide for you?"

"I want to ensure both my daughter and myself are secure, and that Rada is not punished."

"Naturally, I will provide for Rada. Why would I punish her? For following you? She's but a child."

Jadzia threw her hands in the air. "And what of this daughter?" She pointed at the crib. "Unbelievable! I want my own household, staff, and troops."

"Troops!"

"Yes! You've attacked me twice!"

Tikhon's gaze snapped to Bashtan and his hand clenched. "Bashtan, Jadzia and the babe are under my protection and will remain so. Do I make myself clear? If any harm befalls either of them, if you seek to pursue your husbandly... *rights* against Jadzia's wishes, I will see you dead."

"She is sullied. Why would I ever touch her again?"

Jadzia shook with fury. "I'll do as you command, My Emperor, but I'll not bow to the whims of this creature any longer. I'm Zaragarian, not Talak."

Tikhon pinched the bridge of his nose. *May the gods save me from a marriage like this one. Invasion would have been easier.* "You will have it, but Jadzia, your new household will be established here, attached to this house – an adjunct to this building. You'll show a united front. Appearances must be maintained. I'll have papers drawn up for you both to sign."

"She gets everything and I get nothing!"

"You get time to prove you're worth my continued support and when the babe is of age, you will be rid of the marriage."

"Fifteen years!"

Tikhon broke into a predatory grin. "After that time, I'll allow a formal separation. In the meantime, you have Rada to help raise, and I have work for you both."

"I don't see the point in this," Bashtan said. "Everyone will know we live separately. How does this charade serve?"

"Duty is not escaped so easily, Bashtan, as Jadzia knows. And your duty is to your emperor. People will see your loyalty, your adherence to the alliance. They will see my *respect* for tradition and yet my compassion in this arrangement. Compassion for Rada. Compassion in that you both have a kind of freedom."

"Freedom? She gets the freedom, not I. Her own household! She can further disgrace me while she takes lovers and—"

"I have no need of lovers. I'd be happy to go a lifetime without another man."

"That's a long time without a drink for a woman such as you."

Tikhon punched Bashtan in the face. His lip curled in disgust as he glared down at the man sprawled upon the floor, blood streaming from his nose. "Jadzia, if you find a real man, I hope you take him as a lover, but be discreet. Gods know you deserve better than this. You're a fool, Bashtan. My arrangement would keep the status quo, and your position in Talak society. Given your connection to Rodan and the council, it is a position you hold by a thread. If you were clever enough, you could let this appear not as a duty imposed upon you, but as an act of beneficence on your part. This is my command. Think carefully about what you say and how you play your part. Ending you would be a minor inconvenience but one that, at present, I'd willingly suffer." Bashtan prostrated himself before Tikhon. "Out!"

Bashtan rose, his jaw clenched, veins standing out upon his temples. With one hand he tried to stem his bleeding nose while with the other he smoothed his hair into place, and retreated toward the doors, adhering to strict protocol and not turning his back to the emperor. Without another word, he left.

Tikhon sighed and sat opposite Jadzia, stretching his legs out. "How are you feeling?"

Jadzia gave a wry grin. "Like I've had a baby. Although I must confess, I enjoyed that display." Tikhon scowled. "You have work for me?"

"Yes. I need you at the heart of Talak society, not outcaste. I've enemies within father's old guard who lie in wait to see how I perform. Then there's Rodan and Cēdar – they never showed up for the oath of allegiance. I suspect they want Talak independent. I'm sure there are others just waiting in the wings. If Rodan and Cēdar get the numbers, we could have a full-scale rebellion."

"What happened with Rodan and Cēdar in Vēkaria?"

"Like I said, they never showed up." He shrugged. "We had agents watching them back home and you ferreting out all their connections here. There's a reason we break up the troops of satellite states, ship them off and disperse them amongst our own – less opportunity for this sort of thing. Fortunately, it didn't take the Talak soldiers long to learn their new master is better than their old one. Rodan thought he had several Talak cohorts ready to desert. Thanks to our network, we cut off their major source of troops. Yet they both slipped our net. We've a fair idea where they are though, we just have to run them to ground. By eliminating them, I should quieten the old guard, at least for a while. I need you and your spies – I would know what is being said and by whom."

"Talk to Katya. She can fill you in on any developments since my last dispatch."

"As you wish. But she is no substitute for you." He hesitated, leaned toward her, his hand lingering upon her cheek.

She waited, hopeful, for more — words, a touch, the feel of his lips upon hers — anything. Instead, he stood, planted a kiss upon her head, and departed.

"So, it's back to business as usual." A tear slid down her cheek. "Like nothing has happened."

CHAPTER 8

NEEREN JUMPED IN FRIGHT as Bashtan stormed into her room; half his face obscured by a bloody cloth he held to his shattered nose. Rada and Anfisa, eyes wide, bowed their heads and froze.

"You two, out! Go to your rooms!" The girls dropped their dolls and prepared to run. "Wait! Don't you know better than that? Do not leave your things lying about!" he roared. They darted back, grabbed the dolls and clothes, and ran without a backward glance.

"My lord, your face! What's happened?"

Bashtan seethed. "The emperor happened. He has passed judgement." He kicked a cushion, which knocked the contents of the low table onto the floor, his breathing ragged. "The slut must have slept with him!"

Neeren reached toward his face. "Let me look..."

"Don't touch me, Neeren!" Her hands hovered before his face. "Just don't!" She blanched and stepped back, head bowed. "Get me a drink!"

Her gut clenched, a wave of nausea flooded her. She trembled as she poured his wine and it took two hands for her to carry the goblet without spilling the drink. "Here."

He gulped the wine; his face twisted as if it were vinegar. "I'm to remain married to her. After everything! She gets control of her money back. I get nothing." He hurled the goblet across the room, shattering a vase. "Nothing!"

Neeren's jaw dropped. "She can take it back... her dowry?"

"Oh no, not that. It's gone anyway. Oh, and she damn well made sure the emperor knew. She gets all her income from her estate and her family estates. And she gets her own household and guard, but wait... it gets better! It's right alongside this one. In fact, connected to this house. A wife in name only, no obligation save to look the part. We are to keep up appearances until the baby comes of age. To top it all off, he's just issued an edict that every Zaragarian woman of rank who was married off here must now be addressed by their correct title of Stilnassa and given all the honours that conveys."

Neeren was aghast. "What?" *She gets her money! Her own household! Freedom!*

"Stilnassa! You understand what that means? The bitch will outrank me, outrank everyone here."

"What?"

"For the love of the gods, woman, can't you manage anything else other than 'what?' His father wouldn't have bothered; he was content with the tribute." He shook his head. "There's nothing to be done."

Neeren buried her head in her hands. "But she's here... No, no." Tears filled her eyes.

Bashtan tried to embrace her. She shied away, her face twisting in anguish. Shaking her head, she thrust his arms back. He halted, shock on his face. "Shh, Neeren... my love... what..." She shook her head, unable to reply. He stepped forward. She stilled, tense and trembling. He placed his hands upon her upper arms, rubbing them soothingly, and she drew a shuddering breath. "Why are you so overwrought? I won't acknowledge the babe, and her infidelity will be widely known. Her existence here will be miserable. Talak society will shun her. She'll leave of her own accord and no doubt the emperor will forgive her. If he doesn't, so much the better. I'll not have to stay married to her, you wait and see. Then you'll be first wife. We'll still be together and the house will be at peace."

A knot formed in Neeren's stomach. *Yes, we'll still be together... there's no hope that will change. Don't you see?* She sagged against him as despair overcame her.

"Shh, love. Shh." He rubbed her back as if she were a child. "All will be well. Now stop up your tears. You know I hate tears."

Her body stiffened; she nodded, drawing herself upright and regal. "Of course, all will be well. We have each other, that will not change. So... how could it be otherwise?" She graced him with an effervescent smile.

"That's the Neeren I love." He kissed her forehead, his fury of moments ago seemingly forgotten. "Now, I must go. There are... things I need to attend to."

Her stomach roiling, she remained staring at the spot where he'd been. *She keeps all her power here and yet is free. Where does that leave me? Stuck here as second wife. Relegated to a position I didn't deserve. I should've been first wife; in charge. Not someone with no breeding. Gods above! They say she's not even Vēkarian, nor even Zaragarian, not really. Just some upstart peasant stock, some backwoods farmers who sided with a brutal barbarian from some misbegotten tribe. She knows nothing about culture, history, how to act as befits a woman. She doesn't even dress appropriately. Half the time she dresses like a man.* Neeren fingered the heavy fabric of her restrictive court gown.

She attempted to lower herself to the floor cushions, cursing as her skirts restricted her and she could bend no further without toppling. A slave moved to help her. "No! I can do it!" She contorted her body, wobbled precariously, and hiked up her gown as much as she could before collapsing onto a cushion. Neeren tried to pull her skirt down around her legs in some semblance of dignity. She cursed as a vision of Jadzia's striding in loose fitting clothes spiked her memory. *Who does she think she is, running around free as she pleases?*

Bashtan's words replayed in her mind. 'You'll be first wife, the house will be at peace.' Men! All the power and none of the brains. Fool! It was never that simple.

"There is more than one way to win."

———→

Jadzia swayed as the carriage rocked and rumbled across the cobblestone streets of the Talak capital, Bēdarik. Opposite her, Rada knelt on her seat, gripping the window frame and grinning while gawping at their entourage.

"So, you played with Anfisa? Was she nice? Was Mistress Neeren?"

"Uh huh."

"Rada? Look at me and answer."

"Anfisa was nice. Nicer than I thought."

"And Neeren?" She kept her voice light, but the pinched lines around her eyes and mouth revealed her concern; a tight knot of anxiety sat like a weight inside her.

Rada frowned. "She was... nice, but I don't... understand. She's never been like that before." She scrunched her nose up, thinking. "I liked playing with Anfisa... I don't think she is an enemy."

"No." *Leave it be, Jadzia. Let the child have fun. Neeren has no teeth now.*

Rada shoved her head out of the window. Six imperial guards – men and women – flanked the carriage, their traditional blue shadavoc scarves wrapped around their heads and faces revealed only their eyes and protected them from the sun and the dust. They were turned out as if on parade, black boots shining, straight-backed, chain mail hauberks covered with plate coats whose rivets shone on the leather. Grieves protected their lower legs and their vambraces extended to cover the backs of their hands. Ornate engravings of serpents decorated the metal, which glinted in the morning sun. Each carried a spear from which a pennant fluttered with the imperial insignia and a blue shield bearing their individual family crests dominated by the Zaragarian serpent. They wore long swords; axes hung from their saddles and their hands, gloved in dark leather, rested easily on their reins. As they rode, their blue great-cloaks with their wide sleeves rippled like water.

"They look so good, don't they? Do you think I could be an imperial guard?" Rada's eyes grew wider. "Will we always have them now? Can I ride with Akim on his horse?"

"Yes, they do. Yes, you could – if you train. No, we won't have them always, and ask Akim when we get home. He's got a mission right now – they all are."

Jadzia's lips twitched knowing how gossip would fly and the locals would be aghast at the women in the troop – they always were. *But this is our world, not theirs – not any longer and it's high time they got used to it.*

The dark of the carriage offered blissful shelter from the blazing sun, yet little air stirred its interior. Jadzia wiped loose, sweat-dampened tendrils of hair off her brow. The babe in her arms, belly full, slept fitfully. The image of a remote estate in the northern borderlands of Vēkaria arose in her mind. Memories of a stone and timber hall surrounded by a high wall and the outlying village made her heart ache for her grandmother. It was a large holding, but simple, the home of her forebears – once neither Vēkarian nor Zaragarian. *We've come so far.*

"I can see the temple!" Rada turned her excited face towards her mother. "Are we going there first?"

"No," Jadzia said, trying to cling to the thin pulse of hope beating through her.

"I love temple."

"I know."

"Master Pavel says I can start proper weapons training soon." Rada bit her lip. "Will Papi let me?"

"Papi cannot stop the temple."

"Maybe the temple can do all my tutoring?"

"Not yet. You're not old enough. Nor are you without parents to become one of the Mstislavakan and be raised by the Order. Though your tutors must change." Jadzia shook her head in disgust, thinking about her tutors and lessons thus far. *Less Talakian etiquette, more history, mathematics, more tactics, more languages. The best the empire can offer. I failed*

Abaya, but I now have wings. Her lips quirked in a wry grin. *Well, wings of a sort. Enough to ensure Rada will shine. The more knowledge she gains, the more power she may wield. My children will have their place. Abaya is beyond my help. My boys' fate lies in their own hands. Mstislav willing, they will make fine warriors and, in time, leaders.* She placed the now awake baby upon her shoulder, patting her back. *And you, little one... you...* Tears welled in her eyes. *I pray you will surprise us all.*

The carriage halted in the main square of Bēdarik. On one side, the Temple of Mstislav dominated all before it; around the rest of the square lay the largest trading district. Soon all trading would cease during the hottest time of the day, but in early evening it would resume and the square would be full of vibrant market stalls. Akim opened the carriage door and Rada jumped out. "Let's go! I want to see the shops, go to the temple and see the master... Oh! Will we go to Darklina?"

Akim took the baby from Jadzia and she emerged laughing into the bright light. "Yes!" Rada took off at a run toward the Temple of Mstislav. "Wait, Rada! We have other things to do first!" A guard snagged Rada around the waist, swung her about, and set her back down next to Jadzia. Shoulders slumped, she trudged beside her mother. Jadzia had abandoned Talak clothes; instead of a dress, she wore loose, fine-cotton drawstring trousers under a knee length tunic which split at the sides to her waist. Attached to a broad leather belt was her kadag. Over it all she wore a blue, hooded, sleeveless linen outer tunic – the same blue as the guard, but emblazoned upon the back was her family crest. Despite the intensity of the sun, she left the hood down. *Let none mistake who I am.* She slung a satchel over her shoulders and headed off.

"I'll take her now. You need not play nursemaid," Jadzia said.

Akim smiled, handing the baby back. "I don't mind. I miss my little ones, but I admit it doesn't exactly add to my menace."

"And appearance is all, isn't it?"

"You are every inch a Zaragarian Stilnassa," Akim said.

She dipped her head in thanks before striding down an adjoining street shaded by vast shop awnings. Many Talaks were buying goods in a last-minute rush before the shops shut at midday. Slaves loaded with parcels or carrying baskets full of breads, fruits and vegetables stood, subdued, waiting as masters or housekeepers plied them with more.

Akim marched beside her, two imperial guards at her back while the others remained with the carriage. A hush followed her down the street. All eyes turned toward her, then flicked to her escort; heads bent whispering, but always their gaze fell back upon her and the bundle she carried.

As she passed the stall of a fabric merchant, a group of women exited, slaves behind them weighed down with goods. "Lady Jadzia!" a shrill voice called.

Jadzia groaned. She grabbed Rada's hand, tugging her along. "But Mami?"

"Lady Jadzia! Oh my! I mean Stilnassa Jadzia!" The cry was louder this time. Other shoppers stopped to watch the performance.

Jadzia ground her teeth and spun back to the woman. "Lady Irena, what a delight to meet you this fine morning."

The woman's eyes glittered with a fierce joy as Jadzia approached the group. "Do forgive me, I only heard the edict this morning and, you know, old habits and all that. Did I pronounce it correctly? I hope so. I mean, imagine the offence it could cause if I didn't."

"You did well enough," Jadzia said.

Rada bowed. "Greetings, Lady Chandar."

The woman gave Rada a cursory nod. "Stilnassa Jadzia, I'm all admiration that you are up and about so soon after your confinement. And this is your little one." The other women crowded Jadzia, craning their necks for a glimpse of the babe, pushing Rada out of the way. Lady Chandar reached out to stroke the baby's head. A gasp escaped several of the women and she recoiled her hand at the last minute but made a show of wiping her fingers. "You are so brave..."

"Not brave, Lady Chandar, just a good mother."

The woman drew her lips back as if to snarl, instead smiled dazzlingly as Rada pushed her way back through the crowd to stand, arms folded and frowning between her and Jadzia. "You're favoured by no less than an imperial escort." Akim looked amused as she laid her hand on his arm. "Rarely do we see the imperial guard here, particularly one as handsome as this." Jadzia barely restrained gagging. "How long will they remain at your disposal? It must be such a pleasure to have their service?"

"They are not at my disposal and you would do well to remember that they are here at the emperor's pleasure. Given you are eying Akim like he is a piece of meat to be savoured by you," a collective gasp arose from the group, "I feel I should tell you he's happily married with three children."

"Ah!" Chandar's gaze grew sharp. "Well, marriage doesn't always matter in these things, does it, Stilnassa Jadzia? Not when pleasure is involved... be it the emperor's or otherwise."

"Only to some of us, Chandar. To the rest of us, it always matters." Jadzia turned on her heel and proceeded down the crowded street, chased by whispers of, 'cursed,' 'emperor's bastard... wait and see.'

Rada's gaze moved from one to the other, listening, catching only tone not meaning, but with a cunning smile she said, "Good day, Lady Chandar! May Mstislav bring you all you deserve!" She caught up with her mother.

"Rada," Jadzia warned, although she couldn't resist smiling.

"What?" Rada said, skipping ahead and flicking a glance back at her.

Jadzia's gut clenched, her skin prickled and burned under the eyes that followed her, and the whispers that chased them were like the tolling of bells. *Damn them.*

The Temple of Hokati lay at the end of the street, sitting on an intersection that marked the barrier between the more prosperous traders and the less expensive shops favoured by the poorer Talaks. It occupied several blocks, straddling the boundary between two worlds in order to be accessible to both. At a plain gate built into a high stone wall, Jadzia stopped. Etched into the stone lintel was Hokati holding a baby, and the stonework around the door frame featured fruits, flowers and sheaths of wheat. The guild of healers was under the auspices of the temple, and the best healers in Talak would be here, or they would know where in the empire to find them. *Blessed Hokati, help me.*

"I won't be long. Akim, there's no need for a guard here, unless you wish to make an offering and pray. Rada, do you want to come in?"

They entered a vast paved courtyard garden with a long central pond covered in water lilies.

Rada ran straight to the pond and peered into the water, hunting for the small silvery carp that kept it clean. "There!"

Jadzia continued on past row upon row of medicinal herb beds, each step drawing her closer to the central hall with its high shady portico. The door loomed closer and with each step her heart beat faster; bile rose her throat. *Please... please.*

An acolyte stepped out of the shadowed portico, blocking her path. Startled, Jadzia half turned, shielding the grizzling baby.

"Stilnassa Jadzia, welcome." He bowed, not meeting her eyes, his expression neutral.

"I need to see—"

"Follow me please, the Prefect is expecting you."

The baby shivered as they passed beneath two statues of the goddess and then into the main hall. Offerings of flowers and food sat at the foot of another statue at the far end. Double doors and timber shutters along the sides were open, admitting streams of light, and thick rugs lay in rows on the floor for worshippers to kneel upon. The room was light, airy, peaceful and welcoming, yet it did nothing to quell Jadzia's rising anxiety.

Rada raced up. "You didn't wait."

The acolyte paused. "I think it might be best if Mistress Rada waited here... and... prayed."

Rada scowled, ready to erupt.

Her mother's crisp tones silenced her. "Rada, wait here." A chill crept up Jadzia's spine, but she pasted a smile on her face, bent down, and whispered in Rada's ear. "Remember, don't eat the offerings. They're for the goddess, not you."

Rada rolled her eyes, huffed, and kicked the carpet. "I'm pretty sure the goddess doesn't eat them, just fat priests," she said, eyeballing the acolyte.

As Jadzia and the acolyte walked through the complex, the echo of their feet on the stone floors was the only thing to break the silence. Members of the Order stepped aside and refused to look at her. Only one dared to glance at her – troubled and sympathetic.

The Prefect's study was cosy, with soft rugs, tapestries on the wall, a large desk and comfortable chairs.

"Stilnassa Jadzia, Your Holiness," the acolyte announced.

The Prefect stood before a sideboard loading a plate with dried fruit and nuts; she froze, staring at the plate for few seconds before pouring a goblet of wine.

Jadzia waited for a greeting and received none. Instead, the Prefect brushed past her to sit in a high-backed armchair, placed her food on a side table and selected a fig and held it delicately, scrutinising it before taking a bite.

Jadzia moved to the other chair. "Greetings, Prefect."

"Do not sit, Stilnassa. You'll not be here long. We cannot help you."

"You haven't even examined her."

"And I will not, nor will any of the Order."

"But Hokati is the protector of homes and families."

"Yes. And her protection of your young one started the moment she took root in your belly. For the child to be thus, Hokati is not pleased. She has punished you."

Jadzia glared. "What kind of god curses a child to this?"

"What better way to punish a parent?"

"Punish!" Jadzia hissed the words, struggling to contain her fury as she tried to soothe her fussing babe. "And yet this doesn't punish her father! He disowns her and the crime was his! But not under Talak law... Under Talak law, my consent means nothing."

The Prefect blanched, though her eyes widened. "Enough... I don't..." She looked away from the anguish in Jadzia's eyes.

The woman's jaw clenched, her hand gripped the chair's armrest until her knuckles shone white. Staring at the wall, she said. "There is no rape in marriage, you know that. Besides, you're not the first to claim such, and they didn't all have deformed babes. The rumours—"

"Rumours be damned! You're a hypocrite!" Jadzia's voice boomed down the corridors. The babe wailed in outrage. "You're happy enough to take my money every month for your work, and yet you'll not even examine her!" The Prefect refused to meet her eyes.

"I'm not *happy,* as you say. The temple needs funds if we are to provide for those deserving of our help." She shrugged. "But they are not *this* child."

"Not my child, you mean."

"The midwife we sent you was found in a ditch outside the city with her throat cut. Your husband is a powerful man."

Jadzia's fury melded into a hard, cold ball inside her. "Things change, Prefect, but this conversation will not escape my memory. Ever."

➤———————

Rada hadn't spoken since they left the Temple of Hokati; she stalked the street beside her mother, glaring at anyone who dared look at them too long.

"Rada, ignore them. Their words and whispers are but noise on the wind."

Yet by the tightening of her mother's jaw and lift of her chin, Rada knew it was a lie. The girl's scowl deepened; her mouth turned down – she marched on.

They halted before the towering grey stone Temple of Mstislav. A high, thick, stone crenelated wall surrounded it and the heavy iron gates blocked the entrance to a broad paved path. Two young guards stood sentinel.

Rada ran to the gates and pushed on them. "Why are they locked?" Stricken, she looked at her mother and Akim. "Don't they want us?"

Jadzia leaned down, turning Rada to face her and cupping her face with her free hand. "Rada? Why would you say that?"

"I heard you yell at the Prefect." Her voice became a whisper. "She didn't want to help, did she?"

"No, but we're not beaten yet, are we?" She grinned. "Think of what we've done so far. We'll show them all, won't we?"

"Yes!" Rada said. Hands on hips, she stood protectively in front of her mother, her brows drawn into a sharp vee, as if the force of her glare alone would make them quail.

"Open the gates," Jadzia ordered.

"Lady...." the man began, shaking his head.

Akim stepped in front of her. "Lady! Even if you're Talak, you will address her as Stilnassa Maklova! Get this damn gate open before I lose my temper!" Two more of Jadzia's escort moved in behind him.

"Yes, sir! Our orders—"

"Do you see this? It's the imperial insignia."

The gates swung open. The two sentries bowed their heads as Jadzia and her escort swept past them.

"I *really* want to be an imperial guard now," Rada whispered. She rounded on the gate guards. "You really should've let us in. Master Pavel's going to be very mad at you now."

"Come on, Rada," Jadzia said, tugging her on.

"May Mstislav blight them ten times over," Rada mumbled, stomping off.

As was fit for the god of war, it was more of a fortress than a temple. A symbol of power to dominate the city and people. The gardens surrounding the building had been planned for defence and interspersed with only a few trees and strategically placed deep ponds. Low grasses and shrubs gave way to small enclaves for the lesser gods, all of whom faced the temple in abeyance. Two more guards stood outside the double doors that led inside. The tall, lower floor of the temple had no other openings except narrow slits through which to fire arrows. More sentries patrolled the parapet which ran around the top of the lower level.

The second floor balconies overlooked the garden and front entrance. Stained glass windows graced the uppermost levels, though they had heavy defensive timber shutters.

Rada grabbed Akim's hand. "You must stop here and look up. Mami and I do this each time. We love those windows," she said. "Mami taught me all about the stories in them. About the Zaragarians leaving the desert and Aitor I and how we beat the Vēkarians." Rada craned her neck, following the building's design upward to the culminating glory of a statue of Mstislav, the Zaragarian god of war and now head of their pantheon and protector of all lesser gods.

"See? It's the best!" Rada ran ahead.

Jadzia smiled but shook her head. "She's so unlike her sister. Abaya had little interest in such things. Teaching her history, making her understand the importance of our ancient culture – it was like pulling teeth. Without understanding the past, how can we navigate the present?"

"You worry about her?" Akim said.

"A mother worries about all her children. Abaya will do well enough by Talak standards." She shrugged. "She'll survive whatever comes, that much of me she has in her. Rada will be fine..." Her brow creased as she gazed, pensive, at the statue.

"Stilnassa?" Akim asked, rousing her from her contemplation.

"I'll speak with Master Pavel. You'll have time to pray if you want while you wait."

Jadzia hesitated in the doorway as her eyes adjusted to the dark. The austere facade belied the interior. White marble floors stretched to a huge central statue, standing over a fallen enemy – sword poised resting on his sternum. The bronze contours were muscular, athletic. Black scale armour, cast separately and then fitted to the statue, hung to his knees and covered his torso and arms. The body was every woman's dream, but in armour a nightmare. This was Mstislav in all his glory as he had come to Aitor I. It was a smaller version of the one that dominated the Avenue of the Gods in the Vēkarian capital, Dēbar.

Master Pavel bent before the statue, dipping a brush in a bowl of blood and painting it upon Mstislav's feet. He turned to face her, standing tall and straight despite his years. The old man's visage was deeply wrinkled, darkly tanned and weathered; his nose had been broken several times. The warrior priest's uniform included a blue cloak, the same as the imperial guards, but he wore a black scaled leather outer tunic resembling Mstislav's armour. He broke into a grin as Rada raced past Jadzia, slid to a stop, and bowed before him. Laughing, he hugged her with one arm while trying to balance the bowl and brush in the other hand.

"Careful, Mistress Rada, or you'll be wearing this."

She shrugged. "I don't care. It's just nice to see a friendly face. Can I help?" He handed her the basin. Peering at the contents, she asked. "Is it fresh?"

Pavel's eyebrows rose; he put his hands on his hips. "Of course! Are you trying to tell me my job?"

"It's not one of the Darklinan, is it?"

"Never! They know to keep their noses clean."

Rada sniggered and murmured, "They're just too clever to get caught."

"It's just some slave who stole from his master. In a fit of community mindedness, the master gave him to us."

"Good." Rada took the bowl from him and commenced painting the base of the statue. "Master Pavel, could you please address me as Stilniat Rada? Akim says that should be my title since I'm Zaragarian." She continued babbling. "He says it's a bit more important than Mistress. Mistress Neeren wasn't very happy about that..."

"Rada, you didn't..." Jadzia said.

"It just slipped out. I said sorry." She shrugged. "Master Pavel, do you know I'm going to be an imperial guard when I'm bigger?"

Pavel's lips twitched. "Excellent. You'll have to train hard. They don't accept just anyone."

She paused, frowning, mid brush stroke. "Perhaps then you can bless me and ask Mstislav to help me? There's a lot I've got to do and he should probably help."

"I'll bless you," he said, dipping his finger in the blood and smearing a line down her forehead and her chin. "I suggest you pray to him and *ask* him to help you – don't *tell* him. But I think you should ask for some humility first." She opened her mouth to speak, but he cut her off. "And I suggest you do it silently. I think your mother would like to speak to me in private while you work." He ushered Jadzia out of the room.

Rada stared after them. When they were out of earshot, she asked, "Akim, what's humility?"

CHAPTER 9

Jadzia followed Master Pavel into his study. The brightly lit yet sparsely furnished room held only a desk, a set of shelves housing innumerable scrolls and several Matyrani books. To the side sat a stand holding his armour, and a chair rested before a cold, blackened fireplace. Jadzia eyed the maps of Talak and Vēkaria laid out upon his desk and the chain mail draped over the back of the chair.

"You've come out of retirement?"

"You know men like me never retire," he said as he rolled the maps up. "We're just shelved until the need arises."

"The need?"

"The Grand Master sent word; they have mobilised the Order to assist the emperor." When she opened her mouth to speak, Pavel cut her off. "Ask the emperor. Stilnassa, I've been waiting. Bashtan's cronies have spread word about the birth and the evidence of your sins."

Jadzia snorted her derision. "So I've gathered. He's quicker than I gave him credit."

"Rumours flew on the day of her birth. Particularly since the midwife never made it home and the city watch were called to investigate."

"I can't say I'm sorry. He's an idiot. If he wanted rumours spread, he should have let her live. Well, he can sort out that mess on his own, and may it bite him."

"I suspect he thought things would go his way and none would be the wiser. Stilnassa, you should be careful, you're still his wife. Many Talak laws are different to our own, and they accord certain rights and respect be given to your husband. You were lucky."

"How much luck do you think exists in this world? Is not everything the will of the gods?"

"Do you believe you know their will?" His words whipped out.

Jadzia bent her head. "No, of course not, Master Pavel. I've come to ask if you'll perform the naming rite? And... can the Order's medicos aid her?"

Pavel stood, arms outstretched. Jadzia hesitated; a flicker of worry crossed her face. She clutched the baby to her; reluctant to hand her over lest she discover Pavel would reject her too. "Come, Stilnassa," the master said, his coldness gone. "Give me the babe."

He lay the child upon the tabletop, unwrapped her and ran his finger down her cheek with a smile. "She's thrown to your lineage; darker and her eyes have our slope." Looking askance at Jadzia, he said, "I see no Talak in this babe."

"Good."

Pavel shook his head with a wry grin before he picked up the babe's leg, running his fingers along the calf muscle; he cupped her heal and tested the movement in the foot. The baby's face contorted and she cried out, her fists pumping the air as she squirmed.

"Stilnassa, the medicos of our Order deal with the wounds of soldiers, not this."

"Perhaps another...?"

"No. I've served as both warrior and a healer here; I'm old and I've seen a great many things. None of our other healers will tell you any different. She'd be better off without this foot. If she were grown, I'd amputate it. As a babe that would kill her. I'm loath to break the bones of a baby and force the foot into a better position. Take her to the Temple of Hokati. The healers there are second to none."

"Evika!" Jadzia muttered.

"You've already been?"

She gave a sharp nod and, jaw clenched, she wiped away tears. When she met his gaze, her body was rigid but her heart pounded as she asked, "Will you perform the naming rite?"

"I cannot. She's not fit. One day, if she's proven herself, then she may be admitted to the Order and given a new name, but that's unlikely." Jadzia swept up the babe, tucking the blankets around her. "You're aware our ranks are filled with soldiers. Those given the naming rite here as babes are from lines of warriors, or the orphaned whom we choose as Mstislavakan and all must be deemed perfect."

Jadzia's gut clenched. "Can you bless her?"

"I cannot bless her without her having a true name."

"So, no naming rite and not even a blessing. I've been a faithful follower all my life. I've worked for the good of the empire all my life!"

He gave a heavy sigh. "I'm sorry, but you can name her yourself."

"It's not the same." She continued, furious. "And if something befalls her and she dies? What then?" The baby grizzled. Jadzia rubbed the child's back but her actions were hasty, tense and the babe let out a broken cry. "Shh, shh," Jadzia said. She continued in a bitter whisper, "My babe will linger in between worlds, never reaching the afterlife, condemned to wander in the Shadow Lands, trapped, with no hope of return in the next life."

"Stilnassa, I'm sorry."

She bowed her head, her face twisted in grief; when she looked up, the plea in her expression seemed to rock him and he stepped back. She spun and ran out.

"Jadzia, wait." Master Pavel's voice chased her and the sound of her footsteps and the babe's cries.

In the lower corridor, Jadzia slowed and leaned against the cool stone wall. Gasping, she struggled for calm, hugging her child and rocking her gently. "Shh, shh, little one." Her stomach cramped; she fought a wave of nausea and broke out in a cold sweat. "I'll think of something. There has to be a way."

The entrance to the main chamber of the temple loomed at the end of the corridor. *Enough! You weep like some mongrel Talak.* Drawing a deep breath, Jadzia pushed herself off the wall and straightened, once again the tall, proud Stilnassa. The babe slowly settled. Jadzia raised her head to find Pavel staring at her from the base of the stairs.

"Jadzia, there's still something we can do."

Her breath hitched. "What?"

"I can bless you and beseech Mstislav to guide you in your quest to help your daughter. You're already an initiate of the temple and a devoted follower."

It's not enough. Her lips drew into a thin line, and she struggled to keep the sarcasm from her voice. "Are you sure that's what you want to do?" *Be still, Jadzia. You knew this was but a slim chance.*

"It breaks no rules and though it's not what you had hoped, it's all I can offer. Will you take it?"

She hesitated; her shoulders slumped. "Gladly."

Jadzia followed him to the great statue in the temple's main hall and knelt at its base.

Concerned and bewildered, Rada ceased her work and moved to Jadzia's side. "Mami? Didn't Master help?"

"It's all right, Rada." Her daughter wrapped her arms about Jadzia's neck and tucked her head against her shoulder. "Master Pavel is doing what he can. Watch."

"All praise to Mstislav, protector and deliverer," Pavel intoned.

"All praise to Mstislav, god above gods," Jadzia replied.

"Hear my petition. Keep your devout daughter, Stilnassa Jadzia, ever in your eye. I beseech you, as she stays faithful and forsakes you not, to guide her and protect her." He placed his finger in the bowl of blood and smeared it across her forehead, under her eyes, and down her chin. "With the blood of the slain, I bless you. May your courage never waver. May your aim be true, your sword arm strong and your steel never dull. May your enemies fall before you."

Jadzia bowed her head, touching the statue's feet. "All praise to Mstislav, god above gods."

— — — ▶

Jadzia, leaned her head back against the carriage seat and sighed.

"Why are we taking the carriage? Normally, we make sure no one knows where we're going," Rada said.

"I promised we'd go and I can't figure out a way to hide six imperial guards, can you?" Jadzia said.

Rada giggled. "They do stick out."

"Which you rather like, don't you?"

She broke into a huge grin. "It's a bit special."

"And anyway," Jadzia said. "Today I don't think it will hurt if a few people see us." Rada screwed her face up, puzzled. "It's complicated, Rada."

Rada huffed, and pouted. She bent over the wicker basket strapped to the seat, patted her sister on the head, and leaned back against the carriage seat. "I knew Master Pavel would help."

Jadzia gave a tired smile as she rubbed her stomach, trying to ease the cramping. "Master Pavel did what he could, Rada, but it wasn't enough."

"He blessed us, though."

"Yes, but your sister needs to undergo the naming ritual like you did when you were born. If she dies without being named and blessed in a temple, then she'll not go to the afterlife."

Rada's jaw dropped. "The Shadow Lands?" Jadzia nodded. Rada gripped the edge of her sister's basket. "Well, I'll just make sure nothing happens to her then! Will he fix her leg?"

"No. It's beyond his skill."

Rada put her hands on her hips. "Will he even try?" Jadzia shook her head. "Why? I don't understand why everyone who's nice is being mean and everyone who's mean is being nice."

"Master Pavel wasn't mean. He doesn't hate us or your sister." Jadzia sighed. "Though people are rarely what they seem, Rada. It's possible to know someone all your life and misjudge them... or not. It's complicated."

Rada rolled her eyes. "Everything's complicated!" She crossed her arms and stared sullenly out of the window. *Neeren's being nice... I was bad to Anfisa, but now I'm nice. Maybe Neeren was angry because I was bad to Anfisa... maybe she really is nice... I don't know...*

"I hate being litt... a *child*."

Jadzia's lips quirked. "Don't worry. It doesn't last." Jadzia laughed, yet in her heart she knew the weight of those words. *In fact, I fear it will end all too soon.*

The journey ended in a dusty, debris-filled square with a central well surrounded by decrepit buildings. Decades of repair meant a patchwork of different coloured stone and mortar dotted the walls, and the shingle roofs topped the warped and greying timber upper floors like beggar's teeth — more holes than anything else.

The guards' hands tightened on their spears as they scanned the buildings. Jadzia laughed. "Welcome to the old city, Akim. Known as The Bone Yard. We're deep within the poor part of Bēdarik. You needn't worry; I'm safer here than anywhere else."

"If you say so, Stilnassa." Eyes narrowed, head cocked, he scanned the surrounding buildings. "I feel like we're being watched."

"We are. Come, the carriage can go no further and we've still got quite a walk."

"Stilnassa, you're very pale. Perhaps..."

"I'll be fine. I'll rest when we get there." She headed off, calling over her shoulder, "I wouldn't leave the horses unattended, though."

"Evika!" Akim murmured. "You two stay here," he called as he jogged to catch up. "The rest with me."

Rada laughed, racing up to Jadzia. "Mami, Akim just swore."

The streets grew narrower and some were barricaded. Their path lay strewn with detritus from the city – old barrels, crates, a derelict wagon and broken furniture. Out of the corner of his eye, Akim glimpsed shapes shifting in the shadowed alleys before vanishing. A flicker of movement on a roof top caught his eye, but it disappeared in a blink.

"I gather they don't like visitors here."

"We're nearing what was the heart of the Old City," Jadzia said. A rumble sounded behind them as a wagon rolled across the end of the street, trapping them. Each of guards swivelled, spears at ready. "Easy. While you are with Rada and I, you will be safe, but I would advise you to remain calm nonetheless. If they believe we are under duress, then things will be entirely different. Just keep walking."

They halted before a long, low, sandstone building. Above the narrow, darkened doorway was the effigy of a woman's torso on the body of a spider. She spun a large web and its crumbling threads ran around the walls.

Akim snagged Jadzia's arm. Instinctively, she snapped her arm free of him and a fierce, haunted expression flashed across her face. "Forgive me, Stilnassa, but this is the Temple of The Weaver. We shouldn't be here."

"This was once her temple, but it has long since fallen into disuse. Now it's known as Darklina." Akim frowned. "It's Talakian slang for dark heart. The residents have styled themselves the Darklinan."

"Residents?" Akim asked, his voice sharp. Her guard shared quick, worried looks, and their formation around her tightened. "I thought you said it had fallen into disuse."

"As a temple, it has. I assure you, it is no longer a haven for a cadre of her followers."

Akim's jaw clenched and a vein pounded at his temple. "Once a temple, always a temple. The bond with its god can't be sundered."

Jadzia's frowned. "Akim, *no one* could get here to pray, even if they wanted to. The Darklinan won't let others in. Besides, even though Aitor I banished the priests of The Weaver, he didn't make it illegal to walk through the door and pray or make an offering to her, so long as Mstislav is acknowledged as the highest of the gods and none refute it."

"A mere technicality, as you're aware. Stilnassa, just because a door is open does not mean you should walk through it."

"If you're afraid to enter, then I must question your certainty in your faith to Mstislav. You can come or not. I don't care. But if do you come in, guard your gold well, this is, after all, a den of thieves."

Rada smirked. "The Darklinan are the best pickpockets in the city." She sighed dramatically. "I haven't got the knack of it yet."

"What!" Akim's eyebrows nearly disappeared into his hairline.

Jadzia was straight faced. "Rada, don't jest with him. She's actually quite good."

In a high, affected tone, almost perfectly mimicking Neeren, Rada said, "A *lady* needs all kinds of skills." Akim's jaw dropped and she snorted with laughter.

The door swung open before Jadzia could knock. A scruffy teenage girl beckoned them in.

Jadzia smiled at her as she entered. "Hello, Silla."

The girl made a half bow, but her gaze never left the blue-cloaked soldiers. "Coming? Or have the emperor's finest lost their nerve?"

Rada looked back at them. "Well, are you coming, or what?" She ran inside laughing.

Akim ground his teeth and groaned. "Come on, then."

They jogged down a short corridor, catching up to Jadzia and Rada before they exited into a broad courtyard. Unlike the streets outside, this area was orderly; from the long, well-tended garden beds and espaliered fruit trees to the stacked wooden crates by the storeroom door. A gnarled, multi-trunked peppercorn tree shaded the centre of the yard. Sitting in the dappled shade, along a semi-collapsed trunk was a group of children in worn, patched clothes. At the sight of the guards, their chatter ceased and they froze, wide eyed.

"Don't worry about them," Rada called, slipping between the guards. She ran to the children, grabbing the nearest one by the hand and tugging him with her. "Come and see! I've got a sister! Come on!"

The young Darklinan looked warily at each other and hesitantly stepped forward, but Jadzia strode to them. "They won't hurt you. The emperor has assigned them to guard Rada and I for a little while. Soon I'll have my own guards and they'll be gone."

"Did someone try to hurt you?" an outraged boy said.

The others stared at him in shock. Rada's mouth went dry; she refused to meet their eyes.

"Who?"

Papi. Rada's hands twisted her tunic and she kicked the ground.

"Why?"

"Tell us who! We'll fix 'em."

You can't. Nobody can. Rada's stomach roiled.

"Everything's fine now. Don't worry. Would you like to meet the new little one?" Jadzia tried to balance the baby on her knees and unwrap her.

"Stilnassa, allow me," Akim said. The children scuttled back as he placed his cloak on the ground. He winked at the nearest one. "They fed me this morning. I won't bite." The child tucked herself behind Rada.

"Thank you, Akim," Jadzia said, sitting on the cloak, laying the baby down and unbundling her.

As soon as Akim stepped away, the children clustered around, each leaning over the one next to them in order to see.

Rada hovered beside the baby. "She's only little, so you have to be gentle."

"Move. Let me see."

Jadzia uncovered her legs and a hush fell on the group.

"She's like Ivanka and Roman."

"Yes," Jadzia replied.

"You didn't let them take her to the hills."

"No!" Rada said. "Mami and the emperor saved her."

Silence. An awed whisper broke the hush. "The emperor?"

A long shadow fell over them, and the children parted. A lanky boy of about sixteen sat down. He grinned lopsidedly as the babe grasped his finger. "She's pretty for a runt, isn't she?"

Rada punched him. "She's not a runt! Be nice."

He ignored her, instead looking intently at Jadzia. "Are you going to leave her here like the others do?"

"You know me better than that. No one will take my children from me. But you'll be seeing a lot of her, so I hope you look out for her like brothers and sisters should. She's going to need all our help. Agreed?" They all nodded. "Now off you go, leave me with Tav. I have to hear his report."

A thin woman with a harried expression stepped out of a nearby door. Locks of her frizzy hair had escaped her scarf and flour dust clung to them.

"Demenka! I've got a sister!" Rada yelled.

The woman made her way to them, wiping her hands on an apron. The smell of freshly-baked bread clung to her. "Lady Jadzia... oh... I mean Stilnassa!"

"Never mind that, Demenka," Jadzia said, beckoning her over.

"Well bless me, what a sweet little 'un." She put her hand on Jadzia's shoulder. "You look done in, my la... Stilnassa. Like we need to take care of you for a bit."

Jadzia smiled. "Mistress Demenka, that sounds lovely."

"Oh, stop that! You know I ain't no Mistress Demenka!" She chortled, flattered as always.

A small girl took Demenka's hand, whispering. "Did you see? The little one is like your Roman."

Demenka bent down to her. "I did and she's beautiful too, ain't she?" Demenka clapped her hands. "Come on young 'uns," she said. "Lunch! The bread's just about cool enough to eat and you can help set up for lunch. Go on get! Will you stay, Stilnassa?"

"I'd hoped you'd offer. I need to rest a little and think."

"Then you shall have it," Demenka whispered, squeezing her shoulder and kissing her cheek.

Rada cast a worried glance at Tav and moved closer to him, gripping his hand. "Mami?"

"I'm fine. You go help. We'll be there soon."

Rada stood firm. Tav squeezed her hand and nodded. "Go on, Squirt. Safe as houses here, eh?" he said with a twist of his lips.

Rada's cheeks dimpled. "Safe as houses," she said and left; two of the guard followed her. Halfway to the temple door, she turned, chewed her lip and took one step back toward her mother.

Tav made a shooing motion, calling out. "Safe as houses, Squirt." Still, Rada hesitated.

Demenka leaned out of the door and clapped her hands. "Rada, hurry. You'll miss out. You too," she yelled at Akim and the remaining guard with Jadzia. "Get over here! There's none but family here for our lady and Rada. They're safe as—"

"Safe as houses! Yes, I heard! We stay with the Stilnassa." Demenka spat on the ground but retreated. "How many archers have you got on the roof, boy?"

Tav blanched. "None."

Jadzia laughed. "Tav, he's an imperial guard. They're not stupid."

"Three," Tav admitted.

"Good enough," Akim said, nodding curtly. "For us, or regular security."

"Would you feel flattered if I said yes?"

Akim's brow arched and he glared at Tav.

Tav shrugged, letting him wait, and smiling at the babe who gripped his finger. "Not your concern, is it? Would you tell an intruder your security?"

A wisp of a smile curled the edge of Akim's lip. "You'll do, boy. You'll do."

Jadzia sighed. "Behave, both of you. Now, Tav, what do you have for me?"

"Lady Rodan and her young son are prisoners of the Order. Rumour is they snagged them near the border with Nējarak. No gossip on General Cēdar's family. Maybe they got away."

"Hopefully not, but the network is vast. News will come. Anything else."

"The usual. Lord Donak bought a bunch of pretty new slaves and his wife's fairly well pissed off."

"Marvellous! Disgruntled spouses, always an opportunity there."

"Lady Serdag has been overspending in the dressmakers and her husband's been forking out a fortune at the wine merchant's."

"See if they've borrowed—"

"Already done. Sillas, the money lender, was paying them a visit. All dressed up like a lord he was. Still sticks out like dog's balls and probably stinks as bad too."

"Desperate people, lovely. I'm sure I can use that. How was your haul this week?"

"Good enough. Could always be better."

"Spoken like a true rogue. Here." She fished out a bag of coins. "There should be enough in there for Demenka to buy food, but also to get a supply of better clothes and old boots. I wish you could just buy new ones."

"Stilnassa Jadzia, we buy new ones and they'd notice us and think we've stolen 'em. You don't want us noticed."

"True." She remained silent for a while staring at her babe. When she roused herself from her reverie, she said, "Tav, how many of the Darklinan would want to stay here if something better came along?"

"Things are better, but still, some of 'em shouldn't stay. They won't last the distance. Others could go, but won't want to, 'cause here they're nobody's slave. They control their own fate."

"Only to a limited extent, Tav. They've not the skills to do else and this life never makes for a long one."

"Are you offering a choice?"

"Perhaps a way out for those who choose it."

"But we'd still be reporting to you."

"Only for time, then they'd be free to choose... I hope." The baby wailed. "Feeding time for everyone."

Jadzia and Tav headed into the building.

Akim sighed. "Well, we're already in the damn temple, we may as well eat lunch."

Despite the occasional wary glace at the imperial guards, the atmosphere inside was raucous.

Rubbing her temple, Jadzia grimaced and said to Demenka. "I need somewhere private to feed her."

"I've just the place. Tav, you come too. You can stop the little 'uns from bursting in. Give our lady some privacy."

Demenka led Jadzia along a corridor before unlocking a door and ushering her into a small room with a simple camp bed and a set of drawers. "I use this as a sick bay. The little 'uns used to be scared 'cause of that painting." Behind the bed, a life-size image of The Weaver decorated the wall. Long, straight black hair floated behind her and from her spider-half ran a web dotted with small white spots, which seemed to stretch into infinity. She smiled serenely; her arms were open and her slanted eyes seemed to look through you. A delicate, dark web marked her forehead.

Jadzia froze, staring at a likeness she'd not seen since childhood. She resisted the urge to bow her head as her grandmother's litany sprung into her mind. *Bethsinidar – weaver, mother, wise, beneficent and cruel...* She stopped herself, stricken.

"I didn't... It's... different... But I see they got over their fear; someone has been trying to add to it."

"Yep. I keep it locked now. It didn't seem right... drawing on it. I mean, it's her house and..." She scratched her head, shrugging, embarrassed. "Sounds stupid, but it seemed impolite. Now, you settle yourself down and I'll put lunch aside for you before the horde eats the damn lot." Demenka hesitated. "My lady, the rumours... you've been in the wars and no mistake."

Jadzia's face crumpled and she drew a quick, deep breath shaking her head. "I've got soft here, Demenka. I'm not as tough as I used to be."

"Nonsense! You're as tough as they come! You'll bounce back. You know, there'll be doors open to help. Mayhap they've always been there, but you just didn't notice. At least that's what I believe. You'll find them. Now, I'll go sort out some grub for you."

A female guard jogged up the hall and poked her head around the door, saw the image, froze, turned back and waited outside. "Stilnassa?"

"I'm fine," Jadzia called.

Tav looked the guard up and down, brow cocked at the hunk of bread in her hand. The woman had the grace to look sheepish. "Nice to see you've got your priorities right. If I'd been a bad sort, I could have killed her before you got here."

The guard poked him in the chest. "If you think you and that rabble of street rats—"

"Enough!" Jadzia said. "You would do well to remember that those street rats work for your emperor. Do not speak like that again in my presence!"

"Yes, Stilnassa."

"And Tav, stop causing trouble. Go, eat and check that the Darklinan don't fleece the emperor's finest."

Tav scowled at the now grinning soldier and disappeared.

"Well, nothing's worrying you, is it?" Jadzia told the baby as it suckled. "What will we call you? Misha? Marta? Anika?" Jadzia screwed her nose up. "No, I don't think so. We'll have to ponder on it. Perhaps your big sister has an idea. Although knowing her, she'd probably believe Boris was good. We'll find something." She relaxed in the blissful quiet of the room until her babe had finished. Jadzia lay the little one down on the bed and with a sigh, pulled clean cloths from a bag to change her.

Her eyes strayed to the charcoal web drawn by the children that wove around the room. Jadzia's skin crawled. Quickly, she turned and stared at The Weaver. Her eyes danced between her now content child and the open arms of the goddess behind her; a small spark of hope flared in her chest. The door is open... *You can't...* Her pulse raced. *You shouldn't...* She paced the room. *It's an old debt... ancient even. You'll need a pretext for going.* Rapidly, she scanned through scenarios. *You only want help for her... nothing more. It's not like you're starting a revolution. Calm down. Finish up here. The sooner you are home, the sooner you can journey north.*

She finished cleaning the babe, dressed and rewrapped her, before exiting the room. The guard fell into step behind her.

Tav lounged against a wall, waiting. "I've been talking to Rada. She hides it, but she's still a bit shaky. You went into battle for the babe, didn't you? At home I mean."

Jadzia lingered with Tav, her posture stiff. "Sometimes you see too much, Tav." He fidgeted. "What else? Out with it?"

"You're recruiting your own guard, aren't you?"

Her gaze softened. "Do you want to join?" Embarrassed, he crossed his arms and looked away. "Why?"

"Lady Jadzia, you fought for a baby most people would chuck out or hide. You get information from us but you don't have to treat us as well as you do. We don't go hungry, we've got better clothes. Evika! I only steal now to keep in practise. I don't know what's coming, but I get a feeling you'll need all the help you can get."

"My family wasn't always as well off as it is now. I was raised not to forget that." She walked outside into the brilliant sunshine, halting to watch Rada. Tav opened his mouth to speak, but she silenced him with a wave of her hand. Rada stood next to a young boy her age, both had slings and were surrounded by all the Darklinan. Halfway across the yard, two pottery containers sat on a stone bench. The soldiers watched with keen interest.

"Last round. Two all," Silla called.

"Final bets!" A large boy yelled and a flurry of small coins passed hands.

Silla whispered in Rada's ear.

"Hey! No cheating!"

"She's got to do it on her own!"

"Leave off!"

Rada took aim, let fly, and shattered the container. She jumped up and punched the air to a chorus of cheers. The boy scowled and aimed. At the last second, he lowered his hands, shook his head, wiped his brow.

"Bloody showman he is," Tav muttered. "Get on with it!" he yelled. Though he was seemingly focused on the competition, Jadzia saw his eyes keep darting to her. "Stilnassa Jadzia?"

She held up a hand, silencing him, and intently watched the competition. With a cocky grin, the boy with the sling let fly with his pebble. It whizzed through the air, striking the stone seat right next to the pottery and ricocheted into the wall. He stood there slack mouthed; Rada jumped into the air whooped in delight. Akim lifted her onto his shoulders and held out his hand for his winnings.

Jadzia turned to Tav and her gaze bore into him. "Your skill set is impressive, but there'll be a great deal of combat training involved. Are you prepared for that?"

He stood taller, shoulders back. "Yes."

"Who'll take over here?"

He broke out in a grin, pointing at the girl with Rada. "Silla is ready."

"Make sure she is. She must report to Katya for a few weeks. You're coming with me, we're going travelling."

"Stilnassa Jadzia, thank you!" He spun around and whooped for joy.

"Don't thank me yet. What I'm about to do could land us in a lot of trouble."

He laughed. "More trouble than being caught stealing and winding up sacrificed to Mstislav?"

"Yes... same result though."

"I'm in!"

Akim joined them, lowering Rada to the ground.

"Well done, Rada!" Jadzia said. "Come on, home time. Tav, I'll have Katya bring you a uniform. Report to me in two days.

Grinning, he saluted her. "Yes!"

Rada gasped. "Will Tav be with us?"

Tav scooped her up. "Yes, little squirt! I'm going to train to be one of your mother's new guards." Rada wrapped her arms around his neck and hugged him.

Jadzia turned from the main gate. "Oh, and Tav, you'll have schooling too."

The grin fell from his face.

"Don't worry," Rada whispered. "I'll help. I'm an expert."

CHAPTER 10

Bashtan reclined on a long, low couch in the private courtyard garden adjacent to his study. At a wave of his hand, a slave poured him another glass of wine.

The quiet sound of footsteps padding across the tiled floor of his study greeted him. "Neeren?"

"Sorry to disappoint you," Jadzia said.

He slammed the wine goblet down, sending the deep purple liquid over the fruit, cheeses and nuts that lay before him. "Dammit!" A slave rushed to clean up the mess. "Enough! Take it away; bring me fresh." He clicked his fingers, impatiently as one slave rushed to pass him another goblet of wine, while another ran from the room to fetch more food.

Jadzia flicked her hands at the remaining slaves, dismissing them. "Leave us."

"Jadzia... Oh wait, should I call you Stilnassa?" Bashtan said.

"Grow up, Bashtan."

"What do you want, woman? I hope you haven't come here to fight because I'm tired of it."

"Really? You're off to such a good start."

"Evika, woman!" Brows knotted, he made to rise.

She held up her hands. "Peace, Bashtan. In truth, we're both tired of it. The emperor's arrangement suits neither of us and was not my doing," she said. He grunted. "I would have us both free. Neither of us chose this marriage. You wanted Neeren as your first wife, never me."

"Yes." Lips drawn thin, he swirled the wine in his goblet, intent upon it. "I suppose we've got to learn to manage as best we can and stay out of each other's way."

"For Rada's sake, at least."

His hand stilled and his tone was glacial. "Oh, you've remembered that you've got another daughter, have you?"

Jadzia's brow arched, but schooling her features, she laced her hands before her and sat opposite him. "I'm leaving in two days to travel north to see my family."

"Surely you don't want permission to leave? Gods, woman, go!"

"I would like to take Rada with me. It's been a long time since she's seen my family... but I've told her she must ask you for permission."

"So, I'll be the bad one."

"Bashtan, we're both her parents. It might do her good to leave this house for a few weeks and forget the chaos she's witnessed. I hope the break will let everything settle between us."

"It'll take more than a few weeks for that to happen."

Her index finger drummed upon her thigh. Bashtan grinned at the sign of her irritation. To his disappointment she did not rise to the bait.

"Not on my part. I mean what I say." Jadzia drew a deep breath. "When I return, the builder will meet me to discuss plans for my wing."

"*Your wing?* What if I don't grant you use of the land?"

"Bashtan, we've no choice in this. You should view it as a boon. You don't want me underfoot and I'll pay for the extension. When I'm gone, it could be ideal guest accommodation or your own personal playpen." He shot her a venomous glance. Ignoring him, she continued. "Either way, it adds to the value of this property and will eventually be yours. Let's just get along. You and Neeren can play happy families. I'll just show up for official functions, otherwise we'll lead separate lives."

"I'm ordered about in my home." His gaze grew cunning. "You're paying for this wing?"

"Yes."

"It's been enough of a nightmare. Fine, I'll endeavour to deal with this."

"Rada?"

"I'll think about it. But you must abide by my decision."

She ground her teeth. "Agreed. Bashtan, we must start somewhere. We must *try*."

When Jadzia left, Neeren entered the study. "You heard?"

"Yes. My lord, I don't feel it's wise to send Rada with Jadzia. The journey is not without risk."

His brow arched. "How is it risky, my love?"

Neeren's mind raced. *She can't go.* "Jadzia is right, the quiet time would be perfect for Rada to recover from the last few days, but if she were here, it would be an excellent opportunity for you and Rada to regain lost ground. You could win back your daughter."

Bashtan considered this. "Is it so far gone that I must win her back?"

Neeren closed the distance between them, wrapping her arms about him. "She's a child, and she's confused. Right now, you're not her favourite person and you should be. She feels you've betrayed her and your duty."

"What does a child know of duty?"

"Rada is driven by duty and love. That's not a bad thing, though in much else she is misguided."

"I didn't think you liked her."

Neeren gave a musical laugh. "Hardly. We are simply very different and I see potential in her. Potential that only needs the right guidance. I guarantee Jadzia shall rebel against the emperor's edict and expect to get away with it, but he cannot allow that. It shall work in our favour."

"How so?"

"Her rebellion will see her lose favour, at least for a while, during which we can act. Talak law still stands. If she breaks her marriage, the child stays with you. Jadzia is not a fit mother. Rada is but a child. It's not too late to undo the damage done to her education. If I take her in hand now, she'll still turn out to be a fine example of Talakian womanhood. She'll grow to be quite pretty, she has beguiling eyes – she can already turn them to her advantage." Neeren smiled. "I've lost count of the number of times you've let her get away with things because she's given you her wide-eyed innocent look."

"She is six. Her education has been simple reading, writing, languages, basic etiquette, memorising family lineage, the Talak rulers. Nothing to cast blame over," Bashtan said.

Neeren laughed. "Hardly! Her head is full of all the nonsense Jadzia teaches her. Where do you think she gets this rebelliousness from? The ridiculous idea that she can become a member of the Zaragarian guard? Your daughter! It is beyond inappropriate and won't help her in Talak society. If you leave her with her mother, she'll only continue down the same path she is now on."

"Jadzia is her mother, Neeren. She must have some contact with her."

"Of course! But Rada must remain with you and leave her education to me. You know how Sasha has turned out. She already has offers coming in from across Talak and beyond into Nējarak. She will bring powerful alliances to this family and our strength will make us indispensable to the emperor. Jadzia has never had the same values as us and now I would bet my life that she'll not heed what you want for the child. By the goddess Hokati, who'll take Rada unless I can turn her into the jewel she should be?"

He sighed. "She will resent you and me even more."

"It shall not be easy but will need delicate managing. I... we can do it. Enough sweetener can make even the most bitter pill a delight."

➤

Rarely did Neeren deign to visit many of the merchants in Bēdarik other than the dressmaker, perfumer, or toy store, yet today she'd set foot in a dozen stores. She plastered a smile on her face. *Remember your mission. Even if you fail, Jadzia has all but said she'd leave the running of the house to you.*

Neeren breezed into the crowded merchant's store and the prickle of pepper, the sweet hint of cinnamon and cardamon pods along with the tang of spices from across Penīdīen, assailed her. The counters held an array of not only spices, but exotic fruits, preserves, and wines and cheeses. Her nose wrinkled in distaste as a slave proffered a tray carrying a pungent cheese covered in fine blue mould. "Mistress, would you like to sample some fine Rēsphian blue?"

Neeren's hand flew to her mouth, and she shook her head.

"Are you sure?" The slave thrust the tray under her nose.

Neeren groaned and tried to quell rising bile. She pushed the tray away. "No! Get away!"

The shopkeeper hurried over. "Leave the lady alone, you dolt!" He hauled the slave away. "Can't you see she loathes the stuff?" He bowed low. "My profound apologies! You're Mistress Neeren, are you not?"

"Yes, but I don't believe I've met you."

"Oh, my lady," he bowed. "But I've seen you when you've been out shopping. It's hard to forget one so beautiful." Neeren preened. "I try to remember all the members of the notable families, but you, you are so easy to remember. We're honoured."

A wry smile twisted Neeren's lips. "So I gathered."

The merchant froze, realising he'd overplayed his part. "How may I be of service?"

"Lady Jadzia will travel for several weeks, so her duties will fall to me. I wish to review each of the merchants and their goods before I begin."

He paled. "Ah... I see. If there has been any cause for complaint..."

"Oh no! I merely wish to be thorough. I'll not have it said that I've neglected my role while Jadzia is away, and it could be weeks."

Relieved and desperate, he changed the subject. "Really? And where is she going?"

"Oh north, I believe, to see her family. I imagine to find help for her babe as well."

"Ah... yes... I understand... That is..."

Neeren smiled and nodded; a gentle sympathy in her slight frown as she patted his arm. "I know. It is distressing."

His face reddened as he whispered. "Word has spread."

Joy ignited in Neeren; this man was just who she needed. She gave his forearm one last pat and breezed on. "It is tragic, yet such is her dedication as a mother that she'd not see sense." Neeren shook her head. "And such is the emperor's devot... regard for her, he sends her with his own men and under the imperial banner."

The man's jaw dropped. "No!"

"Yes, but they've known each other since childhood, so I don't hold with the rumours."

The merchant leaned closer, whispering, "What rumours?"

"You've not heard? Well, bless you for not being a gossip. If you hear any now, you'll know the truth. They say the babe is the emperor's bastard. In fact, his grandmother was similarly afflicted." His eyes grew wide, glittering, as if devouring his favourite treat. "But as I say," Neeren continued. "I don't think there's any truth in it. I'm mean they're friends, that's all. They've been such *good* friends for so long."

His eyes gleamed. "Yes, yes. I agree. I'll put paid to any rumours I hear, you can be sure of it."

Oh, I've no doubt what you'll do with the rumours.

Smiling, Neeren made her way back to the carriage. *Only one more stop. This should be most rewarding.* She hardly noticed the buildings of Bēdarik as her carriage rolled on. The cobbled streets grew wider and houses larger until they were in the most affluent part of the city. Wealthy landholders who lived more than a day's drive from the city often held town houses in this sector. The views of the surrounding countryside were unsurpassed. She'd begged Bashtan to build a house here, but he refused to spend the money. He'd said given the size and position of his estate, people could be in no doubt as to his status and ancient lineage, so what need did he have of flaunting his wealth in such a way? Living where they did, gave him the same view and infinitely more peace. Her happiness didn't matter.

Neeren's carriage halted before a villa with a broad portico and she ascended the smooth steps to the door.

The chatelaine greeted her. "Mistress Neeren, Lady Chandar and Mistress Sevara are in our lady's private garden. Please follow me."

"They're both here? Perfect." *One might work, but two will ensure this.*

Neeren followed the woman through the ornate villa to an enclosed garden covered with a huge wisteria vine. Long clusters of lilac blooms hung down into the shady retreat, and dappled sunlight hit large rose-pink marble tiles. Reclining on long low settees covered with brightly coloured silk lay two blonde, blue-eyed sisters.

Neeren bowed. "Lady Chandar, Mistress Sevara. I'm blessed you're both here."

Lady Chandar snorted. "We can dispense with the formalities, Neeren, we're all friends here. Sit. Join us."

Sevara's eyes were bloodshot and puffy. She smiled as Neeren curled cat like on the remaining couch.

"Sevara, you've been crying."

"She has. Not that it does any good, as I well know." Chandar rapped Sevara's knuckles with her fan. "Stop it."

Sevara let out a wail.

Chandar cast her eyes skyward and threw up her hands. "Neeren, help me. I've tried to get her to pull herself together."

"What can I do or say? I can imagine how hard you've been hit. Lady Rodan was your friend and—"

"She's dead and her children along with her. Executed by a usurper who now calls himself emperor," Chandar said. "Zaragarian bastard. The sooner we have a Talak ruler, the better."

Neeren was aghast. "All the children."

"Just like..." Sevara faltered, sobbing, "his father did to our king."

"You're sure?" Neeren asked.

"Yes," Chandar said. "All of them – snuffing out the line. Thank the gods he only had one wife."

Sevara smiled wanly. "She never did like competition."

"I always admired that," Neeren murmured.

"Didn't we all?" Lady Chandar said.

"What about General Cēdar's wife?" Neeren asked.

"I believe she made it over the border. She ran earlier than Lady Rodan. If she has any sense, she'll keep running. I doubt Nējarak will keep her safe for long."

"Where could she go?" Neeren asked.

Chandar shrugged. "Matryan maybe."

"I'm so sorry," Neeren whispered. "But are you safe?"

Chandar's eyes narrowed. Neeren rushed on. "Only hearing what you've said and your families are all friends... some may assume you're involved in sedition."

"We're safe," Chandar said.

Sevara opened her mouth to speak, but a warning glare from her sister shut her up.

"But Neeren, your family is amongst this circle of friends too. And we haven't forgotten the emperor is staying at your husband's villa." Chandar's eyes narrowed. "Bashtan walks a fine line between us all."

Neeren paled. "I'm not here to spy on you for the emperor. He hasn't endeared himself to us of late."

"Do tell?"

Neeren laughed bitterly. "You've probably heard everything already."

"Rumours may be delicious," Chandar said, "but the real flavour will be in the truth, I'm sure."

"You're not wrong," Neeren replied before reiterating the events of the day Jadzia gave birth.

Chandar and Sevara's jaws dropped. "They're under his protection?" they said simultaneously.

"Yes, and now she is to travel north to Dēbar, then homeward, I presume. And with an imperial escort and under the emperor's banner no less. She has erred on so many levels and yet comes out with more power." *And freedom.*

"So, the rumours are true. It's his bastard."

"It must be. They've always been close. I've long suspected that if her marriage to Bashtan hadn't been arranged, then she would have married Tikhon."

"And then you would have been first wife."

Neeren's eyes narrowed. "Of course."

"Tell me how many men go with Jadzia?" Lady Chandar asked.

Neeren leaned forward. "Approximately six – men and women."

"Do you know the route they are taking?"

"No, but there are only a few options, especially since I assume she is taking a carriage. I mean, it must be too soon for her to ride."

"Well, leave it to us. You may yet be first wife, after all."

CHAPTER 11

KATYA HELD UP A thick, purple and black rectangular piece of cloth with two long ties. Embroidered golden lynxes played across the fabric and rosy beads jangled across the top. "Do you want to take the baby carrier?"

"Yes, and the wicker bassinet. While I'm carriage bound, the baby can be in that and strapped to the seat. But the stodan root is doing its job. I'll be taking my horse and riding as soon as I'm able. I'll use the carrier then. Damn carriages make me feel ill."

The doors to Jadzia's suite flew open and slammed into the wall; the emperor strode in.

Both women bowed; Jadzia rose, brow arched. "Should I send for another carpenter? Will the doors need replacing again? Or any other furniture in my chambers?"

"Katya, out!"

Katya remained beside Jadzia. "It's all right, Katya. Go to the kitchens and organise provisions before Bashtan thinks to stop us using them."

Katya eyeballed Tikhon as she closed the doors.

A low rumble reverberated across the room.

"Did you just growl? I mean, *actually* growl?"

"I'm emperor and *she* looks at *me* like that. My commands are to be obeyed, by *all*."

"Would you have me with a less loyal servant?"

"No, of course not!" He folded his arms. "What's this about you visiting a temple of The Weaver and who exactly are these Darklinan?"

"The Darklinan are the unwanted of Bēdarik – orphans, bastard children of nobles, children with deformities, birth marks, anything that doesn't fit the Talak's idea of racial perfection. Although the poorer families, Hokati bless them, are more likely to keep their offspring."

"Bastard children?"

"Yes, they don't qualify to be sent to the seat of the gods. As for the others, the love of their families saw them dumped on the streets. For some, the stigma of having to take a child to the seat is too much; they say the baby died and leave it like refuse."

"Gods above and below!" He shook his head. "Though there's kind of wonderful irony in it! A race of mongrels dumping their bastards."

"Many get missed and die, but when the older ones find them, they take them in. Still, a lot don't make it but at least they don't die alone. A woman named Demenka, an innkeeper in the poor quarter, has a child similarly afflicted; she grouped them together and helped where she could with food, though it was not enough."

"And you?"

"The Darklinan are an integral part of my network, they—"

"Are thieves and cutthroats."

"Just what they used to say about the Zaragarians, and look at us now."

"Are you sure you're not just being overly sentimental... maternal?"

Her lips flattened; she put her hands on her hips. "They're a neglected resource here, and I dare say, in Vēkaria. Every society has a class structure; here, theirs has created a world ripe for the picking. Ripe for us to mould. Your father wasn't capable of understanding this."

"Integral?"

"Yes, and on your payroll for years."

He pointed his finger at her. "The temple? Jadzia, couldn't you have used another building?"

She shrugged. "They were already well ensconced in it. It's their home."

"But you need to be careful. Some things I can't save you from. If the Order..."

"The temple is abandoned. There are no priests. Though, as you well know, if people wish to pray to her, they may. No emperor has outlawed it."

"Semantics."

"Master Pavel knows, so I dare say the Grand Master does too. I believe Pavel enjoys the irony that The Weaver's temple is used in activities which benefit the empire and thereby the Order. Did you think I was starting a religious war? Seeking to topple the Order and you?"

His anger faded. "Jadzia, my head is plagued by demons. I see betrayal everywhere, but I would never look for it in you."

A bitter laugh escaped her. "Well, we've been plotting betrayal for a year. It makes you second guess everyone. I do myself, although if I didn't, I'd be a lousy spy master now, wouldn't I?"

"You're integral to my plans."

Jadzia smiled softly. "As you are for mine."

"Ah, now it comes. Just like a woman – a soft, simpering smile and then ask."

"Simpering!" The tunic she hurled hit him squarely in the face.

"Assault on your own beloved emperor!" He tossed the tunic aside and sat, frowning at the pile of clothes on the other chair. "Go on, ask."

"Lady Rodan, did she reveal where her husband may be?"

"Possibly. If she told the truth."

"Master Pavel may appear like a kindly old man—"

"An interesting definition, one he'd find hilarious. A kindly old man with battle scarred hands, a nose that's been broken more than once and—"

"Yes, inestimable skill as a torturer," Jadzia said. "I doubt she lied, particularly if she thought it may save her or the children."

His eyes bored into hers. "People do a lot of things for love."

She refused to look at him. "You've executed them and seized the estate?"

"Yes."

"I want it. I'll buy it from you."

"First assault and now you want to rob me of house and home! I have plans for it and you're meant to be here."

"This will not always be my home and if you let me buy it, the estate will still be at your disposal and working for you and the empire."

"Go on."

"We need to assimilate this land fully. There'll always be men and women for whom the empire is a means to an end: wealth, more power, protection. The Talaks accepted becoming a protectorate because they were afraid, and men like Bashtan have survival and coward firmly stamped on their foreheads but they don't really believe in us, in the empire, in Mstislav. They won't stop following their gods and, to some extent, you can't expect them to. You need to win hearts and minds. We've already twisted their gods into our pantheon, matching them up with similar ones, saying they're the same only with a different name —we're halfway there, but there's more that can be done."

"Continue."

"While you let their old ways go unchecked, while the rich educate their children as they please, they will always be Talak; we will always be occupiers. The children..." She paced. "They're the key. Start schools, curriculum, military training, control the education of the children, instil Zaragarian values, look after them as their rulers did not. All the children: rich, poor, the Darklinan. All of them. There's an underclass here waiting for a better life; give it to them. Improve life here for all — sanitation, education, health. The one who cares, feeds them, saves them, under the auspices of Mstislav as protector and guide; he'll win them. You need to make them love you. Win the children; you'll create a generation who sees you and the empire as benefactor and who will die for you. They will be utterly loyal. The empire will be all."

"So, like the orphans the Order raises to be Mstislavakan?"

"Almost, but not run by the Order. They must have some involvement or you'll run into trouble before you're ready, but *you* need to be all, not the Grand Master. The Order's first loyalty is to Mstislav."

"Despite their oaths to the emperor."

"Yes, and you need to counter their power base."

"I like it. You've given this great consideration. Do you think you can do it?"

"Yes, but it'll be more complex than I've said." She hesitated. "I'll need free rein."

"I'll want regular reports and to be intimately involved in it."

She nodded. "If it works, you'll win most of the Talaks and any reticence by the upper class won't matter. You'll have a generation so loyal they'd turn in their own parents if they dissented. They'll eat, sleep, live and die by our codes without question."

Tikhon didn't answer; his hands caressed the embroidered insignia on one of her coats. "You've all these plans, and yet it looks as if you're leaving when I ordered you to stay."

She reached out and stilled his hands. "I'm not disobeying and not leaving forever. I must travel north."

"North?"

Don't tell him everything. "My family will aid me and I need to find help for my baby. I need to enlist my own guards, ones I can trust."

Tikhon shook his head. "I can get you guards."

"Tikhon, she needs to be named and none here will do it."

"Does it have to be north?" A tightness infected his voice. "Wouldn't it be easier to wait or go into Nējarak?" He crossed his arms, not looking at her, his foot drumming on the thick rug as he thought.

"Would you want one of your sons to remain unnamed before the gods?" she pleaded. Nothing. She went to him, gripping his arm as she begged, "Tikhon, please. I'll be gone only a couple of months. Katya can run the network while I'm gone. I need my family."

He sighed, rubbed his forehead then slipped an arm about her. "I hope my father is rotting in a cell in depths of Ebatov. If you'd married me, none of this would matter... Bashtan could meet with an accident. You could still marry me."

She stiffened and grew still as his other arm came about her. "It's too late. I have no intention of remarrying anyone."

He gave her a lopsided grin. "That's something I suppose."

"And you already have two wives who'd drive me crazy, and Sabina hates me. I'd probably kill them. Thanks to the plotting of one, you've no clear line of succession. Two sons born at the same time! How she managed that, I've no idea. And they are both maestro coquettes." She simpered and batted her eyes at him. "Tikhon, My Emperor, my hero... *please...*" she said breathlessly.

"Oh, for gods' sake!" He laughed. "You can buy the estate! But I'll want a pretty penny for it."

"Excellent!" She rubbed her hands together in excitement. "We can inspect it, work out a price. I'll set Katya and my castellan to taking an inventory."

"I warn you, you'll have to deal with Darcov – he wanted it."

She waved her hand dismissively. "Darcov can have a suite, providing he helps with training when he's there." Jadzia cocked her head. "My journey?"

Tikhon's arms tightened about her; his jaw clenched. He opened his mouth to speak, but clamped it shut and drew her closer. He rested his forehead upon hers and his hands cupped her face; slowly he tipped her chin up and kissed her upon the lips. "You can go. No matter what happens, remember you hold a special place in my heart."

➤——————→

Her mother's words rang in Rada's ears, 'if you want to come, you must ask your father. I'm certain he'll say no to me. But he loves you, so he might say yes.'

A slave bearing a tray exited her father's study. Butterflies danced in Rada's stomach. *No! I'm Stilniat Rada Lujza Ortakli. Daughter of Stilnassa Jadzia Zora Maklova. I can do this.* Rada stiffened her spine, held her head high, chin tilted up – assertive and imperious.

"Where is Lord Bashtan?" Rada demanded.

The slave bowed low. "In his study's courtyard, Mistress Rada."

"Good. Go about your business."

Rada poked her head around the study door and entered. From the secluded garden, voices and a high laugh filtered to her across the semi-dark room. *Neeren is there. That means he'll be in a good mood.* She took a step closer and her confidence dissipated like smoke in the wind. Fisting her hands, she paced up and down, muttering. "Just ask. It'll all be good. Mami is right. Just ask."

Biting her lip, she padded through the study. The cold of the tile floor sent shivers up her body and she hesitated, twisting her hands together. With her head bowed, she stepped forward into the dimly lit courtyard garden. Burning incense kept away insects and its scented smoke snaked its way toward her, hypnotic in the flickering light from tall candles.

"Papi." Rada bowed first to him, then to Neeren, who was lounging on a nearby couch. "Mistress Neeren."

"Rada?" He put his glass of wine down and turned to face her.

She sidled up to the couch he reclined on. "Papi, I... um..." She looked up at Neeren, who smiled encouragingly. "Papi, I'd like to go with Mami to see her family."

"Are you asking me or telling me?"

"Asking, Papi, asking." In a rush, she continued. "Please, Papi, may I go? May I?"

He sat up, holding out his arms. "Come here." Rada ran to him and he pulled her onto his lap. "Now, why do you want to go?"

"I haven't been for ages and I wasn't as big as now and I don't remember what the north looks like." *Don't talk about the baby. You'll just make him mad.* "I've not seen Grandma Galina since I was a baby."

"She is getting old. Mmm... perhaps you should visit Galina and Stepan." Rada's heart leapt. "But I must think about it."

No! Just say yes. Rada's shoulders slumped and she made a little moue.

"It's a long journey, Rada," Neeren said. "My lord, do you have a map? We could show Rada where she will travel."

"Excellent idea." He sat Rada on the couch and fetched a scroll from his study.

"Make room," Neeren ordered. A slave stepped from the shadows and shifted the food off the low table.

Bashtan unrolled the scroll. "Now look. Where are we?" Rada pointed to the north of Bēdarik. "Well done! Watch where my finger goes, for this is the way you will probably travel to Vēkaria. Now, the rivers are low so you can cross here, although the emperor is building a huge new bridge, so soon we can cross anytime." Rada diligently tracked his finger. "The other way is through the forest and mountains. That's much more dangerous – a carriage cannot go there and there are bandits."

"Bandits!" Rada said, wide eyed.

Neeren nodded. "Yes, and you'd be gone for weeks; probably months," she said. "You and Anfisa were becoming such good friends. She'll miss you."

"Weeks?" *Anfisa is fun. Will she not like me if I go? Will she forget me?*

Rada bit her lip, but suddenly smiled. "I know! I'll bring her back a present! Maybe I can bring you all presents – something special."

Neeren clapped. "That would be lovely!"

"Papi, can I go? I'm not afraid of bandits."

Bashtan smiled and scruffed her hair. "I know you're not."

"Besides, Mami will have the emperor's guards."

The smile fell from Bashtan's face. He looked at Rada intently. "Do you know that for certain?" Rada shook her head. "Well, Rada, there's more to worry about than bandits. Some people don't enjoy having a new emperor. I think you'll be safer here. Once things are quieter, you can go."

"But I wanted to see Vēkaria! I wanted to help pick Mami's new guards."

Neeren laughed. "Oh, Rada! How could you help pick her guards?"

Rada crossed her arms and scowled. "I could! Mami always listens!" Rada stamped her foot. "She believes in me!" Her eyes welled with tears. "She needs me!"

Neeren closed the distance between them and reached out to her, but Rada stepped back, glowering at her and Bashtan. "Rada," Neeren said. "We believe in you too, but you're precious and your Papi wants you safe. We'll have fun, I promise, and your mami will be back before you know it."

"I need to keep them safe."

"You mean the baby, too?" Bashtan said.

"I..." Rada swallowed nervously. "Yes, Papi."

He sighed. "It does you credit, but your mother will have her hands full." A bitter tang tinged his words. "I'm sure she'll have the emperor's guards and, if trouble happens, that she'll be safe, but you wouldn't be able to help. You're too little; barely stopped being a babe yourself. Nor can you fight. In fact, having to worry about you as well may cause more trouble for your mother if something happens. No, it's better you stay here with us, where you'll be safe."

Rada glared at him. *I've saved her once already!* "But you don't understand. I can help!" *I've already helped!*

"I said no and I meant it. Now it's late, go to your room. Go to sleep."

"Fine!"

"Rada!" Bashtan's voice whipped her.

She cringed and hung her head. "Sorry."

Bashtan gave her a curt nod. She spun on her heel to leave.

"Don't we get a 'goodnight' and a hug and kiss?"

She ground her teeth, marched back to her father and dutifully kissed him on the cheek.

"Smile, Rada. All will be well," he said. Rada's face grew red; her hands curled into fists. *You're mean. I hate you.* "And Neeren?"

Rada stiffened as Neeren embraced her.

"I'm sorry. Be calm. Hide your anger," Neeren whispered.

Rada gave only the hint of a nod. Her arms stole around Neeren; her breath slowed. She walked calmly from the garden, but once in the corridor, she ran to her room. With each pounding step, she wanted to explode; to smash something,- anything. *You're just mean!* Pound. *You're wrong!* Pound. *I can help!* Pound. *I'll show you!*

She pushed open the door to her room to find her slave waiting. "Get out! I can put myself to bed! I'm not a baby!" Her breath heaved. "Argh!"

She hauled a haversack out from under the bed, opened a trunk, and threw a pair of boots onto the bed. "I'm not too little!"

From another chest, she pulled and discarded item after item of clothing. "No! No dresses." A swathe of pink fabric hit the far corner of the room. "Pants, tunic. Yes. How many? Another one. Those for tomorrow." They landed near the boots. "I'm not useless! Might get cold." A cloak landed on the pile. "Um... over tunic? Yep. I could fight." More clothes landed in the heap. "They need me."

She stuffed the haversack full, excess clothes overflowing out of the top and onto the floor alongside a pile that she had yet to pack.

"Too much. Stupid!" Rada crawled under the bed, her feet wiggling as she inched her way forward. "Got it!" She scooted backward with a dusty duffel bag and shoved the bulk of her clothes in there. Last, she reverently placed her sling in a side pocket of the haversack.

Rada stood with her hands on her hips, surveying her work with a nod. "Good. But I need more ammunition. I could raid the armoury again for lead pellets." She scrunched her face up. "Nope, they nearly caught me last time. I'll get pebbles on the way. Better get dressed now. So I'm ready." Rada donned her pants, tunic and boots and looked herself up and down. She grinned. "Like Mami." She jumped onto the bed and wriggled under the covers. She pulled her teddy bear close. "I'm not a baby, Grokky. We'll show them."

———————▶

Rada awoke and gasped. The pale orange-grey of dawn reached across her room. *"No, no, no!"*

She threw back her bed covers and sprang out of bed. *They were going at first light!* She stuffed Grokky in the top of her haversack, pulled the drawstring tight and buckled the covering flap. "Ugh! No! Sorry, Grokky." She opened the top again to reveal his face. "Better?" The bear looked at her in silent reproach. She frowned, sat him upright in the bag and pulled the drawstring loosely closed around his neck. "Now you can see."

Rada slung the haversack on her back, grabbed the strap on the duffel bag, and hooked it over one shoulder. She opened her door a smidgen and peered into the darkened corridor. The slaves would be up soon. *I've got to be quick!* Rada inched open her bedroom door, wincing as it creaked. Heart pounding, her every instinct was to run, but she drew the door closed and released the handle so it noiselessly clicked into place.

She tiptoed down the dim corridor, hugging the walls as she went, ears and eyes straining for any sign of others nearby. Creeping up to the bend in the hall, she poked her head around the corner and peered along it. Her mother's suite was just ahead. There were no guards outside the room. *No guards? Has she gone already?*

Rada panicked and took off. The duffle bag slid from her shoulder and she struggled to wrap her arm about it. *Not far! One more step.* The bag slipped from her fingers; she tripped and slid on her belly to stop outside her mother's room. "Ow!" Her elbows and knees burned; tears welled in her eyes. Rada pushed herself up, opened the doors. "Mami?" Nothing. Her breath caught in her throat. She left the bag where it was and darted into the bedroom. "Mami?" Rada stared in dismay – the bed was made, her mother's bags were gone. *No!*

Rada ran back, grabbed the duffle bag and dragged it behind her. *Come on! Maybe they're still here.* She gritted her teeth, rushed down the last stretch of corridor, veered right, and the bag smacked into the wall. Rada slid through the main doors.

Outside, she barged through slaves returning to the villa. "Move!" They parted before her to reveal her mother, holding the baby, standing beside a strange carriage, talking with Katya. Akim and over a dozen guards waited beside their mounts. "Wait! Wait for me!" Rada called.

Akim groaned quietly. "Not the child, not on this trip." His hand fisted around his reins.

Rada glowered at Akim. "I'm allowed. Papi said so."

Her jaw dropped as Tav appeared from the other side of the wagon. Taking in his new Zaragarian style tunic, pants and cloak coat, with a grey shadavoc wrapped around his face, she mouthed, *Wow!* He winked at her.

"Rada?" Jadzia said. "I didn't realise you were coming."

Rada stood before her mother, breathless and gulping in air. "I asked Papi last night... He said... yes." *Don't check, don't check. Mstislav, help me. Hokati too... any gods... help.* She grinned. *Don't look away. Keep your eyes on her. If you look guilty, she'll know.*

Jadzia's eyes narrowed. "I wasn't told."

"I wanted to surprise you." Bright eyed, she grinned like a loon. *Keep smiling.* "I even packed for myself!"

Jadzia's lips drew into a thin line. "Katya, were you aware of this?" Katya shook her head. "Rada, are you telling me the truth?"

"Yes, Mami." *Smile. Stare her straight in the eye and smile.* "Papi said I could go because I haven't been in so long. Mistress Neeren was there and I'm supposed to get presents for them all."

"Well, that sounds about right," Jadzia muttered.

"Shall I check, Stilnassa?" Katya asked.

Akim moved over. "Stilnassa, this is a long journey. Perhaps Stilniat Rada should stay."

No, no, no... please... Quick, talk about something else. "Whose carriage is this?" Rada blurted out. The coat-of-arms on the door had been painted over and a slave was affixing a tapestry with Jadzia's crest. The emperor's pennants hung from its top.

"It *was* Lady Rodan's. Now it's ours."

"Can I look inside?" Rada asked. Unable to hold her mother's gaze any longer Rada, jumped up and down trying to see in the carriage.

"Stilnassa..." Akim said, but Jadzia ignored him. Rada could feel Jadzia's eyes upon her so she yanked the door open and tried to pull down the steps.

Katya awaited a reply. "My lady?"

Jadzia hesitated. "Katya, Bashtan won't be awake and Neeren is probably with him. We'll never hear the end of it if we rouse them. If he asks, tell him what transpired later. Rada, it looks like you're off on an adventure."

➤——————→

Inside the villa, Tikhon and Darcov, grim-faced, watched the final loading of the carriage and wagon.

"Are you sure you want to do this?" Darcov said.

"Yes."

"If anything goes wrong, she'll never forgive you."

CHAPTER 12

NEEREN STOOD IN RADA'S room, agog at the neatness. Even after the slaves had cleaned, Rada's room had never stayed tidy for long. She summoned Rada's slave. "Where is your mistress? It's almost evening and I've not caught sight of her all day."

"Mistress Rada is gone, Mistress Neeren. I came this morning and her room was a mess; clothes were everywhere. Katya told me Rada had gone with Stilnassa Jadzia."

"Is that so?" Neeren strove to keep from smiling. "Fetch Katya here now."

Neeren tapped her foot, suddenly stopping, pale. *Rada will be with them when... Gods! If Bashtan finds out... Don't think about it.* She wrung her hands and paced Rada's room until Katya stood before her. "What's this about Rada going with Jadzia?"

"*Stilnassa* Jadzia. You would do well to use her correct title."

"She has been Lady for all these years." Neeren spat the words like poison.

"We've a new ruler. This is his order. Will you defy the emperor?"

"How would he know?"

Katya laughed. "Where to start? Neeren, you have more than your share of enemies. Starting with most of the slaves in this villa. Do you think they would pass up an opportunity to inform on you? And then, of course, there's me." The woman let that hang in the air between them, the corners of her mouth twisted in wry amusement. "But to answer your question, Stilniat Rada came out this morning saying that Lord Bashtan had given her permission to go with the Stilnassa."

Neeren rubbed her head. Dread and delight warred within her. *Bashtan will be furious with Jadzia. If Rodan finds them, he'll kill Jadzia — it solves all my problems. But Rada, she's only a child.*

Katya watched hawk-like as the seconds slipped by while Neeren fretted.

"Rada should be here, safe," Neeren muttered.

It's done...

It's done! It's out of my hands. What will be will be.

"Why would she not be safe?" Katya said with quiet intensity.

Neeren, startled, straightened and smoothed her dress as she pulled herself together before finally looking Katya in the eye. "All journeys involve some risk, Katya." The other woman scowled. "The likelihood of rough roads, carriage accidents and bandits, combined with a child who breeds her own special brand of trouble — of course, Rada may not be safe. And the emperor is but new and things are bound to be unsettled."

Katya's brows rose. "Unsettled? How astute of you."

Neeren waved her hand dismissively. "Bashtan never gave his permission. If you or *Stilnassa* Jadzia had cared to ask, you would have known. Neither of you bothered. Neither of you show any regard for the master of this house. "

Katya snorted. "Everyone in this villa has regard to Lord Bashtan and his moods, as well as yours, which is why we didn't wake either of you."

"How dare you! You desert rat!" Neeren lashed out. Katya grabbed her hand and spun her, twisting Neeren's arm up behind her back and thrusting her against the wall.

"I am sick to death of you and the rest of your mewling race." She lent close to Neeren's ear. "But especially you. You're a snake. You lie in wait like the Alitariya of old. Though you wield no magic, you have their cunning, their malice. Too much of a coward to strike openly. You're tragic, like so many of the women in this land. You cling desperately to scraps of power your men grant you. And what power is that? To rule a house? Say who cooks what, who cleans? To treat others around you as worthless, even your daughters... all in order for you to feel worth something... anything. Yet you can't see how pitiful that is. Or maybe you realise and that's why you hate the Stilnassa so. She didn't just take your coveted first wife position; she holds more power and authority in her little finger than you've ever had. And to add insult to injury, she placed little worth on the role you so coveted. She had no need of it." Katya released her.

Neeren rested against the cool clay brick wall, pale and shaking. She tried to rally, gripping her shawl and drawing it about her as if Katya had stripped her bare, yet she could not keep the tremble from her voice. "You must tell Lord Bashtan."

Katya laughed. "All right then, let's talk to the great Lord Bashtan. Lead the way, Neeren."

Together they entered the central garden where several sets of rugs covered with platters of meat, vegetables, cheese and fruits lay arranged on the grass. Bashtan and his two other wives reclined on cushions, laughing and watching his children playing.

"Neeren, my love, we've been waiting for you to arrive."

She bowed. "Thank you, my lord. First, you may like to speak privately with Katya."

Bashtan frowned, puzzled. "Katya? Why would I want to do that?"

"My lord, it's about Rada."

"Rada? Rada, what've you done, you little imp?" There was no answer. "Rada?" He stood and looked about the garden amongst the other children.

"My lord, she is not here," Neeren said

"Not here... Not in the garden clearly," he said.

"Not anywhere in the villa." Neeren drew a deep breath, mustering all her patience. "Nor, in fact, anywhere in the vicinity. She. Is. Not. Here."

Bashtan was beside them in a heartbeat, his face like thunder. "Both of you come with me now!"

Under the cover of the veranda, he demanded, "Where is she? What's happened? Neeren? Katya?"

Katya stood composed with her hands folded in front of her. "Rada is quite well and in no danger. She's with Stilnassa Jadzia and, of course, under the protection of the emperor's own guards."

"What! I forbade her going!"

"She met us just before departure, saying you had approved of her going and, when questioned as to the truth of this, swore before her mother that it was so."

"Jadzia saw fit *not* to check with you, my lord," Neeren said.

"It was shortly after dawn, Lord Bashtan," Katya said, barely keeping the sarcasm from her tone. "Stilnassa Jadzia considered checking with you, yet knowing your preference for late rising hours, she decided it was important to give you the courtesy of remaining undisturbed."

"Why did someone not see fit to inform me during the day?"

"Why would we, Lord Bashtan? We thought she could go. Given that, until now, no one had commented upon it, or even noticed her absence, I believed she had spoken the truth."

Bashtan's face was crimson; a vein pulsed in his temple. "*Noticed?* You consider me neglectful of my daughter?"

Katya shrugged. "Those were not my words. Now, if that's all, I must return to my work."

"I haven't dismissed you."

"I'm *not* a slave, nor am I some poor indentured servant and you are *not* my master. I serve Stilnassa Jadzia of my free will, and now I bid you a good evening."

Bashtan's jaw worked, but he remained speechless, pacing. Finally, he spoke. "This is my house, Neeren. I'm being dictated to! Defied by my own child! She's become a liar!"

"Rada is young; she tests her limits as all children do. The blame lies with Jadzia."

"She lied to Jadzia. Jadzia believed she had permission."

"Jadzia is no fool. She considered asking you, which meant she had doubts. The early morning was merely an excuse. She knew Rada was lying but wanted her to go along anyway."

"You can't be sure."

"Bashtan, all mothers can spot the lies their children spout. I know when my children are lying, though it is not in their blood to do so often. After all her talk about wanting to get along in peace, to consult with you, she ignores all that, does not check and removes your child from home. What if something happens? Perhaps we should fetch Rada back?"

"Fetch her back and show the world I can't control my child? No. Not only that, it'll look as if I don't trust the emperor's men. No. They'll have made good time and be too far. I do not want another scene played out publicly."

"The emperor has left. He'll not know."

Bashtan shook his head. "I need to think. Rada must be punished, that's certain, and she will be, but whether Jadzia deserves blame is yet to be seen."

"My lord, even if you decide Jadzia has acted honestly, look at the way she has raised Rada. She's wild, she wants to fight, to join the imperial guard and who knows what else! She needs to be taken in hand."

Rada rode behind Akim; her hands gripped the high back of the saddle as she looked about her. The countryside north of Bēdarik was open and undulating. In the distant north-east, clouds surrounded the Central Highlands. Her mother had told her this was a conglomeration of isolated mountains that spanned from Vēkaria, through northern Talak and into Nējarak. A network of rivers, known as The Web, crisscrossed it and condensed into two major rivers in Talak. The first was the Spinner's Run, which originated from an offshoot spine of the highlands that formed the border between Vēkaria and Talak. The second was the Talakmit, which ran through central Talak; both fed Talakmere Lake. For days their party had been following the road which ran along the side of a valley and overlooked the Spinner's Run.

The hillsides were brown, the grass long since having gone to seed and died in the summer heat, but in many places the valley floor was green. Slaves worked booms hauling large buckets of water out of the river and into irrigation channels to water orchards, crops and vegetables.

"Can we go down?" Rada said sleepily.

"Not today. We need to be at camp and set up before nightfall. Here, sit in front for a bit before you fall asleep." He turned in the saddle, hooked his arm about her waist and swung her before him.

"Can I hold the reins?" Her small hands took the leather from him. She transferred the reins into one hand, leaned to the side, turned and shouted, "Look, Tav! I'm steering!" Tav gave her a weak smile. "He's kind of grey," she said with worry.

"He's never ridden so much until now. And after days in the saddle, his behind is probably more purple than a beet."

"I'm all right," Rada said.

"You haven't been riding all day. And you haven't endured the fighting lessons he has."

She screwed up her face. "I want them though. Can I have them? Will you teach me to ride my pony when I get one? I want you or Uncle Tikhon to teach me. What about a sword? Can I start on that now? I mean, I'm good with my sling, but it won't get me into the guard, will it? Do you even use slings?"

He laughed. "We use whatever's handy to get the job done. But you must remember your mother won't need us when she gets her own guards and then we'll have to go back to the emperor." Rada's smile fell from her face. He scuffed her hair. "Don't worry. You've got us for a little while yet."

"I don't want you to go. It's better at home with you or Uncle Tikhon there," she whispered.

Akim's gaze grew soft; he gave her a slight squeeze. "All will be well." He halted the small column. "Now, see where we're going."

The road had been slowly descending to the valley floor and before them the trail travelled between a dense forest and the river. On the other side of the river rose the crags of the Snake's Tail mountain range. In places, its sheer rock slabs dove deep into the water; in others, jagged granite boulders formed an impassable beach leading to broken crags with scrappy shrubs clinging tenaciously to precious footholds as the stone needled its way up to the peaks. On the other side, grassland gave way to scrub and then to the multi-hued blue-green of spiny-leafed conifers that jostled with the deep green of cypress trees. Behind them rose the foothills of a mountain spine that ran from the Central Highlands.

Rada sighed, watching the tips of the peaks turn amber in the final hours of the day. She leaned back against Akim's chest. "They haven't got snow on them."

"No, not in summer, but the Highlands do. The very tops of them always have snow."

"Mmn. I'll go there one day. I want to see them up close. Can we go faster, like yesterday, and beat the others there?"

"No. Not now." He sounded distracted as he scrutinised the forest and the hills, but already the fading light began to veil their path in shadows. "Today we're good soldiers and we stay in formation." She yawned again. He shook his head at something and his body turned to granite behind her. Akim's hand tightened on her middle and tension edged his words. "In fact, I think you can go back in the carriage with your mother."

"But..." she said as he dismounted and carried her to the wagon.

"No buts." He opened the door deposited her in the carriage with Jadzia. "Stilnassa Jadzia, I return your daughter into your care."

Her mother sat bolt upright at his formal tone. "And I offer you my thanks, Captain." Before she'd finished speaking, he'd shut the door and was gone; his gaze never even meeting hers. Rada sat on the seat staring at the floor as the carriage moved off. "Rada, what did you do?"

"Nothing! We were talking, he was letting me steer his horse. We stopped to look at the forest and the hills... It was pretty... But it was like he was off somewhere else. I think he was looking for something."

"Rada, focus."

She shrugged. "I don't know. He just got grumpy and brought me back... Maybe he's sick of me... Maybe he doesn't really like me..."

"Do you really believe that?" her mother asked as she peered out each window, the escorts having moved closer to the carriage and wagon.

"I don't know but remember he didn't want me to come."

Her mother sat back with a jolt; her hand rested upon the sleeping baby in its wicker bassinet. Her mother's face paled and her hand gripped the bassinet. "No..." she mused. "He didn't, did he?"

CHAPTER 13

THEY SET CAMP UP nestled on the edge of the forest with the river to their backs; every instinct in Jadzia riled against it. The supply wagon lay between the campfire and the forest; the carriage behind them facing the road; Akim's troops picketed the horses nearby.

"Tav, don't tether our horses with the others. Leave them and our gear in the carriage."

"Yes, my lady." She quirked her brow at him. "Er... yes, Stilnassa," Tav said, inclining his head.

Rada followed Jadzia to the wagon, waiting while she put feed into two nose bags. "There you go. Take them to Tav."

"I can do it. They'll put their head down for this lot," Rada said, heaving the bags over her shoulders and staggering away.

Jadzia scanned the tree line and hills beyond, worry gnawing at her. *The forest makes perfect cover. Our exits are few.* She retrieved her saddle and tack from the wagon, turned her back on the forest, and returned to the carriage. The skin on her back prickled with every step. Jadzia set her gear next to her tethered horse, out of view of the campsite. *We're vulnerable. Akim knows better than this. Something isn't right.*

Within the carriage, the baby grizzled. "All right, little one." Jadzia gathered her satchel, then took the baby to the river to clean and change her. The child's brow wrinkled in fright at the cold, wet cloth; she screwed her face up and wailed her heart out while her small fists pumped the air. A twig snapped nearby; Jadzia spun in alarm.

Two guards observed her. "You shouldn't wander off alone, Stilnassa."

"Noted. Though you both know the forest is where trouble will come from, don't you?" One guard clenched her jaw, but neither said anything more. "I'm done anyway. We'll return."

A campfire was already alight and Rada sat eating, her eyes glued to Tav as Akim trained him with the sword. Jadzia sat beside Rada and nursed the babe.

"Was I that greedy?"

"You? You were worse."

Tav's sides heaved; sweat dripped from his brow.

"Enough!" Akim said. "You've made a reasonable start. Rest, eat and drink. No more training tonight. One more test, though. Do you remember what I told you about the way ahead?"

"Yes." Tav knelt and sketched the map on the dirt. "The road runs straight and clear for a short bit, then twists about the river. Here, it goes through the forest for a long stretch, then you're in more open country. After that, you're back to following the river for miles before reaching the ford and the site of the new bridge works."

"And?"

"There's a bridle path," he hesitated. "Here! Through the woods and over the hills to Vēkaria."

"Excellent! That same path branches off to a couple of small holdings in the forest and you could also make it almost all the way to Vēkaria," Akim said, clapping him on the shoulder, making him wince. "When able, a good soldier should always try to know the terrain about them. There's a map in the pocket of my cloak. Take it, study it, put it in your saddlebag. Now go, rest."

"It's my turn!" Rada yelled. "It must be! I've waited so long!"

"Go on then, if Akim is ready," Jadzia said. "If training Tav hasn't worn him out."

Akim snorted. "Come on then, little..." Akim gasped. "Forgive me!" He threw his hand on heart, with a dramatic flourish. "For you are *not* little, Stilniat Rada!"

She growled and leapt up, hands on hips.

He grinned at her and tossed her a long stick. "Here's your sword. Let's see what you can do."

She stamped her foot. "That's not a sword, it's a stick. Tav had a sword."

"He's bigger than you."

"Evika!" Rada charged him.

"Rada Lujza Ortakli, use that word again and I'll tan your behind with that stick. Are we clear?" Jadzia said.

"Yes, Mami!" she yelled, taking a swipe at Akim.

He snatched the stick from her and she stood glowering at him.

"Rada, behave," Jadzia said.

"Yes, Mami," she ground out, not even looking at Jadzia.

"I mean it. Take a deep breath." Rada's hands fisted and her mouth clamped shut. "Deep. Breath." Rada's face grew red and she let out an explosive exhalation, straightened and drew in another. "Good. Proceed, Akim."

"All right, hold your weapon like this. Put this foot facing your opponent... yes... and this one like this... Good. Now move like this... Excellent... we don't want you falling over your own feet. Ready? Now watch and copy me. Here are some basic guards – high, middle, low, hanging and back. Excellent."

"Can we fight now?"

"Not yet. Now, hold your sword this way... Pretend you will slice on an angle down through my neck and torso."

Rada rolled her eyes. "You know I can't reach that high, don't you?"

Akim rolled his eyes back at her. "Pretend it's someone your size, then."

She gripped her stick, let out a snarl, and swung. "Wonderful, heads will roll." Akim laughed. Rada pumped her fist in the air and spun about. "Bloodthirsty thing, aren't you? Try again. Don't stick your hands or elbows forward. Lead with your weapon. Your first movement is the tip of the sword, yes? Otherwise, you're vulnerable and dead. Right?"

"Got it. Blade first, not hands or lose hands and dead." She grinned. "Let's do it again."

"Tav, come sit with me," Jadzia said as she nursed the baby. "Here." She passed him a water skin.

His hands shook as he reached for it. "Thanks, Stilnassa. Remind me never to poke fun at the guard again. This is harder than it looks."

She chuckled. "It didn't look easy. You'll get there."

Darkness encroached upon the campsite, dwarfing the flickering firelight. A chill ran down her spine and she surreptitiously kept her eyes on the guards as they laughed and chattered, casual and carefree yet strategically repositioning themselves. "That's enough, Rada. Give Akim a rest. Come, it's time for bed. We've a long day tomorrow." Rada ran ahead to the carriage. She whispered, "Tav, stay close. Put your bed roll under the carriage tonight." His posture stiffened. "Relax, don't act as if anything is amiss."

"Something is?"

"It's just a feeling." They reached the carriage, and she placed the baby in the bassinet. "Tav, bridle and saddle our horses, but leave them tethered here. Then I'll show you how to use the baby carrier." Wide eyed, Rada stuck her head out of the wagon. "Quiet, Rada. Just listen. Don't act differently. Do you understand? Keep smiling. Something's wrong."

"But—"

"Remember how Akim changed when the forest came into sight?" Rada nodded. "He has set this camp up so it looks easy prey. At the first sign of trouble, Tav, we're leaving. You strap the baby carrier to your chest and Rada will hang on behind you. Ride to Vēkaria as fast as you can."

"I can stay and defend."

"No. I'm entrusting you with the safety of my daughters. I'll protect our rear with my bow if need be. Never fear, I won't be far behind you. Now, Rada, to bed. Tav – the horses, then rest. I'll take guard."

She walked back to the fire where Akim sat alone. Other guards lay atop their bedrolls, wide awake and weapons handy despite the chill creeping into the air. Two of Tikhon's troops had vanished. "You're on first watch?"

"Mmm." Distracted, Akim jabbed the coals with a stick.

Jadzia pitched her voice low. "Exactly what are you on watch for?"

He stabbed at the burning wood again. "A good commander always sets sentries, threat or no."

"A good commander would not have picked this camping spot." He grimaced. "Akim, should I worry about my family?"

"Stilnassa, your family is the best protected in the empire."

Half an answer. "Good. Thank you. Your words leave me reassured." *Not at all.*

Jadzia joined Tav on the far side of the carriage near their horses. She strung her bow and belted on her sword.

He raised his brows at her and finished adding extra supplies into his saddlebags.

Inside the wagon, Rada muttered a curse. "Rada, I can hear you. Lie down and at least pretend to be asleep."

Hours later a faint breeze stirred the needles on the pines, their thin whisper keeping Jadzia awake and tense. Her sword rested across her knees, her kadag hung from her belt. Crickets chirped, only to be silenced by the soft stamp of horses' hooves. She peered into the night. The full moon revealed little.

Rada lay sprawled along the seat opposite and mumbled in her sleep. "Not little."

Jadzia smiled wryly. She strained to catch even the faintest sound, catching only the hoot of an owl in the distance. All was still. A distant chink sounded – soft, quick. The hair on the back of her neck rose. By the fire sat the guard on duty. Her head nodded as she struggled to remain awake; around her, the others slept. Jadzia strained to listen. *Again? Was that it?* She shook Rada awake. "Shh. Stay here but be alert." Silently, Jadzia opened the door and stepped into the night. She attached her scabbard and sword to her belt, slung her quiver on her back, and grabbed her bow. Tav slid out from under the carriage. "Wait here." She crept along the carriage's side to peer across to the campsite. *Nothing's amiss.* One of the emperor's guard tossed near the fire and his chain mail chinked. *Maybe that was it?*

Gripping her bow, she approached the fire. The sentry's head remained bowed. Jadzia placed her hand on the guard's shoulder. "Wake up."

"I was awake and you should be back in the carriage under cover," the woman murmured.

Under cover? They're expecting an attack. In her heart and bones, she'd known, yet a wave of dismay assailed her and her gut clenched. Tikhon's words flashed into her mind. 'No matter what happens, remember you hold a special place in my heart.'

He'd set them up.

"Evika! Damn him!" she said, stepping back from the fading glow of the fire.

Her lip curled and venom dripped from her whisper, "If Tikhon were here, the enemy would be the least of his problems." The imperial guards lay, as if asleep, each staring at her, never moving, full of silent guilt.

Shaking her head in disgust, she hurried to her children. A faint *thunk* sounded, followed by a groan. Jadzia spun around as the sentry fell backwards, an arrow in her chest.

"Form up!" Akim yelled, dousing the fire as he and the others rose, shields high.

Jadzia hesitated. A line of soldiers stepped from the trees. They were heavily outnumbered.

She bolted.

"It's her we want! Don't let her get away!"

Skidding around the carriage, she saw Tav already mounted with the baby in her carrier, strapped to his chest and Rada clinging on behind him. Jadzia snatched her reins from him. "Go! Now, Tav! Get them out of here!" she yelled. Tav whirled his horse around and galloped away. *Gods help them.*

Her horse danced about, eager to chase after Tav. She swung up into the saddle. Ready to spur the horse after him, the clashing of shields and yelling halted her. *Help buy them time.*

She turned back toward the fighting. Akim and his troops were battling the attackers. Two enemy foot soldiers broke through and hurtled toward her. Jadzia drew her bow and fired; the nearest fell. She loosed another arrow. Missed.

"Stilnassa, run!" Akim roared and gestured wildly to her right. Horsemen galloped down the road they had arrived on. Two broke off and followed Rada and Tav; the others raced toward her. The remaining foot-soldier was almost upon her. Jadzia fired again, striking him in the neck. She whirled her horse about and took off after Tav.

On her left lay the river, and on her right just beyond a large, grassed verge lay the forest. The river had flooded in winter and damaged the road, leaving it pockmarked and rutted. She caught sight of Tav's pursuers. Jadzia galloped along, the white of her horse's rump clearly visible.

Hoof beats thundered behind her. She released the reins, nocked an arrow, and fired. Her horse squealed in pain as an arrow lodged in its rump. It stumbled, jostling her in the saddle; Jadzia dropped her bow. She regained her balance and drove her heels into its sides, forcing it on.

The horse's gait slowed, grew ungainly, and tossed her from side to side. "Keep moving, you wretched beast!" Jadzia booted its sides and flogged it. It surged forward, uneven and struggling. She kicked her feet from the stirrups and prepared to jump. *If I can get into the woods...*

The horse stumbled and somersaulted headfirst into the road, jettisoning Jadzia from the saddle. She tried to tuck her body in to roll, but her shoulder smacked into the ground; the joint stretched and popped. Jadzia screamed. Her vision wavered, blackened and returned, blurred amid violent orange and reds. The horse lay quivering with a broken leg. Jadzia staggered up and off the road into the trees. She held her uninjured arm in front of her, trying to feel her way forward. Unseen branches struck her, and she floundered her way ahead, slowly making out the darker shapes of trunks and limbs. Jadzia sheltered against the bole of a large sheoak. Her ears rang and the pain in her shoulder made her want to vomit. Blood streamed from a gash over her eye. Her breath heaved, each intake searing her upper body. *Hold it together. Get moving. Gods, my children!*

Dimly, Jadzia registered the sound of horses slowing.

"She's come off!"

"You heard that scream. She's injured."

"Can't have gone far. Must be in the woods." The agonised cries of her horse ceased. "We'll have to go on foot. This way!"

Go! Go! Go! Dizzy, she staggered forward and vomited. *Keep going.*

A harsh laugh chased her.

How many are there?

Jadzia squinted. The way seemed clearer on the right; she stepped onto a narrow animal trail. She stumbled, dazed and struggling to think. The trail disappeared between two massive blackberry patches. She moved between them, catching her top on their barbs, leaving strips of her tunic behind. *Damn!* About to rip it free to hide her trail, she hesitated, left it and moved on. Once through the patches, she doubled back, skirting the clump and moving as quickly and stealthily as she could. She drew her kadag. It's familiar weight, comforting.

"She's injured. Has be. A great Zaragarian Stilnassa leaving a trail, like a wounded bull."

"Even so, don't take her too cheaply."

Debris crackled under their feet and they talked as if out for a stroll. *Idiots think I'll be easy prey. Like some Talak bitch who knows nothing.*

"Nah, she's been with our women too long, I reckon. Got soft like them."

I'll show you.

"Shut up," another murmured. "She can't be too far ahead. The reputation is there for a reason. Right now, she's got nothing to lose."

"Oh, come on."

"Shut up!" The soldier hissed. "You're giving me the shits."

There was no answer.

Jadzia held her breath as they passed between the blackberries patches.

Get to their horses. She crept forward, listening intently. Farther away, she heard a muffled, "I said shut up." Certain they were gone, she stepped on the path and moved toward the road. The air stirred behind her. She swung, lashing out with the kadag, slicing her attacker across the face. She felt the brief resistance and collapse of his cheekbone, then the blade glided through his flesh and down toward his jaw. He cried out, staggering back and falling to his knees, clutching his fragmented face. Animalistic moans spilled from him. Jadzia drew her arm back to strike again.

The haft of a spear crashed down upon her arm. She dropped the kadag.

"That's enough," a quiet voice said. "I should be merciful and kill you now." Cold steel pressed to her neck, a warm trickle of blood ran down her skin. A large hand latched onto her dislocated shoulder and spun her. Her face twisted in agony, Jadzia whimpered and nearly blacked out; she sagged. The sting of a slap bit her cheek. "No, you don't. Wake up."

A young soldier crept into her vision. The spear he held out before him shook as he eyed her.

They pinned her good arm to her side and bound her before putting a rope around her neck. "Watch her while I check him."

The fallen soldier lay quiet, curled in a ball as if expecting further blows. The man turned him and grimaced as he held the torch closer to see. He shook his head. "What a friggin' mess." He rose and turned to Jadzia. "Mercy'd be wasted on you." He slammed his fist into her stomach. She doubled over, gasping, then stumbled forward as they yanked the rope around her neck. "We'll come back for him. Let's get her back to camp." His warm breath and spittle landed in her ear as he whispered. "General Rodan is waiting. You can imagine his delight at seeing you in his wife's carriage. You better pray they don't find your children."

CHAPTER 14

RADA CLUNG TO TAV, and twisted sideways to peer behind them. She could dimly make out the shapes of their pursuers in the moonlight.

"Rada, sit up!" Tav snapped. "You'll fall."

"They're still coming! Mami said she'd get them, but they're still coming!" Rada gripped him with one hand and punched his shoulder with the other. "Tav!"

"I know!"

"We need to go faster."

"We can't." The horse dodged sideways, avoiding a hole. "We'll break our necks."

Their ride stumbled mid canter, jerking them in the saddle. Rada squealed and clung on. The carrier was snug against Tav. He held the reins single handed, while his other hand supported the baby's head. Her mewling escalated and her face scrunched as she readied herself to unleash her fury, a bawling beacon damning them. "We must get off the road."

"Mami said we should run."

"She's wrong. They'll catch us anyway. And unless we can shut your sister up, they'll find us before we're ready for them. I wish I had some poppy juice. I'd dope her to the gills."

Rada smacked him.

Their route twisted and dipped with the river. The forest crept closer here, not quite meeting the road, but at the next bend it loomed over them, forming a dark tunnel. The skeleton of a dead willow, lay on the verge between them and the tree line. Other debris congealed against it, creating a wall of dried mud and sticks dotted with tall, dry grass like hairs on some scabrous wart.

"I can't see them!"

"Good. I've got an idea, but I'll need your help," he said.

Slowing to a trot, he guided their mount behind the willow. The heavy pound of hooves drew closer. Rada screwed her eyes shut, listening, gripping Tav until her knuckles hurt. Their mount fidgeted at the sound of the approaching horses. It threw its head up and lunged forward. Tav reined it in hard, forcing it backwards and making it rear. Rada slid off the horse and landed on her butt in the dirt. The infant wailed; her cries resounding in the night. The horse's hooves hit the dirt, Tav struggled to keep it in place. He dismounted and yanked the reins; the animal pulled away and moved out of cover.

Rada trembled. *Stupid beast! They'll find us!* Akim's words came to her: *'Always act calm to keep them quiet.'* "Tav, calm down!"

Face twisted in fury, fear and frustration, he turned on her. "Evika! Rada, just..." She stepped back, shocked, quailing. He stopped, gritted his teeth, and nodded. Hands shaking, he rubbed the horse's neck and tried to speak soothingly; his voice quavering all the while.

Unable to reach the horse's neck, Rada patted the top of its leg. Her voice hiccoughed, and she thought she might be sick, but she kept her hand steady. "Shh, everything will be fine." The horse's ears flicked as it listened to them and settled, finally lowering its head to Rada. They urged it forward into the shelter of the downed tree.

The baby drew a shuddering lungful of air ready to continue her screaming her indignation into the night.

"Evika, kid! Shut up!"

"Get her out and hold her. Bounce her. Mami does that and she gets quiet."

Tav fumbled with the carrier's bindings. "Evikan bastard of a thing! They're nearly here!"

The ties loosened; Tav heaved a sigh of relief and clutched the child. "Shh, shh." Anxious, he bounced her too much. She screwed up her angry red face and opened her mouth to scream.

Rada thrust her finger into the babe's mouth, startling her. One cry escaped the infant, then she suckled on Rada's finger. "Give her to me!" Rada whispered. She sat on a branch, under the lee of the fallen timber and cuddled her sister. "You must be quiet, Bubba." She rocked them both, crooned to her and shoved her finger further into her throat as she fussed. "Please, Bubba. Please be still, be quiet."

Tav edged the horse closer to the tree. His worried gaze met hers. "Here they come." The galloping horses sounded like thunder to Rada, yet in a few seconds they were gone.

Her sister twisted her head, wriggled and coughed. "Oh! Sorry, Bubba, sorry." Rada had poked her finger too far in the baby's throat, nearly choking her. She kissed her forehead. "Sorry," she murmured. "They're really gone?"

"They know we weren't that far ahead of them. Soon they'll hit a straight stretch and realise we can't be in front and they'll return. C'mon, we need to find a track into the wood. Help me search. There's too much rubbish from the flood piled up here. We'll have to backtrack a bit."

Rada hung her head and hugged her sister. She realised her feet rested on smooth ground, yet all around was littered with sticks and leaves. She knelt down, felt the ground and peered into the dark. "Tav."

"C'mon, Rada. We've got to go. Give me your sister."

She walked off. "Tav, look."

"Rada, we've got to find a trail."

"Tav!" She stamped her foot. "What about this path right here?"

"What?"

Rada followed a narrow trail that ran under the dead branches and disappeared into the woodland where the top of the fallen tree touched the forest's edge.

"Rada, you're brilliant!" Tav tethered the horse so its rump was visible from the road and grabbed a length of rope from his saddlebag. He began breaking branches and clearing the entrance to the path.

"They'll see the track."

"I know."

Rada scratched her head, confused. "Will the horse even fit?"

"No, but nor will theirs. Come on."

"Why are you leaving it where they'll notice?"

"Trust me. You and I are going to fight."

Rada gaped; her brows rose.

"We can do it!" Desperation coloured his voice too bright, made his expression too hopeful.

"Yes," she whispered, wanting to throw up.

Tav led the way. Dense cauliflower shrubs, covered in dusty smelling white blooms hung over the trail and their small, dark green leaves brushed Rada's face. She rubbed her nose, stifling a sneeze. "Poor bub." She pulled the hood over her sister's head. Tiny white petals snowed on them, and Tav explained his plan as he snapped more branches. Not far in, at a clearing, the track intersected with another one.

"This'll be the spot. Have you got it?" he asked.

Rada nodded. "But, Tav, I don't think..." He frowned at her. She gulped nervously and a cold lump formed in her stomach. "What if something goes wrong?"

Tav knelt and put a hand on her shoulder. "You can do this. You want to be a Darklinan?" She nodded. "Are you sure? I mean, you've never lived rough, you've never had it hard. You're practically a baby yourself."

The dread weight in her melted. Rada narrowed her eyes. "I. Am. Not. A. Baby."

He grinned. "Then this is your test, your real test." She readjusted her grip on her sister. "Is she getting heavy? You're only little." Rada ground her teeth. "Come, turn around. I'll tie her to your back."

"No," she bit out. "Put her in front. I need to see her and know she's all right. And I don't want to drop her when I put her down."

The baby grizzled as Tav readjusted the carrier, but once secure, she settled. "Go find somewhere to hide her."

Rada ran down the track.

"Wait. Do you have your sling?"

"Always. Oh, and this." She dug in her bag and held out lead balls. "I pinched them from the armoury at home. They're way better than stones."

He hesitated, then gave her his dagger, fastening its scabbard on her belt. "Remember the plan."

"I'm six, not deaf. And not little," she muttered as she stormed off.

>———————➤

Rada jogged along the path, fending off scrubby bushes that pushed at her and snagged her hair. With each step, the fire in her belly cooled, and she clutched her sister more tightly. The track wended its way like a drunk before descending a broad gully to a stagnant shallow creek. A massive fallen tree had cleaved a gap in the forest canopy, allowing the moonlight in. Rada's footsteps faltered as she stepped into a wall of icy air. The tarnish of the high waterline lay about the gully sides like a noose, leaving the area around the creek barren, with the black stain of the water in the middle. The lichen-covered branches of the downed tree, trapped in mud, lay stretched out reaching for the water like a dying man with thick cobwebs laced between its fingers. A shiver ran down her spine and the hair on the back of her neck prickled as if she were being watched. She spun, seeing only the frosting of her breath in the night.

"I need to hide you, Bubba," she whispered. "There's no time to find anywhere else."

She cast her gaze about, searching. There was nowhere. The shrubs, though with dense canopies, had bare trunks.

The dead trunk originated up the rise on her left. Its broad root ball lay exposed to the elements and elevated the base of the trunk from the ground. Rada scrambled up the slope, following a faint trail. A fine network of webs knitted together the short ferns on either side of her. Dozens of insects and even a bird, its dainty blue wing tip still quivering, lay trapped in silken coffins.

"Spidies, Bubba..." She shuddered and pulled the carrier's hood over her sister. A cold, thin line tickled Rada's forehead. She brushed it away; her hand connected with a thick, sticky web. Looking up, she saw the tail of a rat dangling from a massive web ball. She ducked and bolted under it.

Rada ran up the path until it vanished under broken dead ferns into a narrow gap between the trunk and the dirt. "No, Bubba. It's too small and dark." She peered into the hole left by the upended root ball, searching for a safe hiding spot. The crater was useless.

She bounced on the balls of her feet and bit her thumbnail. "Where? They'll be back soon. I have to help Tav!"

Rada moved around the trunk. The animal trail on this side had been broad and heavily travelled but was now overgrown and the gap under the fallen tree larger. On her knees, Rada pushed aside the rusty, jagged ferns to reveal an old burrow.

"I think it's empty. Whatever used it is gone or dead". The underside of the trunk was black and rotting, with orange fungi growing from it. Rada wrinkled her nose. "No spidies. Good." Carefully, she slid her sister into the hole, leaving only her head and shoulders sticking out. "Sorry, Bubba."

Her back brushed the trunk, flaking off bits of fungus and dislodging fragments of decaying wood. The black spider, poised in the darkened crevice of bark, stirred and watched these intruders in her realm.

The baby flailed her arms; her unfocused gaze drifted across the damp blackened wood. Her grizzling grew louder. "Shh, Bubba." Rada directed the baby's fist into her mouth and the babe sucked on it, frowning ferociously. *This hole is big enough... I could stay here.*

Her stomach roiled, and she wrapped her arms around her middle. "If I crawl under the trunk, I can stay here with you and hold your hand." She reached out and her sister latched on to her finger. "That way, you won't be scared. They might not find us. They'll go away." Rada bit her lip and started crawling under the log. Halfway, she paused, her head resting on the cool dirt. "But a Darklinan wouldn't do that. Tav is counting on me. Master Pavel would be unhappy. He says we must always fight for our comrades and..." She rubbed her eyes, defying the threatening tears.

Rada curled up in a ball, one hand resting on her sister. "I don't want to! I'm scared, Bubba." Her stomach heaved, she groaned, crawled to the side and vomited. Tears streamed down her face. "I can't!" she cried. Hushed, pleading, she said, "Mami, I can't."

A yell rang out through the forest. Rada's breath caught; she spun at the sound and her words came on a tortured gasp. "Tav." She crawled to her sister and sat rocking back and forth, brushing the baby's forehead. "No, no, no," she whispered. "We need help, Bubba." She drew her dagger and pierced the tip of her finger. "Mstislav, help me." Blood welled. Rada smeared a line of blood down her forehead, under her eyes and down her chin. She repeated the liturgy she'd heard so often. "Mstislav, make my courage never waver, make my sword arm strong and my steel never dull, so I may kill my enemies." She deepened the cut, drawing more blood, and a large drop landed on her sister's brow. The baby ceased fidgeting; her eyes blinked rapidly as Rada marked her face. "Mstislav, she is not yours yet, but I am and she's mine – so help us..." She canted her head and looked up at the sky. "Please?"

A deep warmth settled within her, followed by an overwhelming sense of calm. Rada felt the weight of a hand on her shoulder. Goosebumps formed on her arms. Sounds skittered around and through her. Memories flashed through her thoughts. Faint words whispered in her mind. Rustling like dead leaves, taking shape – transforming from rasping to smoothly feminine then to a familiar gravel. *Remember, courage is doing something despite fear...*

"Master Pavel?" Rada spun, searching for him; she could hear his laugh. "Where are you?"

Everywhere.

"Everywhere?"

The problem is fear is a stubborn bastard, but you must remember Mstislav loves the brave. I love the brave. The voice inveigled her.

"Mstislav?" She squeaked and threw herself on the ground. "But I'm not brave."

A chorus of laughter, feminine, masculine, old and young, upbraided her and the skin on her arms crawled. *You want to be a Darklinan? To be in the emperor's guard? You, who lie here snivelling? Who are too little to be of any use to anyone.*

Rada trembled, yet her old defiance rose. "I'm not little."

But you are. Your sister will die. Tav will die, and your Mami...

"No!" Rada snarled.

You asked for help. I can help you. Will you accept this help and all that goes with it?

"Will you make me brave?"

I will make you many things and, yes, I will make you brave, even when you would run. Do you accept my help?

"Yes."

Good. You must do this, Stilniat. Picture a room in your mind... Excellent. Everything Rada feared – Tav bleeding on the ground, her mother and sister dead, failure... her father... all slid into the room. The door slammed shut and a lock, not of her making, clicked into place. Rada blinked in surprise at the emptiness. She flexed her fingers. Her hands were turning purple in the unnatural cold yet she didn't feel it. The tips of her fingers glistened dully with blood.

That is just the beginning. Such is a warrior's path.

Rada's head and back grew warm. She looked to see if someone was behind her then shrugged as if adjusting a cloak about her.

For a fraction of a second, Rada's eyes flicked black, and an ancient presence looked out through her. *Get up.* Rada clenched her jaw, punched the ground, and pushed herself up.

"You must be quiet, Bubba. I'll be back."

Remember, I am with you. Now and always.
Rada sprung up and ran along the trail. "Come on, Rada. We can do this." She had a god on her side. Just like the heroes in the stories Mami told her. How could she fail? Her foot slipped and her arms windmilled wildly. "No! Up! War face, Rada!" She twisted her expression just as she'd seen the soldiers in training do, snarled and ran on. "Hang on, Tav! I'm coming!"

———————▶

Rada reached the intersection where she'd last seen Tav and hunkered down under the draping branches of a bush. She held her sling in one hand; a lead pellet in the other. *It's so dark in here.*

"This way!" The cry came from near the roadway.

The sound of feet pounding down the track reached her. A dim shape sprinted into view, leapt, and spun about, sword drawn.

Tav. All Rada saw was his outline.

The rapid chink of mail and thump of booted feet drew near. A soldier ran into view, stumbled into Tav's trip-line and sprawled face first in the dirt close to Rada. His comrade struggled to avoid him, leaping at the last second and staggering upon landing. Tav rushed forward, swinging his sword. The trooper dodged clumsily sideways, righted himself, and savagely retaliated, driving Tav backwards. Tav struggled to block each blow; his only hope lay in evasion.

Rada watched, a tight knot in her stomach. Her battle snarl twisted to a rictus of fear that melted – locked away. She became a passenger in her own body. Terrified, her spirit cowered before the immense presence that coiled within her.

Watch what you can do. Unbidden, her muscles tensed, her limbs adjusted in readiness.

None will think you a mere child again.
A sickening thrill ran through her.

"You little bastard. Shoot my horse, will you? Think you can take us? I'll gut you, boy!" The soldier's fierce blows almost knocked the sword from Tav's hand. Tav sidestepped, his escape hampered by dense undergrowth. His opponent grinned. "Nowhere to run."

Rada rose, stepped into the path and drew back her arm to cast her sling.

The trooper nearest to her was halfway to his knees; soon he would be in the fight too. The one near Tav moved in for the kill.

"No!" Rada loosed her shot. Amusement and approval brushed over her. *You're not done yet,* whispered the voice. *Get moving.*

The pellet rocketed through the air and sent up a loud ping as it ricocheted off the soldier's helmet. He turned his head toward this fresh attack. Using this distraction, Tav lashed out with his blade, slamming it down. The soldier parried and Tav's sword slid, locking with his blade. Tav's eyes widened in fear. He kneed the soldier in the stomach with little effect other than a grunt from his opponent. They tussled. Tav tried to hook his leg and fell him. Instead, he was hurled on the ground and the air rushed out of his lungs. His sword lay to the side, just out of reach.

The other soldier searched for Rada.

The trooper above Tav raised his blade. Screaming in rage, Rada charged with no idea where to aim. Powerless to control her limbs, she watched her target loom closer. All she could see, all she could reach, were the backs of his thighs. *It's enough. We can do this,* her guide told her. *There is the spot!* Putting all her weight behind the dagger, she stabbed the soldier standing over Tav in the back of the leg. He roared in pain. Unable to let go, Rada's grip drove the blade sideways as he twisted, slicing through muscle. Warm blood covered her hand. Fierce joy sang through her, while her fear railed against the bars of its cage. He clouted the side of her head, sending her sprawling. Rada lay semi-dazed, weapon lost, ears ringing.

Get up! Her guide growled before driving her to her feet.

"Rada, run!" Tav yelled.

The second soldier headed to her. Rada scrabbled away and darted to the bushes, her pursuer close behind.

Tav crawled frantically for his weapon. His fingers closed around it and he pivoted on his knees, thrusting the sword wildly up under the soldier's hauberk. His attacker's leg buckled from Rada's strike. The soldier listed and tilted forward into Tav's blade. A look of shock, horror and pain flicked across the man's face as the blade sliced into his upper thigh and groin. The soldier brought his sword down toward Tav's head, but it dropped from his fingers, and Tav sprawled sideways to dodge the falling blade. It cut through his boot, slicing into his calf. His enemy toppled forward, dead.

Tav lay pale, shaking and cold.

"Rada. The baby." He clambered to his hands and knees, and with great shuddering breaths, tried to collect himself. Rolling his attacker over, he retrieved his sword. "How did she do this? The look on her face. Gods, she was smiling. I just wanted a distraction. What in the name of all that's holy is going on?" Tav grimaced as he put weight on his leg and felt the warm ooze of blood trickle down his skin. "Shit!" The urgency to find Rada beat at him. He tore a strip of cloth from the dead man's tunic and bound his wound.

"It'll do," he muttered, before he limped into the woods after Rada.

The black spider crept from her lair, scurried forward, then froze; her pedipalps twitched. She skittered along the underside of the timber, pausing only when directly over the baby's forehead. With her many eyes fixated upon the infant, she cast a silken thread and spun down, legs outstretched.

A gurgle erupted from the babe at the feather light tickle of the spider as it landed in the blood on her brow.

From cracks all over the timber, the tips of slender legs appeared, tentatively feeling the outside of the log before hundreds of small spiders scuttled forward. They travelled to the broken ferns that had shielded the hole and set to work in an intricate dance that wove a thick barrier, cocooning the baby.

Within the old burrow, eight enormous eyes watched the smaller spiders work, and a large, hairy, jointed leg laid claim to the baby carrier.

Rada's sister lay unnaturally quiet and still.

CHAPTER 15

Rada ran, ducking and weaving and pushing branches aside; her height her only advantage in the thick undergrowth, but he was gaining.

Run!

Her lungs burned, she slowed. "I can hide!"

No! Not here.

Fresh panic filled her while war raged within, and the last vestiges of her free will shredded as her guide took command. Inside the prison in her mind, she screamed, shook, puked and curled into a ball – small and worthless. One wrong move and they'd all be dead. Worse was the dread that the most dangerous foe had already won.

Run!

Brutally propelled along, Rada's legs trembled with exhaustion.

What the night should have concealed, she noticed with sharp detachment – a hiding place, a branch too low for an adult or a hole in the ground to dodge or stumble in.

Here! Stop!

A sea of waist high ferns hid a shallow depression and rough ground fraught with holes; at the bottom lay a thick log with a jagged branch.

Rada skirted it and ducked down in the ferns, listening. Her breathing sounded harsh against the eerie silence. Before she could blink, an oily warmth slid over her, compelling her muscles, and her breathing slowed. In her core, the mouse hurled itself at the bars, powerless. Even that remote sensation vanished, and there was no Rada.

Chain mail chinked.

A twig cracked.

Rada leapt up, a defiant, dark silhouette.

"Got you!" The Talak charged forward. One step. Two. Arms flailing, he smacked into the dirt and crashed onto the log, dropping his blade. She grinned at the sharp crack of the branch breaking as he hit it.

He lay unmoving.

Rada crept to him.

We'll check if he lives; finish him.

Rada gathered a stubby branch. Canting her head, scrutinising, she hesitated then poked him with the stick. Nothing. Relaxing, she closed in and reached for his dagger. "I'll have that."

His arm shot out, and he grabbed her wrist. Rada wriggled, but he held fast. An image popped into her mind. Behind her back, she gripped her stick tighter.

Wait.

The soldier sat up. He rubbed his shoulder where the stick had snapped against his mail. "Here's a lesson for you, kid. Set better traps and never hesitate; kill 'em quick." He yanked her toward him.

"Here's a lesson for you!" Rada jabbed the stick at his face. It glanced off his nose guard, straight into his eye. He roared in pain, and his grip loosened. She wrenched her arm free, snatched up the fallen knife and ran.

"Bloody runt!"

See what you can do? Her guide loosed the yoke that restrained her.

Rada bolted through the ferns and broke onto the path to the creek. The enemy soldier crashed onto the trail at her rear. The thud of his feet grew closer. The air stirred behind her. His fingers brushed her shoulder and he screamed. A wail of pure terror that pierced the night.

She turned to see a black shape clinging to his head. He threw off his helmet and spun while brushing frantically at his head and clothes. The Talak straightened and staggered, weaving at her. She ran a few steps but halted when she a heard thud. He lay on the track, struggling to rise.

"What happened?" she whispered. Rada froze at a rustle in the undergrowth next to her. Several enormous spiders emerged along the narrow trail between her and the downed man. Bile rose in her throat and she trembled from head to toe. Had they noticed her? She could run. She could disappear and find Tav. Together, they were strong.

You will not run. Not anymore. Look at what you've already achieved.

"You did that."

No, it was this body. This little, fragile frame did the work.

Rada's anger rose. "I'm not little."

A chuckle echoed in her mind. *Yes, you are, but you are neither helpless nor powerless, and when they all say 'little', that is what they mean. But I know better. You have proved them wrong.*

"I did, didn't I?"

Yes. Your Master Pavel would be pleased. So would the emperor, so will your mother.

A flicker of pride swelled in her. "Yes."

Keep proving them wrong. Remember, who does Mstislav love?

"The brave."

The Talak moaned; his breath rasping.

Finish him.

"I've never... I've only watched..."

He's your enemy.

"Yes, but..." Her hands shook.

I've made this easy. Impatience, like a whip crack, jolted through Rada.

She held the blade, poised. Rada tried to loosen her grip, only to have her fingers clasp it until her knuckles shone white. Her chest and head ached; a thin line of sweat formed on her upper lip as she fought for dominion, yet she took the first jerky steps of a marionette.

Rada's mouth went dry as a painful surge of energy built within her and she shuddered. "No. Not that. I'll do it."

You know what to do.

She moved haltingly forward.

Don't think. Just do. Lock away everything else.

Within a few strides, her gait changed. She stalked, head down and intent, toward the fallen soldier. His breath scraped in and out; he looked up – eyes wide, panicked, tears streaming and face swollen.

"Wait." He wheezed the word; his head wobbled with the effort of keeping it raised. That look unfamiliar, yet disquieting, tugged at her and she paused.

Like cold skittering across her skin, *'who does Mstislav love'* brushed in her thoughts. So close upon the heels of the threat, it galvanised her.

Do you remember how?

Rada nodded and the path now programmed in her brain opened and she forced fear, confusion, questions, doubts – all emotion beyond that door, barring it closed.

Excellent.

Unbidden, ritual words were pulled from her. "Help was asked, help was given. I must offer thanks. Mstislav, I give you this..."

In a tone that echoed the power inside her, she said, "Kill 'em quick."

The blade moved as if through soft butter. The man fell, limp as a rag doll. Certainty overtook her. It had been necessary. It had been easy. A quiet warmth, gratitude, settled within Rada.

Lesson learned. The male voice dwindled and a feminine sigh whispered on the wind, taking the otherworldly control with it.

Tav rounded a bend in the trail and froze at the sight of Rada holding a knife and standing over a body.

"Rada! Rada!" Nothing. She remained absorbed by blade and the body. Tav took a step toward her and felt something brush against his scalp. He batted it off and his fingers and came away sticky, covered in fibre.

"What the...?" Tav glanced at the remains of a giant web stretched across the track; its torn strands dangled beside him. A soft scuttle below drew his attention. Beside him, a huge spider, one of its legs broken, shuffled into the undergrowth.

Above Rada, a dark shape hovered. Terror filled him. He inched forward. For each step he took, the spider took one too. Eight eyes tracked his every move and, perversely, all he could think of was, *funny how they glisten, even at night.*

The spider hung level with his face. He froze. Tav stretched his arm out to touch Rada's shoulder. The spider raised its fangs, waiting. Beads of sweat pearled on Tav's brow, rolled down into his eyes. He blinked furiously, desperate to wipe them away. He wanted to move, to run, to be anywhere other than here. Rada stood oblivious, a slight frown, and fixated on the knife in her fingers and the corpse at her feet.

Fingertip by fingertip, he gripped her shoulder. The spider placed one foot on her head – poised and watchful. Tav swallowed anxiously as he gently squeezed her.

"Rada?" he whispered. He squeezed harder, careful not to shake her. "Rada."

She blinked owlishly. "Tav?" The spider shuffled away, its foot brushing her hair as it retreated to the edge of its web. She glanced up. "Spider!" Rada squealed, dropped the knife and launched herself at him. "Tav!" He clutched her to him and dragged her away from the web.

A nervous chuckle escaped Tav. "It's been hanging over your head the whole time. Are you hurt?"

"No, but..." Shaking, she turned toward the corpse.

Tav rubbed her back. "It's fine. We got them."

"But I didn't... I mean... Maybe I did, but... something else... Oh... OH!"

"Rada, calm down."

"His face... The spider... Tav... look."

Tav and Rada stole forward. The soldier's entire face was bloated and dark; his eyes swollen shut, his lips huge and his throat swollen.

"He almost had me and then he screamed."

Tav pointed to the tattered web. "He hit the web. The spider attacked him. I saw a spider beside the trail with a broken leg."

Rada gulped. "The spider saved me? ... I... I asked Mstislav for help. See, I cut my hand and made the mark and did the prayer, but... I just hoped he'd make me brave and tough... not this."

"Mstislav maybe, but I doubt it," He eyed the spider in front of them. "It didn't hurt me and could easily have hurt you." Tav's gut churned as he picked up her knife and wiped it on the dead man's pants before passing it to her. "This should be yours now. You're the first to wet its blade."

"It's kind of blurry," she said. "I can't remember it straight and—"

"He would have killed you if he could." Tav interrupted, his words clipped. "And he would have died anyway, so you did him a mercy."

They couldn't stop to think; it could be their undoing. Thinking was for later. He squatted, stripped the man of his weapons and ransacked his pockets, pilfering a bag of coins.

"Master Pavel teaches us the sacrifice must be alive. You can't ask for a blessing and then offer any old dead thing. I've sacrificed a rabbit... but... I haven't killed a person before. I've watched..." Tav's heart sank. "... but... this..."

"Is different?" he finished. She nodded as he continued. "I understand. I'm a thief, amongst other things, but I've killed no one until today either." He took her by the shoulders and stared into her eyes. "You shouldn't dwell on it. Akim would say the mission isn't over. We should fetch your sister. Where is she?"

Rada turned and with a shaking finger pointed past the occupied web. "That way."

He groaned. "I've a bad feeling about this." With one eye on the dark shape hunkered in its corner, Tav peered underneath the cobweb. The way ahead was now a tunnel obliterating the thin moonlight seeping through the trees. Tav shuddered. Rada touched his shoulder and he yelped.

"Sorry," she murmured. "I'm sure they weren't there before."

"You were in a hurry and short enough to have passed underneath without noticing."

"No," she said, certainty ringing in her words. "I would've noticed. They weren't here."

"We'll go around."

"I'm not sure I could find her off the track? What if I muck it up?"

Tav turned to the downed Talak. "Come on, let's get his mail shirt off. I'm pretty sure they won't hurt you. I'm not so sure about me." He donned the mail and stood tall. He took one step and slammed to a halt, hands shooting to his bare head. "Can you find his helmet?"

Rada hunted around and passed it to Tav. "Um... It didn't help him much."

"It'll be better than nothing."

Tav drew a deep breath. Together, they entered the tunnel. He was bent over. "Evika! I can hardly see!"

Rada took his hand, whispering. "I'm here."

"Aren't you scared?"

"Not... too much... Mstislav must have sent them. I'll be fine. And I'll stick close to you, so you'll be fine too."

The air in the tunnel was still, yet occasionally the surrounding webs stirred, creating a cold, airy caress on their faces.

Rada hunched her shoulders.

The branches above them rustled.

Tav sped up.

"What was that?" The webs brushed his back. "Enough! That's it!" He dropped and crawled. It didn't help. His palms sank into inches of leaf litter. Needle-like twigs bit into his skin like a million little fangs. "Never tell anyone about this, will you?"

"It's all right to be scared. They're the biggest ones I've ever seen. The size of puppies... small dogs, even. I bet they can jump too."

"Rada, stop trying to make me feel better."

"Mami always talks to me to make me feel better."

"Then think of something else... not involving spiders."

She drummed her fingers on his back.

"Stop that! It's like something crawling."

"You have to put the Tav that's scared in a box. Don't talk to him until later."

"Is that what you're doing?"

"Yes, and I'm listening to Master Pavel's voice. Remembering his lessons and how to be brave... Mstislav loves the brave." Her words faded into silence. "Am I a Darklinan now?"

"Yes, and more. In your heart you've always been one."

"But now I've proved it?" she asked, and Tav nodded. "Do I get the tattoo?"

"Yes."

"Just the heart? Or am I allowed a pattern around it too? What to use?" She rattled on. "A bird? Horse? Dog? Cat?"

"Rada! I don't..." He trailed off, relief flaring in him at the sight of open ground and moonlight.

"We're out!" Rada chimed. "I made you forget."

Tav collapsed onto his back, heaving in breaths.

Rada popped into view as she leaned over him. "I still want to know what I get to add to my dark-heart tattoo."

He sat up. "It doesn't work like that. The embellishment has to do with your testing."

"Spidies then."

Tav shuddered. "Where's your sister?"

"Follow me." Rada hurried up the slope to the base of the fallen tree, with Tav limping at the rear. "No!" she yelled. A thick cocoon covered the narrow gap under the trunk. Hundreds of small spiders scuttled at her cry. She flew to the other side of the trunk where she had lain the baby in the hole and stood in shock. A webbed wall met her. "No!" Her dagger flashed as she slashed at the cocoon, cutting a hole in it.

Tav caught up with her. "Rada, what? Be careful!" Too late, he reached to stop her. She'd dived into the gap. "She's all right!" The babe lay snug in her carrier, warm and sound asleep. "Ew! What's that smell?" Rada shot out backwards, holding her nose. "It's her." She took two steps backward. "She's all yours, Tav."

"Great. Armed men chasing us and giant spiders you can handle, but a smelly baby and you lose it. Here, let me." He knelt to retrieve her. "Oh, dear gods! No wonder the spiders haven't touched her." He pulled the baby out and held her at arm's length as if she might explode. The carrier fell away from her, revealing her features. Tav gasped. In a choked whisper, he said, "Rada, did you do this?"

The blood Rada had marked her with formed an intricate web pattern across the baby's entire face.

Wide eyed, Rada shook her head. "The spiders?" Rada snatched the carrier, shaking it vigorously. "No spiders." She peered at her sister. "No spiders on her either."

"We have to clean this off," Tav said. "Rada, we can't tell anyone."

"No, Tav, it's protecting her. The spidies didn't hurt her and it was snug and warm in there, not cold like out here. You shouldn't take it off."

"Remember the picture of The Weaver at Darklina?"

"The Weaver starts all our threads. She isn't bad, Tav."

"The temple doesn't believe that. Pavel wouldn't think so. We remove it and you say nothing, not even to your mother."

"But Mami told me about The Weaver."

"Not a word, Rada. We'll clean her up at the creek."

"That water's not very nice."

"It's nicer than her!"

"We haven't got a nappy."

"We'll use the shirt off the dead guy. Let's just clean her and pray she does nothing else before then, or I might leave her in the tunnel."

CHAPTER 16

TAV TIGHTENED THE CARRIER around his chest. The baby worried him; she'd not uttered a sound since they'd retrieved her from her hiding place. Their enemies' horses stood quietly, tethered to the fallen tree where Tav had left their one.

"Rada, have you ridden alone before?"

"Papi said I wasn't old enough yet. Sometimes Mami would lead me around."

"Well, you're going to ride now."

"On my own?"

"Yep. Your horse will probably follow me. I'll lead the other one. In case something goes wrong, I want you to take the reins, and I don't want a lead rope loose around your horse's legs if things go to shit."

"But aren't we safe now?" She took his hand and peered into the night.

"No, Rada. They'll wonder where those men are and come looking. If we let the horses go, they could run back and the soldiers might come looking quicker." He lifted her up onto his horse and shortened the stirrups. "I can't make them short enough." He flipped them over the top of the saddle so they hung criss-crossed. "How's that?"

Rada held the reins loosely and tested her feet in the stirrups. "Better."

He readjusted her grip on the reins. "Hang on to them properly and shorten them a bit. You don't want to haul miles of them in if you need to stop or turn."

Tav latched onto a saddle, his weight on his injured leg. A long groan escaped him as he tried to push off to mount. "Evika! Friggin' leg! Friggin' horse!" Resting his head against the side of the saddle. *I'm failing! Keep them safe! I don't know what I'm doing.* He bit back a sob. "There has to be a way."

"Tav? Use the tree, Tav," Rada whispered. He looked up at her, eyes moist. "It's what I'd do. I need to climb up things all the time."

He stared at her open-mouthed, before turning away and wiping his eyes. "You're right." He led the horse to a thick part of the trunk. "I should've thought of that."

"You're bigger. I suppose you don't need to think about it as much."

He grunted as he mounted, leaning over the neck of his horse for a moment, hiding his pain. Righting himself, he flicked a grin at her. "Are you saying you're little?"

Concern vanished from Rada's face. "No!"

Chuckling, Tav unhooked the remaining horse to lead it. As quick as it had come, the anger left her face; she looked pale and impossibly young to be in this situation. He couldn't believe she'd done as well as she had.

Voice tremulous, she said, "Where are we going?"

"Akim made me study that map, remember?" Tav said. "Soon we'll be off this road and into the track through the hills."

"What about Mami?"

"I don't know. Your mother's orders were to get you and the baby to safety; to her people."

"She should be here. Something's happened. We have to help her."

"Rada, there's only two of us. We've just survived by the skin of our teeth as it is. We can't help her." Rada clenched her jaw. "Do you understand? We'll die! Your baby sister will die! Think of her! Remember what your Mami wanted."

She burst into tears, and Tav pulled alongside her. "I'm sorry, but we can't do this now. Rada, we don't even know how far this goes; how big it is. This could be a takeover – the emperor may be dead." Rada sobbed uncontrollably. "Rada! You're a Darklinan now and we've a mission. My job and yours is to get your sister to your mother's people. Concentrate only on that. Then we can scream and rant." He drew a shuddering breath and wiped away a tear. "Then we can cry until we've no more tears to give." He leaned over and squeezed her hand. She blinked furiously, gulping in breaths, trying to stifle her sobs. "After, we'll take revenge. Remember how you said I should shut the frightened Tav away?" She nodded. "We both must shut away our fear and our sorrow. We'll talk to them later, but not now."

"Not now," she repeated, wiping her face on her sleeve.

"Are you ready? Come on, let's see how you ride."

Darkness thinned and black shapes transformed into tall grey trees whose true colour was bleeding back in with the encroaching dawn. The track doubled back and then meandered the foothills of the mountain range, climbing and veering amongst rocky outcrops.

As they rode, Rada saw Tav scan the sides of the path, looking for another trail heading north. They were quite far inland from the road, but by his reckoning, still heading in the camp's direction. Tav reined his horse in. "Rada, I don't know where we are exactly. But the camp will be down there somewhere. We've got to be careful. There might be men in the woods. We'll have to stay quiet."

Rada nodded. She was too tired to want to talk. Her bottom had gone numb; her feet too. Walking was easy. All the trotting almost rattled her teeth out of her head. She wriggled in the saddle, trying to ease the ache. The horse's head and thick neck bobbing along comforted her. *I don't feel like I'm going to fall off anymore. I can even rise a now... a bit.*

Tav's horse dropped out of sight as the path ahead vanished over the edge of the steep slope. Rada stood in the stirrups, trying to see what lay before her, but all she saw was Tav's head. Jaw set, she plopped back down and tightened her hands around the reins. She hauled on the leather, stopping at the hill's crest. Rada's jaw dropped; the path plummeted.

Tav was halfway down, but he turned and grinned up at her, nodding encouragingly and waving her forward.

"Wait, what do I do?" she hissed, a squeak of panic tainting her words.

The horse took his first downward steps. "Oh!" Rada clutched the pommel, the reins under her hand but hanging loose. Her mount stretched his neck down as he tackled the track. The saddle seemed to hang in mid-air. *His head's gone! His neck's gone! The saddle will slip off. There's nothing to stop it.* "No, no, no! Tav!" She squealed, pushed against the stirrups, and leaned back. She watched in horror as the horse skidded and stones rolled down the hill before her. Rada shut her eyes. At the bottom, the horse jumped the narrow gully and broke into a canter as the track wound along the side of the slope toward the top. She lurched back in the saddle and snapped open her eyes, seeing only faint grey sky through the trees. The reins slipped from her hand. She pulled herself up and scrabbled for them. With each stride, the reins slipped further away. The horse jumped a small log. The reins flicked up in the air, and Rada snatched them. She bounced in the saddle, a rictus fixed upon her face as she clutched the pommel and reins.

"Pull on the reins!" Tav called.

Rada pulled on the reins, leaning back to do so, and bounced sideways. She squealed and scrabbled at the saddle again.

The horse crested the hill and the trail broadened. "Tav! Help!"

He urged his horse up after her. Tav took his hand from the baby and reached out for Rada's reins as he drew closer. The baby let out a howl, and Rada's horse tossed its head and gathered speed. "This won't work! He thinks it's a race!" Tav backed off. "Pull the reins harder!"

Rada gritted her teeth, reeling in the reins, before clamping her hand on the saddle as her body lurched. The horse slowed, bouncing from canter to trot. It pig-rooted and Rada shot forward. "Hey!" Her temper exploded. "That's enough!" She yanked on the leather, stopping the animal. "You evikan horrible horse. I hate you." Shaking, breath heaving, she waited for Tav. A tremulous smile crept across her face. "Tav, I did it!" she shouted, but he wasn't in sight yet. "And I didn't fall off." She poked her tongue out at the horse. It wrenched the reins from her hands and put its head down to eat. "You're a grumpy horse," Rada said, trying to pull its head back up without success. "Maybe the worst horse ever." The horse's head shot up. It fidgeted and spun about.

"He's a big horse for someone so little," a rough voice said.

The smile fell from Rada's face as she stared at two of General Rodan's cavalry watching her from a side trail that led downhill. "I'm not little!" Their horses surged forward. One of them tried to grab Rada's reins. Her horse threw its head up and the man missed. The other rider blocked the track. Rada kicked the horse and, though her legs didn't hang past the saddle, it took off.

She clung on, looking back in panic. "Good horse! Faster!"

They gained on her. One drew a bow. Terrified, Rada ducked low in the saddle and hung on.

Her face froze in shock as three horsemen loomed before her, blocking the trail. The two in front had bows drawn. Arrows sped toward her. She held her breath as they flew past and into her pursuers. One toppled off his mount, but the other regained his seat. Another arrow whizzed by and struck him. He sagged and fought to turn his horse.

Wide eyed, Rada watched soldiers pour from the woods, surround Rodan's men, finish them and capture the horses.

The familiar blue of their uniforms registered with her. Her wild-eyed horse slowed, was caught, and strong hands reached out, wrapped about her waist and plucked her from the saddle.

"Hello, my lioness."

Rada looked up into the familiar, worried, dark eyes of the emperor and threw her arms about him.

"They've got Mami! I've lost Tav and the baby!"

"Shh. Here comes Tav now."

Tav trotted up the road surrounded by soldiers, the baby snug against him.

"Mami?"

He hesitated and his lips drew into a tight line. "They still have her... She lives. But now we get her back."

———►

In the grey light of dawn, Tikhon lay on the ground peering through the undergrowth at the campsite. Rodan's Talakian rebels sat around the camp; they expected no reprisal. Clearly, they assumed Tikhon remained waylaid and battling forces led by Rodan's friend, General Cēdar, or that Tikhon had lost and been executed.

Tikhon cursed inwardly. Intelligence had underestimated Cēdar's forces and placed him elsewhere. He'd not expected to get ambushed on the way here. *It could be a simple error, or we could have a traitor in our ranks. Gods know what else they've fomented. We should have been here long ago. It shouldn't have gone this far.* Darcov's words returned to haunt him – *'she'll never forgive you.'*

The bodies of his fallen troops lay piled away from the camp. *Too many dead.* Even though the number of corpses bearing Rodan's colours outnumbered the Zaragarian troops. They'd put up a good fight. A few of his troops still lived, beaten and bound, placed next to their slain comrades and surrounded by guards. Other than the sentries and the prisoners' guards, the rest of Rodan's soldiers slept, though in a few hours the entire camp would be active.

Jadzia lay on her side unmoving, hands and feet hogtied, with the end of the rope forming a noose about her neck. So long as she could keep her back, arms and legs arched, she'd be fine, but if she failed to do so, she'd strangle herself.

Rodan shoved her with his foot. "Wake up, bitch. I'm not letting you die that easily. Once your children are here, we can start. I'll put them to the knife before your eyes, just like that old bastard Pavel did to my wife."

An agonised groan escaped Jadzia.

"She's failing." Tikhon dug his hands into the soil, every muscle coiled, fighting the urge to charge in and rescue her. He hung his head then looked up as her groan transformed into animalistic rage.

"She's still holding on, my friend," Darcov whispered. "We've not got long. He's got to be wondering where the men are that he sent after the children. Once he figures they're not coming, he'll kill her."

"I know," Tikhon bit out. They crept back on their bellies and retreated to their awaiting warriors. His mind raced; analysing, calculating risk, discarding scenario after scenario and always coming back to the same conclusion. He pushed his misgivings aside; useless reminders of his guilt. *There's no choice and time is running out.* "We need a distraction to draw them away from the camp and her. Otherwise, he'll kill her as soon as we attack."

Darcov put his hand on Tikhon, waylaying him, his gaze hard. "Just what kind of distraction did you have in mind?"

Tikhon schooled his face, his voice cold and flat. "One they won't shoot on sight. Two teams. Darcov, you take one, release those captured and take down the enemy left at the campsite. The rest will be with me. We'll join you once we've killed those who fall for the bait."

"I can go," Tav said. "Let them see me. Maybe they'll think Rada and the baby are nearby. Maybe I can lure them off."

"You can't run far or fast, boy, not with that leg."

"You don't want to free the others and go straight for Rodan?" Darcov asked.

"No, I need to protect the distraction."

Worry creased Darcov's face. "Tikhon?"

An iron dread lodged in his gut. "Rada, come here." She trotted over and he pulled her onto his knee. "Do you want to help save your mami?"

"Yes."

"You're going to need to be braver than ever, and you must do exactly as I say or this won't work."

She looked up at Tikhon, Darcov, and all the blue-clad guards around her. "I can be brave."

CHAPTER 17

TIKHON STOOD BEHIND RADA with his hand on her shoulder. His men had dispersed. She wanted to turn around, hang on to him and never let go, but could not turn her gaze from the campsite.

"They don't expect an attack. That man is—"

"General Rodan," Rada said. "He's a friend of Papi's, but he had a fight with Papi and hasn't been to the villa in a long time."

"Mmm, your father showed rare, good sense there."

Rada snorted. "Mami yelled at him and told him he was a fool if he kept being his friend."

"Your mother's wise."

Rada shrugged. "Yes, but she says most men are a bit stupid."

He knelt beside her and turned her to face him. "Rodan has your mother and he's hurt her. He's not getting you or your sister. Do you remember the plan?"

Rada nodded. Her stomach flipped and burned inside her. She wasn't sure if she'd be sick or have to run into the bushes before she soiled herself.

"Who does Mstislav love?" Tikhon asked.

"The brave," she whispered. Fear clawed at her insides. She shuddered, waiting for the god to reprimand and control her. Nothing.

"Rada, you can do this," Tikhon said. "You are my lioness, brave and powerful. Already, you've proven it. No one will ever call you little again. Don't be frightened of the battle. We're here. We'll save her."

"I'm not frightened of that."

"No?"

She shook her head. "There are worse things."

Tikhon rubbed his chin. He looked at the field before him and back to Rada, nodded, and let the silence stretch between them. "Remember your lessons." The word hung like a noose in the air over her.

Proven, little, lessons, brave. Rada gaped at him. Mstislav's words. Was he here? In uncle?

She nodded, frantic, tried to gather her fears and bundle them up, but it was like chasing marbles rolling down a hill – always one escaped. *Get into the room!* Her face scrunched in concentration.

I can't tell anyone. They'll think I'm weak, little, and useless. I have to get this right. Everyone is depending on me. Everyone. Her mind raced and her heart pounded; all movement around her appeared sped up, and an ache built at the back of her skull. Noises from the birds faded, and Rada wondered if the leaves normally had an orange-tinge as her vision blurred. "Everyone is counting on me," she whispered.

Tikhon squeezed her shoulder gently. His voice filtered through her fugue. "Because we know you can do it."

Because he knows I can. Pop. It all stopped. The door slammed shut.

"I bet you've lost count of how often you've play-acted at home to get what you want?" Rada's lips quirked. "You trick that fat man and get your mami back. Remember your orders. They'll trust you because they think you're little. But we know better. You're not little Rada anymore. You're Rada the Brave, Rada the Warrior; Rada, the youngest imperial guard ever! Wear her face. March to her beat! Trust her! Tell yourself this again and again." Rada nodded. *He knows I can do it.* "They're our enemies. Your mami's enemies. We'll make them pay."

Rada stepped out of the wood; behind her back, cradled in her palm was her loaded sling. She murmured a prayer that it would unfurl smoothly and the lead pellet would stay in place.

No one noticed her stepping out of the tree line. One step... Two steps. Nothing. *What's wrong with them? Are they blind?* One of the enemy glanced in her direction and nudged the other; murmured conversation reached her, but no one stood. *They see me, but they're pretending they don't. They're tricking me.* Her steps faltered. *Rada the Brave.* Her mouth grew dry. *Rada the Brave. Rada the Brave... No shaking! No blubbing! Rada the Brave!* She kept walking until she was halfway to the campsite. *No further, Uncle said.*

Rodan stood.

Rada stopped.

Her eyes widened at the sight of Akim and the handful of Tikhon's warriors who remained alive, tied up, beaten and bruised. Wary, she scowled at the soldiers who were awake, standing and staring at her. Two men flanked Rodan, obscuring her mother's body, another draped a cloak over her.

Rada ground her teeth. *They think I'm little and stupid.*

"Softly now, men," Rodan murmured. "We don't want her to run off and get lost again."

Rada made a mental eye roll. *Do they think I'm deaf too? Lost? I'll give you lost. Let's reel you in, just like a big, fat fish.* She stood there with her thumb in her mouth, forlorn, dishevelled; her face dirty and blood smeared, hair tangled with twigs and springing from its braid. Every inch of her the lost waif.

Her breath hitched as she let out a sob, sniffed, and rubbed her eyes. In a plaintive whisper she said, "Where's Mami?"

"She's gone looking for you. The emperor sent us to chase the bad men away. You're safe now," Rodan assured her, stepping forward. She scuttled back, alert, distrustful. "We only want you safe, I swear it."

Rada scratched her scalp and frowned, squinting at him. "Why have you tied up Akim and our guards?" Two soldiers were attending to their attire, making a show of chatting to their comrades, all the while moving closer. Rada tracked their movements, like a deer tensed for flight.

"Gentlemen, desist. You're frightening Mistress Rada." He held up his hands. "You're safe now. These men weren't loyal to the emperor. They're traitors. Every one of them conspired to hurt your family. Where's your sister?"

Rada nodded. "He did act funny... He was just pretending to be our friend?"

"Yes. The world is full of liars. You need to learn who to trust," Rodan said, stepping toward her. "Where's your sister? We must keep her safe."

Rada shuffled her feet, reddened with embarrassment. "I fell off the horse and lost them."

Rodan's expression darkened. "We'll find them for you. What way were they going?"

"North. That's what Mami said to do."

"Six of you go. Bring them back safely," Rodan ordered.

"Wait! I came off when we left the main road and went on the forest track. They should go there." She jutted out her chin and stamped her foot. "Tav didn't stop. He's a coward! He left me!"

The men mounted and rode off at a gallop. A bubble of happiness swelled in her. *Uncle Tikhon was right. That was easy. They don't believe anyone can hurt them. Wait 'til you see who's coming for you.*

Rodan smiled at her, all warmth and reassurance; kind and fatherly. Cautiously, he moved closer. "You'll all be reunited soon enough."

"I don't care about Tav. I'm mad at him. I just want my sister."

Rodan laughed. "You've got a temper, little one. I wouldn't want to be him when we bring him back. Come," he held out his hand to her.

Rada remained motionless. She clenched her jaw and fought to stop snarling. *I'm not little.* She gripped the smooth lead weight in her sling. *Just a few steps more.*

The camp was busy now and the smell of food wafted on the air. The men chatted and laughed but stole glances her way.

"You've had a long night by the look of you and must be hungry. I wish my men had found you earlier."

Rada waited.

Rodan took a step toward her.

"Your men..." She hesitated, then chortled. *This'll be fun.* "Your men are dead."

Rodan's hand fell and his lips shifted into a stern line. The soldiers around the camp stopped what they were doing and listened.

"The spidies got them. They started at their heads and they swelled up all purple and black." Rada grinned, relishing the shock on Rodan's face. "Then they finished at their fingies and toesies." She continued in a singsong voice. "All gone. Dead. Gobbled up. Dead and gone. They're never coming back." She giggled, high, girlish, coldly gleeful, yet the memory made her queasy.

"Spiders? Rada? What nonsense is this?" he said.

Rodan took another step.

She relaxed her hold on the sling, waiting.

"Now is not the time for games."

Rada canted her head. "Everyone likes games. You've been playing games with me."

"Rada, your mother will hear of this!"

"Do you know how often I've heard that?" Rada said.

"Now, look here!" Rodan snapped and...

Took one last step.

"You must think I'm stupid. I want my mami. Now!"

She let the sling unravel from her palm, felt the reassuring weight still secure in it, and hurled it forward. The lead weight hurtled through the air, colliding with Rodan's eye, driving it out of its socket. Rada gaped as it flew like a small, soft-boiled egg, blood and viscera trailing in its wake.

He roared and doubled over, clutching his face. "Evika! Little runt!" he bellowed. "Get her."

Rodan's men charged.

Rada gawped at where his eyeball had landed on the grass. The pound of boots broke her stunned fixation. She bolted.

Only a handful of his men remained guarding Akim and the others.

Heart pounding, arms pumping wildly, Rada's breath burned in her throat. The darkness of the trees swallowed her. The sound of snapping twigs and branches dogged Rada as her pursuers entered the forest. *Where's Uncle? He should be here.* Rada screamed, realising one of them was nearly upon her. *Run, run, run!* She launched forward.

Emerging from behind a tree, Tikhon stood before her, feet apart, hefting a short axe. Rada squealed and dived between his legs, skidding on leaf litter. He hurled the axe, embedding it in her enemy. She rolled and came to her feet. Rada loaded another lead pellet into her sling and peeked out from behind the tree.

A volley of arrows shot out from the woods. The Talaks stumbled, staggered, some fell, and others turned to face the emperor's troops with barely enough time to draw their weapons.

The confines of the forest hindered the Talaks with their long swords, and Rada watched the brutal melee. She bit her lip, relief and frustration warring within her. One Zaragarian leapt onto the back of a rebel, attempting to drive a dagger into his neck. Rodan's man threw him off and the pair grappled, punched and kicked each other. In a frenzy, the Zaragarian caved the Talak's head in with a rock.

A sword-wielding enemy lunged at one of Tikhon's troops. The woman side-stepped and drove her axe down on his arm. His mail remained intact, but his arm broke and the sword fell from his limp hand. The next blow hewed into the base of his unprotected neck. Blood gushed from the wound.

Fighters punched, kicked, wrestled and hacked into each other. Tikhon's force snuffed out life in any way they could. Each individual victory renewed Rada's confidence. Near her, an imperial soldier lay pinned by his opponent, striving to fend off a dagger. The blade drew ever closer to his throat.

Rada loosed her sling, smacking the enemy in the temple. He reeled, insensible, and the imperial trooper thrust him off and stabbed him.

Mstislav loves the brave. She grinned maniacally, loaded her sling, and looked for another target.

In front of her, Tikhon battled another assailant. The man charged, striking out with his sword. Tikhon thrust out his small shield, redirecting the blow. The blade stuck into a tree trunk, and Tikhon swung his axe down into the man's side. The Talak screamed, and Tikhon landed a final blow to his skull.

Rada spied another rebel heading to attack Tikhon from the rear.

"No!" She whirled her sling, shooting a pellet at the man. She didn't aim. She didn't think. It was her worst throw. Time seemed to slow as she tracked it. He ran forward, sword raised. His face twisted in pain and he faltered, dropping his weapon and clutching his throat, struggling for air. Blood seeped between his fingers. He fell to his knees and gazed in horror at Rada.

"Well done, Rada!" Tikhon said as pulled his axe from the skull of his first assailant. "He's the last of them."

An imperial guard stepped forward to finish the enemy Rada had felled.

"Hold!" Tikhon ordered. The guards thrust the man to the ground. "Rada, come quickly." She ran to take his outstretched hand.

Face pale, eyes wide, blood seeped from between the downed-man's fingers as he watched them approach. His lips twitched and he moved his mouth in silent prayer.

"Rada, a warrior would finish him."

"He could be a slave?"

Tikhon knelt beside her. "He's rebelled against his emperor. What's the punishment for that?"

"Death." A flash of a dark tunnel, a swollen face, a hand holding a dagger – her hand and yet, not; a dagger that moved without her volition. Rada swallowed, almost wishing Mstislav would control her again so she wouldn't have to think, and half terrified that he would. "I'm not sure how. I don't really remember last time."

"I understand." He rubbed her back. "Come, I'll show you. Draw your dagger, my lioness."

As each finger embraced the cold handle of her knife, a chill settled deep within her and she trembled until the warmth of her uncle's hand covered her own. She looked up, smiling in relief at his blood-spattered face.

Two of the guard restrained the ashen Talak. Tikhon moved Rada's hand so that the blade of her dagger rested just behind his collarbone. The soldier no longer gazed in fear, instead he glared, struggling to speak. Impassive, Tikhon said, "Push." When her hand didn't move, he pushed the dagger down with excruciating slowness, trapping hers, ensuring she couldn't let go. Rada winced as the dagger slid with hideous grace into the rebel's flesh. "It doesn't have to go far. That's enough. Well done, my girl."

The red didn't bloom until the dagger was removed. *I did this.*

The Talak managed one word. "Monsters."

➤

Darcov and his team stole their way forward and hunkered down amongst the undergrowth at the edge of the forest. He watched, momentarily stricken, as Rada stepped out of the tree line.

What was Tikhon thinking? Mstislav help the child. He couldn't believe Tikhon would do this. The risk hadn't seemed to bother him, at least not for long. *No, that's not true. It bothers him, but he's locked down his emotions so tightly that no one else would guess.* The end goal was all. This was like the first emperor, rather than his father, and the path Aitor I trod was bathed in blood... and, Darcov had to admit, glory.

Jadzia lay unnaturally still. Darcov wondered if she'd died. What then? How would Tikhon cope? Guilt, rage, and a good dose of self-loathing? How would that play out?

He shuddered. "I pray we don't find out."

Rada hurtled a shot at Rodan and a gut-wrenching cry of agony filled the air. The general doubled over in pain, clutching his face. His guard ran to his aid, but he waved them on yelling, "Little runt! Get her!"

Jadzia stirred at the commotion, suffered a kick to the belly, and remained motionless. At the general's bellow, at least half of his men had run to pursue Rada.

When they disappeared into the forest, Darcov said in a harsh whisper, "Now."

They surged out of cover. Darcov led the charge to Rodan. Cries of alarm rose and Darcov sped up, running full tilt at the general and the two guards who were bent over him, assessing his injuries. Stunned, they drew their swords. Rodan staggered to his feet, reaching for his weapon.

Darcov lunged at the first Talak soldier protecting Rodan. The man parried at the last moment and the clash of their blades rang out, joining the harsh cacophony of fighting around them. Darcov's sword slid along the other blade into a bind. He smacked a hand into the Talak's elbow, forcing his torso to twist and driving his enemy's blade down and away. With a deft manoeuvre, Darcov rammed the pommel of his sword into the man's face. The man staggered and Darcov kicked him in the groin, felling him. He drove his sword through the enemy.

Nearby, Darcov's aide had taken on the remaining soldier who had stood defending Rodan. Sword and shield clashed. Darcov swung his sword at the unprotected back of the man's knee, severing most of the bone and toppling him. He kicked the Talak in the head and knocked him sideways. His aide struck the final blow.

Rodan swayed on his feet, face twisted in pain, but he had drawn his sword. He attacked. Darcov blocked the swing, sidestepped, and slammed a fist into Rodan's injured eye socket. The man reeled and collapsed.

Around them, the last of the Talak soldiers were slain.

Darcov's troops joined him. "Did any escape?"

"No. They're all dead."

"Good. Bind him," he said, giving Rodan's prone form a kick. "Justice for this one will be slow."

CHAPTER 18

RADA HELD TIKHON'S HAND and Tav stood beside her with the babe strapped to his chest. Together, they surveyed the campsite. Bloody bodies of the fallen lay scattered about. She looked down, her nose wrinkling as she kicked a severed hand away.

Bound and kneeling, Rodan awaited his fate.

Three female imperial guards knelt, bent over a figure on the ground. "No!" Rada shot forward, dodging the slain. "Mami!"

She broke stride and stumbled as a series of high, gut-wrenching wails sliced through the air. Terrified, Rada crept the last few steps, leaning forward to peer around the shoulders of the troops. A guard turned, muttering a curse, her lip curling in disgust as she tossed a coarse rope to the side. Upon seeing Rada, she blocked her view of Jadzia, murmuring, "She's alive, Stilniat, but you should wait before you see her."

Rada shook her head.

Tikhon and Tav caught up with her and Tikhon lay his hand on her shoulder, drawing her back a step and restraining her. He nodded and the soldiers parted to reveal Jadzia's prone form. Her arms hung limp, yet they and her legs still lay swept backwards as they had when she'd been hogtied.

"Proceed," Tikhon said.

Together, they rolled her mother onto her back. She let out one long scream and moaned before passing out. Jadzia had a blackeye, and a bruised, swollen cheek. Stark bands of raw skin encircled her neck, wrists and ankles. Her torn trousers were low and loose about her blood-stained thighs. One of her hands was swollen; her fingertips ragged, raw and inflamed where the nails had been torn out – a little finger and the one next to it broken and double their normal size. Her mother's torso, shoulder and upper arm were mottled purple. "The shoulder is dislocated... backwards."

"Quick, do it while she is still out," Tikhon ordered, grim faced.

The soldier held Jadzia's wrist. "Wait," Tikhon said. "I'll do it." He gestured to Tav, who replaced him in restraining Rada. Grimacing, Tikhon knelt, gripped Jadzia's wrist and flexed her elbow before taking hold of her upper arm. A guard held Jadzia's torso still. The third held her feet. Tikhon manoeuvred her arm slowly.

Jadzia awoke with a harsh cry. "Get off me, you evikan bastard!"

"Stilnassa, you're safe. It's the emperor. He's putting your shoulder back in. Please try to lie quietly."

Recognition dawned on her face, yet the look of fury did not diminish. Her mother gave the briefest nod. Her scream rent the air. The skin bulged, and the joint popped back into place. Tikhon stepped back, scrutinising Jadzia as the women tied her shirt, but left a cloak concealing her lower half. One raised Jadzia's head and pressed a water flask to her lips; she guzzled it down.

"Mami?" Rada looked on, horror-struck at the sight of the woman she loved and idolised, the one constant guiding light who understood her as no other, who laughed, played, scolded, praised and stood firm against all her childhood demons real and imagined, lying broken and battered before her.

Rada stepped closer. "Mami," she whispered.

Jadzia lay on her back, staring stonily into space, breathing shallowly.

Rada fisted her hands. A snarl erupted from her. She pivoted, drew her dagger, and charged Rodan. "I'll take your other eye! I'll kill you! You evikan—"

Tikhon swept her up before she reached Rodan. "No, Rada. That right belongs to your mother. Go sit beside her. Talk to her. Let her see you are well."

"Rada," Tav said, taking her hand. "Come." He drew her along and they sat beside Jadzia's head. "Stilnassa Jadzia, Rada and the little one are well." Nothing. "They're here. They're safe."

Rada leaned over her mother and touched her cheek. "Mami, everything will be all right. I'll take care of you."

"Rada," Jadzia whispered hoarsely. "Hold my hand. I can't move my arms much yet." Trembling, Rada cradled her mother's good hand with both of hers. Crying, she looked away from her mother's battered state.

Tav moved the baby into Jadzia's view. "See. She's safe and sound. Though a bit on the nose... again," he added.

Jadzia's lips twitched as if she'd smile, but they twisted into a grimace of pain. Noting the surrounding warriors looking anywhere but at her, she mumbled, "I am shamed."

"No, Stilnassa, you are not," a woman said. "Never. You are alive, you have endured. Your courage is clear. No fault lies with you."

"I know that." Her words carried on shallow breaths. "That's not what I meant. My ignorance, my naivete, did this." Jadzia groaned and clutched her abdomen. She spat out the words, "I must wash. Help me up, please?" The female guards prepared to aid her, but Tikhon waved them away, crossing to Jadzia's side. She recoiled. "No! Not you."

"Jadzia..."

"No!"

Tikhon retreated, gesturing for the women to continue. Two of them put their arms behind her shoulders and lifted her into a sitting position. They held her there while she shook and her head drooped forward.

"Mami!"

"It's all right, Rada. I've been lying down so long that I'm a bit dizzy." She lifted her head and gave Rada and Tav a tired smile. "I just need to sit for a bit. Thank the gods for your safety."

"Thank Mstislav," Rada burst in. "I prayed and made an offering and..."

"Rada!" Tav whispered.

"And he heard and..."

"Not now, Rada!" Tav said.

Rada's expression fell and she faltered. "And he helped us," she finished quietly.

Jadzia marshalled her wits and scrutinised them. Neither held her gaze. Tav focussed on the baby, jiggling her as if she needed soothing, and Rada fidgeted with her sling. Jadzia took in their wild, dishevelled states, and savage joy and pride crossed her face. "I think you've a tale to tell me, yes?" Rada glanced at Tav then peeked at her mother from under her tousled hair, nodding.

"Tav, take the babe, clean her up, change her. Rada, you go with him and find some other clothes for me in the carriage." To the third female guard near her, she said, "Go with them and get the clothes, please."

"You'll be proud of them both, but Rada in particular," Tikhon said. Jadzia ignored him. Anxious for some acknowledgment, chasing for a hint it was not him she hated, he continued; his words became avalanche threatening to bury him. "She rose to the challenge, and even at her age the battle-light shone in her eyes. Rada's deadly with that sling and she saved me."

Jadzia raised her battered face to him. Venom dripped from her words. "Battle-light? Even by our standards she is too young for this. Have you asked yourself, *My Emperor*, how this jaunt to the north became an ambush? Whoever is responsible deserves punishment."

Tikhon's posture grew rigid, but after a moment he stepped toward her, hand outstretched.

She recoiled.

Turning to the guards, she said, "Help me to the water." She flashed a glare at Tikhon, adding, "I need to clean the stink off me." Gently, the women raised her, waiting patiently as she tested her legs. She sagged, unable to stand. The two women linked arms to carry her. "No. I should move. It hurts no matter how we manage it, but I must try." They supported her as, clutching her tattered trousers in place, she forced herself to walk and began a torturous trek to the river.

Tikhon glowered. "To work all you!" he bellowed. "Get the camp cleaned up. Tend to our wounded. Salvage what weapons you can." The warriors moved off, leaving him and Darcov alone.

Tikhon took a step to follow Jadzia, but Darcov snagged his arm, whispering, "I warned you. I wouldn't follow. Not unless you want to be publicly flayed alive by the woman you love." Tikhon clenched his jaw. "Only a fool would approach her now. I've seen that look. I'd be surprised if she wants any man near her for a while."

"She didn't have a problem with you."

"Yes, but I've got more charm than most," he said with a wink. "Admit it, I tempt even you."

"Keep dreaming." Tikhon sighed.

"You won't want to hear this, but your people and your troops will judge you on how you handle her, my friend. Jadzia is not just any Zaragarian Stilnassa. She is of the First Circle and amongst them, her family was the first to support your ancestors. Rumours of your love for her have become damn near an epic tragedy in the telling, and her children are Zaragarian under our blood laws. If all had gone according to plan, and they had been unscathed, they would hail this as a brilliant tactic, but..."

"I know. At least we got Rodan and Cēdar. The others will crumble, believing me to be the most ruthless bastard that ever walked the earth. Even more so after I take the Talaks in hand. The rest I can deal with."

"The rest? I assume you mean Jadzia... My friend, I don't think..." His words stalled as a group of riders cantered into the campsite, leading six horses all with bodies draped across them. "They're the ones Rada diverted and the last of them.

She really is the most remarkable child," Darcov said. "Pity about her father."

Tikhon grunted and spat on the ground. "Every time I think about Bashtan, I could kill my father all over again. Things should have been different." A fierce, hard, desperate look consumed his face. "No matter what, she'll always be *my* family, her and her sister. They are *my* little Stilniats." With each 'my', he jabbed Darcov in the chest, making him step back. "And they are blessed in their mother."

He stalked toward the battered and trussed figure of Rodan. Deep in thought, Darcov watched his retreating form. *My family, my little Stilniats? Both of them?*

"Never again," Jadzia muttered as she hobbled to the river. The two guards supported her, but with each step she grew more determined and bore a little more of her weight. "Never again will I be so used."

The water had seemed so close last night. *Was it only last night we set up camp? Rada practised her sword fight with a stick.* A desperate laugh escaped her. *Gods above, she'd begged for a real one. She needed it. Bastards. Rada will never suffer this fate. I don't give a toss what Bashtan thinks about what evikan Talak ladies should do. This is a Zaragarian world and my daughter will know how to protect herself – fighting, tactics, politics. She'll wipe the floor with those that oppose her. She'll never be a victim. Never at the whim of some man.*

Jadzia winced at the intense needling pain from her ruined fingers. Her feet burned from being caned; the fire travelled up her legs, through every bruise, every graze, every bit of raw skin. She shuddered. Jadzia recalled their hands, their weight; smelled their breath and heard their jeers.

"I need to wash," she said. Panicking, she broke from the women and tried to run to the river, wanting only to be clean, to have its icy depths wash away her memories. A near delirious smile of relief crossed her face as the water covered her feet, her calves. She staggered and the women caught her before she fell. Jadzia stifled a cry at their grip on her battered body.

At the water's edge, she let go of her trousers, shuffling the pants aside with a shudder and a look of pure revulsion. Her hands shook, a cold sweat broke upon her brow. She fumbled with the ties on her shirt. "Gods damn it! I need it off! Get it off!" She tugged at the fabric, unable to grip it with her damaged fingers. "Get it off, *please*," she begged.

A dagger flashed and a guard sliced through her shirt ties. "Be patient, Stilnassa. Let us help you."

Jadzia hung her head, nodding. "Thank you. What's your name?"

"Stilnassa Adana, this is Stilnassa Regansh," Adana said as she slipped the tunic top free.

Jadzia waded knee deep, sobbing in relief. Regansh stood behind her, ready to offer support. Hunched and scrubbing ineffectually at her legs with one hand, searing pain shot through Jadzia. "Gods above, I can't even wash myself!"

She moved deeper into the river, submersing herself and shuddering as the cool water washed over her skin. Jadzia held her breath, eyes scrunched, praying the cold would numb her, praying the gods would help her... begging. Gods, how she hurt – flesh, bone and soul! Her lungs cried out for air; she burned inside and out. Jadzia thrust her head and shoulders out of the water and screamed her frustration to the sky. "Evika!"

She spun in alarm at a soft touch on her shoulder.

Adana stood next to her. "Please, let us help. Stand up. There's none but Regansh and I to see. Let me wash you. You'll feel better if you're clean of them."

"I'm not sure I'll ever mend. I feel like a piece of meat that's been... served up to wolves."

"It will get better, trust me," Adana whispered. She nodded to Regansh, who helped Jadzia to stand. Adana picked up Jadzia's sodden, discarded shirt. "Stilnassa, I will wash you."

Mired in memories, horror and grief etched on her face, Jadzia was deaf to all else.

"Stilnassa? Jadzia? I'm going to wash you. I must touch you... Do you understand... Jadzia?"

Jadzia's eyes focused, and she gave a small nod. She flinched as Adana gently bathed her, and she tried to curl in upon herself seeking protection – at once both fearful, outraged at her injuries and disgusted at herself for her weakness. "Stilnassa Adana, I will never forget this kindness."

"Mami... I have your clothes," Rada called.

Her daughter stood on the shore, accompanied by a female guard. "Rada," Jadzia ducked beneath the water again. "Good girl. Just leave them. Return to the camp."

Rada clutched the clothes, gaping.

"Rada, go back to the others now." Still, the child stared as tears rolled down her face. "I'll be back at camp in a minute. All will be well again." Jadzia's patience was fraying. To Adana, she whispered, "I can't have her see me like this. I've failed her." Adana rested her hand on Jadzia's shoulder; comforting, protective. "She needs a job to do. Keep her busy. Keep her away until I'm more... myself," Jadzia whispered, unable to look at Rada.

"She might help with the injured? If she were in training, it would be required," Adana murmured.

Jadzia grasped the notion like a lifeline. "Rada, have you checked on Akim and the others?"

"No."

"You should. They were our defenders and we owe them now they're injured. Go back and help tend their wounds." She smiled, trying not to grimace as her lip split further. "This is the first part of your training as a warrior. It's as important to know how to heal your comrades as it is to inflict damage upon the enemy. Can you do it, my Stilniat?" Rada rubbed her nose on her sleeve and nodded. "Good girl, now go." Nothing. "Do as I say, Rada. Go!" Rada dropped the clothes on the grass as if stung, spun on her heel and ran.

Jadzia sighed. "Please go with her," she asked the female trooper standing on the bank. "Help her understand that I'm not angry with her."

"Yes, Stilnassa." The woman departed, leaving Jadzia with Adana and Regansh.

Jadzia shook, head bowed, as Adana bathed her. Gradually her posture straightened, her jaw set and righteous anger chased the grief and vulnerability away. Regansh held her cloak out wide, blocking the view of Jadzia from the campground.

"I'm finished, Stilnassa."

"I would scrub myself raw," Jadzia replied. "But thank you. Call me Jadzia. We're the same rank, Adana."

"That may be, but you are..." Regansh cleared her throat. Adana looked up and stepped aside from Jadzia, making a quick bow toward the bank.

Jadzia turned to see Tikhon standing on the riverbank. Her lip curled, and she angled away. Words – dark, angry, deadly – writhed for release within her.

"Leave us," Tikhon ordered. The two Stilnassas left without a word or backward glance.

"Jadzia."

Keeping her back to him, she fought for control; her face pinched and her jaw clenched. Fury roiled through her. She faced him, arms to her sides, hiding nothing, her voice bitter. "Is this what the emperor's protection buys?" Jadzia turned full circle. "Well, is it?"

"I'm sorry."

"Don't you dare pretend you're sorry."

"You are most precious to me—"

"Rubbish. The most precious things to you are your crown and your heirs. Am I right?"

"Jadzia, come out of the river. Let me help you."

"You betrayed me and my children! I had no choice then and I have no choice now, do I? You've dismissed Adana and Regansh. There's no other to help me. So, unless I want to return to the campsite naked, it must be you." Her gaze narrowed. "Perhaps I should walk there like this. Then everyone can see what your choices wrought."

He flinched, waiting, holding a cloak out for her as she waded to the shore. Each step tore at her, but by all the gods she was done with this man; she'd not falter now. Jadzia stood before him and lashed out with her good arm, slapping him across the face. "That was only a taste of what you deserve." She gritted her teeth and her eyes watered at the flare of pain in her arm.

Tikhon braced himself for another blow, and when it didn't come, he dropped the cloak around her shoulders. He grabbed a cloth from the pile of clean clothes and held it up. "Will you allow me?" he asked.

"No."

"I can command it."

"You evikan bastard!"

He nodded. "Yes. Being emperor requires cunning, manipulation, brilliance and bastardry." Without waiting for her consent, Tikhon dried her body.

"What happened, Tikhon? Or did you intend to sacrifice us all along?" Her accusation sliced through the air.

"They were smarter than I gave them credit, or else there's a traitor in my scouts. Cēdar was not where we thought he'd be. Rodan was rumoured to be northeast of Bēdarik in the hills, but nothing was certain."

"So, you drew them out with us as bait. In your damn arrogance, you probably thought nothing would go wrong." Her stomach roiled, and she fought the urge to vomit. She was cold and yet her skin burned where he touched her. Jadzia strove not to tremble.

He took the utmost care, each move slow and gentle, wary of causing more hurt.

Her heart broke, but she wrapped it tightly in iron, knowing it for the fragile, traitorous thing it had always been.

"Cēdar delayed us. We killed most of his men, but he escaped. I could have pursued him but worry drove me here."

"You caused this! You used us! We were expendable!"

Tikhon held up his hands. "Know this, Jadzia, my plan should have gone smoothly, but Rodan was already here waiting. The signs of his passage were days old."

She frowned. "He was already here?"

"We let it be known that you were making a journey, but not where. We didn't make the passage of your caravan known until after you had left. By all rights, he should have been following you. My spies and scouts caught no sight of him. Would your servants, your slaves, have spoken out?"

She shook her head. "None other than Bashtan and Neeren knew where I was going."

Tikhon finished drying her. He fished a small wooden pot, sealed with cork, a stoppered flask and bandages out of an oiled canvas bag. "Hold still," he said. "Jadzia, your fingers are a mess. They'll need more attention than we can give." He began treating her wounds, starting at her torn wrists before moving to her thighs, dabbing dark brown liquid on each of her cuts and grazes, delicately blowing on them until the liquid dried.

Jadzia watched him kneeling before her, stoic in all but her eyes. "Stop." She stepped back. "Just stop. Someone else can treat me."

He met her gaze, implacable. "No." He took hold of her leg before she retreated. "Do you think Bashtan contacted him?" he asked as he bandaged her worst cuts.

All thought fled her as he held her trapped and her profound sadness almost overwhelmed her. "Who?"

"Bashtan. Would he have got word to Rodan or Cēdar?"

"He's essentially a coward. He wouldn't be upset if either you or I were killed, but he wouldn't act. Even as a council member, he sits in the middle and waits. Besides, he, at least, wouldn't risk Rada."

"Are you sure? Rada said you had words with him about his choice of friends." Tikhon bandaged her injured shoulder joint.

"No, I can't be sure until I've talked with my spies, but Bashtan is a scavenger not a killer. Neeren though..." She paused, contemplative. "I could have misjudged the extent of her hatred."

"Neeren?" Tikhon held a pair of trousers for her to step into.

"She's jealous of my position, desperate for recognition and, I suspect – though she doesn't even understand it – that she chafes against the restrictions placed on her as a Talak woman.

Like all women, she's capable of anything, but I've not been watching her movements closely; she's inept. My resources are finite and there are more valuable targets, but I'll talk with Katya when I return. Of course, you can do that yourself if you're returning there."

He fastened the drawstring on her trousers, then eased her arms into a loose, long shirt. His fingers fumbled on the buttons. "I'm better at undoing them," he said with a crooked smile.

"Not something you'll need to concern yourself with," she said, all ice and iron.

"Apologies. That was inappropriate... considering." He slid her outer tunic up her arms. "My Stilnassa..."

"I'm no longer *your* Stilnassa."

He froze.

"I am still, however, your loyal subject, *My* Emperor." She made a tiny bow in his direction.

He ground his teeth as he moved her jacket to rest across her shoulders; his hands hovered over her, flexing as if to caress her and he rested his forehead on hers, but dared not touch her with his idle hands. She stiffened, every muscle and joint ramrod straight, yet her heart was a trembling bulwark. A tortured expression twisted his face before he stepped away from her and impassivity became his mask. "Jadzia, they'll pay. I swear it."

"You can swear all you like, but I understand the worth of that. My memory is long, so is my reach. All those involved shall pay. I thank you for your kindness and compassion." She spat at his feet. "But I never want your hands on me again."

Jadzia brushed past him, walking to the camp without a backward glance.

CHAPTER 19

RADA CAST WORRIED LOOKS back at her mother. *Mami. They hurt Mami. She was all bruised and cut and crying – really, really hurt.* What had they done to make her so frail? Adana caught up with her. "I want to go back to Mami. She needs me to take care of her."

"No, Stilniat. She wants you here helping."

"But she needs help, she—"

"You will help her. We all will while she recovers, but right now she has the emperor and you're needed here." Adana gestured at the soldiers who were cleaning up.

Rada wrinkled her nose. "It smells bad."

"Blood, guts and shit. It could be worse, but the dead aren't yet rotting."

"They don't put that in the stories."

Bodies were being dragged well away from the campsite and dumped in a pile. Three bound prisoners knelt, awaiting their fate, a bloody log before them. Several troopers stood behind them, one with a long sword in hand. With insane joy, he snapped out a command and the captured Talak lowered his head to the log. A prisoner next to him jerked sideways, watching, crying, pissing himself as the soldier swung the blade down upon his companion's neck. The body toppled forward with the head only partially severed. The soldier scowled and cursed. He stepped forward to finish the job, but a man wielding an axe stepped in and hacked the head free then tossed it aside as others hauled the body away.

The next man cowered, tied hands raised imploringly, lips moving rapidly. Rada couldn't hear him; she didn't need to. She'd never seen someone begging for their life; for food, yes. To be spared a whipping, yes. Their life? Never. It was different somehow. The level of desperation fascinated her; fatalism streaked with a thin thread of will that refused to succumb.

The prisoner turned his head, crying out, pleading, and looked at her. She swallowed hard. She'd seen that look before. Those eyes, that bloated face in the moonlight. He'd been begging for his life from her. Why hadn't she noticed last night? Why now? Her pulse pounded in her ears, the surrounding noise, the laughing soldiers, the prisoners, their fear, their eyes, the smell of blood and shit from the dead faded, and once again she stood in the moonlight, a dagger in her hand. A dagger she couldn't release. Arms and legs that moved not of her own will. Her skin crawled. The sensation of being trapped, of being controlled, nearly overwhelmed her. She bent double, fighting nausea. *No, no, no! Lock it away! It won't happen again. Be brave and Mstislav won't do that again.*

The ground came into focus and the surrounding noises resolved themselves into speech. She straightened, returning to the present. The Zaragarian soldiers were arguing and the axe-wielding soldier shook his head, gestured to the next prisoner and pointed at himself. A few more guards nodded their approval. A kneeling prisoner tried to crawl away. The guard with the axe laughed, kicking him in the back with his foot, sending him sprawling face first into the blood-stained earth next to his friend's severed head.

Tikhon's troops hauled him to his knees and shoved his head forward onto the log. The axe wielder lined up a blow, swung and severed the head in one go. He let out a wild whoop and held the head aloft. Money changed hands amongst those watching. The victor tossed the head beside the other decapitated bodies and beckoned for his share of the winnings.

The remaining prisoner bent forward and vomited. Darcov, face set like granite, strode through the group, wrenched the man's head back and cut his throat in one smooth motion. He barked a command at the others, who slapped their fists to their chest in salute and hauled the dead to the growing pile.

Rada had seen that efficiency in the temple. That was more like Master Pavel.

"It's different," she said.

"What is?" Adana asked.

"The killing."

"Killing is killing, Stilniat. Same result, no matter what."

"No, it's not. In the temple, they don't look like that. They don't wet themselves or poop. They're not scared."

"That's because the temple drugs them, and they are starved for a few days prior to the rituals. By the time they get there, they don't care about anything anymore. It makes for a cleaner spectacle."

"Oh."

"Sometimes death comes on swift wings; calm, serene even. Think of the old who slip into his arms in their sleep. But here it is most often like this; smelly, bloody and brutal, and the end is all the same. No matter what, they all beg if you give them time. It's better to do it quick. It's the one kindness you can do for them and for yourself."

Rada said nothing. That face. Those eyes. She'd hesitated. That was bad. It wasn't quick. It wasn't brave.

"But you have to remember they're only Talaks and traitors," Adana said.

Rada's feet froze. *Only Talaks.* Her mind processed this. The casual dismissal, the derision. If they'd been slaves... but they weren't. *Only. Talaks.* "My Papi is Talak. I'm half Talak."

"You're also half Zaragarian. That outweighs the other, *and* your mother has raised you right."

Rada's brow creased. "Tav is Talak."

"Yes."

Short and sharp, the words slapped her in the face.

Adana walked on, stopping only when she realised Rada had not followed. "Come on, Stilniat," she said, looking back and smiling. "We've work to do, and this begins your training."

Rada worried at the icy knot which had settled inside her. *Later. I'll ask Mami later. Lock it away for later.* Rada looked up to see the woman several paces ahead, waiting. "Training?"

Adana nodded and Rada slowly smiled. She trotted to catch up, taking the woman's hand as they went to where the wounded were being tended.

She handed Rada a wad of multi-coloured bandages; at Rada's frown, Adana said, "We'll have stripped their supplies and kits, but must have needed some extra padding and bandages." She shrugged. "They've no use for their clothes now and they'll make fine bandages."

"Akim!" Rada ran to him and looked on, dismayed, as his ribs and abdomen, mottled grey and purple, were bandaged.

"Don't look so worried, Stilniat Rada. I'll be well. See? No cuts, just a few bruises and cracked ribs. They'll soon heal. Not the first I've had, nor the last."

"I'm glad you're still here." She sat and rested her head against his arm. "I don't want you to call me Stilniat Rada. Just Rada would be nice. You're like family."

"I'm low born and you're not. It's proper."

Rada snorted. "I don't care. Mami wouldn't either."

He patted her head. "We'll see. Now you've helped fix me up, there's still more to do."

Together they moved to a woman Adana was treating. "Now, Rada, pour this on the wound. Just a little. We can't waste it."

"What is it?" Rada asked.

"Vinegar. We each carry a small bottle of it in our kits."

Rada took the flask and drizzled it into the gash on the woman's thigh.

"Sorry," she said to the wincing soldier.

"Stilniat, it must be done."

"Now, Rada, pass me the cat gut and needle," Adana said. "Watch while I stitch this up."

Next to Adana was an unrolled oilskin cloth. Within its small pockets lay a fine-bladed knife, curved bone needles and an off-white fibre.

Rada passed Adana one needle and catgut, yet her gaze kept straying toward the river where her mother was.

"Rada? Watch," Adana instructed. "One day you'll have to do this. When your formal training commences, you'll learn all about basic healing."

"And weapons and fighting?"

"Weapons and fighting too, of course."

"Good, as long as I don't have to wait to learn to fight properly. Next time I'll be ready."

"From what Tav told me, you did well enough this time," Akim said.

"No, not well enough." Her voice hitched. "They hurt Mami. They hurt her bad and they hurt you and the others. Next time I'll stop them." Rada inspected the wound. "Why isn't it bleeding much?"

"It's missed the blood vessels," Akim said.

"What are those white squidgy bits? Some are kind of roundish," Rada asked.

"Have you watched the goats or pigs being butchered at home?"

"Yes."

"Have you seen white squidgy bits on them when the skin comes off?"

The soldier being sewn up muttered through clenched teeth, "I'm not sure I like where this is going."

Rada bent close to the wound, screwing up her face in concentration. Her eyes widened in recognition. "Oh! It's fat!"

Akim snorted with laughter and grimaced, holding his ribs. Adana paused in her stitching, a wry grin spread across her face.

The patient groaned. "Oi! I've got a hole in my fat leg, just get on with it." To Rada, she said, "I'm sure there's others need your help. Here comes your mother."

Rada shot up, her face brightening at seeing Jadzia returning from the river. Her mother held her head high, but her walk was ungainly, her face pale and brittle as eggshells. Rada's smile vanished; her hands fisted.

"Go on, Rada," Akim said. "Go to her. Show her you are whole and hearty. Don't let her walk into camp alone."

Rada ran. "Mami!"

Jadzia bent and embraced her with her good arm. "Rada, my fierce, lovely one!" She kissed her cheek. "I'm so glad that you're well."

"I am. Mami, I helped rescue you."

"Mmm, I heard you talking to Rodan." Jadzia took her hand and they walked toward the campsite. "You were very, very brave. Rada, there are adults who could not defy a man such as him in the way you did! Were you scared?"

"At first, but Uncle Tikhon gave me my orders, and I knew that if I just did what he said that it would all work out." She shrugged. "Besides, I knew Uncle wouldn't let anything happen to me ever! He wouldn't, would he, Mami?"

"Never!" Jadzia said, though her smile never reached her eyes.

"I knew it," Rada nodded. "Uncle said Rodan was stupid and would think I'm little and helpless, which I'm not and we'd fool him." Rada laughed. "And we did!"

"My brilliant, brave girl!"

Rada beamed. "And I knocked his eye out with my sling! You should have seen it fly! Kind of like a gooey marble. I looked for it, but I think it must have got squashed in the fight."

"Why did you look for it?"

"I've never seen the back of an eyeball."

Jadzia chuckled. "Rada, there is no one else like you!"

Rada canted her head. "That's good, right?" Without waiting for a reply, Rada looked behind her mother and waved her arms. "Uncle Tikhon!"

Jadzia ploughed forward toward the first aid area, Rada trailing in her wake. "Akim, how are you?"

"I've been worse, Stilnassa." He gave her a sympathetic half smile. "Rada, we've still got some work to do. Will you keep helping?"

"Of course!"

Akim led her away.

Jadzia moved on to the injured guards, murmuring to each of them. She halted beside Darcov as he treated a soldier's arm.

Tikhon shadowed her. "Jadzia, your fingers need tending and your arm should be in a sling. Let me help."

She kept her back to him. "There's no need for you to do it. I'll wait my turn here."

Tikhon opened his mouth to argue with her.

She saw Darcov look up from his stitching and cast a warning glance at Tikhon. "I'm done here. Jadzia, sit, I'll treat those fingers and we'll sling the shoulder." Tikhon glared at him, only to receive a beatific smile in response. Jadzia stifled a satisfied smirk as Tikhon growled, spun on his heel, and left.

"Thank you, Darcov," Jadzia whispered as she sat beside him.

"He'll keep trying." He bent over her fingers before lifting his head and calling out, "Get me something I can use as a splint for this hand. This is a total evikan mess. Bastards!" he muttered. "I need more vinegar."

"We're out," Adana said.

"There's red wine in my supply wagon," Jadzia said. Adana hurried away to fetch it, returning with a wooden bowl full of wine as another soldier handed Darcov two small, straight sticks. "No," he said. "Find something big enough to support two fingers. This long, so it goes up under her palm. Shave it down so it's not a damn tree trunk." To Jadzia he said, "Put your hand in the wine and leave it there."

After a few minutes, he lifted her hand, dabbing it dry. He smoothed a thick salve on her fingers and she hissed in pain. "Sorry, but this will be worse." Examining her broken fingers, he said, "This is beyond us. The middle joints must be smashed."

"There'll be help in Vēkaria. It's not so far. I can wait."

"Jadzia, it'll take longer than you think. They should just come off."

"No. We'll wait. Once the swelling goes down, it will be easier to tell what should be done. As my grandmother would say, those who act in haste oft stumble into Ebatov."

Darcov snorted. "Ebatov may await us all, but if you leave them, then your judgment day may come sooner than you think."

"It would cripple my hand; make me useless."

"Do you think your babe will grow up useless?"

Jadzia bristled. "Of course not!"

"Of course not!" he mimicked. "That's why you're travelling halfway across a continent to give her a chance you think she deserves. Yet you think two fingers will cripple you. Being a bit of a hypocrite, aren't you?"

Her lips turned down. "I hate you, you know. Couldn't you just tell me I'm overreacting instead of dressing it up in a lesson?"

The guard returned with the piece of wood. "That'll do," Darcov said. "Are you ready?" Jadzia nodded and he put the splint under her fingers. Harsh pants escaped her as he straightened her little finger and the one next to it and bound them to the wood. He then bandaged the rest, ensuring it would remain still. "That shouldn't move." Darcov shook his head as he worked. "That shoulder needs strapping, but—"

"It's fine, just sling it. Supplies are short."

He fashioned a sling and eased her arm into it. "How're your feet? Do you need a cane? A staff?"

"No. They're manageable. For something so excruciating, it always surprises me that people can walk after caning."

"Then you're done. At least for now but remember what I said. Check the hand daily." He kissed her cheek. "You don't hate me, I know it. And I love you too but mind my words."

She rolled her eyes. "Yes, sir!"

He grinned. "That's more like it. I've longed to serve you a lesson for years, but you're such a damn paragon of Zaragarian virtue that I can never find cause."

"Never change, Darcov. Promise me that."

"I'm too old to change and having too much fun... usually."
He focused on packing the materials in front of him. "We must
resupply."

"You're not expecting more trouble, are you?"

"Hopefully not. Tikhon will have more plans in hand,
especially after this." He sighed. "We should have been here.
Cēdar ambushed us on the way. He lost but escaped. Evika,
Jadzia, this should never have happened."

"No, it shouldn't."

Darcov grimaced and all trace of humour fell from his face.
"He won't give up on you, you know. He's sorry."

"If a hunter uses bait, he's always prepared to sacrifice it.
We were the bait. Tikhon may regret it. In fact, I'm sure he
does, but he knew the risks — ultimately, he was prepared
to sacrifice us. There is no forgiveness for that. There never
will be." Bitterness twisted her face. "Worse, I understand his
strategy, but I just wished he'd used someone else's family for
it."

➤————————→

Rada watched as Tikhon's soldiers stripped the enemy of
all their possessions. Akim and the few remaining men
and women who had defended Jadzia were claiming prizes
amongst the weapons and armour.

Rada sat beside Tikhon. "What are they doing?"

"They're taking their spoils of war. The victors do this after
battle. These men and women get first pick. They're owed
this and more. Often, a ruler or commander will divvy out the
spoils to those they think the most deserving. These troops
who fought to defend you and your mother have first pick
here and they can choose from among the horses if they wish.
Spare horses will go to new recruits."

She nodded sagely. "Tav should get something, Uncle.
Because he saved Bubba and me."

"And so he shall. Akim, make sure the boy gets to choose too. Stilniat Rada commands it."

Akim beckoned Tav over and helped him select a sword and dagger.

"And you, Rada, what about you?"

"I have a dagger. Tav gave it to me. He said I had drawn first blood with it, so it should be mine. All the swords are a bit big."

"I'll have a sword made for you. You'll need one when you begin training. Is there anything you'd like? Your bravery has won you the right of a prize."

A slow smile blossomed across Rada's face. "A horse. I want a horse of my own." Her gaze darted between her mother and uncle.

"Of course! Every warrior should have a horse."

"Tikhon," Jadzia warned.

Rada turned pleading eyes on her mother. "Mami?" Jadzia sighed and nodded. Leaping up, Rada said, "Let's choose one!"

"What? Now?" Jadzia said.

"Yes! There're spare ones now. The enemy won't need them. Uncle said they're for warriors to choose from." She took off at a run, calling over her shoulder, "Come on!"

Jadzia groaned.

Tikhon offered her his hand. "Shall we?" His smug smile vanished when she struggled to her feet on her own.

"My Emperor," she ground out. "These are war horses, not suitable for a small child to learn to ride."

"Jadzia, humour her." He stopped by the supply wagon and grabbed some apples. Tossing one in the air, he caught it, took a bite, and shrugged. "She's unlikely to find a suitable horse here. You can get her one when she's home, or in Vēkaria."

As they followed Rada, Jadzia said, "So, what is my reward? My spoils of war? For surviving?"

"I suspect you'll tell me."

Rada halted in her tracks behind the long picket line of captured horses who stood flicking their tails. Her gaze travelled from hooves the size of dinner plates to their enormous, muscled rumps. They all towered over her; she swallowed nervously and stepped back. "Maybe... No!... I can do this!" She took a few steps.

"Rada, wait for us," Jadzia called.

Two of Tikhon's troop tended the horses. They hastily stood to attention, arms straight and stiff by their side before bowing.

"At ease. How are they? Anything special?"

"A couple of beauties, My Emperor," the older woman said.

Tikhon laughed. "That sounds as if you've already got one picked out for yourself, Jemilla."

"I'll not deny it, My Emperor. There're a few here that are spoken for, with your approval, and a few that Horse Master Melor will probably think suit new recruits. Their stock is not as heavy as what we're breeding now. But it's still good. Rodan's stallion is excellent, of course, and rumour has it the breeding stock at his estate is fine. I'll bet my last piece of silver Melor will be interested in them."

Jadzia smirked. "Rodan's horses are excellent. Perhaps I can see my way clear to selling some to the imperial stables. Since I own the entire estate."

"At a good price I hope," Tikhon muttered.

"Market rates," she quipped.

He leaned in, whispering, "I'm to pay in more ways than one, am I?"

She held her ground, though her body went cold at his closeness. "We're talking about horses here."

"Good thing I've seized more than one estate, thanks to this rebellion." He smiled at the officer. "Otherwise Stilnassa Jadzia would beggar me." He arched his brow at Jadzia. "Or perhaps you merely want me on my knees begging?"

The guard's eyes widened at the tension between the two and she elbowed her compatriot. "Here. Help me look at this hoof, will you?"

"But we've already—"

She smacked him on the back of the head. "Do as I ask," She hauled him aside where both became unduly intent upon the horse.

Rada ran to Tikhon and her mother and bounced up and down. "Ready? Come on, please?"

Tikhon laughed.

"Fine," Jadzia said. "We'll inspect them with you but take your time. They're not puppies. They will not want to be yours straight away."

"Watch their back feet, don't get too close," Tikhon said, shepherding her. "Let's move to the other side so you can see their faces. Start at the end of the line and we'll see which ones you like the look of."

Rada walked the line of horses, her hands clasped behind her back and her face screwed up in concentration. Now and then she'd stop and hunker down, peering at a horse's legs, or lean sideways trying to see the horse's flanks amongst the line. Few of the animals paid attention to the small girl.

"Mmm... maybe," she said, but then shook her head, moving on.

"Our expert horsewoman at work," Tikhon murmured with a wink.

Jadzia struggled to keep the smile from her face. "Rada, what are you looking for?"

"A kind eye. Akim said you can see what a horse is like by their eyes, and a kind eye is good."

"They're war horses, Rada."

"But I'm not the enemy and we're not in battle. So now I should see their true selves."

Jadzia's brows rose, and for the first time in her life, she was speechless.

Rada stopped at a bay with a long, full mane and tail. "Pretty," she said. "Hello, horse." The horse's ears flicked, but it didn't deign to lower its head to her. Rada rose on tiptoes, stretching out her hand. "Hey! Hello!" She scowled. "It's a bit hard to see if you've got a kind eye when you won't even lower your head." She stomped to Tikhon and Jadzia.

Tikhon handed her an apple. "Here, maybe this will help them show their true selves."

"Good idea!" Brightening, she walked back to the horse. Despite the apple, the horse refused to reach down to her.

"Odd," Tikhon said, moving beside her. He held out a piece of apple and the horse took it, nuzzling his hand for more, but ignored Rada.

"Try another one, Rada," Jadzia said. She chose a horse shorter than the rest. "What about this one?" It was rubbing its head into Jadzia's hand.

Rada held out an apple to the horse. It shifted its focus, took the apple, then jerked its head away before she could pat it.

Tears welled in her eyes, but she brushed them away angrily. "I don't think any of them like me at all."

"What about the one you rode yesterday?" Tikhon asked her.

"No. He wouldn't listen. If you hadn't been there, he probably wouldn't have stopped until he hit the ocean."

"Rada," her mother said. "No matter what horse you get, you'll have to work hard at riding and gaining the animal's respect. You can't give up."

"Yes, Mami, I know, but there has to be something special you like about them. Even if it's a little something. So you know you can work and it'll be worth it."

Tikhon smothered his laugh with a cough.

Jadzia glared at him, her lips a tight line.

Crestfallen, Rada said, "I can't believe *none* of them want to talk to me. Back home, they'd knock me over for an apple."

Jadzia bent, cupping Rada's chin in her hand. "Never mind, Rada. We'll look in Vēkaria. I'm sure there'll be some at Grandma's. The horses we breed are second to none. It doesn't have to be right this minute."

"It won't be the same..." She broke off, shaking her head and biting her lip.

"Rada?"

"If Uncle... *the emperor* gives me a horse and tells me I'm to learn to ride then..." she swallowed, wincing and looking about, whispering, "Then Papi can't say no. He can't stop me. He can't say that it's not a thing for a... a..." She wiped her tears away in irritation and stamped her foot. "For a little girl or a lady." Half indignation, half fear, she plunged on. "And he will. Just like with my sling and swords and bows and knives and spears and everything..." Rada faltered and, in a wavering voice, finished, "Everything that can keep us safe."

"You are—" Tikhon began.

Jadzia cut him off. "We'll find you a horse on this trip, because the emperor has ordered it as your reward."

"The horse," Tikhon cut in, "will still be a gift from me, so none will take it from you and you'll become a member of the temple. You'll learn to fight as a Zaragarian should. No one can stop either of these things. Do you understand?"

Rada gripped their hands. "Promise?"

Jadzia looked Rada in the eye. "I promise." Rada leaned her forehead against her mother's. "I'm sorry I didn't keep you safe," Jadzia whispered.

"I know you stopped most of them chasing us." Rada wrapped her arms around her mother's neck and hugged her.

Tikhon flinched, his fist clenched and his mouth drew into a stern line as he beat down the leaden sensation of unaccustomed guilt. He reached out, wanting to embrace them, certain Jadzia would not rebuff him in front of Rada, but that trap would cost him even more; he withdrew his hand and stood mute before the pair of them locked in a silent tableau.

A roar of pain shattered the quiet.

Jemilla rushed over to a soldier lying on the ground, clutching his leg, and dragged him away from a dark-brown horse tied to a tree. The horse struck out; its hoof narrowly missing Jemilla's head as she hauled the downed man to safety. The animal spun and eyeballed them, snorting and pounding its front foot into the ground.

Tikhon, Jadzia and Rada made their way to the guards.

"What happened?" Tikhon asked.

"Damn beast, just let drive!" The man looked up, adding hastily, "My Emperor."

Jemilla examined his leg. "Fool! I told you to be careful. You'll live, but you're bloody lucky your leg's not broken." She shook her head. "Idiot! The horse is tied up on his own because he's a foul old beast. Hated being tied up with the others and belted them, tried to take pieces out of a few of the men. I'd keep your distance, My Emperor. He'll settle now he's alone, but it wouldn't do for you to be newly crowned and then felled by a cranky rig."

"I take it nobody wants him," Jadzia said.

"No, Stilnassa. Though there's one or two of the young bucks, like this dolt," she nudged the wounded trooper with her foot, "who think they're up to taking him on, but I'll take odds on them coming off the worse for it. He's not near so angry with the women. The beast's old hand, but he's sour on the world."

"I wonder what his history is?" Tikhon said.

"That, I think I can tell you. He was Rodan's, he bears his brand. Rodan had a stallion he used for years in competitions. They had a formidable reputation. If it's the same animal, Rodan made a name for himself on this beast. The horse was injured and spelled for months. I remember seeing it with Horse Master Melor during one of our stints in Talak. Animal was lucky to live."

"I'm surprised Rodan didn't get rid of him then," Jadzia said. "He's not known for his kindness."

Jemilla shrugged. "Sometimes people surprise you. This fellow was getting a bit long in the tooth and by then Rodan had finer stallions in his stables. I'd wager he was a damn handful in the paddock, so he gelded him and kept him as a packhorse. All I can think is that Rodan couldn't bear to part with him."

"Or saw an investment that could still turn a profit," Jadzia said.

"Maybe. A crime really, and bloody stupid if you ask me. He'd have to be the last horse in a string or you'd have a nightmare of time."

"Poor old soul," Jadzia said. "From proud warhorse to pack animal."

As she spoke, the horse kicked out at a sapling. There was a resounding crack and the young tree listed sideways, almost grubbed out of the ground. Rada gaped. Tikhon laughed. "It would be a shame to waste all that natural talent."

Jemilla said, "In his prime, I'll bet he was a ripping horse in a fight. If he was on your side, you'd be as safe as houses." She spat on the ground. "Now, who knows? I'll ride him. See what we've got under saddle. Mstislav, help me." Jemilla sighed. "I take it you want to keep him, My Emperor?"

Tikhon nodded. "We'll see. He could be a perfect training mount for cocky recruits. Leave him, Jemilla. I'll ride him tomorrow." He winked at her. "See what odds you can get on me."

"I know where I'll be placing my bet, My Emperor."

Rada remained fixated on the horse. "Safe as houses," she whispered.

She stepped toward the animal.

"Rada!" Jadzia said, halting her.

The horse's gaze snapped to the child. He ceased fidgeting, ears forward, interested. She rolled her apple along the ground and it stopped under his nose. In an instant it was in his mouth, juice frothed from his lips and bits of apple fell to the ground; he snatched them up greedily. He stretched his neck out to her and tossed his nose up and down.

"Rada, you may have found his weakness," Jadzia said, smiling.

"It'll take more apples than that, Stilniat Rada," Jemilla said.

"How many apples?"

"Probably an entire tree full and then some," the woman said.

Tikhon and Jadzia moved off. "Come on, Rada," Jadzia called.

Rada followed, but her gaze kept travelling back to the dark, scarred horse who lashed out again, flattening the sapling and then belting it with its back hooves.

CHAPTER 20

"IT'S TIME, MY STILNASSA," Tikhon said, gesturing to where Rodan lay trussed up and guarded by Darcov. "First, I must ask, what did he get out of you? What did you tell him?"

Jadzia laughed bitterly. "Tell him? Nothing! He never asked me anything? It was never about information, only revenge. I doubt he'll tell you much."

"Everyone talks. Though I'm not prepared to linger here for that. Retribution and making an example of him will be enough."

He walked ahead of her.

Coldly, she eyed his back. "Yes, retribution may just be worth it."

She wiped the look of resentment from her face as he turned to her. "Come. You wanted to choose the manner of his death."

Jadzia nodded but hesitated before hunting around in the undergrowth and withdrawing a knotted, straight stick about an inch wide and the length of her forearm.

"Do you want me to take it?" he asked as she struggled to grip it.

"No. I've one good hand," she said sharply. "I'll keep it. You interrogate him, I need to hone it in the fire, so it's perfect. It should have the desired effect."

"What's the stick for, Mami?"

"Never mind, Rada."

Rada's chin jutted out, and she screwed up her nose. "But..."

"No buts." Jadzia's words whipped out.

Rada stomped behind them, kicking dust up with each step.

A fire burned near Rodan and on the ground lay an assortment of implements including pincers, a hammer and fine nails.

Rada bent down to the trussed up Rodan and with a cocky grin said, "Hello. How's your eye?"

"You wretched, demon-spawned, misbegotten miscreant. If I was loose, I'd—"

"If you were loose, I'd take your other eye!" She kicked dirt into his face. "I hate you! You hurt Mami!"

Red faced, spitting dust, Rodan said, "Get... Oomf." The air rushed out of Rodan as Darcov drove his boot into his stomach.

"Rada, return to the others," Jadzia ordered.

"Are you going to kill him now?"

"Yes."

"Can't I stay?"

"No. This is not a simple sacrifice. It will be a long time before he dies. Go to Tav."

Rada folded her arms and planted her feet.

"Akim! Tav!" Tikhon yelled. They ran to him. "Take Rada away."

Rada yelled as Akim wrapped his arm around her and hauled her off. "I want to see him die! He needs to die!"

Jadzia's gaze remained fixed on Rodan. "Tav, tell him to keep her busy. Take her back to the horses," she whispered.

Tikhon reached out to her. "Jadzia." Concern laced his voice. She sneered at him and he lowered his hand.

"Trouble in paradise?" Rodan asked with a vicious grin. Darcov kicked him again, but Rodan continued. "She's a little girl. You're no mother! You've raised a monster who's baying for blood. She should be home playing with dolls, wanting pretty dresses, learning the arts, music, dancing. Learning how a woman should—"

"Act? Your way would have her in another kind of prison. Peg him out!" Jadzia roared.

Four men untied Rodan, stretching his arms and legs so he lay splayed upon the ground. His face twisted in pain at the sudden movement of his limbs. Stakes were hammered in the ground and his limbs were bound to them.

"My daughter is magnificent. She's already had your blood, and she's only six. Imagine what she'll be like when she's grown. My daughters will be subject to the whims of no man."

Rodan chuckled. "Hear that, Tikhon? I guess she didn't like being used as bait. May the gods help us! Tikhon, if you'll do that to your family, then what will you do to the rest of us?"

"Your instructions, my Stilnassa?" Tikhon said with a bow.

"Start with his hands and feet."

Tikhon picked up a nail. Rodan gritted his teeth, curling his fingers. Darcov forced his hand open. Tikhon grabbed one of Rodan's fingers and slid the metal tip just under his fingernail. Rodan's brow twisted as he waited for the pain.

"You know how this works. I ask questions. You answer. Simple," Tikhon said.

"You'll kill me anyway," Rodan said.

"I'm not going to kill you. Jadzia is."

Rodan laughed; short and brittle. "How? State she's in, she can barely wipe her own arse."

"The emperor has granted me the right to choose your death, Rodan," Jadzia said.

Bitterness permeated Rodan's voice. "Lucky you. I'm sure it'll be spectacular then."

"Yes," Jadzia smiled. "It will rival the death of Daeldun at the hands of Seraphine." Rodan's pupils dilated in fear. *He may not be so hard to crack.* They just had to keep him talking. Once they opened their mouths, they then seemed to spill their secrets quickly, usually after they spilled their bowels. Jadzia wrinkled her nose. She always preferred when they'd not been fed for a few days. "It may still be quick should you answer the emperor." Rodan's jaw clamped shut, and he stared up at the sky. "Then to work it is." Her dishonour must be seen to be revenged. Reputations amongst her kind were made or lost on less. Despite her weariness, a weight of grim satisfaction settled upon her – each of the injuries he'd inflicted would be revisited tenfold upon him.

Tikhon's voice ended her musings. "Who else besides you and Cēdar was involved?"

Rodan said nothing. Tikhon shoved the metal up under his nail. Rodan let out a strangled cry between clenched teeth, and veins bulged in his neck.

"Let's try that again, shall we? Who else?" Tikhon laughed, patting Rodan's cheek. "You'll break your own teeth if you're not careful. Can't have you doing that." He picked up the pincers. "That's my job."

Jadzia cleared her throat and shook her head, forestalling him. "Ah. As the Stilnassa commands – hands and feet first. Now, let's start again."

>——————▶

"It's not fair!"

"Behave yourself! Or regardless of orders, I'll tie you to a tree until you settle down and Tav here can have first pick of the horses."

Rada's worried gaze shot to the dark, motley, bay horse. Straight faced, Akim continued. "The pick from *any* of the horses." Rada nibbled her lip. She stopped squirming, limp in Akim's arms. "Are you going to behave yourself?" he asked, placing her on the ground.

She sighed melodramatically. "Yes, I'll be good." Her head rose, and she stared at him wide eyed, innocent, and batted her eyelids.

"Ugh! Rada!" Tav said. "You nearly had it. I keep telling you, don't bat your eyes!"

"Why? I see the wifelings do it when they want something, and Papi gives in. I even saw my big sister do it to a guard and he caved in like soggy sponge cake."

Tav reddened. "Rada, older girls do that to make boys interested in them."

"Interested in them?"

"You know... They're after something else... Are interested in..." Desperately, he looked at Akim for help, only to be met with a wide grin. Tav reddened, and his words rushed out. "Like to be their boyfriend,"

Rada's jaw dropped. "Boyfriend."

"Yes or..." He blushed. "Or um... Marry."

"Marry!"

"You shouldn't use it and anyway, only stupid men fall for it."

Akim laughed, clapping Tav on the back. "Not just stupid men. We all fall at some stage – men, women, one and all."

"Not me! I'm not marrying anyone! Celedane, take me if I lie!" Rada said, hand on her heart.

A roar of pain arose from the direction they'd come.

Rada spun back. Another agonised scream pierced the air. Her face paled.

Akim grabbed her shoulder, turning her. "Come, Stilniat Rada, let's take a second look and see if we can find you a horse. These will all have had an excellent education. They must, to be used in war. They're a warriors' prized possession, but they may be too much for you at this stage." She dragged her gaze from the direction of the camp to him, brow knotted. "You know if you pick one you like, you can keep it for later when you are not so little. Most little girls need gentler little mounts. To match their size." Rada's jaw clenched. "So don't worry if there's not one amongst these big ones that you can ride now; especially with you only being little." Rada turned beet red in fury. "Once you reach your mother's family, I'm sure you'll have the pick of the small ponies."

Rada swallowed hard, tamping down her rage. She bestowed a beatific smile upon him. "I already know which one I want. I need some apples." Rada raced to the carriage, snatched her backpack, upended the contents, then ran to the supply wagon.

"That's one way to throw down the gauntlet," Tav said. "You almost laid it on too thick. It's a wonder she didn't explode. She hates being called little."

"I know," Akim said. "Now she'll focus on this and not on the butchery back there."

⇒———→

Rodan's shirt had been torn from his body and he lay bathed in sweat. Scorch marks dotted his chest. The smell of burning hair still hung in the air. Shallow, short breaths hissed through his gritted teeth.

Jadzia ignored him and placed the stick in the fire's glowing coals. Rodan turned his head, sickeningly hypnotised, as she carefully rotated it in the heat.

A tug at his hand broke the spell. Arching his back, he tried to wrench away, but it was useless. He stared beseechingly at the sky, howling in agony as Tikhon rammed another bit of metal under his nail.

"Who else, Rodan?"

Nothing.

"You've got big feet. Plenty of surface area to work on. Should be interesting," Tikhon said. "Darcov, which would you try first?"

"Why not ask that evikan bitch?" Rodan ground out.

Jadzia smiled as Tikhon said, "She'll have her turn."

Rodan's head lolled sideways to stare at Jadzia. She'd removed the stick from the fire and was honing its tip into a point on a flat rock. Another woman joined her. They murmured together and glanced at him, then the other woman took over working on the stick. Tears slipped from Rodan's eyes as he watched them.

"We'll start again. Who, Rodan? Who told you where to find the Stilnassa?"

Defeat and exhaustion were clear in Rodan's voice. "It was common knowledge on the street that she was travelling."

"Someone got word to you specifically. Who?"

Tikhon's hand clenched around the pincers, applying enough pressure on them to break the skin on Rodan's little toe.

"Lady Chandar."

Tikhon looked at Jadzia, brow raised in query. She nodded. "Plausible. Neeren is her friend."

"Thank you," Tikhon said before forcing the pincer handles together. Rodan screamed. Tikhon tossed his severed toe into the flames.

Jadzia gestured to the woman with her, who rose, sharpened stick still smouldering.

"Roll him," Jadzia ordered.

>————→

Rada ran back to Akim and Tav with the backpack bulging.

"How many apples do you need?" Tav asked, incredulous.

"I don't know. I've never done this before. Better to have too many than not enough." She took off to the horses.

She gave all the picketed horses a wide berth and aimed straight for a scrappy bay tethered alone.

Akim's eyes narrowed. "That can't be good."

"Rada! Wait! Damn it!" Tav yelled.

They jogged to catch up with her.

Rada pounded toward the horse. He spun at her approach. His gaze flew from her to the men pursuing her. He reared, pulled back on his tether and the young tree he was tied to listed sideways.

Rada skidded to a stop just out of his reach and unslung the backpack. She carried it in front of her, an apple in her hand. The gelding had flattened all the vegetation around the tree and he'd dug a trench with his pacing. The horse stilled at her approach — cautious, curious, his nostrils flaring. Slowly, she moved toward him. "Hello," she whispered. "I'm Rada. Look what I've got for you. See?" She rolled an apple along the ground and it rested in the shallow trench. He sniffed it, snatched it and, chomping, sent juice, slobber and bits of apple dripping from his mouth.

Akim and Tav were almost upon Rada. The horse's attention snapped to them; he pawed the ground, snaked his head at the men and paced on his short tether. Tav took a step forward, but Akim restrained him. "Rada, come back. You should pick another horse. This one is not for you."

"I'm not too little," she stamped her foot, and the horse focused on her. "You'll see."

Akim muttered, "This is not what I had in mind."

Tav pushed forward. "Akim, maybe he's more concerned about us than her. Rada..."

"You think? Maybe! Meanwhile, the Stilnassa's daughter... Gods help me... They'll kill me."

She ignored them, stepping closer to the beast.

"The other horses didn't like me. Will you? I've got lots of apples, see?" She tilted the open pack, displaying the cornucopia of food she'd stolen. Rada rolled another apple. It stopped short. "Evika!" she muttered. The gelding stretched his neck out, unable to reach it. "Hang on." She peered at him. "Will you be good? I'll get it for you if you're good."

She swallowed nervously and glanced back at Akim and Tav.

Akim stepped toward her and the horse reared, striking out. Akim retreated.

"By all the gods! Rada! Remember what I told you in the stables? Be calm and you'll help keep him calm. Talk to him soothingly."

She nodded, took another apple, and slung the pack back over her shoulders. "I can be brave." Her insides churned. "You're huge." She took a few steps, aimed a kick at the apple, but, trying to keep her eyes on the horse, she missed. Rada huffed in exasperation. "Evika! Stupid girly kick." Unthinking, she strode forward. "Just keep being good, you hear?" She bent, seizing the apple to roll it, and he snatched it out of her hand. Rada stood there stunned, eye to eye with the gelding while sticky juice, chunks of fruit and slobber rained down on her hands. He snatched the other apple from her hands.

"Piggy." She giggled, half turned to Akim. "See, he's not so bad. He just wants a friend." The horse shoved her, trying to get into her backpack. "... and... food," she added.

"Stay here, Tav," Akim approached them. The gelding pinned his ears back at Akim, but aside from the odd snort and a shuffle at his approach, the horse was intent only on Rada.

Akim touched her on the shoulder, drawing her away from the animal. He tilted her chin, forcing her to look at him. "Rada, you should have waited. You don't know this horse and could've been hurt. Did you consider why he's tied up on his own?"

"He doesn't like the others."

"So you knew that and kept *going*?"

She looked away, but he grabbed her shoulders and gave her a shake. The bay's head shot up in alarm. "I'm disappointed in you. You were foolhardy, but what's worse, you didn't even think about Tav or I, did you?"

"Wh-what? Why?"

"What do you think your mother or the emperor would do to us if something happened to you?"

Another of Rodan's roars of pain from near the camp reached them. Rada's panicked eyes met his and her lip trembled when she glanced to where Tav waited. "I'm sorry. I'm sorry. I'll be good. I promise."

Akim nodded. "Excellent. Now we'll examine the other horses first."

"But—"

"No buts." Akim grabbed her by the hand and hauled her off. The horse's pacing raised a cloud of dust behind them. "Tav needs to choose a horse and you need to take a second look with me helping. Yes?"

Subdued, she said. "All right."

Rada dragged her feet behind them, kicking up dust and clumps of dried grass and letting them get far ahead of her.

The beat of hooves drummed up behind Rada. The bay, dragging a remnant of the tree he was tied to, cantered up to her, picked her up by the rucksack and shook her. She squealed in terror as her feet left the ground and he jostled her from side to side.

The backpack tore apart, spilling apples and carrots everywhere. Rada fell onto her hands and knees. Scrambling around, she saw the horse grabbing the fruit off the ground.

A kernel of indignation grew within her, and fury lit her face as she jumped up. "Hey!" she yelled. "You can't have them all! Greedy pig!" She dove forward and frantically grabbed at the food. "You only get it if you're good!" She hauled as much of the fruit and vegetables to her as she could. Her hands shot forward, snatching food. At the same time, the horse lunged to the pieces, his feet coming down within inches of her fingers. A mad dance of hooves, hands and scrambling child ensued, raising a small dust cloud.

"Evika! Evika!... Bad horse!"

Akim and Tav raced to her. They slid to a halt as the horse threw kicks in their direction. The dust cleared. Red faced and covered in grime, Rada was on her knees, half hunched over a pile of food. One carrot remained in the open between her and the bay. Her gaze travelled from it to the horse. The horse was utterly still, fixated upon the child.

Rada's mouth grew dry. Silently, she counted. *One...* Her fingers twitched. *Two...* The horse snorted. *Three.* She launched herself forward, hands outstretched. Airborne, she watched in dismay as the horse's teeth closed around the carrot. Her eyes widened in panic as the horse's front legs blocked her flight path. She squeezed her eyes closed and braced herself for impact. Rada hit the ground, bumped her head, and the air whooshed out of her lungs. Horsehair brushed her arms, and she heard the stamp of hooves next to her. Curled in a ball, she whimpered.

Nothing happened.

She cracked open one eye. Her ears rang and a short distance away stood the blurry forms of Tav and Akim. She blinked and gradually their alarmed faces came into focus. Their lips moved, but she couldn't make out words. They took a step closer. Dust stirred around her. Rada half rolled and looked about. A spike of fear stabbed her. Looming over her was the horse's belly. "Evika," she whispered.

The horse, however, was intent upon Tav and Akim. Even the small pile of fruit and vegetables she'd abandoned in her fury and determination, lay untouched; his insatiable greed forgotten in the face of a threat.

Akim stepped closer, motioning Tav to remain. The horse fidgeted and his feet barely missed Rada. Akim stopped, retreated, and returned to Tav. The horse relaxed, lowered its head, and looked at Rada.

"What's are you doing?" Tav asked.

"Shh," Akim said. "You might be right. For whatever reason, he may like children more than adults."

"He just picked her up and shook her," Tav said in a harsh whisper.

"He grabbed the backpack, not her. And in all the commotion, he never hurt her."

Tav's jaw dropped.

"Move out slowly, Rada."

She nodded and wriggled sideways to clear the horse. He shuffled sideways, keeping her under him. Rada tried again, to no avail. He flicked his head and snorted at her before returning his attention to the men.

"He wants me to stay put," Rada said, her voice trembling.

"Rada, it's a horse. It doesn't think like us."

She stared at the rugged patchwork of scars on his leg and belly. The webbed lines blurred and swirled; a pattern emerged and vanished. Rada rubbed her eyes, squinting, refocusing — a tendril of memory from the forest snared her. On one knee, she reached a trembling hand out to touch the web of scars on his leg. A bitterly cold sensation shot through her fingers, numbing them. She jerked her hand away, skirted out from under him, and stood on shaky legs, rubbing her arm to ease the sensation of something crawling along it. Ready to bolt, yet entrapped by her own reckless curiosity, she stood there warily, unsure what to do but unable to leave. The horse turned and nudged her until she tentatively patted him. "If Mstislav sent you, then you should be nice to me." His ears flicked back and forward with her every word. "Will you be good?"

The stiffness left Rada's posture as she patted the enormous horse; her shoulders relaxed and a small smile tugged at the corners of her mouth.

"Rada, he's still got half the sapling tangled up in his lead. We need to fix that," Akim said. "I'm coming to you."

The horse moved between them.

She poked her head around the animal's side. "He doesn't like grown-ups." Rada stepped forward, grabbing the rope. "Be good." The horse snorted but allowed her to step beside his head.

"Rada, I don't think he likes anyone," Akim said.

As if to prove him wrong, the horse rested his chin atop her head. "He must have liked his owner. Jemilla said no one would keep him otherwise."

Akim approached, heading to the timber entangled in the long lead, yet acutely aware the bay was watching him. "Keep talking to him, Rada."

"Akim is good. You should like Akim," Rada said. "And Tav too. And the emperor and Mami... You should like them really, really a lot."

Akim kept his gaze off the horse, talking in a soothing voice while he unravelled the rope from the remnants of the tree. That done, he worked his way closer until he could pat him.

Rada beamed. "See? You can be good. Tav, come on, say hello. He's a good boy."

At this, the horse yanked his head and towed her to the food on the ground.

"Oh, no you don't," Rada said. She locked her legs and slid across the dirt on her heels. Dropping the lead, she ran and jumped in front of him. Wagging her finger, she said, "No! You don't get it unless you're good."

The horse stood back, shaking its head.

Akim grabbed the lead while they argued.

Tav gritted his teeth and joined them and put the last of the apples in the remains of the rucksack before giving it to Rada. She hugged the ruined bag to her.

The horse nudged her in the back repeatedly. When no food was forthcoming, he pulled her braid.

"Ow!" She spun to face him. "No! Bad horse!" She stamped her foot. The bay stamped his foot.

"Enough!" Akim said, his voice rumbling with command.

Horse and child snapped to attention.

Sighing, Akim said, "Now, tell me why you want this horse."

She looked at her feet, at Tav, and then around to see if anyone was nearby to hear.

"Come on," Akim said, picking her up. "You can whisper why in my ear."

"Uncle and Jemilla said he knows how to fight. That with him on your side, no one could touch you. I can learn to fight and he'll keep me safe, and I can keep Mami and Bubba safe and it won't matter that... that I'm only little. No one will touch us."

Akim hugged her. "Are you always so much trouble?"

"Yes," she and Tav said in unison.

A long, soul tearing scream ripped past them.

Rada paled and clutched Akim. "I've never heard anything like that." She trembled. "Are the enemy back?"

"No. Now, back to business, my Stilniat. You definitely want this horse?" Clutching him, she nodded. "Well then, you've got a lot of work to do. You'll have to prove you can handle him. That means you have to brush him, bridle him and get the saddle on his back on your own by morning. Can you do it?"

"Yes!"

He set her down. "Let's get to work then."

Excited, Rada said, "Where will I get a brush?"

"Go ask Jemilla. She's over there by the other horses."

Rada ran off calling, "Jemilla! Jemilla!"

Akim scrubbed his face with his hands. "She'll be upset in the end, but it'll keep her preoccupied for a good while."

"You don't believe she can do it," Tav accused. A short back of laughter escaped him. "You don't know Rada. She won't give up."

Tikhon tossed a bucket of water over Rodan, who woke moaning.

Jadzia prodded his face with the bloody stick.

"Finish it," Rodan said, words scraping and clawing out of him.

"We will. You know there was never any getting out of this."

"Mercy," Rodan whispered.

"Mercy would have been doing it first, but I'm all out of mercy. There is only one death for your crime against me. The kadag-talir will be your end." Jadzia passed Tikhon her kadag. Grim, he tested the curved blade's edge.

Jadzia knelt beside Rodan's head. "Know this, Rodan. We have wiped your line from the earth. Your wife, weak as she was, spilled what information she knew the moment we threatened her child. They died in horror and fear because of you. The rest of your family: your brother, your sister, their children – their lives hang in the balance. We will arrest them. Maybe by then I will feel like mercy, and I may petition the emperor on their behalf." She paused, head canted, thinking. "But if they survive, they'll be watched. At the slightest whiff of dissent, their lives will be forfeit. What kind of life would that be? With the blade hovering over their necks?" She shook her head. "No. With any luck, all the threads of your misbegotten clan will be severed. All. Because. Of. You. Your estate is now mine. My children will grow and thrive there and I will teach a generation of Talaks to love, fight and die for the empire. You don't realise what you've done. The events of the last twenty-four hours will change history."

She nodded to Tikhon, who crouched beside Rodan's groin. The man closed his eyes, tears streamed down his face. Tikhon gripped Rodan's scrotum, stretched the skin. The dagger in his hand flashed down once... twice. The Talak's scream shredded the air. Anger, loss, pain, defeat and hopelessness became a wail that faded with each beat of his heart as the blood pumped out of him.

Jadzia studied his face, memorising every expression as the life left him and his final breath whispered into the air.

Grim faced, Tikhon said, "Do it."

Darcov beheaded Rodan, forced open the severed head's mouth and stuffed the genitals into it.

"Bundle it up. We'll take it back to Bēdarik and mount it in the square."

CHAPTER 21

THE DAY WAS DRAWING to a close; Rodan was dead, yet Jadzia felt no relief. Instead, a weight had settled in her belly and it chilled her to the marrow. Tikhon had betrayed them – all of them. Their safety should have been assured, yet she saw how much of an illusion that had been. Power, inheritance, legacy, and the stability of an empire. What was love compared to that? A necessary sacrifice? Perhaps Bashtan was right. How much had Tikhon fought for her when they were young? Emperor versus man. There was never a contest. She should have known better. Jadzia shook her head. Later. There'd be time later. Tomorrow they would move on to Vēkaria. There, they would be safe while the Order and the emperor dealt with rebels. Her future would lie in her value to the empire, not the man.

Jadzia went in search of Rada, stopping in her tracks at the sight before her. "Akim? Explain why my daughter is with this horse. Rada, come away!"

"But Mami, he's just got used to me and he's a good boy, really. I think he likes me."

"He's been with her for hours, Stilnassa. He's shown no real malice towards her. I'm guessing he doesn't know what to make of her, either that or he likes children."

"I wouldn't imagine Rodan let his children near him," Jadzia said. "I'm thinking I shouldn't."

"Please, Stilnassa, watch," Akim said. "You wanted her occupied, and I told her she could have him if she could bridle him and get the saddle on his back herself."

Lips drawn in a tight line, Jadzia crossed her arms and tapped her foot. Finally, she nodded. "On with it."

Akim's face remained neutral. "Watch."

Rada climbed the supply-wagon's wheel to stand on its back with the bridle in one hand. She shoved a carrot into a crack in the boards and laid the bit next to it with some more carrots around it, while she held the brow band up. "Be good, BC." The horse gave a snort.

"I swear he understands her," Akim said. The horse ambled over, reaching for the carrots. Rada studied him as he ate, carefully timing her action. She pulled the bridle up, hooking it over the dark bay's ear, but misaligning the bit. Jadzia blinked in disbelief as the horse shifted his mouth and took the bit up.

The horse moved sideways. Rada teetered on the edge of the wagon, one hand still on the bridle. The other reached out to stop him, and she wound up clinging to his neck as he pulled back. A high squeak escaped her as she hung over his neck, her legs flailing in the air.

Jadzia moved in to help. "You two should be closer in case something goes wrong. What if she lands on her head?"

"Wait, Stilnassa. Watch. He's not so keen on us, though he's improving. His first reaction seems to be defensive with most people other than Rada."

Rada got one leg hooked over his neck. The horse threw his head high and Rada slid down his neck. Her hand released the bridle as it slipped over his other ear and she pushed herself into position on his back, clutching the reins like a lifeline.

"I've never seen anything like that," Jadzia said. "Well done, Rada." To Akim, she said, "If it distracts her from what has gone on here, good, but let nothing happen to her." Jadzia approached the horse, her gaze avoiding eye contact, her hand outstretched. The horse sniffed her hand, then relaxed.

Rada leaned down, patting his neck. "See, he's the best boy. Can I keep him?" she asked as Jadzia patted the beast's shoulder.

"I'm not sure. You still have to saddle him. And you, beast, if you hurt her, I'll send you to a glue factory," Jadzia said before returning to the campsite.

"Good thing she didn't see the first six attempts," Tav murmured.

Excited, Rada called out, "Tav, can you put the saddle in the wagon?"

"No help saddling him," Akim said.

"But he's not saddling him, he's only putting it in the back. You never said he couldn't do that,"

"You're bending the rules," Akim said.

Rada grinned. "You should have been more specific."

"Well then, boy," Akim snapped. "Get on with it."

Tav looked at two saddles. One was a heavy military one with high cantle and pommel, the other a much lighter one Stilnassa Jadzia used for general riding. Tav chose that and, trying not to smile, he hung the saddle over the wagon's side and returned to Akim.

"I'll bet you three kellig she does it," Tav said.

"Boy, do you even have a single kellig to your name?"

Affronted, Tav produced the coins. "Satisfied?"

"You're on. Easiest money I'll ever make."

Rada whispered to the horse and, face contorted in concentration, reined him alongside the wagon.

"Good boy!" she whispered. She swung her leg over his back. Dangling, her feet wiggled in the air as she strove to touch the wagon bed. She let out a squeak, closed her eyes and let go, landing with a *thunk* on the timber.

"Come on, move this way." Rada jiggled the reins and cajoled the bay alongside the saddle. She slipped his reins into a metal ring, tying them loosely.

She lifted the sweat-encrusted saddle pad up. Rada teetered, used the horse to balance while she threw the saddle pad at his back. It landed sideways, barely over his back. "Evika," she muttered.

"Language, Stilniat." She snuck a look at Akim who stood, arms folded, brow raised in disapproval.

Teeth gritted, she grabbed the pad's bottom edge and pushed it farther over his back.

Hands on hips, she eyed the saddle and the horse. Rada tried to pick up the saddle, groaning as she lifted it all of a few inches. She scratched her head, lifted the flap and lay it on the horse's side.

She flattened the saddle flap against the horse's side, attempted to lift and push the saddle up his back. Her arms strained and her feet scrabbled on the wooden floor of the wagon.

"Stay still," Rada pleaded with the horse. She gave up and allowed the saddle to slide down, grunting as she hoiked it back onto the wagon's side.

Akim let out a huge breath and smiled broadly. "Well, that was a good try, but I'm sure you'll find a lovely little pony more suited to you once you reach your mother's family estates."

Rada scowled, muttering, "A little pony for a little girl." A growl escaped her. Her mind raced and her gaze travelled around the wagon, alighting on a rope. "I'm not done yet!" she said as Akim grabbed the horse's reins. "Wait!" she pleaded, eyes wide. "Please."

"Mstislav, save me," Akim said.

Rada grabbed the rope, threaded it through a stirrup and tied a series of simple knots that resulted in a tangled conglomeration.

Akim put his head in his hands. "Remind me to teach you how to tie a knot."

She pulled with all her might. "It'll work," Rada said before slipping and landing on her butt.

"I think it's tight," Tav said with a laugh.

Rada threw the rope over the bay's back. She bent to push the saddle up again but stopped. "No, that won't work."

"Rada..." Akim began.

"Wait, wait, wait." She jumped from the wagon to fetch a fallen branch. After sliding the branch onto the wagon, she clambered back in. Again, she pushed the saddle, lifting the flap flat against the animal's ribs. "Stay still, stay still," she murmured to the horse. The horse snorted and with half-closed eyes appeared to doze. Grunting, on tiptoes, she moved the saddle no higher than her first attempt. Red faced, digging the branch into the leather, she shoved the stick, raising the saddle two inches more. Rada forced the branch into a groove in the wagon bed, holding the saddle in place.

"How is that even working?" Tav asked.

Together, he and Akim moved in front of the horse, canting their heads in unison. Both stood slack jawed.

"I don't believe it. He's actually leaning against the saddle. That cranky old bugger is helping her," Akim said.

"He's keeping it in place," Tav said.

Rada jumped from the wagon and ran to the other side of the horse. She wrapped part of her tunic top around her hand and pulled on the rope, trying to haul the saddle over the horse's back. It barely moved.

"Evika!" Rada grabbed as high on the rope as she could and lifted her feet off the ground, using all her tiny weight to shift the saddle. It moved a few more inches. Grinning like a loon, she slid down the rope a little and kicked off with one foot, swinging like a pendulum. The horse snorted again and bent one front leg, lowering his back. The saddle shot into place. Rada landed on her backside in the dirt under the horse. The horse groaned, shifted its hind legs and arched its back.

"Rada, move, quick!" Tav yelled.

Rada shot out from under the horse as a powerful stream of urine landed where she'd been sitting. "Ew!"

Akim turned away, struggling to hold back his laughter.

Nose wrinkled, Rada waited until the bay finished. Face twisted in disgust, wary, she leaned under his belly to grab the girth strap. Unable to reach, she moved under the horse to grab the strap. Another squirt of urine spurted out. She shot back. "You're mean." Rada stood in front of his chest, reaching between his forelegs and shifting her position and grip until she stood by his side, girth in hand. "Ah! See! Who's the boss now!"

Rada tried to bring the girth strap to buckle. It wouldn't reach. "I'll make it longer on the other side." She untied her mount and attempted to move him away from the wagon.

"Come on." Nothing. "Come on," she coaxed. He planted his feet and refused to move. Her shoulders slumped, but her eyes narrowed. She tried to undo the rope on the stirrup, but the knot wouldn't budge. Fishing out her dagger, she cut the rope, leaving the great knot dangling. Tying the new piece of rope to the buckle on the girth, she pulled it to the girth strap, frowning at the realisation that there were only small holes for the girth buckle and no hope of tying a rope. "I'm not finished. None of you will win." She drew the rope through the stirrup to fasten the girth to it. She leaned back on the rope, pulling it as tight as she could. The gelding shot his head around and tried to bite her as the stirrup contacted his belly. Rada yelped, dodging, and the rope slackened. The horse turned his head away. "It's all wrong, I know!" she whispered to him. Tears threatened, and Rada pushed her palms into her eyes and leaned her head against the horse's shoulder. "But I can't do it properly. I'll leave it loose. Maybe Akim won't notice and then Tav will fix it."

Akim's eyebrows shot up, nearly disappearing into his hairline.

"We're almost done. Be good... please?"

The horse shook his head, moving off to a snatch at a green weed. Rada drew the reins over his head and leaned over his neck. "Once more. Come on." She plastered a smile on her face as she looked around at Akim and Tav. "Mstislav, help me. Hokati? Any god will do," she whispered. "Come on, you can understand me. You must! Mstislav sent you." She poked his neck. With a snort, he tossed his head. She clung to his neck and slid down into the saddle.

"I'm done! I saddled him! On my own! Can I keep him?"

Akim walked around them, critically surveying the result. His lips twitched, but he did not laugh. The girth was attached to a stirrup and hanging several inches below the creature's belly. The saddle blanket was askew and barely under the saddle. Atop sat Rada, grinning, triumphant, but anxious. Her worried eyes tracked him and her smile faltered a little with each passing minute as he made her wait.

"All you said was, I had to get the saddle on," she burst out. "I did. I got it on. You didn't say anything about getting the straps done up right. Just the saddle." She lowered her head. "I did it," she finished quietly.

Akim sighed and shook his head. "Beaten at my own game by one child." He handed Tav some coins. "And robbed by the other."

"So, I can keep him?"

"Yes, if he'll put up with this, you might just make a team," Akim said. "Tav, help her unsaddle him and tether him out of kicking distance of the others, then come to the fire. It'll be dark soon." He walked away, shaking his head and murmuring to the heavens for help.

Rada patted the horse's neck. "You hear that? Good boy, BC. We're going to be a team."

"BC?" Tav asked.

Rada giggled. "BC – Bone Crusher!"

The horse gave one great shake. With a squeal, Rada hit the dirt and the saddle landed beside her.

⮕

The fire burned brightly, everyone had eaten; soldiers not on guard duty had bedded down.

The baby grizzled and her fists flailed as she lay in her basket. Jadzia reached for her; wincing, staring at her damaged hand.

Adana and Regansh came to her side. "Stilnassa, let us help." Adana picked up the baby.

Regansh helped Jadzia to her feet and seated her away from the others with her back to them. Gesturing to Jadzia's coat and buttoned shirt, she said, "May I, Stilnassa?"

Jadzia gave a weary nod. "I can't manage them."

Regansh unbuttoned Jadzia's shirt, revealing her battered torso. "Give yourself time, Stilnassa. You must heal. Once you reach Dēbar, you'll be able to purchase a wrap-around top, which will be much easier."

Adana placed the babe within her crooked arm. Jadzia sucked in a breath; her voice shook. "I can't. My shoulders... my hand. I can't bear her weight."

Adana altered her position and held the baby in place, guiding her to suckle. "The other side will be worse. Gods help me, I cannot even feed my baby unaided. They've taken even that from me." Jadzia smiled down at the baby through silent tears. "Praise Hokati, it's a miracle that this little one survived."

Adana chuckled, watching the baby feeding greedily. "She doesn't seem the worse for her travels. It bodes well for her future if she is such a tough little nut. With you and Rada, she will best all challenges that come her way. Have you thought of a name yet?"

"I've some ideas," Jadzia said.

Rada sat next to Tav, rocking herself with her arms tightly crossed around her middle as she eyed her mother huddled between the two women.

She sprung to her feet. "Tav, will you help me?"

"Do what?"

"Dark is coming." She fidgeted, casting her eyes into the ever-lengthening shadows from the forest. "I'm not sleeping in the carriage again. We'll bring all the blankets and your bedroll over here with everyone else."

"Your mother might be more comfortable in the carriage," Tav said.

Rada shook her head. "Our bedrolls are in the wagon. I checked, and there'll be extra around now, since... since."

"Since the battle," Tav's whispered.

Rada nodded and rushed on. "And there's the enemy cloaks. We can pile them up and make it cushy for her. We need to be here. This is safer... much safer."

She paced, biting her lip as she waited for Tav's reply.

"All right." Tav followed her and they brought arm loads of gear from the wagon. Jadzia and the others returned to the campfire as Rada began organising their sleeping arrangements. Rada laid one well-padded sleeping spot and glanced Jadzia's way, sizing up the wicker basket that sat at her feet. Next to the adult's space, she left a gap with a smaller child size pallet below it – her place and the baby's. Opposite her mother, she left room for another sleeping adult pallet.

"Tav, you sleep there." Rada pointed to a spot close by. "Mami will be here, Bubba here." She ran off and dragged Akim back. "Akim, you sleep here. And Adana and Regansh here."

Jadzia's throat went dry; her stomach somersaulted.

The pallet opposite her site remained unallocated.

The guards allowed this little general to arrange them, recognising the deep fear driving her. Rada ran to Jadzia and said, "Mami, there's a spot for you. It's soft as we can make it and the fire's close, so you shouldn't get too cold."

Jadzia nodded. "I can see that."

"It's nearly dark. You should come now."

"In a minute."

At the look of panic on Rada's face, Jadzia said, "I'll come. Can you manage carrying your sister over there in her basket and get her settled?" Rada wrapped both hands around the handles and lifted. She gritted her teeth and took two steps, but the extra width of the basket made it difficult for her to carry it and keep it upright. A large hand reached over her and took the basket.

"Come on, lioness. Where do you want your sister?" Tikhon said.

She trotted ahead of him. "Here. Next to me and between you and Mami."

Jadzia's words came tight; thin. "No, Rada."

The cocky grin fell from Tikhon's face at her words. He knelt beside Rada. "Why do you want that, Rada?"

For a moment, she gazed down at her feet. "It's just..." Rada gulped and looked everywhere but at Tikhon. Finally, she gripped his arm and met his gaze. "It's safer. You'll keep us safe. See, I've laid everything out. We're in the middle. Mami and Bubba will be safe... and me."

He nodded. "I see. That's a very sound strategy and well thought out. You'll make a fine general." He saluted Rada, straightened and looked at Jadzia, his eyes a fleeting mix of sorrow tinged with desperation.

Jadzia scowled. "No, Tikhon. This is not..."

He shrugged. "What? She's right. It's safer." With that, he spun and deposited the babe where Rada instructed. "Permission to get my bedroll, general."

"Granted," Rada said with an imperious nod. She took her mother's hand and shuffled her feet, rocking from side to side, as she followed Tikhon's progress.

Tikhon laid out his bedroll and sat.

Rada clapped her hands. "Good!"

A lump formed in Jadzia's throat as she looked at the pair of them beaming up at her. Tikhon's darkly-tanned skin and brown eyes seemed to glow in the firelight. For a moment, he looked like the same boy she fell in love with years ago. He murmured to Rada and, with his gaze averted, she took in the familiar outline of his jaw, his aquiline nose; the short hair curling at his nape. *He'll be sick of that soon.* She used to tease him about his curls when they were young. Once he let his hair grow, just enough for her to bury her hands in. It was during one of many tours across the tribal lands where the appearance of the crown prince demonstrated the emperor's love of his desert homelands and the tribes that still dwelt there. Months of ample time to themselves between duties. Months of freedom to be just Jadzia and Tikhon. He turned to her; the movement showed his dark hair flecked with silver. Time returned. Her eyes welled with tears; her throat burned. She longed for those days before politics and greed came crashing down on them. They'd known it would happen, but the plan was for them to be together.

"Mami?" Rada frowned and took Jadzia's hand.

"Rada..."

"It's all right. We made your bed nice and soft. Soon it'll be full dark, but uncle is here. He'll keep us safe. Won't you?"

"Always," Tikhon said.

Stark silence descended upon the remaining troops. Akim's mouth formed a tight line as he turned from view.

Jadzia remained frozen next to the bed. Her face crumpled before becoming a rigid mask. "All right, sweet one."

She lay on the bedding, allowing Rada to cover her up with cloaks.

"Comfy?" Rada asked.

"Yes, mother."

Rada lay down between Tikhon and Jadzia. Tikhon pulled a blanket over her and rested his hand on her chest. Rada clasped it and sought Jadzia's hand as well.

"Mami?"

"Yes, Rada."

"Mami, I'm not little."

"No, not anymore," Jadzia whispered. She stared at Tikhon over Rada's sleepy form.

The child's grip loosened and Jadzia slipped her hand free. Tikhon reached for her. He didn't flinch at the hurt and betrayal etched upon her face as she snatched her hand away.

"Never again," she whispered before rolling over and ignoring him.

CHAPTER 22

RADA TOSSED BETWEEN JADZIA and Tikhon.

No moon shone, yet an eerie glow emanated from all the living things that surrounded her. Approaching hoof beats vibrated through her feet into her chest. The enemy was catching up with them. Their ghostly faces twisted in rage.

Tav had to ride faster.

Why wouldn't he ride faster?

Bubba, what about Bubba? She'd bounce to bits.

And Mami?

They had to help Mami!

They had to save Bubba!

The world swam around her. Iridescent tendrils of fog brushed against her skin, sending thousands of tiny pinpricks along her arms and scalp, chilling her to the marrow before vanishing with a barely audible whisper. Exposing her. Opening doors that had been slammed shut and bolted tight.

Rada followed a path, tangled and twisting, through the scrub. She held her sister in her harness, but the baby weighed nothing. Rada had to hide Bubba and get to Tav. A skittering sounded above. Gigantic spiders, hundreds of them; all the colour of moonlight. She stared in dread fascination as more joined them and sat poised; their palps and forelegs twitched in silent communion. Rada rushed forward, and they trailed in her wake. She threw herself on the ground, cowering, covering her eyes.

Peeking, she noticed spiders of all shapes and sizes joining the larger ones. A pattern emerged as they moved in sync to form a larger shape. Rada whimpered, realising she now lay under the abdomen of a spider the size of a house.

She rose and tried to run, knowing the spiders shadowed her overhead. The path grew softer, boggy. Thick black mud crawled up her legs, trapping her.

Tav cried out in the distance.

A dagger was in her hand.

She stood gazing at the bloated, purple and blackening face of Rodan's soldier. Blood spurted from his slit throat, coating her hands. He stared back at her and whispered, "lesson learned."

The weight of a thousand eyes bore down upon her, and she didn't need to look up to know the spider loomed overhead.

Rada bolted, branches snagging her clothes, tearing her face. The shadow chased her. Her emotions lashed her.

Where was Tav?

Bubba?

Terror.

Uncle's here – joy, hope, relief.

Mami battered and bruised – BROKEN.

Battle.

Victory – JOY.

Rodan's final scream. The queasiness, the relief... the satisfaction.

They were safe. They were safe. They were safe.

Were they?

They were not safe.

Gasping for air.

NOT safe.

NOT SAFE.

Her vision blurred. Living fog ensnared her in its web. Voices chopping and changing, sometimes melding before coalescing into one – Pavel? Mstislav? Yet under it all the hush of a woman's voice, a touch on her mind like a dip into an icy stream – exhilarating, numbing, overpowering.

Rada's eyes snapped open, and she screamed.

With a million tiny, quick steps, Neeren hurried through the halls of the villa, her narrow skirt restricting her stride. Rapid, shallow breaths flew across her parted lips. Red in the face, she fanned herself as her tight bodice restricted her breathing. Unbidden, a thought of Jadzia's flowing skirts or loose pants and long, split, frock-coats came to her. "Evika!" she muttered. The tittering of two junior wives reached her and she turned, seeing the pair of them grinning at her. "I will find both of you later!" They fled. "Not a brain between them; pretty, vacuous darlings. They've no idea our world is about to change."

She stopped outside Bashtan's rooms and met his personal slave. "Lord Bashtan is not here, Mistress."

"Where is he?" The slave hesitated. "Well?"

"He is in the bathing rooms, Mistress."

She nodded. "Go about your work." He hesitated. "Go!"

Neeren whirled and left.

He watched her departing back with a smirk, whispering, "But he doesn't want to be disturbed."

She descended into the lower stone corridor. The bathing-room slaves stood in the garden at the end of the hall, enjoying the sunlight.

"What? Why are they not...?" Her pace slowed. Her urgency to speak with her husband evaporated with each step. She contemplated abandoning her quest but shook her head and continued. In the vestibule between the hall and the bathing room, she faltered at the feminine giggle followed by moans of pleasure.

She knew which one it would be – Gilda. It was always her lately. She'd like to kill Jadzia with her own hands if she wasn't sure the woman was dead already. A twinge of guilt niggled at her that Rada was surely dead too. *That wasn't my fault. I did all I could to stop her. Mayhap she is alive. I must look after my girls.*

Another groan of pleasure and the sound of water sloshing. Her fingernails dug into her palms. *Bastard! I shouldn't tell him. Let him miss the opportunity. But then I miss it along with my girls. Damn him!*

She stiffened and walked into the pool chamber.

Bashtan's bed slave, his silpara, sat astride him in the water. He lifted his head from her breast. The woman ran her hands over Bashtan's shoulder and chest, kissing him and sliding her hips closer to him. She arched her back, presenting him with her breasts. He caressed them, an indulgent smile upon his lips.

Neeren clasped her hands behind her back, gripping them until her fingers purpled. "Bashtan."

"Tell me you're here to join us and not harangue me."

"You know I don't share my time with you, besides you wouldn't keep up with the two of us."

Gilda laughed. "I hear the words of a jealous tongue."

"Mmm," Bashtan said, chuckling.

Neeren strode to the pool's edge, grabbed a handful of the slave's hair and yanked it. The woman squealed and gripped her hair her below Neeren's hand to ease the pressure on her scalp. Neeren kept pulling, forcing her to rise. She grasped the silpara's dangling earring, twisting it to hasten her out of the water.

Bashtan sat relaxed, arms resting on the sides of the pool, enjoying the spat playing out before him. Neeren sneered at the woman, now kneeling before her. She released Gilda's hair, but gripped the earring tighter, wringing her earlobe.

"Don't damage her, love. She's flawless. I want no blemishes upon her."

Neeren's hand shook. She did not let go and a smile as sharp as a blade curved her lips. A drop of blood fell to the floor.

"Neeren!"

One finger at a time, Neeren released the jewellery. "Out, whore."

The slave rose, regal, proud, beautiful, with creamy skin, cornflower blue eyes and long blonde hair. Her breasts were firm, round. There were no dimples on the backs of her thighs and no stretch marks from childbearing. Nor would there be. These women were sterilised; given enough of the herb moonbane once they'd developed fully, to stop their monthlies. Selected at a young age for their looks, they served as house slaves in the silparat schools, where they also trained in the intimate arts, music, history and literature. They were better educated than many noble women. As they matured, any who failed to meet beauty standards were culled into the general slave populace or sent to lesser houses, but not this girl. Jadzia had picked well. This silpara was the epitome of Talak beauty, and Neeren hated her.

"Your days here are numbered," Neeren said.

Gilda grinned. "I'm no whore and you can't get rid of me. Lady Jadzia owns me, not you. Nor are you in charge of this household. She is."

Bashtan watched the women argue over him with a half-lidded gaze and bemused expression.

"Soon I'll wear the mantel of 'Lady' and you'll be gone."

"Even were that true, my lord would not be without me. Have you considered why he needs a silpara? Ah, I see by your face that you have. You should feel no shame, Mistress Neeren. The presence of a silpara in a house shows status, not... failure."

Neeren lashed out to slap her, but Gilda caught her hand, whispering, "Though you may have a better understanding."

Bashtan gave a long-suffering sigh. "Enough, leave us." Gilda bowed and left, swaying her hips and casting a mischievous smile at Bashtan over her shoulder. "Wait in my chambers. Explain yourself, Neeren. How are you going to become 'Lady'?"

"Word is all over Bēdarik – General Rodan killed Tikhon."

"Word is all over Bēdarik that Lady Jorgen is a virtuous woman, but we both know that's a lie. Don't believe what you hear."

"It's true. One of Tikhon's men escaped and made it back, wounded, covered in blood, panicked and near babbling. Everyone knows. Now the temple is locked down. People are hanging gold banners for our old king from their windows."

Bashtan snorted. "The old king and his offspring are dead. They'll find no hope there."

"Of course not. It's simply defiance, a rallying call. Think, Bashtan! A new ruler will arise. Don't you see? This is an opportunity."

"An opportunity for death."

"Bashtan!" Neeren stamped her foot.

"Fine. So how many are hanging banners? All the people? Is every house in Bēdarik flying the gold? I'll bet the poor quarters aren't."

"They don't matter. No one cares for them; they're powerless. The nobles are hanging banners, that's what matters."

"How many of the nobles?" She hesitated. "See, you aren't even sure. I want confirmation. I'll not act on a rumour spun by housewives." He shook his head. "You should stay out of politics, Neeren. You've not the head for it."

Her jaw dropped.

"Tell me, how does this affect Jadzia?"

"Rodan attacked Jadzia's convoy."

"What!" He sprung to his feet, exiting the bath to stand before her.

"You heard me. I suppose it was revenge for his poor family. The emperor went to her aid and his force was decimated."

"What about Rada?"

"If the emperor fell, then most likely they've been captured."

"Most likely? You mean you don't know?" He gripped her arms and shook her. "Neeren, answer me."

"There's no news about them. The city is abuzz with news of the emperor's death. No one cares about a Zaragarian bitch and her whelp."

Bashtan slapped her, knocking her to the ground. "I care! Rada? Whelp? By the gods, woman! She is my child! How can you dismiss her fate so carelessly? Is becoming the lady of this house all you think about? I see the glee barely contained on your face! Gods, I've got to find them."

"Them? Jadzia too?"

"She is still my wife! And for all that has passed between us, I owe her something."

He grabbed a towel, wrapped it around himself, and headed for the door.

Neeren rose to her knees and snagged his arm, looking imploringly at him. "Bashtan, wait. You're wrong. I care. Those are the words of the crowd on the streets; not mine. I was carried away with the news of the Tikhon's fall. I didn't think. Forgive me."

He refused to look at her, shrugged his arm free, and hurried out.

"Bashtan, wait!" Neeren's hand cradled the side of her face. She shook her head. "Fool. He'll see us all condemned."

CHAPTER 23

NEEREN SAT IN THE garden at Lady Chandar's, morose and resentful. Nearby, Mistress Sevara lounged, goblet in hand and a half empty wine carafe before her.

"But, Neeren, we couldn't have done it without you," Sevara said.

"Yes, your information was vital in killing Tikhon. Surely, you'll be rewarded."

"I didn't do it for reward."

Lady Chandar laughed. "Come now, Neeren. You don't expect us to accept that, do you?"

"I just want Jadzia gone."

"Well, I'd say you got that wish. Even if Rodan has left her alive, I'm sure she won't last long. She'd make a fine example before the city, and to the Zaragarians, of what happens to our enemies."

Neeren startled as a chorus of loud male voices reached them in the garden before an interior door slammed, cutting off the din.

Chandar frowned as she noted Neeren's curiosity at the intrusion. She enclosed Neeren's hand in her own, drawing her attention back to their conversation. "Neeren, you're clearly troubled. Tell us. We're your friends."

Neeren fidgeted in her seat. "I understand it was the right thing, but... Bashtan... You should have seen his face. He still loves her, I'm sure of it. I thought it was impossible. And the child. I do regret the child. He's furious; devastated at the idea she's dead. Do you really think she is?"

"Of course, he's devastated," Sevara said. "She *is* his child... Isn't she?"

"Stop, Sevara. She's not a pure-blood; anyone can tell that. She has to be his," Chandar snapped.

Neeren groaned and held her head in her hands.

Chandar rolled her eyes at her sister and shook her head. "Naturally, we know you didn't want harm to come to the girl. I mean, Neeren, you tried to stop her."

"I... yes."

The bell-pull sounded and through the door to their enclave, Neeren saw a slave admit several richly dressed men.

Noticing the direction of her gaze, Lady Chandar said hurriedly, "Nothing stops gaming day. All the men meet, play rhakrum, eat and drink far too much." She waved her hand dismissively. "It will hold their attention all day."

"Amongst other things," Sevara said, smirking.

"Enough, Sevara!" Chandar set her cup down, slopping water over the low table.

Neeren tapped her foot, held out her wineglass whilst a slave filled it. She sipped at the wine. "This is lovely. Tabar, isn't it? From Rēsphia?"

Chandar nodded. "Of course."

"You're not drinking?" Neeren asked.

"No, not today. I find the lemon water more refreshing in the heat."

Sevara snorted, raised her glass to her, but said nothing.

"Ah..." Neeren paused, her eyes darted between them, taking in Sevara's semi-drunken state and the fine tension lines around the eyes and mouth of each woman. Curiosity and worry curled in her gut. "I don't remember Bashtan mentioning gaming day."

Sevara studied the drink in her hands, and Chandar smiled. "I believe he was asked."

Again, the entry bell rang, and a harried slave admitted men Neeren recognised – Lord Drayton and his two elder sons.

The men slid a look in their direction, giving a brief nod to the gathered women.

Neeren's interest flared. "I wasn't aware Lord Drayton was a gambling man."

"All men will gamble if the time is right," Sevara said, fatalism in her tone.

"Close the door," Chandar ordered a nearby slave. "I'd like my peace. Bring Mistress Sevara peppermint tea. She's had enough of the wine." Sevara made a face and downed the last of her drink. "Neeren, in truth, you should rest easy regarding the girl."

"Yes," Sevara said. "It's not your fault she was so wilful. Neeren, you always tried to do your best for her. You saw the potential her mother let go to waste. You, well... you tried to guide her; to steer her toward the correct path of a Talak woman."

Neeren nodded. "Yes, I did. I suppose I can't help Rada's nature. There is a wild taint in that Zaragarian blood."

"Zaragarian, please! Jadzia was Vēkarian! She just said she was Zaragarian to put on airs. Whatever else we say about her, her family knew how to feather their own nest. They were backwoods farmers in the borderlands of Vēkaria; outsiders utterly unaccepted by their own kind until they allied themselves with the Zaragarians. For the love of all that's holy, there are rumours those folk in the Snake's Tail have more in common with the hill clans in Matryan than the lowlanders." She shuddered. "From the way Jadzia acted, you'd think they were royalty."

"They are now. It shows you how the threads of fate can twist and change." Curiosity unfurled to suspicion, and Neeren stared at Lady Chandar. "This is one of those times when we may change the course of our lives."

Lady Chandar stiffened. "Go on."

Neeren laughed, emboldened; trusting her instincts and the knowledge they could not have killed Tikhon without her help. "Do I need to explain? You're far more astute than I. We have no royal family and a power vacuum. Now is the time for new leaders. Now is the time for showing true colours and acting."

"Particularly if you want a place in the new regime," Chandar said. "Neeren, you're forgetting. Tikhon may be dead, but the empire remains and they regard us as *theirs*. There is still a vast army to fend off. Not to mention the temple."

Neeren's face fell. "So, we just wait for a new ruler to take over? Another Zaragarian? Can't we enlist aid from our neighbours? Rēsphia? Nējarak? Any of them would like the Zaragarians gone."

Lady Chandar's fingers drummed on the arm of the chair. "Action has been taken, Neeren, and your efforts will not be forgotten." She fell silent, staring at the doorway.

Neeren turned in her seat to see Lord Eadan, Chandar's husband, standing next to a burly man. "General Cēdar!" She shot to her feet.

"Mistress Neeren. Or should I say Lady Neeren?"

She smiled and flushed. "I'm surprised you remember me, General. I'm doubly pleased you have returned unscathed from your battle."

He scowled. "We lost many men. Only a handful of us escaped. Farmers delivering new thatch to the Temple of Hokati smuggled me into the city."

"It's a good thing no one pays attention to that part of the city," Neeren said, hand upon her heart.

"The abbess at the temple is my cousin; she sheltered me."

"But you'll continue to fight? You must; so many are buying gold cloth. Surely, they'll join you."

He smiled indulgently. "Lady Neeren, they may want freedom, but most would like others to sacrifice for it."

"So, you'll do nothing?"

"We are marshalling support and troops from amongst the noble houses."

Neeren sighed with relief. "So, you will oust the empire."

"Our sources say Tikhon's death has thrown the Zaragarian clans into disarray. Leading families are vying for the title and wanting a clan moot to decide the next emperor." He laughed. "Their own traditions will be their undoing. I'm certain our neighbours will aid us. Particularly when they witness most of the nobles are behind us. Until then, it will take only a small force to blockade the temple here and we can prepare to defend our nation. We've already had soldiers on leave desert to us. More will surely follow."

Lord Eadan took her hand, placing a kiss upon it. "Lady Neeren, lovely to meet you again. I'm sorry Bashtan couldn't find the time to join us today. We sent word, and he declined."

Neeren blushed and dipped her head, not meeting Eadan's gaze. Lord Eadan tipped Neeren's chin up and guided her to a settee.

He sat beside her, never releasing her hand. "Lady Neeren, we need your help. You must convince Bashtan to side with us. If we have his support, the remaining lords will surely side with us. Then we'll have the numbers. We will have our chance. Our old allies will see the country is united and surely help. We have so much for which to thank you; so much we will reward you." Neeren nodded, his fervour igniting the ambition within her. "Lady Neeren, will you help us? Will you persuade your husband?"

"I'll try. Already I've attempted to convince him of the opportunities before us, but I fear he'll not listen."

"Without Jadzia, he is free. He can be the true patriot we all know him to be. He has one of the larger personal guard. We need him to mobilise his forces for us."

Neeren shook her head. "Bashtan is a patriot, but he is ever cautious. I fear the only thing that could make him mobilise his guard is to bring Rada home."

"Rada?" Eadan asked.

"The second youngest of his daughters, with Jadzia," Chandar said.

"No," Neeren said. "The youngest. The last is not Bashtan's. I would stake my life on it. Bashtan refused to acknowledge her until the emperor forced him."

"How does the child figure into this?" Cēdar asked.

"She was with Jadzia, both were. Bashtan was distraught at the idea that—"

"But the child is safe," General Cēdar said. "Rodan is not like Tikhon and the temple, he would not— *has not* harmed the girl. I've word she will be returned to her father."

"Truly?" Neeren sagged in relief. "But..." Her gaze went to Chandar and Sevara.

"These ladies have said otherwise?" Cēdar asked. "Who will you believe? Them? Or the man who knows Rodan best and has word from the battle?"

"Well... you naturally, General," Neeren said, abashed.

"You must go home and tell Bashtan. Tell him all you've heard. Be sure he understands we remember our friends," Cēdar said.

"Yes." Neeren's voice quavered; she bit her lip before continuing. "But he is not aware I gave you Jadzia's route."

Eadan and Cēdar smiled. "Understood."

With that, Eadan rose, guiding her to her feet as he did. "Come, I shall escort you home. You can speak with your husband first and then if he has questions, which I'm sure he will – cautious man he is – then I can answer them."

"Yes," she said more firmly. "I shall."

With a bow to those gathered, she left the villa.

"Do you think the child is still alive?" Sevara asked, amazed.

"Not a chance," Cēdar said. "Rodan would butcher every babe in their empire to sate his revenge."

"Poor soul," Chandar said. "Neeren believed you so readily. She has overweening ambition, but she is a simple creature at heart." She shrugged. "It will give her a momentary peace, I suppose."

"It had damn well do better than that," said the general. "We need Bashtan's troops. Will it convince him to stop sitting on the fence?"

"Maybe, but he'll want something for it."

"Well, we can let him keep his seat on the ruling council and not hang him for the traitor he is."

Every fibre of Jadzia ached, but her fingers burned like the very fires of Ebatov. Rada stirred beside her, rolled and snuggled down into her bedding, sleeping after another evening of nightmares. Tikhon had risen and was nowhere to be seen. The fire from the night before had died down to the charred carcass of a large log. One of the guard prodded it with a stick and it disintegrated into coals, black with a hint of red in their depths. He put a smaller branch on them and drew the fire to life again.

Jadzia struggled to her feet and limped into the bushes. She was damned if she knew how she was going to manage, but there were some things she wasn't ever going to ask for help with. When she returned, Rada was sitting bleary-eyed, wrapped in a cloak, and Tikhon was passing her a strip of dried lamb while he stirred a pot hanging from a tripod.

"I didn't know you could cook," Rada said.

"I wouldn't call it cooking, but I can make porridge." He handed her a bowl and spoon.

"Papi can't."

Tikhon snorted at that.

"Nor can my brothers. I don't think my sister can and not me either." She looked up as Jadzia approached. "Mami, can you?"

"Of course."

"And your brothers can probably whip something up," Tikhon said. "They're in my legions. None of my soldiers are so useless as to not be able to fend for themselves."

"Useless, but..."

"Don't worry, you'll learn," Jadzia said. "I'll teach you some old family recipes once we're in Vēkaria. If you're lucky, your grandma may even teach you." Jadzia folded herself down on the sleeping pallet.

Akim, Adana, Regansh and several others were rolling up their bedding.

"You're sending them away?" she asked Tikhon.

"They're going with you. You're leaving today."

"Am I?"

"Yes. You'll only have ten to escort you, but it should be fine."

"Should be? Like it was going to be fine for me to leave Talak?"

At the harsh clip of her words, Rada eyed each of them, hand hovering, spoon shaking, porridge forgotten.

"Go visit your horse, Rada," Jadzia said.

"What's wrong? Don't fight."

"We won't," Jadzia replied,

"You will. I can tell. But Uncle saved us!"

"Go." Flat, uncompromising; Jadzia kept her eyes fixed on Tikhon. Rada pouted, placing her bowl down and rising. "Take the porridge with you. Breakfast is important and you'll need your strength since the emperor has deemed that we will travel today."

Head bowed, Rada skulked away to Akim, who waited, hand outstretched for her.

The campsite was empty.

"I don't understand what the problem is," Tikhon said. "You wanted to keep travelling, didn't you?"

"When I chose. Not," she muttered, "when some man dictates it to me."

"Some man?" He kept his expression neutral. "Your emperor, you mean."

"How can I forget, My Emperor?" She swept her hand out before her and inclined her head in mocking submission. "And where would you like me to travel, Your Imperial Majesty? North? South? East? West? Vēkaria or back to Talak?"

"Not Talak. Not now."

"Worried about us being in danger now, are you? It's a little late for that."

"Enough, Jadzia. We can hash this out in private when this is all over, but not here in front of my troops. You're safe," he hesitated. "You will heal." Softly, he continued, "I was convinced I could keep you safe and being out of Talak now would be a good thing."

"You're not heading off to cower the good citizens of Bēdarik?"

"No. Not yet. We'll let them think I'm dead and discover what rats come out of the woodpile. Meanwhile, the

Zaragarian Firsts will be on their way. They were clearing out bandits in the hills southeast of Dēbar." His lips twisted in a wry smile. "Which is convenient. I've sent a rider to them. They'll join me soon and the Vēkarian Foxes will follow. Then we'll see what the Talaks have been up to."

Jadzia blinked; her jaw dropped, and she stared at him in disbelief. "The Firsts? On their way?" She snorted in derision. "Clearing bandits? An elite legion? You evikan bastard. You've been planning this for a long time."

"Of course." He averted his gaze. "Any change of power results in turmoil. The Firsts were assembled and positioned where they could quickly respond to rebellion, wherever it arose. Once the Order's support was guaranteed, any usurpers in Zaragaria or Vēkaria could be dealt with by the main Vēkarian legion."

"And the clan moot?"

"Posturing. A few old supporters of my father worried they're next. Once I've squashed the Talaks, the moot will be nothing. I've been hoping rebels there would stick up their heads. Then we can clean them out." He held a bowl of porridge before her. "Can you manage the spoon?" Nothing, merely Jadzia's unseeing gaze. "Here," he loaded the spoon and held it before her, waving it about.

Jadzia snapped back to awareness. "No!" she said, knocking away both spoon and bowl. "You mean to tell me they were nearby? Why weren't they lying in wait for this battle? We would not have been endangered. It would have been over in a blink. My daughters would not have been risked! Your men? Your injured men! Why?" The last came as a lingering cry.

"Jadzia, see sense! You're enough of a tactician to know in your bones what I did was right. Hiding a legion in the woods is not feasible. We weren't sure how far Rodan's eyes reached. Better that they be seen to be simply ridding us of bandit vermin. The alteration in their movement to the narrow mountain pass may have been tracked. And any hint of a trap and we would've lost Rodan. He would remain a snake in the woodpile. That was unacceptable. As it stands, we lost few troops."

"Few troops," she murmured. *Few. Troops.* Her mind whirled and twisted, chasing down gnarled, rotten thoughts. "I loved you."

"Loved? Is there no love still?"

She shook her head, grief etched across her face and the ire in her words. "I feel it faded; it lies shrivelled - a blackened, bitter seed in my breast. No matter what you try to lavish upon it, it will never grow. Years it flourished, despite distance, despite opposition, despite my marriage. A marriage you could have prevented. I sometimes think your father did it to test if you had the balls to defy him. If you were man enough to rule. It was a test you failed. I didn't see it then, but I do now. For years I lived in stolen moments and threw myself into serving the empire in order for you to be crowned... Years. Years because it was worth it since you loved me. Yet it's gone."

"I refuse to believe that." He reached for her and she shrunk back. "Jadzia," he pleaded. "We've time. We can build something better. You can divorce Bashtan, live where you want, do what you want. Only don't turn your back on me."

She rose, standing over him. "It's done."

Jadzia went to find Rada without a backward glance.

CHAPTER 24

JADZIA WINCED AS THE carriage rolled over the rough road and wiped a fine sheen of sweat from her brow. The baby lay in her wicker basket, which was strapped to the seat. Rada fanned Jadzia's face, altering her grip on the delicate bamboo fan.

"Rada, stop fanning me and stop looking at me like that. I'm mending well." Jadzia drew her kadag smoothly. "And look. See? Practise makes perfect, or nearly. Soon I'll be as fast with this hand as the other."

Rada laughed hollowly, as she scrutinised her mother. "In a fight, no one will know and you can switch hands and get them! Then we should give you a special name like Danika Justice Bringer had."

"Jadzia Justice Bringer?"

"No. Mami, for it to be proper, it needs to be just for you; not a copy."

"You must think of one."

"Mmm, it's hard. I don't want it to sound silly. Maybe Tav can help. The Darklinan are good at names. I miss them. I miss Anfisa too."

"Really?"

"She's got good dolls, and she's not like Aunty Neeren."

"She's not your aunt," Jadzia snapped.

"Mistress Neeren. Anfisa doesn't do much else other than dolls and she... Um... Can I tell you a secret?"

"Of course."

"She won't ever do anything really fun in case Mistress Neeren finds out. It's strange. She looks like she wants to do other stuff, you know, when I tell her stories but...."

"Perhaps she's just being good."

"I think Anfisa's scared a lot."

"Remember, not everyone is brave like you."

"But I don't think it's good to be scared of your mami."

"No, but that's something for them to work out. I can't interfere with the child."

Rada blew a strand of hair off her face and continued fanning her mother.

"Rada, stop. I don't need you to fan me like a slave."

"But you're always hot. I can see it. You don't look right."

"Rada! Enough! I'm fine. Rest yourself. Sleep for a bit."

"I don't need to sleep." Rada squirmed in her seat. "I don't want to," she mumbled.

"Close. Your. Eyes. No one will hurt you. You've got Grokky. He'll help. You must try to sleep. If you sleep, you can ride BC later."

"Only a baby'd think Grokky could help." Rada folded her arms. "He's just a toy. I won't sleep."

"In this world, he's just a toy, but in the dreamworld he's a bear. An enormous bear, stronger than ten men, with huge teeth and claws. He will shred whatever seeks to do you harm. That's why so many children have bears like Grokky." Rada pouted, stared out the window and pretended not to listen. "Hokati gives them powers to defend children in the dream world. You must learn how to call upon him."

"How?"

"Take him with you. Hold him tightly and think only of him as you drift to sleep. Walk with him in your dreams. If your dreams scare you and you wake, go back into them with Grokky and defeat the demons that lurk there."

"He hasn't come before."

"It takes practise. I know – Grokky used to be mine, and he slayed my bad dreams."

"Did he?" Rada shook her head. "You're sure?"

"Yes. I'll teach you how to take Grokky with you into your dreams, as my grandmother taught me."

"Really? Lessons?" Rada's shoulder's slumped. She kicked the seat. "Promise I can ride BC?"

"Yes, and it's not that kind of lesson."

Rada huffed. "All right. I'll try. But it won't work." Rada clutched the bear and lay along the seat, grumbling as she curled up and stuffed her cloak under her head.

"Now, take a big breath in, hold it and let it out. Good girl. Breath in, hold it, scrunch up your body tight, let out your breath and let the tightness go. Excellent. Keep breathing in through your nose, out through your mouth. Bury your hands in Grokky's fur. He is your friend; a guardian bear, blessed with power from the gods; brave beyond measure. Wherever sleep takes you, he is there – a spirit with tooth and claw to protect you. He walks beside you..."

Rada slowed her breathing, relaxed her limbs and pretended to sleep. Through her lashes she could see her mother rub her abdomen before shifting the bandaging on her broken fingers to inspect them, only to cover them up again quickly.

"Imagine you are both in a meadow beside a stream. Hear the trickle of the water over the rocks. The grass is soft under your feet. You lie down and watch the butterflies dancing through the flower stalks. All is light and peaceful..."

I'm not sleeping. No way!

Rada burrowed down into her cloak, pulled Grokky close and curled around him.

Her mother's soothing tone continued. "The sun is warm on your skin, and your eyes and limbs are heavy. Grokky's fur is soft, warm, long. Bury your face in it and hug him, love him. He will stand watch..."

Jadzia's words faded as Rada drifted into sleep.

A one-eyed man reached for her as blood streamed down his face from a stick she had shoved into his eye. A voice told her she should have pushed it harder and farther; then he'd be dead. Rada spun to race away, and a swollen, purpling face loomed at her. Ducking under reaching, rotting fingers, she ran. *Mami! Grokky! Grokky! Grokky!*

The carriage jolted, sending Rada tumbling forward, squealing, onto Jadzia before sliding into the footwell.

Jadzia awoke with a roaring battle cry, drawing her kadag. She kicked out at her assailant and drove the dagger down. Rada screamed and scuttled backward to tremble, wedged in the carriage's corner with Grokky held over her head.

"Mami, no! It's me!"

Feather-stuffing fell like snow in the cabin as the blade plunged through the bear, striking something hard. Rada cried out and was silent. Jadzia's laboured breath was the only sound in the carriage. The dagger shook as she struggled to control her trembling hand.

Her face froze in horror. "Rada! Rada, are you all right?"

Nothing.

"Rada?"

Nothing.

Jadzia snatched the dagger back, the bear coming with it.

Rada's knees were drawn up to her chin and her eyes were scrunched closed.

Jadzia fell to her knees. "Rada..."

"Mami?" Rada said, raising her face to reveal a small lump and faint bruise on her forehead.

"Oh, thank the gods. Mstislav, Hokati, every damn one of them, thanks. You're well."

"Y-yes. Just a bump."

At the sound of a horse cantering to the window, Jadzia hid the dagger and bear under her cloak.

"Stilnassa, what's amiss?" Akim asked as he put his head through the open window.

"Nothing. Just bad dreams for us both, and then the last rut tipped us out of the seats. We each let out a battle cry, didn't we, Rada?" The child nodded. "But, as you see, we landed here. Hardly in a position to engage the foe." Jadzia gave a weak smile. "We'll pause for a break here, Akim."

Akim took in the feathers on the floor and their clothes, narrowing his gaze but nodding and calling out to the troops. "Rest break! I'll have some food and drink brought to you."

"No need," Jadzia said. "We both need to stretch our legs; we'll come for it."

Once Akim left, Jadzia sagged. "Oh, sweet one! I'm sorry. I didn't realise it was you." She held open her arms.

"I don't want to hurt you."

"You won't."

Rada scooted over for a hug. She wrapped her arms around her mother's middle and laid her head against her breast. Jadzia stroked her hair. "I'm sorry. We're both a bit of mess, aren't we?"

Rada nodded. "But it's all right, Mami. I know you didn't mean it, and Grokky saved me."

"Grokky?" Jadzia uncovered the bear. She drew the dagger from the bear to find it wedged in a piece of wood. Jadzia turned it over in her hands. It was carved in the shape of a heart and decorated with etchings of a long-haired woman on one side and a web on the other.

"That's The Weaver, isn't it? The lady on the wall where the Darklinan live?"

"Yes." She ran her fingers over the detail in the wood and brought it to her lips with a smile. "My grandmother made me this bear. Once it was common to place these tokens in favourite toys like Grokky that were held close... cherished."

"Why?"

"Protection."

"But didn't you say the power came from Hokati?"

"Yes, but The Weaver came before all the other gods."

"I don't understand."

"A follower of Bethsinidar will tell you she is the only true god or, if they value their lives, they will say that she bestowed power on other gods because they are her children."

"So Great-Granny followed The Weaver?" Rada whispered.

"Yes, and she paid for it. One day when we are alone, I will tell you about her. Tonight, though, I will help you fix Grokky. We'll put this heart back in, don't you think?" Rada nodded. "Good. It has served you well. But you must tell no one, not even Tikhon."

"All right."

"Good girl."

"Mami, will the dreams go away?"

"Eventually, but we'll keep practising this every night before you sleep and you will learn to control your dreams. In the meantime, we have to tell ourselves that they are only dreams. They cannot hurt us in real life."

"Really?"

"I would not lie."

"But Grokky will be there, so I won't have to do what Mstislav said." Rada clapped her hand over her mouth. "I... I wasn't supposed to say. Tav said not to tell."

"Rada, what weren't you meant to say?" Jadzia's voice held a sharp edge. "I won't be angry if you have done something. The only thing that will anger me is if you lie or do not tell me."

"Um... Mstislav showed me how to lock away my fear. It was good, but scary. He, um..." Her voice shook. "When I was too slow, he made me do stuff."

"What stuff? Mstislav?"

"Tav said no one would believe me; that they'd think I was crazy."

"When did thi..." Jadzia halted as Akim approached and spoke through the window.

"Stilnassa, we've prepared a site for your repast," he said.

"Excellent."

He opened the door. "Do you need my assistance?"

"No, and we'll be along shortly," she said curtly.

He bowed and left.

"Rada, where was this? How did Mstislav 'tell' you?"

"In the forest, the night they attacked us," Rada replied in a rush. "He talked to me, and then there were the spiders."

"Spiders?"

"Big ones, some dinner-plate size and some like dogs. They were good though. They saved me and Bubba. Tav was scared, but I wasn't."

Jadzia put her hand over Rada's mouth. "Shh. Akim and the others are waiting, and not that far off. I need to hear all about this, but we need somewhere private." Together, they left the carriage. "Tav was right to tell you to keep quiet about this, but you should have told me." Rada limped beside her. "I'm sorry, Rada. If I'd known it was you, I would never have kicked you."

"I know, Mami. It's because they chase you in your dreams too. It's just a bruise. Doesn't even hurt that much. Not like when I jumped off the stable roof, and that got better quick, so this should be really quick."

"At least you don't think you can fly anymore." Jadzia's lips quirked.

Rada kicked the dirt. "Mami, that's not fair. You said you'd forget it. I was only little then and I was sure I'd flown around my room that night. I mean, I saw everything from the air; even saw me in bed."

"That should have been a clue that it was a dream, not incentive to leap from the roof."

"I was little then!"

Jadzia laughed. "Rada, I'm teasing. Oh, it's good to be out of that carriage." She arched her back and stretched sideways, surveying the surrounding landscape. "See those mountains? Just beyond that is Vēkaria. We'll soon be home. You'll be able to see your grandparents."

"Do we climb the hills?"

"No, from here, the road travels down to the river and winds through a gap in the mountains to enter Vēkaria. This mountain is the last we cross." Jadzia was flushed.

They reached the soldiers; a few stood watch but most of her small retinue were seated on the ground, relaxing and eating.

"Rada, do you want some bread?" Jadzia said.

"No. It's gotten like a rock."

"We must toughen you up," a guard said. "This bread is nothing. Wait until you're on campaign and there's just hardtack, or not even that."

"You'll find out when you train for the imperial guard," Akim said. "Oh, and then there's the Order's training. They're all about making your suffer."

Rada gaped. "Suffer?"

"Never mind that," Jadzia said. "There's plenty of time before your training begins and before you have to worry about such things. Your early training will be with weapons and hand-to-hand combat, and you will not be one of the Mstislavakan. The training you have will take a different course, particularly if you want to be one of the emperor's own."

"Really?" Rada asked.

"Yes," Jadzia said. "The imperial guard train in a separate facility to the Order. Much of the basic training is similar, but it diverges once someone chooses to serve the Order."

"But doesn't every soldier pray to Mstislav?"

"Most, yes."

"Don't they all serve the emperor?" Rada asked. "Why is there a choice about serving the Order or being an imperial guard? Doesn't the Order always serve the emperor?"

Jadzia's harsh intake of breath was the only noise in the silence that followed. "Ah, well, that is a longer conversation for another day."

"But?"

"Rada, all I'll say is that, yes, the Order serves the emperor while their interests align." Jadzia said.

"So..." Rada canted her head. "They mightn't always serve Uncle?"

Jadzia sighed. "Akim, how far to the next campsite?"

"Only a few hours, Stilnassa."

"Good. Time enough for me and Rada to stretch our legs before we need to head off in that infernal contraption. Come on, Rada."

Adana rose to accompany her but Jadzia held out her hand, forestalling the Stilnassa. "No need. If I'm not mistaken, there is an old path that heads up to the lookout farther up this road. We'll meet you there. Come, Rada."

Together they headed through the scraggy wattle, their passage sending showers of tiny yellow blossoms cascading to the ground. Jadzia headed through the trees, finding the trail with ease.

"You're not limping as much, Mami. That's good."

"Very good. With such an excellent nurse, how can I not get better quickly? Perhaps your future lies with the Temple of Hokati."

"No!"

Jadzia laughed. "You're so easy to tease! Don't worry. I'll never place you with that bunch of hypocrites."

"Good. Anyway, Uncle said I could join the imperial guard." Rada thrust her hand out, slashing an imaginary sword. "Then I'll be one of the emperor's own!" She laughed. "But Master Pavel will be disappointed. Are you sure I can't be both?"

"Yes. The Order will give you some training and continue your religious education but you are not Mstislavakan. You are not an orphan and I will not sign you over to them. For you, there'll be a choice when you become sixteen – the Order or the legions and then the imperial guard. I warn you, the path to the guard is difficult. They're chosen from the elite of the legions and so far, only full-blood Zaragarians. You must fight hard for a place. If you fail, you will have to be satisfied with the legions, which is an honour in itself."

"But Uncle said—"

"Enough!" Jadzia bent over, red faced before straightening, holding her side. "I've become soft! Now, Rada, listen. What you said about the Order serving the emperor is theoretically correct."

"Theoretically?"

"It means it is what should happen, but their highest loyalty is to Mstislav. If they feel a conflict between the two, then they will choose Mstislav."

"But Aitor I made the Order. An emperor made them!"

"Yes," Jadzia said before heading along the rising rocky path, "because the Mstislav appeared to him. He is the only god to do so in centuries. Many believe Aitor's victories were due only to Mstislav not because he was special, and if they see an emperor who does not honour the god as they feel he should be—"

"But they should choose the emperor."

"Rada, you must understand this, and we will never talk about it again. The Order helped your uncle overthrow his father. And who was he?"

"The emperor," Rada whispered.

"Correct. This is the crossover of religion and politics. The Order has grown huge and has temples and members everywhere."

"But Akim and the others all go to the temple."

Jadzia nodded. "But they are not members." Breathless, she struggled up the well-worn path which wound through enormous grey boulders as it rose. The trill of birds silenced as they neared, only to resume as they passed. A warning cry of a deer sounded off to their right, and the clatter of its hoof-beats and sliding scree reached them as it made its escape.

Jadzia leaned against one boulder. "Worshipping at a temple is not the same as being a member of the Order. You pray at the temple and are not a member. We have prayed to Hokati and left offerings and are not one of her nuns."

"Oh, I suppose. So, I can still pray and see Master Pavel?"

"Of course. And you can take all the combat training with them you want but do with it as you choose. You don't have to follow their path. Rada, you are lucky to have choices for your future."

Rada surged ahead, no longer limping. "Come on. How far is it?" She stopped and spun back to her mother. "There are other choices?"

Jadzia groaned. "Yes! Being a wife and mother with a..." she panted, "...talkative, mischievous child is one!"

Rada snorted with laughter. "No way!"

Jadzia arched her brow and wagged her finger at her daughter. "Mostly it is rewarding, though sometimes you test me! I also have been able to work behind the scenes for the empire."

"Like with the Darklinan?"

"Yes, the Darklinan and you are the best part of my role."

"What about Vlas and Abaya?"

Jadzia halted in her struggle along the path. "Of course, they are important and they have my love, but they are grown. They have made their choices." She shook her head. "Life is full of sacrifices, Rada. Some paths we move down are the start of a slow rot and after years, you don't recognise yourself." Rada's jaw dropped. "Argh! Not you, I don't mean you or you brothers or sisters. I had dreams, like you, of what my future would hold, and they came to naught. This you must remember – that no matter your choice, you are expendable to the empire. Better to be a soldier. The rules are clearer, and in many ways, you will be more free."

"But Uncle will—"

"Don't." Jadzia's chest heaved and she wiped sweat from her brow. "Do not say Uncle will protect me or Uncle will look after me. Don't."

Rada stood slack-jawed.

Jadzia's brows drew into a deep frown. "I swore I wouldn't tell you this, but..." She bent and rubbed her abdomen. With a grimace, she straightened, not meeting Rada's eyes. She said flatly, "Your uncle knew General Rodan would strike at us."

"What? No. That's not right." Rada backed away, shaking her head.

"Yes. He counted on it. We were like the cheese in a mousetrap. We were the bait."

"Uncle wouldn't do that!"

"He did. He wanted to catch Rodan, and we were the bait."

"But... but... it was all right. It worked. He got him!"

"Yes, he got him, but we all nearly died. Your sister would have if not for you and Tav."

Rada bit her lip and sagged. "We were the cheese?" Jadzia took Rada's hand but was shrugged off. "But Uncle loves us." She wrapped her arms around herself and paced. Rada shook her head and looked beseechingly at Jadzia. "He loves us."

Jadzia gazed sadly at her.

Rada fell to her knees and rocked herself. Her hand closed on a stone and she hurled it at her mother, striking her in the chest. Jadzia grunted and staggered back but said nothing. "You shouldn't lie, Mami!"

Rada leapt up, her hands fisted by her sides. "I hate you! Mami, you always fight with everybody! You're just mad at Uncle! You're being bad! You're mean."

The child picked up another pebble. Arm raised, screaming in rage, she swung her arm back and hurled the rock into a tree.

Rada spun at the sound of soldiers coming through the undergrowth.

"Stilnassa?" Akim called out.

"Leave me alone!" Rada lay curled in a ball in the dirt. "Everyone go away!"

"All's well! Turn back," Jadzia called out. Nevertheless, Akim and Adana burst from the trees. "Rest easy. Rada has just learned some unpleasant truths. Return to camp. We will meet you at the lookout as planned."

"No!" Rada leapt up and bolted through the scrub, never once looking back, yelling only, "I hate you!"

Akim ran to where she disappeared and parted the bushes to follow.

"Stop!" Jadzia's voice rang out. "*I* will find her."

Akim hesitated. "Stilnassa?"

"Leave, Akim."

"What did you tell her?" he asked.

"Return to the wagon. Now, Captain!" Jadzia ordered.

Adana tugged Akim's arm. "Come, this is not our place."

Reluctantly, he allowed Adana to drag him back the way they had come. They had not gone far before he shrugged Adana off and stared at the spot Rada had vanished.

"Go," Jadzia said tiredly. "There is nothing you can do. We will meet you back at the wagon."

When they were out of sight, Jadzia let out a sob and hung her head. She stood like that for some minutes before straightening and following in Rada's wake.

Jadzia tracked the trail of broken branches and stumbled onto an offshoot of the path they had been travelling. She gazed about her with a slight frown and looked up the hillside to see a huge rocky outcrop next to a lone pine at the top. "Is it? It looks the same. This, of all places?"

Her chest heaved as she climbed, and her eyes grew glassy. With one hand rubbing her stomach, she struggled up between the boulders as the track skirted around the granite outcrop at its crest. Her gaze flitted to the lee of the massive outcrop and the dark, beckoning entrance remained just as it had when she was a child. At the pine that clung to the cliff face, she found Rada sitting on a rock, hurling stones into the distance.

Rada stood and turned at her mother's approach, a snarl poised on her lips and a stone in her hand. Jadzia perched on the edge of a boulder and caught her breath. "You are acting like your father; you've got his temper."

Rada dropped the rock.

Jadzia approached and put her hand on Rada's shoulder.

"Uncle loves us," Rada whispered, her voice thick with unshed tears.

"Yes, but he loves his empire more."

"Like the temple loves Mstislav more?"

"Yes."

"Maybe he thought it would all go well and we'd be safe?"

"Maybe, but Rada, when you put the cheese in the rat trap, do you expect to get the cheese back?"

"No, but Akim and Adana? They were cheese too?"

"Yes. That is often the lot of a soldier."

"Did they...?"

Jadzia waited for her to finish, but she never did. She opened her mouth to speak, to reveal one final act of betrayal but seeing the knowledge lurking in her child's eyes, she remained silent.

Rada turned to Jadzia and wrapped her arms about her as sobs wracked her body. Jadzia held her for an age, fighting the growing dread inside her with this cherished moment. Rada released her, rubbed her eyes and wiped her grimy, tear-streaked face.

"You are a sight! I've seen urchins on the streets of Bēdarik look more presentable than you." Jadzia smoothed the many wild strands of her daughter's hair and plucked a twig from her plait.

"Why did you tell me?"

"It's the most important lesson you can learn."

"But I know Uncle loves us."

"Not enough." The bitterness was gone from her tone. What remained was resignation and a near overwhelming fatigue. "Love doesn't solve everything. Your papi loves you and he'd sell you off in marriage if it meant more power for him. You must gather as much power for yourself as you can, Rada. Train, learn, develop unique skills that make you indispensable."

"Unique? Indispensable?"

"Special. Skills no one else has, or that you do better than anyone else. I tried this with the Darklinan. They are now the empire's eyes and ears and they answer first to me."

"I thought you liked the Darklinan."

"I do, but my work served two purposes. They needed help and I gave it. They've repaid me and the empire by providing information. I will make sure they become much more important. I will ensure them a future." She rubbed her side, and a brief flicker of pain crossed her face. "I was raised to be more than a wife. As a Zaragarian Stilniat, your future should be broader... have more scope than other women. I've tried within the role they thrust upon me, but from now on we make our own path. We'll serve the empire in *our* way; under *our* rules." She doubled over in pain, clutching her abdomen, and crumpled to her knees. She bit back a cry as her hand hit the ground.

"Mami!" Rada knelt beside her. "You're all hot and sticky. That's not good."

Jadzia slipped her arm out of its sling, shed her tunic top and sagged back on her knees. "I just need a moment..." She arched her head back, staring into the blue sky. Her limbs shook and her vision swam. Rada wiped her brow and tried to fan her face. Jadzia's breath heaved, but slowly the spasm ebbed. "I'm fine. I just needed a rest. Sit with me for a bit. Now we're alone, tell me about the night you saved Bubba."

Rada spun the tale of her adventures and her mother listened as Rada's face shifted from terror to amazement and back again, but Jadzia could not look away from the cave and an ancient voice whispered in her memory.

"Mami... Mami?"

Jadzia blinked and shook her head, returning to the present. "You say you didn't understand whose voice it was at first, man or lady, but it turned into Master Pavel?"

"Yes."

"Did you see anyone? Or just hear the voice? "

"No, Mami. Just the voice."

"And the spiders... They made no move against you at all?"

"No."

"You never saw them again?"

"Never."

"Rada, I don't think it was Mstislav who helped you."

"Huh? But Mstislav is my... our god. I prayed to him."

"Why didn't you hide in there?" Jadzia said, pointing to the cave.

Rada's gaze slid away from the sight and she shuddered. "Gives me the creeps."

"Mmn." Jadzia struggled to her feet. "Come with me."

They walked to the cave, into the shadows. Grey-green lichen covered this colder, darker side of the stone except around the cave entrance. Here, moss had been cleaned off the rock in order that a carving remained untouched. Etched into the ancient stone lay a web and caught in the web were the figures of trees, animals, flowers, people and stars and spiders.

Rada stepped back, her voice tremulous. "Spidies."

"Yes, Rada. Mstislav didn't help you, Bethsinidar did."

Rada's eyes grew round and her voice trembled. "Will I get in trouble?"

"No. Even so, we shouldn't tell anyone."

"Why The Weaver? Why not Mstislav?" she pleaded.

"I don't know, sweet one." Jadzia put her hand out and touched the web, a tiny frown on her brow, yet the trace of a smile on her lips. "Someone still tends this shrine, My great-grandmother used to bring me here," she said wistfully. "We walked this trail for miles. This used to be called the

Pilgrims' Way, and it ran from the shores of Vēkaria to the home of the Hill Clans of Matyran. Now much of it is overgrown; the mountain ways impassable." She traced her fingers along the web pattern. "Though obviously not all of it is disused. I wonder..."

"Wonder what, Mami?"

"Nothing, Rada. Let's see the inside, shall we?"

Rada tucked in beside her and clutched her mother's pants. Together, they bent down and entered the shallow cave. It was about six feet deep and pristinely clean. A figure of the goddess rose out of the rear stone wall.

"It's like the picture at the Darklinan," Rada whispered. "But... this one... She's got an extra eye."

"Yes, Bethsinidar is sometimes depicted like this, particularly in old shrines. The goddess is said to see all."

"Probably needs the extra eye, then." Rada gave a nervous giggle.

"Rada? Are you all right?"

"The eye is creepy."

"I'd say that's why the newer images don't have it or the spiders... just The Web. But this place is ancient, Rada. The temples on the Pilgrims' Way are the oldest in Penīdīen. I don't think anyone knows who built them. Aitor I destroyed many of the others. I don't think he could be bothered with these, not once he'd banished the sect to the Senner Isles. Perhaps he thought no one would come here."

"But Mami, someone's left food, look." In a basket on an altar before the goddess lay flat bread and some apples. "Who would come? No one lives around here, do they?"

"It could have been someone passing through. Someone who knew the shrine was here. That's all."

"But who would know?"

"I did. Others would too. And out here there is no one to care."

Rada fidgeted, rubbing her arms as she stared at the sculpture, before whispering, "I don't think I liked the voice, Mami. He... um, she helped, but I wasn't me... It wasn't me...

Sometimes." Rada shivered. "I couldn't do anything. I was locked up."

"No, nobody would like that," Jadzia murmured. Her hand shook as she touched the statue, her lips curved in a sad smile. The breeze rustled the leaves outside and stirred up a mini tornado of pine needles. Rada clutched her mother's sleeve. Jadzia remained silent, lost to the past.

"Mami?" Rada tugged Jadzia's tunic. "Mami?"

"Mmm?" Jadzia only half listened to her daughter. "What Rada?"

"Will it happen again?"

"I... I don't know." A tear rolled down Jadzia's cheek. She wiped it away quickly, shook her head as if waking from a dream. "But if it does, do what the voice tells you. The gods can wreak powerful revenge. Be dutiful."

CHAPTER 25

BASHTAN STOOD OVER A map on his desk, talking with his second-in-command. "Have you been able to find out where they were attacked?"

"No, but they wouldn't stray from the route. It won't be difficult to find."

"General Cēdar will know where they are," Neeren said from the doorway.

"What?" Bashtan straightened and glared at her. "Well? What are you talking about?"

"Cēdar. He is here in the city." She approached him, confidence growing with each step; certain this would prove her worth.

He narrowed his eyes at her. "What?"

"I—"

"Wait! Clear the room. Everyone out!" Bashtan ordered. "Not you," he said to his commander. Once the slaves were gone and the door closed, he nodded to Neeren. "Continue."

"I've seen Cēdar. He was at Lady Chandar's. I just spoke with him." She rested her hip against his desk and fingered the edge of the map. "There's no need for this though."

"Evika, woman!" The words rumbled from him like a growl. "None of your damn games. Speak plainly!"

She plastered a careless smile across her face. "You. Don't. Need. This." She flicked the edge of the map. "You don't need it because Rada is alive and will be returned to you. Cēdar said so. He had word of the battle from Rodan himself."

"Alive!" The word rushed out of him, and Bashtan collapsed into his chair. "Alive?" he whispered. Tears welled in his eyes. "By the gods, I can't believe it." He bowed his head, covering his face with his hands. "If only it were true, I swear I'll be a better father to her. Are you sure?" He could not look at her.

Gently, she touched his shoulder. "Quite sure." His shoulders sagged, and he leaned back in the chair, rubbing his face tiredly. "She's fine. Cēdar swears it. Eadan had a message for you. He said they remember who their friends are."

Bashtan narrowed his eyes. "What do they want?"

"They are moving against the empire. They need you and your guard to add to their cause. With you, the remaining noble houses will join."

"They don't have the numbers. It's suicide. Then there's the temple."

"The few members of the Order here are hiding inside the citadel. Cēdar says a small force can blockade the temple and starve them. I think he means the rest to defend the borders, along with our old allies."

Bashtan laughed. "Our old allies are just that – old and useless. They didn't help years ago when the Zaragarians invaded. They won't help now."

"But Cēdar said."

He shook his head. "I told you, I want proof that Tikhon is dead. Anyway, what is to stop Zaragarian troops pouring over the border tomorrow? It can't be done. We'll never be ready."

"The Zaragarians are fighting amongst themselves for who will be leader. They've demanded a clan moot, and it will give us time."

"You seem very well informed, Neeren. They've been in your ear, coaching you. How deep in their pockets are you? What other secrets are you hiding?"

"You know this is the course of action I was urging you to earlier. They have not swayed me, merely confirmed my belief."

"Well, I want more than the ramblings of a woman to convince me."

Neeren stood ramrod straight, heat rising in her cheeks. "Would that be your response had Jadzia delivered similar news?"

"What?"

"If the situations were reversed and Jadzia was bringing you strategic news of my location and..." Her voice trembled, words deserting her briefly. She blurted out, "I don't know – news of impending politics!"

"Impending politics!" Bashtan threw back his head and laughed. "Neeren, for a start and for good or ill," he muttered, "Jadzia had training in strategy and political manoeuvring. Unlike you."

Neeren's face flushed. "So, yes, then. You'd listen to her!"

The sound of a throat clearing brought their attention to the now open door. Eadan stood there, a slight, sheepish smile curved his lips. "Forgive me, Bashtan. I thought it politic to make you aware I was outside before you continued your discussion."

Bashtan shook his head, jaw clenched, foot tapping an impatient rhythm on the hard floor. His furious gaze moved from Eadan back to Neeren. Dripping sarcasm, he said, "Not in their pockets, eh? Anything else you've neglected to tell me, Neeren? Is Cēdar himself waiting out there?"

Neeren said nothing, only held his gaze briefly before lowering her eyes in shame.

Eadan stepped farther into the room, closing the door again. "Cēdar can't walk around Bēdarik, Bashtan. At least not yet. You understand that."

"Neeren, what have you got me into? No, don't answer that. Leave. Find something suitable to occupy yourself." She left, never once raising her eyes. Bashtan glanced at his second and gestured toward the door; with a salute, the man departed.

"Don't be too hard on her, Bashtan. And we didn't twist her to our cause. She was damn near pleading with Chandar for us to fight; using this time to shed the yoke of the Zaragarians. She's right."

Bashtan moved around the desk to stand before the man, arms crossed. "What do you want, Eadan? Say your piece."

"There are only a handful of lords who have not sided with us, but like you, they are amongst the older families; those who've done well under the empire. Those with the most to lose."

Bashtan's mouth formed a grim line. "My family is one of the oldest titled in Talak. We've always..."

Eadan waved Bashtan's words away. "Yes, yes. Your pedigree is well known. What is also common knowledge is that your forebears squandered any real wealth you had and made an enemy of the old king." Bashtan stepped toward him, hands fisted. "Now, now, calm yourself. I've not insulted your honour, merely stated truth. All the blue blood in the world does not change the fact you'd become little better than farmers. Certainly, that's how you survived. It's astounding what a few woolly mountain sheep can do for a family. Who could foresee you'd produce some of the finest fibre in all of Penīdīen. I admire your resourcefulness, Bashtan. You built a reputation for yourself as a shrewd businessman. And you were slowly rebuilding your family's finances, trading with other countries – Rēsphia, Nējarak, Matyran... even Zaragaria." He paused. "You've done rather well out of the Zaragarians, haven't you? Fortune restored, position on the governing council..."

"That was my right!"

"Not how the king thought."

"Mitos was a vindictive, ineffectual man. Once I paid my debts and he couldn't domineer me, he wanted me gone. He wasn't one to surround himself with any who'd give unbiased, worthy, and frank advice."

Eadan roared with laughter. "Frank advice! Why would he take advice from a man who dealt with the enemy?"

"We were not at war. All I did was trade."

"Tell that to the council; to the rest of Bēdarik who've seen your rise and your marriage to a Zaragarian of the First Circle. Regular visits from the emperor. Although the motive for those is the source of much speculation, none of which helps you. I can go on, Bashtan."

"My marriage was forced upon me."

"Forced? You could have walked away, but the lure of money was too much. And how many children with Jadzia? Six? Can't all have been such a chore."

Bashtan seized Eadan by the shirtfront, shaking the man and shoving him backward.

"Action at last!"

"Shut up, Eadan. If I hadn't taken the opportunity offered to me, then one of you would have and you know it. I've never acted against my country."

"You've never acted at all. This display is the most decisive I've seen you. Well done."

"Get out!"

"Are you sure you want that? Change is coming, Bashtan. We've a golden opportunity to oust the bastards. The clan moot is arguing over who should rule them. Our allies will come. We need to buy time. You've sat on the fence long enough. It's time to choose."

"You're taking a huge gamble. Why would our allies be any quicker now than in the king's day? Are you even sure of your sources? First, I need to get my daughter. The rest? Well, I can sit back and wait. By the time I've got her back, it will be clear whether you're right. There is no need to do otherwise.

"You can't sit on the fence as usual! You must make a choice now! Or be accused of treason and collaboration with the enemy when we win. Join us and retain your current standing. You need to pick sides, Bashtan."

"I need time. I want my daughter home."

"You've my word your daughter is on her way home. If you delay, she'll have nothing to come home to. Some want you dead sooner rather than later. They'd prefer not to wait to see which way you jump. They'd still get your troops, who, let's face it, without you will need employment and your death may scare the others into following."

"It may also make them oppose you."

Eadan shrugged. "Your support would fare us better."

"So, follow you or die?"

"Yes."

"And if you're wrong, the Zaragarians will kill me," Bashtan said.

"Well, take comfort, if I'm wrong, they'll kill us all."

"Come back at dusk. You'll have my decision then." Bashtan rang a bell, and his commander and two guardsmen stepped into the room. "Our meeting is done. Lord Eadan is desirous of his home. Ensure he doesn't get lost on the way out."

Eadan gave a deep, formal bow before the guards ushered him out, leaving Bashtan alone with his captain of the guards.

Bashtan leaned on the desk, staring at the map. "Thank you. It was good thinking to have the guard ready. How much did you hear?"

"Not a lot, but I guessed at trouble. I returned quickly just in case."

Bashtan explained what had passed.

"What are you going to do, my lord?"

"A bit of juggling, but I'm calling his bluff. We're getting Rada."

>———————→

The small column threw up a low haze of dust with its passage along the road. Undulating grasslands stretched on either side of them before the dirt road climbed again. The central highlands, with its jagged mountains and river systems, known as The Web, dominated the view to the east.

Her mother's carriage travelled in the centre of the column, flanked by Adana and Regansh.

Rada sat astride BC. He'd tried to bite her every morning since the battle. She snickered. *I was too quick after the first time.* She didn't care; he was hers. Won by right in her first spoils of war. Now she just had to learn to fight and no one would hurt her family. She giggled. No one was coming close to her now, anyway. He kicked just like a good war horse should. Tav and the others were a whole length behind her. She patted him, lent forward and wrapped her arms round his neck. "I love you, BC."

"Careful. He'll drop his head and dump you again," Akim said.

Rada laughed. "No, BC's starting to like me." The horse flattened its ears in annoyance.

"Let's test your control. Take him out from the mob and to the back and stay there until camp. It's Tav's turn for a lesson. Remember, use the stick if you have to."

Akim had given Rada a slender, whip-like branch stripped of all the leaves save a tassel of them at the end. She hadn't used it and didn't want to. She didn't think BC would like her more if she did and niggling at the back of her mind was what he'd do if she smacked him with it.

Rada twitched the rein and the big horse peeled off from the group. She turned him toward the rear with a huge grin on her face. "Good boy!" She kicked his sides. Nothing. Her feet didn't come past the saddle flaps. With each kick, his ears flicked back and forth and he stayed where he was. Kick. "Come on, everyone's watching." Kick. KICK. The horse tossed its head and trudged off. Rada sagged in relief, neglecting her reins. His stride quickened as he took advantage of Rada's inattention and stretched to bite the other horses as he passed.

She struggled to steer him and the orderly column kinked sideways as riders gave him a wide berth. Her face screwed up in frustration. They were all watching. She was failing. Her shame turned to anger at BC and the stick burned in her hand. When he shunted his rear sideways to kick out. She yelled, "BC, be good!" and swatted his rear. He pig-rooted. Rada somersaulted through the air. Dizziness assailed her as the world turned upside down then righted itself. She landed on her feet, holding the reins and the stick, facing BC. The horse tore the leafy tassels off the stick and ate them, snatched the branch, broke it and then stepped on it. The bewildered look never shifted from Rada's face. "What happened?"

Jadzia's voice rang out. "Halt!"

The carriage door opened and her mother emerged, bent like a little old lady. She gripped the door frame with her good hand. A curse escaped her as she leaned against the timber, eyeing the drop to the ground.

Adana dismounted, flipped down the carriage steps, and helped Jadzia out. "Stilnassa?"

"Gods above, I could kill that bastard all over again!" Jadzia alighted from the carriage and turned to face Rada with a grim look. Akim reined in next to Jadzia and they exchanged words with repeated glances at Rada and BC.

"No, no, no," she whispered to BC. "You've got to be good or they won't let me keep you."

"Rada? What happened?" Jadzia asked.

"I..." Rada hid a hand behind her back and crossed her fingers. "I was giving him a hug and I... fell off."

Jadzia's lips pursed. "He didn't throw you off."

"No," Rada said too quickly. "No, no. BC likes me. He wouldn't do that... Ever." Her fingers crossed more tightly. The horse shoved her in the back, sending her sprawling.

Rada picked herself up. Her lip trembled and her hands fisted around the reins when she reclaimed them. There was a lengthy pause while Jadzia eyed the pair, her hand tapping on her thigh as she considered them. Rada stared at the ground.

Finally, Jadzia said, "Well, then. On you get."

Rada jerked her head up in hope. "Yes! BC, head please?" The horse lowered his head for a carrot and she drew the reins over his ears and clung onto his neck. He shook as if to rid himself of her. When that failed, he snorted and tossed his head up, carrying her into the air. She wriggled her leg over his neck as he moved, then slid back toward the saddle, hoicking her herself over the pommel into the seat.

"Akim, I will ride. We're near to the Vēkarian border."

"Are you sure, Stilnassa?"

"I'm tired of being an invalid. I'm being bounced to bits in that carriage."

Anxiously, Rada asked, "What about Bubba, Mami?"

"Tav, you'll carry the baby." Tav dismounted and went to the wagon, where he bundled the infant into the carrier and tied her to himself.

Akim led a spare horse to her and boosted her onto it. She winced as she hit the saddle, adjusted her seat, and tested her weight in the stirrups.

Grave, Akim whispered. "Stilnassa, you don't..."

"I refuse to enter my homeland hidden in a carriage as if defeated. There's value in this, Akim. Let my people, from here to the capital, see what those damn Talak bastards did; what they would have tried to do to me and my children. It will take little to provoke them; remind them why the Talaks need to be brought to heel. Let them see I may be battered and bruised, but I'm not ashamed or cowed. I'll enter as a warrior who's battled and won, not as a victim. It will stir both their indignation and pride, which will aid the emperor." Akim's bow hid both his shock and awe. "Akim, we will ride at the head of the column. Tav and Rada, you'll ride behind us. My family will be proudly on display – undaunted. Rada, this is your test. BC must behave! No kicking or biting! Can you do it?"

"I think so."

"No 'I think so.' Do it, or I'll sell him at the first meat market I come to."

Rada gulped. "Yes, Mami."

"Good girl."

Over the next rise, the city of Dēbar, capital of Vēkaria, came into view at the end of a broad road that split the undulating countryside.

Rada gaped at the size of the city. "It must be twice as big as Bēdarik!"

"Bigger than that," Jadzia said.

"How long will it take to ride there?"

"At least several more days," Akim said. "Stilnassa, surely it is only necessary to ride into the capital? That will still serve your purpose."

"Akim, I know my mind. This is necessary."

He moved closer to her horse and held its reins. He whispered, "You're unwell and you are not improving." Jadzia avoided his gaze. "You know it. It's that finger, isn't it? It must come off." Her jaw clenched. "You will kill yourself. Why? All this will be for nothing. What will happen to Rada? A life with Bashtan? The baby?"

"I will not become a cripple. They will not see me as weak."

"A cripple!" He struggled to keep his voice low. "You fight for the life and rights of your baby, who'll never walk properly, who will face more challenges than you've ever known." His voice rose. "You hypocrite! It's a finger! One finger! You will recover. You, of all people, can cope and be stronger for it. And it shall be your badge of courage; a reminder to all of your dauntlessness. But, no, you are being a coward. They'll remember you as weak. You'll lose your reputation. They will have won."

The stillness of the grave entrapped the group. Not a whisper of sound escaped the riders and horses. The imperial guard sat, emotionless masks on their faces.

"Are you finished?"

"Yes."

Jadzia opened her mouth to say more, but Rada cut her off.

"Mami, it's all right," Rada murmured, snapping Jadzia's attention to her, Tav, and the baby. "Mstislav loves the brave."

"He does indeed, Stilniat Rada." Akim arched his brow at Jadzia.

Rada and Tav moved into formation behind them, and the column moved forward.

Amid the chink of harness and the rumble of the carriage wheels, quiet conversation returned amongst the riders.

Eyes ahead, Jadzia whispered harshly, "I won't tolerate another such outburst. My finger is healing and you—" She ground her teeth before continuing, "you have caused only more worry for a girl who has seen enough."

"Mami?"

"Rada, there should be a healer in the next village. I will consult with her there. All will be well."

CHAPTER 26

KATYA LEANED OVER THE table in Jadzia's suite, staring down at the plans for the new apartment the architect had drawn up according to Jadzia's wishes. A soft knock sounded on the double doors of the room.

"Enter."

The castellan edged the door open and closed it with barely a click.

Katya continued to stare at the plans, anxiety twisting at her gut. Would he have news of Jadzia? She feared if she looked up and met his eyes, she would see the truth. So, she stared at the diagram as if her gaze could set it afire when what she really wanted was to burn this whole Talak monstrosity to the ground.

With each nearing footstep, her hand fisted and her breath came in sharp, shallow bursts.

"Mistress Katya."

"That's Stilnassa Katya to you."

The castellan dipped his head in acknowledgement and withdrew one step. "I have information to report."

"About Jadzia?" The words were brittle enough to break.

"No. Bashtan."

Katya expelled a long, low breath before sitting. She gestured for the castellan to sit and poured him a glass of peppermint tea, handing it to him with a tight smile by way of apology.

"Lord Eadan escorted Mistress Neeren home the other day," the castellan said.

"I know. Neeren was damn near thrown out of the room and has been sulking since."

"They're not speaking."

"I know, too, that he spent some time with Bashtan. It's that conversation I want to hear," Katya said.

"Bashtan was planning to fetch Mistress Rada home. Cēdar is in Bēdarik. They cleared the room of slaves, so none can be sure what they said. When the talk became heated, the gardener overhead fragments of conversation outside the private courtyard walls, as did a slave in the corridor. Piecing it together, Eadan gave Bashtan an ultimatum of some kind. Since then, the commander has been quietly organising supplies for at least ten men."

"What type? For how many days do you think?"

"Dried goods: beans, charqui, dried fruit, flat breads. They're travelling light. No supply wagons."

"And I'd guess fast. So probably off to find Rada. Meanwhile, the household troops...?"

"Are training as if war will break out."

"He's no hero. I'll warrant he won't commit until he knows who the winner will be, and use Rada as an excuse to vacillate with Eadan."

"Poor child would be better off wherever she is."

⟶

"What about Lord Eadan's offer?"

"Damn Eadan's offer. I want my daughter back safe."

"But you could be on the new ruling council and save your position. You could save us! What about your other children?" Neeren's pitch rose with each word like a boiler about to explode. "Have you considered them? What will happen here, to us, without you, when Eadan finds out?"

Bashtan grabbed her arm and she winced in pain. "Shut up, you stupid woman! You've not been listening. I'm taking my personal guard only and leaving in the dead of night. I'm leaving Macario in charge. He knows what to do. If Eadan is watching this house, he will see our troops being readied and intensely trained. He'll think that I will side with him."

"But..."

"No, Neeren! If I find Rada and discover the emperor is truly dead, I may side with Eadan. By then, we'll know if reinforcements are coming from our neighbours."

"You're risking everything!"

"When he discovers I've left, tell him I've gone to retrieve my daughter. If I am to follow him, I need my child safe with me and not behind enemy lines."

"Rada is most likely the emperor's bastard, just like the last one."

Bashtan slapped her. "Enough! I have raised her! Rada is mine, and you will never speak of this again. You continue to disappoint me."

She hung her head. "I meant no disrespect. I worry for our family. Rada will most likely be safer where she is."

"Neeren!"

"But if you choose to go, my lord, I will support you. If you do not support Eadan now, so be it. But..."

"I must know if Eadan is telling the truth. He is a blind patriot, and he's made it clear he regards me as an upstart. Nothing is guaranteed. I also don't believe they can win against the Zaragarians. Tikhon was popular. Even if some of their old guard didn't like how he took power, they liked the return to the old ways he represented. Tikhon is... was more like Aitor I than anyone realises. If he's alive, Tikhon will see the fires of the Ebatov rain down on us if we rebel. If he's dead? Well, either way, they will be back. We're their link to the rest of Penīdīen. All their trade comes through here."

Neeren opened her mouth to speak.

"NO!" Bashtan shook his head and rubbed at his temples. "Don't you understand? There is no good choice here! One way or another, war is coming! We will be on the winning side, providing you don't use your brilliant intellect to throw us into the fire! You will sit tight and wait for my return."

⟶

Katya knelt in obeisance in the Temple of Bethsinidar in the Darklinan compound. At the sound of running feet, she rose to see Silla, Tav's second-in-command, breathless in the doorway. "Report."

"My lady, there's talk Stilnassa Jadzia and Rada are dead. There are rumours all over the city of their slaughter in an ambush by General Rodan!"

Katya stood silently, eyes closed, hands clenched. Many more feet pounded down the corridor and a group of grotty urchins lingered in the doorway.

"Is it true?"

Katya waded through the clamouring crowd and walked to the dining area; they trailed in her wake. "Look, we've got *rumours*. It would make sense with all the increased activity we've been seeing that something was... is afoot. But we don't know they're dead. The Stilnassa is tough, and Rada can cause more trouble than any other child in existence. So, let's just focus on what's happening here. Let's do our job for Jadzia. Have you all reported to Silla? Good, then outside with you. Silla, I need today's updates."

Silla bowed deeply. "Yes, Stilnassa Katya."

"You needn't bow to me. Now give me the daily roundup."

Silla delivered the latest observations from the network. "That is all, Stilnassa." Silla turned to go, but Katya stopped her.

"No, don't go. We'll discuss this."

"But I'm not—"

"I need a second-in-charge who can think and plan. I realise this may not have been asked of you previously, but Tav may be dead, as may be our Jadzia. We both must step up and continue their work. So, what skills you don't know, I will teach you. Can you read and write?"

"Yes, a little. Tav taught me."

"Well, we'll continue. Over the last week, we've had ten of the wealthiest families; no, correction, fifteen noble houses out of thirty, gathering. Gods they're like rabbits, aren't they?"

"Rats more like," Silla mumbled.

"Mmm, fifteen noble houses all meeting," Katya mused.

"All. I mean, they all had parties or whatever, but it's not just them. There've been more social calls made in the last few days than we've ever seen and between families who would never give each other the time of day. Merchants and nobles having social chats, being best buddies. At least six merchants closed shop and left on restocking trips to Matyran."

"Smart enough to run and not pick a side. Let's start with Neeren," Katya said.

"She had a long visit with Lady Chandar before Lady Jadzia left, and also after."

"Yes, and after the last visit, Lord Eadan escorted her home. I always told Jadzia she dismissed Neeren too easily. And Neeren knew Jadzia's route."

"We've not been able to identify everyone who entered Chandar's Villa."

"But we should be able to cross-reference from spies in other houses. Come, you can help me."

"Stilnassa Katya, that's not—"

"Still saying that's not your place? We've had more scurrying about in this city in the last week than ever. It's clear alliances are being made. Good work, keep watch."

"Oh, there's one more thing, and it's really strange," Silla said.

"What?"

"I heard one merchant telling a customer all of his gold cloth had run out. I thought nothing of it, but I tailed her and every stall she went to said the same thing. No gold cloth."

Katya's face fell. "Evika!" She handed Silla her coin purse. "Stock up on food, get as much here as you can *discretely*. Stuff that will keep a long time. Talk to Demenka. I'll get more money for you tomorrow. I need to get word to Master Pavel." Before Silla could ask why, Katya said, "Gold is the colour of the old king. We're going to war."

CHAPTER 27

THE RIDERS DESCENDED THE sloping road and entered the small village. The soil of the central square was churned into powder and their horses' hooves cast pale clouds of dust into the air, which eddied around their mounts.

Rada sneezed.

Akim dismounted beside a well, but before he could draw water, a sharp nasally voice said, "If you want water for your horses, you have to head down to the river."

"Are you denying the emperor's own?" Akim demanded.

"I'm not denying anyone. I'm just saving you're wasting energy. The well is dry. You'll have to wait for it to refill. The bloody Firsts were here. So many of the buggers they damn near raised a dust storm. Well, at least they had the sense to go to the river. The rest have got brains the size of a peanut! The supply wagons, lazy buggers, didn't want to trek for water. On a mission, they said, didn't have time to go bashing through the scrub when a fine supply of water was just here. Cocky pricks, they are. Always have been. So, the silly buggers tried to fill here and drained the well." The skinny, sun-brown man with saggy, wrinkled skin and a bush of snow-white hair hawked gob of phlegm and spat. He laughed. "Evikan fools! They drained the well and then had to take the wagons down to the stream anyway! I tried to tell them there's an evikan road. But did they listen? No. Whiny bunch. Not breeding 'em as tough as they used to."

"But the Firsts are the meant to be the best!" Rada said. Several throats cleared around her and she reddened. "They are second only to the imperial guard!"

A couple of quiet chuckles greeted this along with a murmured, "Exactly."

At this, the old man raked his eyes across the troupe before him. "At least you lot look like you've earned the dust and scars that come from a hard journey and damn harder fight."

The entire unit levelled steely gazes at him and, to his credit, he didn't flinch, just spat again.

"Do you have a healer in this village?" Akim asked.

"Depends."

"On what?"

"On how bad you need one?" His canny eye rested on Jadzia. "There's old Biny, but she's older than me and damn near blind. Her great-granddaughter, Bree, is still learning, but we make do with her for most things."

"Most things?" Jadzia asked.

"Well, some things is beyond her. And then... well, what happens depends on how desperate you are. You die, or..." He spat again. "Or you see the Sennerese chit. Lives way out in the woods." He nodded in the road's direction down which the army had gone. "Keeps to herself, thank the gods. We don't need her type around here."

"Sennerese? What is a woman from the Senner Ilse doing on the mainland?" Akim asked.

The old man shrugged. "Don't know. Don't care. Long as she leaves me alone. She says they kicked her out, but once a spider lover, always a spider lover. We should have wiped them out an age ago."

"Where will we find Bree?" Akim asked.

"With everyone else down by the river goggling at the Firsts."

"How will we recognise her?"

"She's about this high, long brown hair in a braid. Slim."

"Is that all?" Akim fingers drummed an impatient rhythm on the pommel of his saddle.

Rada stood in her stirrups, scowled, kicked her feet from them and stood atop the saddle.

Jadzia laughed. "Akim, let's go down to the river. Rada wants to goggle."

The track opened up to a broad field flattened by the Firsts and littered with rows of campsites that were being packed up. Horses lined the broad, sandy riverbank as they dipped their heads to drink.

Tav and Rada gaped. Tav sat straight but looked self-consciously at the babe strapped to his chest. Jadzia smiled at him, "You have a most important duty, Tav, but rest assured, when we reach Vēkaria, I will engage a sword master for both you and Rada. Your training will begin in earnest and you will feel less like a nanny. Remember how important your role is. Remember, my daughters live thanks to you."

Rada spun in the saddle. "What about me?"

Jadzia rolled her eyes. "And you. You are a team, but without Tav, you would have failed. Listen, both of you. These are not the imperial guard who know you. This is a large army, full of all sorts, and you will both stay with this group and the guard. Do not stray."

They rode on.

"A sword master for the boy? Is there something I should be aware of about him?" Akim murmured.

"No... Not yet," Jadzia whispered. With a grin, she said, "Maybe never."

"There's so many," Rada said.

"Yes," Jadzia said, squinting. "And they don't appear as if they've had a rush journey. Akim?"

He glanced away. "I'm merely a guard, Stilnassa, not privy to the emperor's plans."

"That's convenient." Jadzia stopped a passing soldier. "Tell me, when did you depart Dēbar?"

He looked at Akim, who sighed and nodded. "Tell Stilnassa Maklova."

His eyes widened and he gulped. "We left over a week ago, pursuing bandits in the hills." Jadzia snorted. "Then we formed up here."

"All of you for bandits?"

"Different groups in various spots. Others made their way here being on manoeuvres."

"Well played, Tikhon." Her lips formed a tight line.

"Can we go closer?" Rada asked.

They moved on with Rada twisting and turning in the saddle, gawping at the surrounding host. "Which ones are the Firsts?"

"Those wearing deep-blue cloaks."

"What's the black mean?"

"The black capes are Mstislavakan."

"They've got black swirly bits on their armour too... fancy."

"Yes," Akim said. "They like being fancy. The grey cloaks are enlisted men and women in the regulars. Any silver insignia, regardless of unit, denotes an officer."

"What about the ones with red on their cloaks?"

"Think of them as being like the city watch," Akim said.

Rada screwed up her face. "Why does an army need them? Don't they watch everything anyway?"

"They deal with soldiers who step out of line."

"Step out of...?"

"Misbehave, Rada," Jadzia said. "They bring those who behave in ways unbecoming, or those who do wrong before the officers for punishment."

"Do they fight too?"

"Fiercely, they are all dedicants of the Order," Akim said.

A small group of men and women stood together, lightly armoured in leather lamellar breastplates and multicoloured cloaks of grey and pale brown with a small blue insignia on their collars. Rada opened her mouth to speak and Akim cut her off. "They are trackers and scouts. The blue shows their elite status."

As they rode, groups of riders were wheeling off from the water's edge and reforming in columns in the vacated sections of the field as campsites folded. At the far end of the open ground, a larger dark tent was being dismantled and a cluster of officers stood talking animatedly with a lone soldier in the imperial guard blue. Upon seeing them, the speaker broke off, mounted and rode to Akim.

Face flushed and his eyes glistening with excitement, he asked. "Do you have further orders?"

"None, other than make haste."

The young soldier stepped back, indignation flitting across his face. "Cut it out," Akim chided. "If you've delivered your orders as you should, any delay is not your fault. You," the word jabbed toward him, "are merely the messenger."

"I..." He reddened but controlled himself as Akim's brows rose and his fingers drummed against his thigh. "I passed on the emperor's orders verbatim and though it may seem we are all here, over a third of the company has filtered out."

"But we didn't see them," Rada said. The soldier ignored her. "Akim?" Her voice quavered.

Akim lent forward in his saddle. "Humour me, explain to our Stilniat Rada."

"Forgive me, Stilnassa," he said to Jadzia. "Er... Stilniat Rada, forgive me." Rada nodded, wide-eyed, with no idea of the power game being played here. "You see, the emperor is brilliant. These troops arrived here in groups, some in the day, many at night and from a wide range of locations. No one in the capital would expect them all to come together. And since the emperor's new orders, they have left to reach him in the same manner."

"Hiding from spies!" Rada said, startled. "There are spies in the capital?"

"Emperors who live the longest assume there are spies everywhere," Jadzia said. "Whether from rivals, or other rulers, or those who've forgotten they lost and their best days are behind them."

"Talak?" Rada frowned, her gaze troubled and thoughtful. Her usual litany of questions died as she exclaimed, "Mami, that's our coat of arms!"

"Where?" Jadzia turned her gaze in the direction Rada pointed. "That can only mean one thing. Your Uncle Dimitri is here."

"Oh! I have an Uncle Dimitri? Can we say hello?"

"No." The sound slapped the child. "We do not have time."

"But... Have I ever met him?"

"No, and with any luck you won't," Jadzia murmured. "He and I are not on the best terms."

Rada stared at the emblem fluttering from the black tent, face contorted in thought. "What's the other symbol?"

"Mstislav as the god of death, though I doubt you've seen that depiction."

"His sword looks like... a bone? What's happened to his fingernails? They're long, like... knives? I get why he's standing on a skull." She scratched her head. "But I don't see how any of the rest can work. I like the one in temple better."

Jadzia laughed. "True. It belongs to the Mstislavakan. Your uncle is their preceptor. Akim, hopefully he won't realise we're here. Let's find a clear, quiet spot away from all this to water our horses."

"As you wish, Stilnassa, but we should find that healer as well."

"Akim, you're like a dog with a bone."

"So my wife says as well."

Jadzia chuckled. "Probably the least she says? What was the description of the healer, about so high, with long brown hair in a braid, slim?"

Groups of villagers stood arrayed where they could survey the might of the Firsts. Amongst them were many young women, almost universally with long brown hair in braids. "This must be all the people from this village and every other village nearby. So much for the discretion of Tikhon's Firsts. Well, if you rule out the chubby ones, and there's few of them, that's a start. Good luck finding the healer amongst this lot."

Adana spoke up. "I'll find her, Stilnassa, and bring her to you." She rode off to question the villagers.

Akim cantered away and questioned an officer in the distance who gesticulated directions. On his return, they headed through the middle of the camp. Riding past the tent of the Mstislavakan, Jadzia's eyes remained fixed ahead. Rada, however, craned her neck, trying to take in their banner.

They followed a narrow path through long grass and rushes. "They did not use this section. We should be out of sight and left in peace."

The horses' hooves sank into thick mud as they crossed the run-off of a spring, its many fingers trickling to the river. Rada squealed as BC bunched his haunches and thrust out of the bog. They pushed forward toward the tree line. Akim stood beside Jadzia's horse. With one hand, he held its reins while he held out an arm. "If you can swing off, I'll catch you."

"My thanks, I have the balance of a duck with a broken leg. You may need two hands."

Akim dropped the reins, reached up and gripped her waist, supporting her as she dismounted. On the ground, she leaned against the side of the horse, shaking. "Was it worth it?" Akim asked.

"Yes," she said, though a wry, pain filled grin crossed her face. "I am nothing if not proud; today they saw a Zaragarian Stilnassa unbowed and undefeated by the enemy."

The guard took the horses to the water and Jadzia sank to the ground, resting her back against a tree. Tav passed her the baby, who was fussing. "Tav, relieve Regansh with the watering of the horses. I'll need her help here."

Rada sat next to her mother, caressing her sister's downy hair; she leaned forward and placed a kiss on her head. "I can help, Mami."

"All right, unbutton my shirt. Good, we need to unwrap your sister a little– we have her laced in."

"For safety!"

"Yes, of course. Can your nimble fingers release her?"

Rada lay her sister along her legs and bent to her task. She looked up from unbinding the child, pulled a face at her, leaning close and made popping noises with a finger in her mouth, startling the newborn whose head lolled sideways, her dark eyes filling her face.

Rada giggled. "She's a bit weird. Her head's as floppy as a rag doll and she doesn't look in the right place."

"You were the same. When you're tiny, the world takes a little while to figure out."

"I can hold her while you feed her."

"Regansh is here. She can help. I think after a day in the saddle, your arms might tire. I'd like you to rest."

"Not tired."

━━━▶

Rada dug holes in the dirt with the heel of her boot and eyed the tall feathery grass nodding in the breeze. She sprang to her feet and ran to a clump before using her dagger to pick a handful and moving onto a patch of wild black and yellow daisies. Once back in the shade, she set to work, deftly weaving stalks together, her brow knit in concentration. With a grin, she flourished her finished product. Rada darted back to her mother and crowned her with the floral tribute.

"Harvest Crown?"

Rada shrugged. "No. Just a crown. I think you deserve it."

"I thank you for your gracious gift," Jadzia said.

"I made one for Bubba too." Rada lowered the second grassy halo and scowled, her shoulders slumping when she realised it was far too big. "I got it wrong. Her head is teeny tiny."

"Will it fit you?" Regansh asked.

"I don't think so. I tried to make it teeny for Bubba."

Regansh flicked her fingers. "Here, pass it to me and sit. I think I can make it work. Can you manage for a moment, Stilnassa?"

"Rada can help support the baby for a moment," Jadzia said.

"Yes!" Rada knelt and assisted her mother.

Regansh ran her fingers through Rada's hair, separating out sections, and plaiting a series of braids that intertwined with the floral circlet.

"There! Done!" she said.

Rada reached up and patted her hair, tracing her fingers along the interwoven braids and crown. "Wow! Thank you, Stilnassa Regansh. Have to see!" Rada raced to the river's edge and bent over the water, turning her head from side to side. "I can't see it properly." She pouted.

"It looks beautiful," Jadzia said.

"Thank you, Mami," Rada said with an exaggerated bow.

"Yes, beautiful indeed. Like a perfect little flower of Talak," a deep voice said. A tall, lean man deeply tanned with a pockmarked face, stepped out of a gap in the rushes. "Did you think I would not see you, Jadzia? The runner from Emperor Tikhon said you'd be arriving with an escort of imperial guards, although from the look of you, it appears they have not been terribly effective."

Every guard assigned to Jadzia stiffened and turned to him in outrage.

"Ignore him. My brother was ever the tease. That we are alive at all is due only to their dedication."

"And some fine archery from yourself, I believe. You see, I hear all."

The hair on Rada's arms was standing up and a queasy knot formed in her belly. This was her uncle? She marched over and stood at her mother's shoulder, putting herself between them. "Hello, Uncle, I'm Rada."

"I thought this little flower of Talak beauty might be my niece." He bowed with a theatrical flourish of his hands.

Rada narrowed her eyes at him. "I'm not little!" She wrenched the floral circlet from her head, sending the intricate braids awry. "I'm going to be an imperial guard. I've already started training." She rested her hand on her dagger.

Dimitri's lips twitched. "Really, little Mistress? Is that dagger a gift from your escort? Such weapons must be earned. Honestly, Jadzia, to give a little girl such a gift! You'll spoil her! She'll expect that her position, such as it is, will get her whatever she wants."

Rada stood silent and scarlet, her hands clenching and unclenching above her dagger.

"Rada!" Jadzia barked out her name. "I forbid you to make your uncle your next kill."

"Kill?" Dimitri laughed, but then sobered when confronted with the serious nods of Akim and the others. "Really?" He bent forward, scrutinising her.

"I wouldn't get too close. She stabbed one through the eye with a stick," Regansh said.

"And knocked Rodin's eyeball out with her sling shot at twenty paces," Akim added. "What's more, I don't think she likes you."

"Well, that must be some kind of record for a Talak child."

Rada stamped her foot. "I'm not little! I earned this! Uncle Tikhon said so! You can't have it!" Dimitri stepped backward, hands raised. She scowled at him, hands on hips. "Mami, can I go for a walk? I need to go for a walk, or I might say something bad."

"Go, but not far," Jadzia said.

Rada stalked away.

"Well, Dimitri, you've made a friend there," Jadzia said

"The opinions of a child, let alone a Talak, carry no weight with me. You, more than anyone else, should understand what they are like."

Jadzia narrowed her eyes at him. "She is half Zaragarian and under law has all the rights of a full blood."

He snorted in derision. "At the moment..." He paused, then raised his brow and surprise. "You haven't told her there's a difference? You've done her no favours raising her in ignorance."

"She knows there are small-minded people who do not understand the overwhelming influence of Zaragarian blood – our blood, my blood – but she has been raised to know her worth and her correct station."

A faint smile twisted into a snarl on his face. "Small minds? Those words could be easily misconstrued."

"Oh, Dimitri, just stop! We are all servants of Mstislav here and should you question her, Rada will satisfy even you with her loyalty and devotion. All you need is to ask Master Pavel, and he will attest to this."

"There's a reason Pavel is in Talak – he's more tolerant of their kind."

"No, Dimitri, he is there because a powerful presence of the Order was needed and he has done his job." Dimitri remained quiet, thoughtful. "So, did you merely come here to insult my daughter, or did some freak of brotherly affection draw you here?"

"Truce?"

Jadzia ignored this overture.

"So be it. I came to see your new arrival. Rumour travels fast, sister, that you've given birth to the emperor's bastard; the only one." He knelt beside her and watched the baby feed. "She looks strong." He moved to brush the baby's cheek and Jadzia shifted sideways, preventing him.

"She is strong," came her abrupt reply.

He canted his head, eyes narrowing. "Good and no one will mistake her as a Talak. But why did you travel with her so soon after your lying-in? Surely you realised the dangers?"

"It's been too long since I've been home and my duty is done."

Lines around his eyes tightened as he listened. "The old emperor and our father dealt you a bad hand, but you've made more from it than anyone alive could."

She inclined her head. "Do I hear respect?"

"Let's not go too far. Now, I must head back. Hopefully, my stray young charges have returned and readied themselves."

"Stray? You've lost them?"

He laughed. "Of course not. You know how young men are; they'll be off amusing themselves. They're loyal to a fault and most likely waiting for me."

CHAPTER 28

DIRTY FROM DAYS OF riding and camping, Bashtan and his guards reined their horses in at the sight of their scout signalling them from a clearing by the roadside.

Bashtan wrinkled his nose at the remains of the burn pile, where a charred hand lay reaching for the sky.

"This is where they camped and the battle fought," the scout said.

"Yes, but we don't know who won," Bashtan said.

"There's no wreckage."

"They could have used the carriage to fuel the pyre," Bashtan said. "We'll ride on to the next village and ask if they've seen them. If they haven't, then maybe Rodan has her. We'll just have to find him."

"That may commit us to war."

"I don't care. I'm not prepared to give up on finding my daughter. The day is nearly done. We'll camp here."

Once they'd settled for the night, Bashtan lay on his bedroll. Rada was so keen to leave with her mother. A spark of anger flared in him, quickly quelled by guilt. He dwelt on all the times he'd lost his temper, but she was so unruly! The Zaragarian in her needed taming. A smack never hurt. He'd had plenty of them. The boys had left as soon as they could to join the army, without so much as a backward glance. Jadzia made sure their eldest daughter, Abaya, had married into a family in Nējarak. Abaya never caused trouble; she was the sweetest. Jadzia made sure they all left.

"Bitch," he murmured. "Hokati protect my home and rid me of her."

The guard on watch pretended not to hear, preferring to huddle into his cloak and listen to the sounds of the night.

In the forest, one of Tikhon's scouts rose and headed back to his master.

⟶

Neeren greeted Lord Eadan in her husband's study. "Lord Eadan, so nice of you to take time to come during this difficult period."

"Of course, Lady Neeren." The polite smile never reached his eyes. "Given that you are such a good friend," he said; Neeren simpered. "I will do you the honour of getting straight to the point." His smile vanished. "Where has your husband gone?"

"H-He's gone to find Rada and bring her home."

"I see. What about our cause? What about helping to rid Talak of these bastards?" Eadan strolled the room, eying in the furnishings appreciatively, picking up precious ornaments as if appraising them.

Neeren stood tall and looked at him indignantly. "He has left the bulk of our household troops here, taking only his personal guard with him. Those that remain train every day."

"Really? That is interesting, but your husband fled."

"He has not fled. He is looking for his daughter, whom he loves very much."

"His Zaragarian daughter."

"Yes, gods help me. I cannot stand the girl, but I find I cannot fault a man for loving his child."

"Mmm, we'll see. General Cēdar has assured me things will change for children like her under our new rule, so you should not worry on that front."

"Change?"

"Yes, they will all be disinherited under the law. They and their mothers are being rounded up as we speak. So, you see, your children will receive all the benefits of this estate."

Her eyes widened and a faint smile crossed her lips. "I've no objection, but you'll have to work upon Bashtan."

"Never mind him. Rodan has probably killed the girl anyway."

"Killed her?"

"Of course. Surely you realised that?"

"Well...I hoped. I mean... it's just that she's only a child. She's half Talak. With the right training she could be brought around and..." Neeren bit her lip, her gut clenched. "Jadzia was one thing, but I hoped —"

Eadan shook his head. "Wake up, Lady Neeren. Did they spare Rodan's family?"

"No. No they didn't," she whispered.

"This is war. You did the right thing for your country. All you did was provide information. You are not responsible for the actions of others."

Neeren nodded, one hand over her mouth while the other pressed her stomach trying to quell her rising nausea. *I'm not responsible. I didn't kill her. I would've helped her had she lived and treated her as my own. This is not my doing.*

"The others? Once you imprison them all, what are you planning to do with them?" Neeren asked. *They kill them too. Hokati, help me – redeem me. I have one chance.*

Eadan shrugged. "We've not decided."

"Why not sell them in the slave markets of Rēsphia? You'll never need to worry about them again and they'll turn a pretty coin too."

Eadan laughed. "You are ruthless, aren't you? It's an excellent idea."

The knot of guilt inside her unravelled. *They'll live.* "Have you heard from General Rodan?"

"No, but I've no doubt he is making his way here as we speak and gathering forces from the loyal Talaks in the countryside. I suppose that leaves you in charge?"

"Yes," she said with a hint of pride.

"Excellent! Someone with some sense and courage to work with."

Neeren blushed.

"I'll need your household troops turned over to me," Eadan said.

For a fraction of a second, she hesitated, recalling Bashtan's words. *No! I am right about this. My instincts are correct. This is our chance... my chance to prove my worth. I've had enough!* "Come, I'll introduce you to Macario. Bashtan left him in command of the household guard."

Together they made their way to the barracks, where Macario was training the men.

"Macario," Neeren said. "Lord Bashtan has left me explicit instructions in his absence, and I am now putting the household guard at Lord Eadan's disposal. It is time we Talaks took back our country."

Macario stood at attention and bowed to Lord Eadan. "We are at your disposal, Lord Eadan. The men will be up to the task."

Eadan smiled. "I know. Your reputation precedes you. Your strong arms and blades will be instrumental in freeing Talak."

Neeren beamed. "I shall send the chancellor to you both, for I am sure that there will be more you require from this household and he will take care of it. I shall personally help hang the gold of our old king from the windows, so all of Bēdarik will see them and know we are true patriots."

"There is one more thing," Lord Eadan said. "Where is Jadzia's servant Katya? We have a special fate for her."

⟶

Bashtan woke to the sound of metal hitting the ground and the press of cold steel against his throat. His eyes flew open.

"Good morning, Bashtan," Tikhon said, giving him a nudge with his boot.

"My Emperor," Bashtan croaked, rolling over and prostrating himself before Tikhon. "How have I offended?"

Tikhon spat on the ground. "That would take forever. Get up."

Bashtan rolled to his knees, saw his entire guard disarmed and some of Tikhon's troops cooking breakfast with his supplies. His face bloomed red and his hands fisted; his men hung their heads.

"Don't be too hard on them," Darcov said, munching on a piece of spicy, smoked sausage. "We're very good at what we do. This is superb. Your own pigs?" Bashtan nodded. "Thought so. The recipe tastes—"

"Enough, Darcov," Tikhon laughed. "Now is not the time for your culinary critique."

One of Tikhon's guard ensured Bashtan was unarmed and removed the weapons near his bedroll, placing them on a pile away from the camp.

"Now, Bashtan, what are you doing here?"

"Looking for Rada. Rumour is rife in Bēdarik that you and Jadzia were killed by Rodan and that he has Rada."

"So, you came to join Rodan?"

"No! No, I came for my daughter."

"But by logic you'd have to meet Rodan and—"

"I have no idea where Rodan is," Bashtan snapped.

Several guards took a step toward him. Tikhon forestalled them with a wave of this hand.

"Rodan attacked Jadzia's group. He is dead. You should know he was planning to kill them all, including Rada. We saved them. Rada and the baby are alive and with Jadzia. They should have reached Dēbar by now."

Bashtan's shoulders slumped. "Thank the gods. I prayed to Hokati to keep her safe."

Tikhon nodded. "I'm sure you prayed equally hard the other two were dead."

Bashtan glared at him. "Yes."

Tikhon punched him in the face, knocking him to the ground.

"Can we just kill him?" Darcov asked.

"Not yet. Get him up. You are going to tell me how Rodan knew where Jadzia was. Someone had to get word to him."

Two of the guard held Bashtan, kneeling, before the flames.

"He's right-handed," Tikhon said.

Darcov, wearing thick gloves, grabbed Bashtan's right hand in his and held it close to the fire.

"Did you pass information to Rodan regarding Jadzia's trip?" Tikhon asked.

"No," Bashtan said. At a nod from Tikhon, Darcov raked coals forward and held Bashtan's hand on them. Bashtan howled in pain. "I told no one!"

Darcov pulled Bashtan's hand back, wrinkling his nose at the smell of burning flesh. "Smells like roast pig."

"Did someone in your household do this? For you, perhaps?"

"No!"

He screamed and writhed, trying to break the guards' hold. "No! I... I don't... perhaps."

Darcov released Bashtan's hand from the coals. "Who?" he said.

Bashtan whimpered. Veins stood out on his neck as he rocked back and forth.

"Who?" Darcov roared at him.

"Maybe... Neeren. She's a gossip and visits women like Lady Chandar. She may have said something. I did not. Why would I? You were going to let us separate. I'd no need to want her dead."

"You'd like the babe dead though."

"Yes, but how many of them die naturally before they are grown anyway? And I'd made it plain to all that she wasn't mine." He cast a resentful glare at Tikhon.

Darcov grabbed him by the neck and shoved his face near the fire.

"Darcov, let him up. I'll deal with Neeren later. Now, Bashtan, tell me the state of affairs in Bēdarik. How were things when you left?"

"Nothing had changed, Your Majesty," Bashtan said, tears rolling down his face as he cradled his hand.

"Nothing? Would you like your other hand in the fire too?"

Bashtan hung his head, then straightened and looked Tikhon in the eye. "There was rejoicing in a few quarters, but none are out on the streets dancing or planning to revolt. It would be foolhardy of them to even consider it," he said. "There is no match for the might of the Zaragarian army and there is still the presence of the Order."

"Good, you'll return with me."

"My Emperor, I want my daughter back. She did not have permission to go."

"There'll be time for reunions later, Bashtan. Though when you meet her, you'll find her changed. Your daughter fought and killed in defence of her family. Her journey as a warrior has begun. Eat, Bashtan, we'll head out soon. Darcov, come with me."

They walked some distance from the camp.

"He has to be lying."

"Yes, if not, why even mention revolt?"

"What are you going to do with him?"

"Let him hang himself. If we could get to Katya, we'd know exactly what was going on, but I doubt a Zaragarian at the moment would get in undetected."

"What about Pavel? Surely, he'd send word."

"Pavel wasn't aware of my plans. He only had a holding force at the temple. I sent the rest to track down Cēdar. If rebellion is in the winds, then he's probably going to concentrate on holding the temple. They can last there for a long time."

Darcov grunted.

"We'll meet up with the army, keep that idiot with us so he doesn't let on that I'm alive, then see what mischief the Talaks manage in the interim. When they've got their courage up and revealed themselves, we'll put them down and ensure they never rise again. Like my father should have done years ago."

CHAPTER 29

RADA STOOD ON THE riverbank casting stones across the water. "Evika! Not again! Tav said this was easy!" Peering at the stones littered on the ground, she said, "Maybe, it needs to be flat. Ah! There!" She seized a pebble and turned it over. "You seem good." Closing her eyes, she whispered a prayer. "Mstislav... er..." Looking over her shoulder and seeing no one, she continued, "Bethsinidar?" She waited, expectant. With a sigh she said, "Hokati?" Her shoulders slumped. "Anyone will do. I just want the stupid stone to skip."

She waited, listening intently – only a lone raven cawed.

Rada growled, curling her lip in frustration. She leaned sideways, trying to make her torso horizontal to the water, drew her arm back and flung the stone with such force she toppled to the ground. Landing hard on the pebbled shore, she rubbed her arm. "Evika! Stupid! Stupid!" She rose and kicked a curtain of stones into the air.

"I don't think I've ever seen a child with so much fury inside her. Well, at least you're letting it out," said a chuckling, raspy voice. "Nothing worse than bottling things up. They say it cuts years off your life, so I guess you're going to be truly ancient."

Rada spun, looking in panic for the intruder but saw no one. The hair on her nape stood on end and a shiver ran down her spine. "Mstislav?... Beth... sin... idar?"

"Goodness, child, do the gods call on you often?"

Rada stood, slack jawed. "I... um..."

"Ow... Bloody damnation. Get over here, will you? I'm stuck."

"Probably not a god then," Rada murmured, but remained rooted to the spot. "Where? I can't see you." Rada's insides twisted like knotted rope.

The top of the shrub rustled. "Here."

Rada loaded her sling. She crept forward, veering left along the narrowing beach. An enormous amount of flood detritus – sticks, branches and a long dead tree – blocked her path. She pocketed her sling. "Higher ground. Uncle would say that's strategic. Up." She clambered over the mound, her feet slipping into holes and breaking small branches. At the top she balanced, wobbling, with her feet apart – one on a clump of clay embedded in a branch and the other resting on a limb no wider than her wrist. Her hands gripped a narrow branch. She took slow, shallow breaths, too scared to move.

"Oh, good grief! Child, what are you doing?"

"Higher ground," Rada said, letting out a squeak as the branch she held cracked, and gave way. She landed, on her belly, spreadeagled like a cat, one fatal move off testing her nine lives.

"Higher ground?"

"Strategic."

Another chuckle. "You must be Zaragarian. Though you don't look it. It'd be a lot more strategic if it was actually solid."

Rada grunted and turned to see an elderly woman staring up at her. Her smooth skin held a golden hue and her dark eyes were slanted. The only hint of her age was her steel grey hair, though many laugh lines creased the corners of her eyes.

"Why are you in the middle of a blackberry patch?" Rada asked.

The old woman pursed her lips, holding up purple stained fingers. "The berries were best here, of course."

Rada looked at the plump dark berries remaining on the bushes and her stomach rumbled. "I like blackberries too. Our garden has a patch of raspberries and blueberries, but I'm not allowed in there anymore."

"Why?"

"It doesn't matter."

"Oh, well, if you help me, you can have some. My plait is stuck in this bramble. I can't reach behind me to untangle it."

"Why not? My arms would do it."

"You are quite a bit younger than me."

"Yes. But—"

"Old people are often not as flexible as the young, surely you've seen that," came a whiplash reply.

"I don't know many old people. How do I get to you?"

"You could slide down. You'd be straight in here."

Canes with thorns like a million little daggers poked up at Rada. "Er... no. You'll be all right. Just cut your hair."

The woman narrowed her eyes. "Cut my hair. Never! We from the Senner Isle do not cut our hair. I should have known a little girl, and a Zaragarian at that, would not help me."

"I'm not little!"

"Since you're up there, crawl along the pile you're on to the end of the trunk and clamber down the base. Push through some tea tree in this direction and from there you will see a deer trail. They've been coming in for the berries. Buggers got the best ones too."

"You had to go into the middle," Rada muttered as she crawled along the pile of rubble, standing as she neared the bole of the tree and the clay encrusted roots. From the vantage point she spied the deer trail on the other side of a dense cluster of spiny-leaved shrubs with small pink flowers. She climbed down the exposed ball like it was a ladder.

Rada pushed her way through the prickly undergrowth trying to reach the deer trail. She snapped off branches that clawed at her. "Why am I always grubbing through the woods! At last!" Rada hit a clear path. "Right!"

"Hurry, child, I'm not getting any younger!"

"All right!" Rada jogged and slid to a stop in front of an enormous tangle of briars. "How did you even get in?"

"Crawled," came a mumbling, munching reply. "I knew the berries would be good."

Rada dropped to her knees and peered down the tunnel through the berry canes, bits of fur clung to the thorns from passing wildlife. "Even I'm not greedy enough to crawl through that." She unwound her grubby scarf from her neck and wrapped it around one hand to protect it. With her bound hand she gripped a cane, bending and cutting it with her dagger. Rada strove ahead, cutting a channel slightly wider than herself. Canes dug into her trousers, the material on her bound hand, and snagged her hair. She yanked, hacked and stomped on them.

Sweaty, strands of hair poking from her braid at all angles, her face scratched and her clothes askew, Rada stood before the woman. "Evika! I hope there's some berries for me!"

"Yes, of course." She handed Rada one.

"Is that it? Where's the rest?"

"Well, I had to do something while I waited."

Rada stamped her foot. "That's not fair. I worked hard." She held up her scratched hands.

The old woman grinned and passed Rada a small cloth bag. "Here."

With a scowl Rada took it and peered inside suspiciously. Her eyes lit up. "You lied," she said happily and stuffed a plump, dark-purple berry in her mouth. She reached in for another one.

"Before you get carried away, can you get my hair free?" Rada reached up with her dagger. "Don't cut my hair!"

Rada rolled her eyes. "I know! I won't." She stood on tiptoes. Her hand hovered in the air as she noticed the old spider webs clinging to the cane. A shudder ran through her body. "I'll cut the cane and you can fix your hair later," she said. "There. Done!" She flicked a spider web from her hand. "Erg! Let's get out of here!" Rada ran through the gap she'd hacked and stood bouncing on her toes. "Come on!"

The woman wound a bright scarf around her hair and made her way out.

"Why didn't you do that around your head the first time?"

"It slipped off." She sat down on a log. "What's your name, child?"

"Rada Lujza Ortakli. Daughter of Lord Bashtan Ortakli and Lady Jadzia Zora Maklova." Rada bowed. "What's yours?"

"Makiko."

"That's it? Nothing else."

Makiko chuckled. "The length of a name signifies nothing. How many lords have you met who were jackasses or as stupid as a stump."

Rada screwed her face up and scratched her chin. "Mmm some, but names have power."

"True names have power. Only The Weaver gives them."

Eyes wide, Rada looked over her shoulder. "Shh. You could get in trouble."

"I'm too old to worry or for anyone to bother with. Sit beside me for a bit while I wait. Here have some more berries."

Rada sat down and ate. "What are you waiting for?"

"A girl from the village. She has to collect an unguent from me."

"Huh?"

"An ointment. She's picking up an ointment. What do they teach you in school?"

"Hey! I'm only six! That sounds like a big word."

"Only six, but *not* little," Makiko said, eyes twinkling.

Rada stiffened, her back ramrod straight, hands fisted as she digested this comment. "Um... that's right. But I don't go to school. I've a tutor."

"Your parents should sack him or her."

"Well... to be fair. I hide from him. A lot. I've never met anyone from the Senner Isles."

"Sennerese is the correct term, but I'm not surprised. There's few on the mainland now and we avoid most folk. People fear us or hate us or both. It's not even safe if you are a dimashne." At Rada's puzzled expression, she explained. "One who has abandoned The Weaver and her ways."

"Why would someone fear you? You're old."

"And you're little..." Rada leapt to her feet and Makiko held up her hands. "Stop, let me finish. You're little, but I'll warrant you're not harmless. Little is just size, not what's in here." She touched Rada's chest. "In here you are a lioness, so hold that in your mind and don't get so angry every time."

"You're old, but... I suppose wise."

Makiko chuckled. "Well, thank you, I think."

A stick cracked and they both looked up to see a slim, young woman with a long, brown braid. At the sight of Rada, she turned to leave. "Wait, Bree," Makiko said. "Rada is fine. You don't need to worry. Here, come take the unguent. It must be placed on the cut several times daily, then bandaged until the skin has closed." Bree snatched the clay jay with a trembling hand. "Good grief, girl, what ails you today?"

"The soldiers... they um..." She noticed Rada staring at her. "Never mind. It doesn't matter. I lost them. Thank you, Makiko. I wish we didn't have to meet like this... That you could just be a part of the village. They'd be so much better off with you healing them."

"Are you the healer? We were looking for you," Rada asked.

"Yes, but I'm only learning. Makiko is the real healer."

"Makiko, my Mami needs your help."

"There she is! I told you that pretty thing went this way."

Three young men in the black of the Mstislavakan stepped into the clearing. "And look who she has with her. An old Sennerese hag and a Talak brat."

"I'm not a brat. I'm not Talak. I am Zaragarian!"

They laughed. "Liar! You're nothing like a Zaragarian!"

"You shouldn't lie to us, little girl!"

Rada loaded her sling. "I don't like you. You need to leave."

"Rada," Makiko whispered. "Be careful. Be calm."

The colour drained from Bree's face and she trembled. Two Mstislavakan closed in on the group. Bree rushed forward, trying to dodge them, but the boys caught her. They laughed. "You've got to be quicker than that." While one gripped her arms from behind, another lifted her skirt. Bree wriggled, trying to break free.

"Enough!" A boy drew back his hand to hit her, but yelped in pain and staggered back, holding his head.

"No!" Rada yelled and shot another pebble at the one holding Bree. She hit him in the temple and he dropped to his knees, blood streaming down his face. Bree fled.

The remaining soldier laughed. "Felled by a baby!"

Rada shot again. He lunged sideways, avoiding the stone. She reloaded again, fumbling in her ammunition bag for her next stone. He was upon her. The boy knocked the sling from her hand and slapped her across the face. Rada flailed sideways. He snatched her up and shook her. "Deal with her," he said and threw Rada toward his friend, who had staggered to his feet. "Don't kill her yet. She needs to learn a lesson first."

Rada hit the ground. The air whooshed out of her lungs. Dazed, she spat dirt from her mouth and tried to rise to her knees. Hands gripped her legs and dragged her face first across the leaf-strewn forest floor. "Search her."

Hauled to her feet, she stood swaying while the blurry figure before her frisked her. "Evika! Look at this, dagger."

"That's mine," she mumbled.

"Not anymore."

Rada felt a tug on her tunic, heard a tearing noise, and they bound her hands and feet before pushing her back down against a tree.

"You watch her. Can you manage that? She damn near shot a hole through your head."

"Yeah."

"Don't kill her, no matter how much you want to. Remember Feyan's orders." The soldier left and joined the other one in front of Makiko.

"Well. Your kind is the last thing I expected to see here. I suppose it makes sense. A backward shit hole like this is just where you can bide your time and scheme."

"What exactly do you think I'm scheming?" Makiko said. "It is not illegal for me to be here. I am dimashne!"

"I don't care. The old emperor should have wiped all of you from the map. You yellow slope-head!" Feyan spat on her. "You need to be cleansed from this land."

"She's dimashne!" Rada said. "And she's freeborn, not a slave. You can't treat her like this."

Rada cried out as a slap knocked her sideways.

"Strip her. See if she's still got the tattoo. I'll bet she has. If she's burned it off, then..." he bent down, yanking on Makiko's braid. "Maybe we'll let you live." He twisted her hair and sliced her braid off taking a small piece of scalp with it.

Through tear-streaked eyes, Rada watched as they stripped Makiko's clothing from her. The old woman stood proudly, silently. "Arms up! Turn around!"

"I can't see it, Feyan," the boy said.

"No, but there's no burn scars either. Bend over bitch." Feyan shrugged. "On the ground. Spread your legs."

Makiko straightened, and Rada thought for a moment that she appeared taller than either of the Mstislavakan. Feyan punched Makiko in the stomach. She doubled over and he hit her in the face, sending her sprawling sideways. Tears streamed down Rada's face as she watched them. With each kick, Makiko's moans grew softer.

"Rada!" Tav's voice rang true and clear through the trees.

"Tav!" Rada screamed out his name. "I'm here! Help!"

Her guard struck her.

"Shut her up!" Feyan said.

A hand clamped over Rada's mouth, and he pressed her back into the bark of the tree. Hate-filled eyes from a blood-stained visage glared at her. "Shut it, you little bitch."

Rada bucked under his hand, clamping her teeth into the flesh of his palm. He whipped his hand away.

"Tav!"

"Gods damn it! Help him!" Feyan said to his friend.

His companion hurried over, but before he could do anything, Rada yelled, "Tav!"

"Shut her up!" Face twisted in a snarl, he aimed one last, savage kick at Makiko's head; it flopped sideways. Makiko's sightless eyes stared at Rada. She screamed.

Tav burst into the tiny clearing. "I've got her! She's here!! Akim!"

He drew his sword and advanced. One soldier intercepted him. "Bastards!" He lunged at the boy, who parried his blow and side stepped. The soldier stood poised but squinted at Tav's uniform and insignia. A frown formed on his face.

"Feyan... I don't think..."

Tav attacked, his blade slicing through the air toward his enemy's head. The Mstislavakan raised his sword, blocked the blow and kicked Tav in the belly, sending him sprawling back. As Tav staggered, his opponent cried out. "Feyan, no!"

Rada screamed as a sword skewered her friend from behind. Tav's blade fell from his fingers and he looked surprised at the steel protruding from his chest before the light left his eyes. Feyan withdrew his weapon and pushed him away with distaste.

"Evika, Feyan! Look at his insignia. We're in shit now." They rolled Tav over and a snarling lynx encircled by the Zaragarian serpent met their gaze.

Feyan paled. "Kill her and let's get out of here. No witnesses."

Rada wriggled away and tried to squirm along a gap under more blackberries. A Mstislavakan seized her by the waist and hauled her back, pushing her down against the tree.

"What about the other girl? She's probably the reason he's here."

Feyan shrugged. "We weren't to know. We were just cleansing the Senner bitch, keeping the little one out of harm's way and he attacked you." His friend groaned, holding his head in his hands. "No. You're right, it won't work. We'll kill her, find the other one and get rid of her too. Even if she's talked, without her at a tribunal before the commander, then we'll be fine."

"Tav!" The sound of several mailed bodies breaking branches reached them.

Feyan stalked to Rada.

"Feyan, no!" His friend stood between them, but Feyan pushed him aside and swung his sword at Rada.

Akim plunged into the clearing. He hurled a short sword through the air. It sliced through Feyan's back like a knife through butter. The Mstislavakan dropped his sword, and it fell point forward straight at Rada's chest. She squealed and rolled sideways. The sword nicked her tunic and the tip buried in the dirt next to her.

Rada squirmed backward, only to hit dense undergrowth. One of the black-clad boys reached for her. "Leave her. We'll get her later."

They drew their swords.

"It's refreshing to see such optimism in the young," Akim said, glancing at Regansh who stood at his side. "Mine will fall first."

"You lost last time," Regansh said. "Same prize?"

"Seems fair."

One boy stood, jaw clenched, while the tension in the other leaked out of him as he shifted from foot to foot, white-knuckled grip on the hilt of his sword.

Akim and Regansh stood, swords ready, waiting. The Mstislavakan uttered a prayer; Akim's lips quirked in a half smile. "When you're ready, children," Akim said. One boy bristled, straightening, and launched himself at Akim. The other attacked Regansh. Like an arching bolt of lightning, Akim met his attacker, dodging his blade as it plunged toward him and shifting his own cut to slice into his opponent's inner thigh. Red blossomed along his blade. The boy's eyes widened in shock. He staggered; Akim's blade skewered him and he crumpled to the ground. Regansh's victim fell seconds after.

Rada sat, knees drawn up to her chest; trying to use her bound hands to undo the restraints on her feet. Sobs broke from her as her fingers fumbled on the cord.

"Hold still," Akim said, cutting the ropes. She leapt into his arms. "I'm here," Akim said as he scooped her up and stood. She buried her head in his shoulder.

"Tav," she wailed.

"He's gone."

"Makiko?" she whispered.

"The Sennerese?" Rada nodded, but still hid her face.

"Neck broken," said Regansh.

"She was nice. She liked blackberries too."

"Rada, here's your mother," Akim said.

Jadzia entered the small clearing, face tight with worry. Bree and the remaining guards accompanied her. "Akim, is she hurt?" He shook his head. She sagged, putting a hand against a tree to steady herself as a long breath left her.

Akim put Rada down. "Go to your mami." Rada ran and wrapped her arms about her mother's waist.

"Sweet girl. It's good to see you well." Jadzia pushed her back a little to survey her appearance. "A lot of scratches and I think you'll have an enormous bruise on your cheek, but that will fade. You're tough, aren't you?"

Rada nodded, sniffing, wiping away tears and smearing dirt further across her face.

"Where's Tav?" Jadzia asked.

Fresh sobs erupted from Rada.

"He fell defending your daughter," Akim said.

Jadzia looked stricken. "No, not so soon. He had so much before him... His life was about to change." Her eyes fell on the black-clad figures. "Evikan, bastards!"

"They killed Makiko too," Rada said.

"Who?"

Rada pointed to the battered body of the old woman. Her words fell like an avalanche. "She was stuck in the blackberries. She like blackberries too, like me. And I got her out. She was funny looking, but nice... and... and they came looking for the girl... um... Bree. Then..." Rada's voice quavered. "Then they were going to hurt her and Makiko. I didn't like that. They weren't slaves and they didn't do anything wrong. I think they were just bullies. Mstislav loves the brave, so I tried to be... only... Only it didn't work." Her bottom lip trembled.

Jadzia held her hand and inspected the bodies. "I see this one has a nasty lump and cut on his head. This looks like the handiwork of a skilled markswoman. You did this? Then you were amazingly brave, again. You stood up to them and I am so very proud of you. You are a lioness."

She moved to the Sennerese woman. "Why was she here?"

"I don't know why she was here to begin with, but she was teaching me," Bree murmured.

"Teaching?"

"I wanted to be a healer. If I could be a healer all the time, then I wouldn't have to tend the fields and the work would be easier." She shuddered at the sight of the dead youths. "And I might be left in peace."

"So, the Sennerese was the real healer?" Jadzia asked.

Bree nodded. "I didn't have time to learn everything. We had to meet in secret. If the villagers knew..."

"We won't tell them. You should go now. Say nothing of what happened here."

The girl ran back to the village.

"Stilnassa, what would you have us do?" Akim asked.

"Bring Tav back to where I rested. There were plenty of rocks there. We'll build a cairn."

"And these?" Akim nudged a black carcass at his feet.

"I'll tell Dimitri where he can find them. Come, Rada, let's find a spot to lay Tav to rest and pray the gods grant him peace."

"What about Makiko? Shouldn't we bury her?"

"No," Jadzia said. "We cannot. If we bury her, a Sennerese, and not them, there will be repercussions." Before Rada could question her, Jadzia continued. "She is Sennerese. Her burial would show preference for one of their kind over one of ours. That is trouble we don't need. We will pray for her journey in the afterlife."

"Who to?" Rada asked.

"Anyone who'll listen."

⇒⟶

When they had left the tiny clearing, a shadow rose like smoke from Makiko's body and coiled into the figure of a woman with long dark hair – Bethsinidar. She knelt by the body, brushed the hair from Makiko's face. "I took the pain from you, but I thank you for your sacrifice." She gathered the severed braid and rested it against Makiko's scalp, where the skin and hair knit back together. Murmuring to herself, she placed her hands over the woman's heart and drew forth a glowing blue orb of energy. Cradling it to her face, she whispered, "Go join the Wild. Know peace. Know freedom. Mayhap you will be born anew." She blew upon it, sending it scattering into the air where it danced in a million tiny stars, rippling the leaves before it faded into nothingness. She placed her hands on the ground and the soil opened up. Roots from trees encompassed Makiko's body and dragged it to the shelter of the earth's embrace.

Bethsinidar stood, a look of infinite sadness upon her face. "If only this was the end of it."

CHAPTER 30

THE SUN BEAT DOWN upon the streets of the semi-derelict buildings of the Boneyard, Bēdarik's poorest and oldest section of the city. Katya kept to the shadows, and glared at the prickly straw hat in her hand she'd used to hide her face and wished she could just stomp on it and never put it on again. She'd stashed her usual attire at the Darklinan compound and tried to lighten her skin with ground whitlock powder before she'd donned simple leather sandals, a long Talak skirt and a loose shirt, sashed by a worn-out leather belt. Her long braid was hidden by a scarf.

Movement on a rooftop caught her eye and she slunk back into a doorway, watching. A scruffy head popped up and signalled her, so she back tracked and entered a narrow alley between two buildings. Katya wrinkled her nose at the stench of urine as a small, very young Darklinan darted into the alley.

"Stilnassa Katya, they're rounding people up! You'll get caught!"

"What?"

"I was in the market and the City Watch came and arrested a Stilnassa. They took her and her daughter away. I saw them take another one too. Only she yelled at them and hit a Watchman and they killed her. Right there on the street!"

The little boy trembled and pressed himself against the wall in the deepest shadow, as if hoping it would swallow him.

"Take a breath. Slow down or you'll draw attention to yourself."

"I'm not the one to worry," he said. "Your powder's running."

Katya put a hand to her face and it came away white. "Evika! It's because I'm sweating. How bad is it?"

"Um... bend down and I'll stick some dirt on those bits," he said. "There! Best I can do. I hope they don't look too close."

"It's all right. Return to the Darklinan. Tell them to keep the other little ones close. I'll be back as soon as I can, but I must get to Pavel and fetch some things from the villa."

He nodded and was gone.

Katya's mouth grew dry and her gut clenched; a bead of perspiration ran down her face. *Focus.* She closed her eyes, controlled her breathing, and felt the knot inside her gut loosen. *Bethsinidar, help me.*

She donned the hat. Just another worn-down Talak worker about her business. Katya slumped, and her walk slowed to a weary gait.

Gradually, the streets grew wider and the buildings were no longer a patchwork of repairs. She passed Demenka's tavern, seeing her husband busy with customers, and continued on. The other stores in this quarter were still trading like nothing was wrong in the city.

Katya passed through Bēdarik's workers with no trouble, most were too preoccupied with their business or gossiping about the events of the day to pay attention to her. She bumped into one customer who spun around, but before the rebuke fell from her lips, she cast her eyes down and quickly resumed her shopping.

Katya's shoulders tensed, but she continued. She took a circuitous route to the Temple of Mstislav, halting in a shady lane to stare across the broad plaza at the building. The market looked as if nothing was amiss. Hundreds of Talaks went about their business. It should be simple to get across with so many people. Katya stepped out and sauntered through the crowd. Every instinct in her screamed to run, but she kept her head down and wove her way through the people.

Halfway across the plaza, a voice yelled. "Hey! There's another one!"

Katya froze momentarily, but no one grabbed her.

Across from her, a woman dressed like a Talak, carrying a basket of food, had a scarf ripped from her head. The shoppers pushed her to the ground and spat on her. Another woman kicked her.

"We don't want you here!"

"Go home!"

The woman scrambled to her feet and drew a dagger. Her attackers stepped back. The silk merchant, a burly older man, stepped out from behind his stall, cudgel in hand. The woman eyed him warily. "Leave her be!" he roared and said to her, "Run!"

She took off and headed straight toward the temple.

Two members of the crowd spat at the stall holder. "Traitor!" They chased the Zaragarian woman.

She made it past the stalls and into a clear area with the mob following. Master Pavel exited the main gates with a group of six guards. They ran toward the woman surrounding her and tried to retreat to the temple fort. At the sight of the armed Mstislavakan, the crowd slowed.

"What are you waiting for?" a man yelled. "We're a hundred at least."

The woman bolted for the gates. Archers along the Temple wall took down those who broke off to pursue her. She made it inside before they shut the gate again. The mob fell upon Pavel and his force. Swords flashed and bodies fell. Arrows rained down from the few bowmen yet the seething mass of Talaks kept on and shortly the Zaragarian swords were held aloft in Talak hands, and the crowd parted to reveal the body of Master Pavel and his men.

Katya remained transfixed. A hand touched her shoulder. She swung around, dagger drawn. The silk merchant leapt back, hands held up.

"You've left running too late. They'll see you now. Come inside the stall. We're packing up. We'll hide you in the cart under the silks and get you out of the city."

Her eyes strayed back to the crowing, cheering mob, now tossing Pavel's head around. "Thank you."

Inside the stall tent that half hung from the large horse-drawn cart, Katya hunkered amongst bundles of silks as the merchant and his son packed up. "Why are you doing this? They'll kill you if they find out."

"I travel all over Penīdīen in my trade. I've met many kinds of people, from all kinds of faiths and lands, and we've more in common than different. No race is all bad. Besides, no one deserves to be ripped apart by that lot."

His son added, shaking his head at his father. "He can't help himself. Well, we weren't going to hang about here anyway. There are safer markets in the east."

"I'm grateful, but I don't want to leave the city," Katya said.

They both stopped what they were doing and stared at her. "I need to get to the Ortakli villa."

"You're a fool if you try. I've got a delivery of yellow silk to take near there. We can drop you off, but that villa is on a hill with clear ground around. How do you think you'll get in?"

"Just get me as close as you can and leave the rest to me."

➤——————▶

Katya shivered as she waited under the stone bridge and peered through the dense, tall reeds that surrounded it. Many torches lit up the gardens and outbuildings of the villa. There was still too much activity up there for her to sneak in undetected.

The household guard had left hours before. Neeren seemed to have the villa in an uproar and visitors had been coming and going since Katya had reached her hiding spot.

Lady Chandar was still there. Her personal escort waited by her carriage. *How long can those two prattle on? My feet are numb.* She closed her eyes, leaning her head back against the cold stonework of the bridge.

The rumble of heavy wheels and hoof beats woke her as Chandar's carriage rolled past. She waited until slaves extinguished the torches around the house before sneaking through the vineyard to the villa. Skirting the main house, Katya made her way through the kitchen gardens and tried the kitchen door. It opened.

The kitchen was empty. She crept through the room and up the stairs under a covered walkway. The central garden courtyard was also empty. Swiftly, she climbed the stairs to the next level, pausing at the top to peer down the hall. A slave, back to her, turned into the far corridor and was gone. Katya stole along the passage, stopping outside the new door to Jadzia's suite. She thought of the battle they'd fought in here, all for the babe. It seemed so long ago.

The door swung silently. Moonlight lit the chamber. Neeren had ransacked it. There was an odour of soot in the room.

The rack, which normally held Jadzia's weapons, was empty. Katya inspected the fireplace and saw the gut string from Jadzia's bow in the ashes.

Hunting through the detritus, she found a backpack emblazoned with Jadzia's crest and hugged it to her. Katya was certain Neeren would have stolen any jewellery. They scattered all the clothes from the massive timber wardrobe across the floor. Katya rifled through the clothes, most had been ripped apart. Katya picked up a suede vest, a shirt and pants, and put them in the backpack. She stepped inside the wardrobe, moving her hands until she felt a join in the timber and pressed. Two faint clicks sounded and the back of the wardrobe swung in.

Jadzia tugged on it, revealing a compartment containing a short, curved bow, sword and dagger, along with a bag of gold. She donned the weapons and stowed the gold into her pack.

She hesitated. *Neeren.*

Katya picked up the remains of a shirt bearing the Jadzia's sigil. She walked to the curtains and removed the cords which bound them back.

In the corridor, Katya turned in the direction the slave had gone and prowled down the hall. She passed a balcony window and hugged the wall as she peered below to the villa's main door. Two guards, one asleep, were stationed below. She continued on. A soft shuffle sounded behind her. She drew her dagger and spun. The pounding of her heart filled her ears. Head canted, she strained to hear the noise again. *There!* Footfalls in the corridor below. A door clicked.

Silence.

Bethsinidar, I know Jadzia served Mstislav and you've no love for those who follow him, but she was my friend. She protected me. Please help me with this.

A slave slept on the floor outside Neeren's room. Katya rested the backpack against the wall and crept forward. In one sleek movement, she fell upon the slave, squeezing her legs to cage the writhing body. She clamped her hand over the girl's mouth and drove the dagger up under her rib cage into her heart. The slave stilled, startled eyes frozen wide. Katya curled her into a sleeping position facing the door.

Katya gathered her pack, pushed the latch on the door and entered Neeren's rooms. The sickly-sweet scent of incense filled the space and an offering of fruits lay before her personal altar to Hokati. Neeren lay sprawled on the bed in a sheer nightgown, her long hair unbound.

Katya's boots sank into the plush rug on the floor.

Jadzia would never have this in her room. A cohort could march through here and you'd never hear them.

Katya skirted a small table, but her sword tip knocked two porcelain ornaments. They wobbled and chinked against each other.

"Bashtan, my love," Neeren mumbled, before rolling over, closer to the edge of the bed. Katya considered the difficult angle of her neck with a frown. Neeren moaned and rolled onto her back. An empty wine jug sat on her bedside table.

Katya stood beside the bed. *She's drunk. It would be so easy to just kill her now. It's not enough.*

Gingerly Katya put her pack down and withdrew both cord and the shirt bearing Jadzia's coat of arms from it. She placed them on the table.

Katya leapt upon Neeren and clamped her hand over the woman's mouth. Neeren's eyes shot open and she bucked under Katya's weight. The Stilnassa pressed the tip of her dagger against the Talak's throat. Neeren grew still - wide eyed.

"Hello, *Mistress* Neeren. Or have you begun calling yourself *Lady* now?"

Blood welled along Neeren's neck and a rivulet tricked into the sheets. Neeren whimpered.

Katya smiled. "Scream and I'll kill you right now. Do as I say and it'll just be a warning."

She grabbed the shirt and cord from the table and, still pinning Neeren down, said, "See this?" she held up Jadzia's symbol. It is the most exquisite embroidery." Katya shook her head. "It's a shame to waste it. Open your mouth."

Neeren shook her head. Katya sliced a shallow line along her neck. "A touch deeper and you'd die."

Neeren opened her mouth and Katya shoved the shirt into it. Neeren's cheeks bulged and her jaw stretched. The woman gagged and her eyes watered. Her nostrils flared as she panicked and tried to rapidly inhale. Jadzia's sigil hung like bloated tongue from between Neeren's lips.

The Stilnassa touched the coat of arms reverently. "Jadzia was worth so much more than you."

Katya punched her squarely in the face. Bone crunched under her fist and Neeren thrashed under her. Katya clamped her legs around Neeren's torso and pinned her shoulders down. Her hands clawed at Katya's forearms. The Talak's face crimsoned and her eyes bulged as she struggled to breathe through her shattered nose. Neeren writhed, nearly bucking Katya off. Snarling, Katya pressed her down, smiling as Neeren's strength ebbed. The woman's fingers scrabbled weakly at Katya. Neeren's skin became grey, her lips blue - her eyes blood red. Finally she lay still.

Katya put her ear to Neeren's chest and heard a faint, slow beat. She wrapped the cords around each of the woman's hands and bound them to opposite bedposts. Neeren lay splayed on her back. Katya ran her dagger slowly down each of the Talak's forearms, severing her arteries from elbow to wrist. With the tip of her knife she carved a Zaragarian serpent on her breast.

Katya let out a sob.

It will never be enough, but it will do.

CHAPTER 31

JADZIA AND RADA STOOD before the cairn. Rada, eyes red and puffy, laid a small bouquet of wild daisies upon the stones.

"I got him killed," Rada said.

"No," Jadzia said.

"But I called out to him."

"You did not get him killed. The Mstislavakan killed him, hoping to cover their guilt. Come, we must go." Akim steadied Jadzia as she mounted her horse. When they crossed the field, the tents were gone, as were most of the soldiers; only Dimitri's black tent remained and it was being disassembled and placed onto a cart.

He stood, back toward them, speaking with one of his officers. "What do you mean three are missing? Who?"

Jadzia rode her horse toward him and the group followed her. Dimitri's men turned to greet them, bowing slightly to Jadzia. Dimitri stiffened and faced her. "Sister?"

His gaze took in Rada's dishevelled appearance. "What's amiss? Has my niece had some accident playing?"

Jadzia levelled an iron gaze at him. "Hardly. Your little wolves strayed too far from the pack and played where they should not."

He quirked a brow at her.

"I suggest you head down that path and take the deer trail on the left to the large blackberry patch. You'll find your missing men there. Keep your other recruits on a shorter leash, Dimitri, lest they meet the same fate."

"Fate?" His voice held a cold, brittle edge.

"Dead, Dimitri."

"What do you mean?" He reddened.

"They thought to rape a local girl, a free girl. Rada saw them. She defended her, and they were about to kill Rada to cover their indiscretions. Fortunately, the problem resolved itself most satisfactorily."

Dimitri approached her horse and gripped its reins. Jadzia's guard surrounded him. Her brother took in their number and dropped the reins. The Mstislavakan officers stepped forward to aid their chief.

"No! Stay where you are," he told his men. "All is well. Just a minor squabble with my sister. The Emperor's Own are merely being cautious."

Jadzia grinned at him.

"You had no right!" he hissed at her. "They should have been brought before me, for our own justice."

"And what justice would you have rendered upon them? A slap on the wrist? Chastised them for getting caught? The Mstislavakan should represent the best of the Order, Dimitri, not the worst. And to be bested by a six-year-old." Jadzia shook her head. "Standards are slipping."

"You have overstepped your bounds, Jadzia. You think you still wield the same power you once did? There will be consequences to this."

Jadzia shrugged. "You are not emperor, Dimitri. Nor are you the Grand Master."

"No, but you have been too long in Talak. Things have changed in Vēkaria." He leaned closer. "It was the Order who throned your Tikhon. Be warned, Jadzia, now you understand where the true power lies, you would do well to remember it." He barked a command at his men. "Go find their bodies, bury them."

She nudged her horse's sides, pushing the mare on, and the others followed. Looking back over her shoulder, she called out. "Safe travels, Dimitri. May Mstislav bring you glory."

Once they were out of earshot, Jadzia said, "Does he speak true, Akim? I had not thought the power of the Order had risen to king-making."

"They have backed the emperor in his ascension while the council collects its wits. They merely hold fast if needed in the outer reaches of the realm."

"You mean Talak."

"Yes."

"While Tikhon plays his games and manoeuvres his other pawns."

"Yes."

Her lips drew into a thin, straight line. "Of course. Akim, I hope the guard have replenished our supplies. We must make all speed to Vēkaria. I long to see home and rest. And you, my girl, will meet your grandparents. They've not seen you since before you could talk!"

"Stilnassa, first I insist on examining your finger," Akim said. "Regansh, fetch the young healer, Bree, she may be of some use."

Stern, worried faces met Jadzia's gaze.

"Mami, you were going to get a healer anyway."

Jadzia sighed and when they reached the carriage, Bree was waiting.

She bobbed a curtsey to Jadzia. "Stilnassa, I will try my best to aid you."

Jadzia sat on the step of the wagon while her hand was unbandaged and the makeshift splints removed. Bree turned her hand over, gently examining the broken fingers.

"The swelling has gone down," Jadzia said. "But they itch damnably."

"The itching is a good sign. Your body is healing. It looks like the bruising is fading. I'll bath and re-splint it. I've clean bamboo here for splints which are lighter and finer for the fingers, so it should be more comfortable for you to wear. This arnica ointment should help with the bruising on your face and fingers. I have another salve for the wounds on your neck."

"You see, Akim, I told you I was mending."

Bent over Jadzia's hand as she worked, Bree whispered, "I know enough to see that you are not well. Something else ails you."

Rada, leaning against the carriage watching intently, said, "Mami, gets tummy aches."

"I'm fine," Jadzia said.

"Bree, they did bad things to Mami and they tied her up hard," Rada whispered.

"I should examine you properly, Stilnassa. Please, if not for yourself, then to put your daughter at ease."

"Mami, please," Rada pleaded.

Jadzia nodded. "But not here. I want privacy."

"Of course, but the carriage is too dark. My house is not far." Bree finished salving the wound, splinted and bandaged it. "Come."

Jadzia and Rada followed her, accompanied by Adana and Regansh. Bree kept glancing over her shoulder, scrutinising Jadzia's walk. Nearing her small house, they saw Bree's mother in their vegetable garden. Bree ran to her and they conversed in hushed tones. At first the woman shook her head, eying the group suspiciously, but Bree gesticulated wildly, pulling her sleeve up, revealing bruises. Her mother grabbed her arms and shook her, before pushing her away and shaking her head.

Rada moved closer to Jadzia. "Mami?"

"Just wait."

Bree returned. "My mother... is very private. She doesn't want you in the house."

Adana and Regansh stepped forward. Jadzia stopped them. "They've had an army here and are more than right to be wary."

Rada dropped her mother's hand. "But Mami needs help!"

"Stilnassa, I can bring some sheets and we can rig up a screen near the carriage to shelter you."

"It's not necessary," Jadzia said, turning to leave.

Rada spun and ran through the garden to Bree's mother. "My Mami needs help. We won't hurt you. We're not like the..." She bit her lip. "Like the Mstislavakan." The woman straightened, leaned on her rake, and turned to Rada, who rushed on. "These are imperial guards. The Emperor's Own. Please, can Bree look at Mami here? I think if she doesn't then Mami won't do anything about it. But her tummy hurts, and she's always sweaty, but not hot. Now she's cold."

The woman took Rada's chin in her hands and tilted her head, surveying her injuries. "You are the one who defended my Bree."

Rada gulped. "I tried, but it didn't really work."

"Bree is alive."

"It all went wrong and… my best friend. He's… he's gone."

"What's your name, girl?"

Rada stood at attention. "Rada Lujza Ortakli. Daughter of Lord Bashtan Ortakli and Lady Jadzia Zora Maklova." She bowed.

"Maklova. A child of the First Circle bows to me." She clamped her lips together, but the corners of her mouth quirked. "Why did you not use your rank first? Many would?"

"I…" Rada hesitated. Why didn't she? She was proud of her name. It always got her what she wanted. "I don't know." Her hands fisted around her pants, twisting the fabric. "I just want Mami to get well, please help," she begged.

"Then you better get her," Bree's mother said. "Tell her there's no one in. She'll have her privacy."

The presence of the guards made the small kitchen oppressively crowded.

"Out!" Jadzia ordered the guards. "You too, Rada."

Adana took Rada's hand. "Come, we'll wait outside."

The moment the door closed, Jadzia sat on a stool and doubled over, clutching her abdomen, panting.

"How often does that happen?" Bree gathered a clean cloth and water from the kettle that sat at the side of the fire and washed the table.

"It's a constant ache. Feels like a rock in there." She drew a deep breath. "Sometimes this happens."

"Sometimes?" Bree shot a glance at Jadzia. "There! As clean as it will get. Remove your clothes, Stilnassa." Bree paled when she caught sight of the bloody muck on the wadding Jadzia had between her legs.

"I recently gave birth. This is but the aftereffect of that."

Bree nodded, rubbing the back of her neck as she surveyed Jadzia's injuries. "Gods! You'll need a bucket of that arnica!" She cast her gaze away at the sight of the bruising on her thighs. "Tell me what happened."

Jadzia's words came, raw, fragmented at first, then in a deluge, filling the home with horror and bleeding through the door.

Bree paced, arms wrapped about her middle, clasping herself. When, at last, the torrent was over, Bree stood with her back to Jadzia. She shuddered, drawing in a sob and wiping her eyes.

"It's all right, Bree."

"It could have been me."

"But it wasn't. I'm not sure how much the dimashne taught you, but I need you to do the best you can. She must have seen promise in you or she would not have started to teach you."

Bree nodded and turned to Jadzia. "All of your outside wounds, nasty as they are, are healing. You say you washed in the river, but we'll heat more water and give you a proper bath and treat the rest of the cuts. First, lie on the table, Stilnassa." Bree palpated Jadzia's abdomen, causing her to wince. "It is hard and you're too hot."

"I feel cold all the time."

Jadzia stared up at the roughhewn, smoke-stained ceiling beams. There were no cobwebs anywhere, except in one corner. *Why clean every web except that one?* Thoughts roiled through her, along with a sickening notion that numbed her. Bree rummaged through a chest containing herbs and tinctures.

"Has this been your family home for long?" she asked.

"Yes, for generations."

"You and your mother are diligent housekeepers. This place is spotless."

"Thank you."

"Except for that cobweb up there. Does your mother think it will hide The Weaver's symbol?"

Bree froze, horrified. The sachet she held fell back into the chest. "I..."

Jadzia gave a twisted smile, hand clutched to her belly. "I can't see it. I guessed. This place is small. Your mother must have wondered where you were gaining your new skills, and it would be hard for that old Sennerese to survive without help."

Unable to look at Jadzia, Bree clutched her supplies to her chest, but did not move.

"You have my word. I'll not reveal you. I don't care if you worship Bethsinidar. Shall we continue?"

Bree slowly resumed her tasks and mixed up a solution of vinegar and a dark tincture with warm water into which she soaked a clean rag. "Hold still." Grimacing, she cleansed the wounds and bathed Jadzia's genitals. The rag came away bearing pus and bore a cankerous odour. Bree grimaced and continued to cleanse her patient.

"How is it?" Jadzia asked.

"You must know... your clothes. You had to have seen."

Jaw clenched, Jadzia nodded.

"The infection is inside you. I... I can't help. I'm not certain if it's from the birth or if there's a bit of the stick in there. All I can suggest is a bath in this mixture and we hope enough enters to help cleanse you, but... I'm sorry... I just... I wish Makiko was here. She would be more help."

"Perhaps, but she may not be able to do anything either. We'll try the bath. At least the warm water will be nice." Jadzia wrapped her cloak about her.

Jadzia emerged, pale and shaking. She turned to Bree, who stood on the threshold. "Know this, you did your best. You were unsure, frightened, but you tried and you examined me with efficiency and I saw your fear disappear when you worked. Makiko was right to train you. You should leave this place and seek another healer to apprentice yourself to. The

Mstislavakan will find out who their recruits were pursuing and you don't want to be here when they do. There are many excellent healers in the capital and if you journey there, seek my family's home. I will leave a letter of recommendation for you."

Bree's jaw dropped. "Stilnassa, I..."

"Just do it, girl."

Bree curtseyed.

Rada ran over but stopped midway, eyes wide. "Mami?" she whispered.

"What's wrong, Rada?"

"You're not better." She directed her rage at Bree. "You should have made her better!"

"Rada!" Jadzia snapped. Then in a lighter tone, she continued. "Bree did excellently! And I had a bath, so I'm feeling better than I have in ages!"

"You're paler."

"That's what happens when you wash the dirt off!" Jadzia limped to Rada and hugged her.

"You smell like the kitchen garden at home," Rada said.

"That's lavender and rosemary."

"Oh." Rada hugged her loosely, afraid to hurt her, stepped back and patted her uninjured hand.

"Now, you and Regansh go back to the others and make sure Akim is ready to go," Jadzia said.

Rada nodded, racing off, forcing Regansh to run after her.

"Once we are out of sight of this village, I will ride in the carriage again," Jadzia said to Adana. "This breeze is icy. I'm chilled to the bone."

➤——▶

The capital of Vēkaria, Dēbar, sat within a broad valley in a break in the Snake's Tail mountains and straddled The Tearfall, the only river flowing from Teardrop Lake in Zaragaria. Forests bordered its northeast all the way to the coast. Two large, opposing buildings overlooked the orderly city. On one side sat the blocky, towering fortification of the Order; on the other, traversing a slope, lay the sprawling imperial palace, its golden dome gleaming in the sunlight and surrounded by lush, colourful gardens; once a fort, now a monument to indulgence.

Rada sat speechless astride BC.

Akim and Adana laughed. "It's the first time she's been quiet for days."

Jadzia's carriage rumbled to a stop beside them. She leaned on the window, gazing at her homeland. "It's been far too long. Akim, I managed to finished it for you."

He rode to the carriage and Jadzia passed him his blue cloak. "Rada, we have a gift for you."

Rada nudged BC over. "But that's your cloak."

"Not quite. Every one of the guard here decided it was time you had your own cloak as an honorary member of the imperial guard." He unfurled it to reveal the same imperial insignia. "It is part of my cloak, but your mother has fashioned it to create one for you."

Her mouth formed dropped open, and she took it with reverence. "For me? Really?"

"Put it on," Adana said.

Rada dropped the reins and draped the cloak around her shoulders, and Adana leaned over to fasten it. "Now you are one of us."

Rada's lips trembled and she let out a huge sob. "Thank you!" She hugged it to herself and ran her fingers over the fine fabric.

"This too. Lean over." Akim wound a blue shadavoc around Rada's head, the tail of which draped under her chin. "When the weather is bad, we hook this tail higher to cover our face, except our eyes," he informed her. "Now you look the part!"

The guards let out a high trill and held their fists in the air. Rada coloured, grinning from ear to ear.

"Mami, look!" Rada cantered BC, turned him and raced back, cape flowing behind her in the bright sunshine.

"I can see. You look amazing!" Jadzia's vision wavered and briefly she saw her daughter, grown, sword drawn, the sounds of battle ringing in her ears.

"Stilnassa, do you want to ride?" Adana asked.

Jadzia remained transfixed by Rada.

"Stilnassa?"

"No, Adana. I just want to stay here where it's warm."

Adana inclined her head and joined Akim and Rada at the head of the column. She shook her head when she approached Akim. He wrinkled his brow.

"You'll get worry lines," she said.

"I've got more worry lines on this mission than I've ever had before."

"Where's Mami?" Rada asked in a small voice.

"She's staying in the carriage."

"Again? She's cold, isn't she? Still? But the sun's shining. And she doesn't eat much."

"No," Akim said, meeting Rada's gaze. "Maybe the healers in Dēbar can help her."

"Do you think so, really?" Plaintive hope tinged Rada's words.

"The gods alone know."

Rada cantered BC back to the carriage to ride alongside her mother.

Akim rubbed his face. "I'd rather ride into battle naked than this."

"They might help her."

Akim snorted in disbelief. "She's dying. We all know it. Whatever those bastards did to her have broken her inside. Without her mother, Rada will be left at the mercy of her prick of a father and that mewling shrew, Neeren."

Adana's scowled. "Hopefully not."

The road turned from dust into cobblestones worn smooth by traffic into the capital. Carts before them moved aside and let the small procession through. The sight of battered imperial guards and the carriage displaying Jadzia's family crest drew stares and whispers.

They passed a wagon filled with vegetables. A woman sitting on the front seat nudged her husband, who drove. "The lynx and the viper," she whispered. "The Maklova crest. Who?" Her hand flew to her throat. "Stilnassa Jadzia? By the gods, she is home." Her voice rang out, "Stilnassa Jadzia, it is good to see you return."

"Sit down, before you fall out," her husband groused. "Look at the state of them."

Jadzia leaned forward and peered out of the window, hollow-eyed, and nodded a faint acknowledgement to the woman. "Rada?" She beckoned her daughter closer. "You are my representative. I wanted to ride in here triumphant and show them the mettle of the Maklova women, but you must do it. Remember who you are, use your name and be proud. You are my lioness." Rada's gaze darted around the horde of people, and she fidgeted with the reins. "Go, I can see the city gates. Ride up to Akim and Adana and announce us."

The column slowed and Rada tried to push BC through the crowd. People jostled around her. "Move," she said.

Nothing.

"Big horse for a little girl," the snide remarked snaked its way to her. Rada ground her teeth.

"Make way," one of their escort joined her.

"I can do it," Rada said, reddening. BC pinned his ears back at the crowd and bit the shoulder of the nearest person. "Get out of the way!" Rada yelled. "You had your chance. Now move. If I let him, he'll level you all!" The big horse snorted, kicked out, and danced his way forward, parting masses with ease. In short order, Rada reached Akim and Adana. She hugged BC. "Good boy!!"

"Straighten your uniform," Akim ordered. Rada dropped her reins, rearranging her cloak and shadavoc while BC bared his teeth and snaked his head at the crowd.

"You'll do nicely," Akim said proudly.

At the main gates, three of the city watch halted them. "The emperor's own are lowering their recruiting age, are they?"

"And their standards, clearly. Taking on little children now, are we?"

Rada fumed.

"The little girl's not for fighting," one snickered.

Akim kicked him in the face.

The nervousness in Rada's stomach subsided as indignation flared within her. Fuming, she stood tall in her stirrups. "I am *not* little! I am Rada Lujza Ortakli. Daughter of Lord Bashtan Ortakli and Lady Jadzia Zora Maklova of the First Circle! I wear this because I fought!" Her voice choked, but those around her fell silent.

"Go on," Akim said.

"General Rodan and his men tried to kill Mami, my sister and me!" Righteous anger fuelled her words. "Our guard fought bravely and Mami fought with them, so Tav and I could escape." Her eyes welled with tears. "But they got her and... they hurt her... badly." Whispers washed through the crowd.

"Silence!" Akim bellowed. "Let Stilniat Rada finish."

Rada's mouth was dry. "The emperor found us and I fought with him and the other imperial guard to free Mami."

"Here me," Akim called. "Stilniat Rada is an honorary member of the imperial guard. Every word she has spoken is true. She served well and with more courage than I've seen in many a soldier. The emperor has personally honoured her bravery."

"So, the Talaks are rebelling."

"Rodan and Cēdar certainly. What else has transpired, I cannot say." Akim gestured at one of his troops and said, "Get their names and stay here until I get decent replacements sent for the gates. You three are going to wish you'd never been born."

CHAPTER 32

THE NEWS OF THE attack upon Jadzia and Rada rippled its way through the crowd, gaining in momentum with each word spoken, and the traffic on the streets parted before their small caravan.

Dēbar was an ancient city, and no longer resembled the sleepy backwater it had once been. Once a border Vēkarian trading town, it was now a vast metropolis.

Rada craned her neck, trying to absorb the sights before her. She'd gawped at the brightly canvassed stalls in the main marketplace, where the haggling over prices pierced the air like the shrill squawking of gulls. "I need to explore here," she said. "There's so much..." Her voice trailed off as she swivelled left and right in the saddle.

An aging fruit seller saw her and stepped in front of the procession. He addressed Akim. "Is that Stilniat Rada? The one they're all talking about? Stilnassa Jadzia's daughter?"

"I am," said Rada.

The old man bowed. "Here." He proffered her a small bag of fruit. "We've all heard tales of how you fought. You must be tired and hungry after such a journey."

Rada took the bag. "Um... thank you."

"I've a bag here for the Stilnassa too."

"I'll take that and make sure she gets it," Akim said. "Now, move out of the way."

Rada peeked in the bag as they rode on. "Oh!"

"What's wrong?" Akim asked.

"Blackberries," she whispered, passing him the bag. "I don't think I can eat these."

"Just as well," he replied. "Otherwise, you'd greet your grandparents covered in purple juice and what kind of impression would that make?" He ate one berry and passed the bag along. "Pity, Rada, they're very good."

She shook her head. "Akim, what are my grandparents like? I don't really remember them."

He scratched his chin. "Well, yours is an old family. One of the oldest and one of the first to support Aitor I, probably because you're all from up in the hills right on the border with Zaragaria. And they're rich. Got farms, vineyards, horse studs. You name it and your family will own it. And they're loyal, through and through."

Rada's thoughts drifted back to her mother's talk about her great-grandmother and Bethsinidar. She clamped her lips shut.

"Akim, that doesn't tell her what they're like," Adana said, rolling her eyes. "Your grandparents have a reputation for being..." She hesitated. "Firm but fair. Stilnaat Maklova likes to follow the rules, and he's very concerned about the family's reputation."

"Oh." Rada paled. Butterflies danced in her stomach. "Will Mami get better?" she whispered. Adana and Akim cast a glance at each other and stared ahead. She drew a shaking breath. *They think she'll die and I'm too little to tell.* In her mind, her mother or Tav was always beside her in this strange place, and now she felt more alone than she ever had.

The rattle of the hulking great carriage behind them jostled her from her thoughts. "He likes to follow the rules? I'd better be good then," Rada said with a cheeky grin, pretending she'd never asked what she feared the most.

Akim laughed. "It will be the most difficult thing you've done yet."

The market gave way to broad, paved streets lined with shops whose shutters were open. A baker placed a basket of freshly-baked pastries in a holding bracket in a window. Her mouth watered.

"Do you want one?" Akim asked.

"No. I don't want crumbs on my clothes when I meet Grandpa and Grandma." She frowned. "It's silly to put them there. They'd be very easy to steal, you know."

"Better pickings at the market. It's more crowded and the sellers there are less likely to demand your hand gets cut off."

"They cut off your hands for stealing?" Rada squeaked.

"Just the hand that stole. Usually there's a caning for a first offence."

Rada gulped and kept her eyes straight ahead. "How far to the house?"

"Do you remember where the palace was on the hill?" She nodded. "Well, your grandparents' home is not far from there."

The convoy rode over Tearfall River along a broad bridge bordered with intricate end-pillars carved in the shape of vipers.

"That's the widest bridge I've ever seen!" Rada said.

The merchant district fell behind them and houses with vast walled gardens graced either side of the road.

"Rada, there is the house," Akim said, pointing to a sprawling estate.

A large copper dome glistened in the centre of the main building and smaller ones winked on towers at its corners. A flag bearing the lynx encircled by a viper flashed its golden threads in the breeze. Rada kicked her feet out of the stirrups and stood up in the saddle to get a better look.

"Sit down now!" Jadzia's voice whipped through the air.

Rada grimaced and dropped back into the saddle.

"I'll bet you twenty that she doesn't stay out of trouble for a day," Adana said to Akim.

"There is no way I'm taking that bet."

The main gates opened and guards wearing grey uniforms stood at attention. Trees in blossom dotted the front gardens, lavender and roses lined the drive and the faint hum of bees filled the air as they approached the house.

"There will be a short welcome ritual. I'll present you after that and you can dismount," Akim said.

At the wide steps of the main house stood a barrel-chested old man sporting a moustache and beard with small braids in it. He wore tall black boots, and loose trousers. Under his wrap-around tunic was a high-buttoned white shirt. Beside him stood a short, thin woman with long grey hair in intricate braids, the same practical boots as her husband, and a three-quarter length, high-collared dresscoat over pants. Both remained where they were until the carriage stopped in front of them. To their rear stood several uniformed servants.

The guards dismounted.

"Stilnaat Stepan Maklova, Stilnassa Galina Maklova," Akim said, bowing to each. "We deliver to you Stilnassa Jadzia, Stilniat Rada, and her new sister."

"Captain." Stepan nodded in return. "We thank you." Servants rushed forward with sliver cups of wine and offerings of sweetmeats, presenting them to Akim and the others. "With this, we bid each of you welcome to our home and would offer the comfort of a few days' respite and the care of our physicians before you return to duty."

Akim took the goblet in both hands. "May Mstislav bless you for your kindness." The others did the same, drained their glasses and ate some of the food. Adana and Regansh bowed before moving to the carriage. Galina made to follow but her husband put a hand out, forestalling her.

"This is not tradition," he said.

Rada remained astride BC, trying to be as still as possible and invisible. A bee landed on her shoulder. She turned her head and blew on it, sending it flying toward BC's ears. He flicked his ears. It moved on, landing on one of his whiskers. Rada could feel his sides expand. BC stomped his feet, pushed Akim aside, and placed Rada right before her grandparents, just as BC snorted snot all over her grandfather. With a rictus grin, she gave a small wave.

"Stilnaat, may I present your granddaughter, Stilniat Rada," Akim said, lips twitching.

Her grandfather pulled out a handkerchief and wiped his face and clothes, glowering at her. "You need to control that horse!"

"It was the bee," she murmured.

"Are you not sitting on him and holding the reins? You are meant to be in control."

"I—"

"Why are you on such a horse, anyway? Who allowed this?"

"I did!" Jadzia said as she stepped down from the carriage. "And the horse was a gift from the emperor, so don't even think of taking it from her. You can get down now, Rada." Jadzia shuffled forward. Adana hovered beside her, supporting her, while Regansh carried the baby.

Stepan paled at the sight of his daughter, but he remained where he was.

"Tradition be damned!" said Galina, leaving her husband and running to Jadzia's side.

Jadzia gave her a wan smile, and Galina replaced Adana in supporting her. At the base of the stairs, Jadzia said, "I can do it. Go up there with him."

Jadzia, hunched now, took the steps as if they were mountains, but made it to her father. "Greetings, Stilnaat Father and Stilnassa Mother, I honour you. May the blessings of the gods rain down on you and may Mstislav strengthen your hand in times of strife. I return to the home I love, to the hospitality and warmth of family." She quirked a brow at her father and winked at her mother. "And introduce you to your newest granddaughter."

She sagged and Stepan leapt to her side. "Well done." To the servants, he bellowed, "Get the guard housed and feed them well. Summon healers to attend to them. And get my medico to meet us in Stilnassa Jadzia's rooms." He scooped her up and carried her inside.

Stilnassa Maklova knelt before Rada. "And you must be, my—"

"Yes, I... er..." Rada drew a deep breath, remembering her mother's words. "I am Stilniat Rada Lujza Ortakli, I honour you. May the blessings of the gods rain down on you."

The corners of her grandmother's lips curled in a smile. "I think I'll just call you Rada."

Regansh passed Galina the sleeping infant before bowing and leaving. "You're a dark little love, aren't you?" she said, running her finger along the babe's downy cheek, waking the child, who began a slow grizzle. Stilnassa Maklova's intent gaze drifted between Rada and the baby, cataloguing their differences.

Rada hung her head, murmuring. "What would you like me to call you, Stilnassa?"

"I think Granny will do, don't you?" she said, offering her hand.

>——————→

Almost all the noble's houses bore gold cloth hanging from balconies or windows, as did many of the shops in the richer part of the city; the poorer quarters of Bēdarik did not. The frisson of excitement and wave of whispers that flowed through the upper city were absent in the lower one. Katya lay on a rooftop and surveyed the plaza. Eadan's forces had surrounded the citadel, trapping those few members of the Order of Mstislav who had not gone looking for Cēdar.

"How long can they last?" Silla asked.

"A while. That place is more fort than temple, but Eadan will need to take it before the rest of the Order give up looking for Cēdar and return."

The pair left their vantage point and stole back to Darklina. In the courtyard of the Temple of Bethsinidar, Demenka herded the children in for lunch.

Katya inspected their storerooms, now piled high with food and blankets. She entered their first aid room. "Who built the shelves?"

"Darius," Silla said. "Stilnassa Jadzia got him an apprenticeship with a carpenter in the lower city, but he's still one of us. Demenka must have stacked it all away."

A troop of urchins entered and emptied their bags on the bed. "We hit the motherlode!" the smallest of them said. "Silly buggers left a little window open in the distillery."

"And we got what you told us," added another. "You should have seen the stash they had. Nick a bit here and there and they'll never miss any of it."

Katya grinned at them. "The motherlode, eh? Let's look." She inspected the supplies. "Excellent! But did you take all this from the one healer's shop?"

The three children's jaws dropped. "What! Do you think we're dummies? 'Course not, there's three big ones in the upper city and they're all totally hopeless about windows out the back."

Katya laughed. "They need to ventilate the area they prepare in."

"Do you reckon we're just about full up now?" the smallest said.

"Yes, now off you go and eat up big." Katya grabbed a scroll from the shelves as she and Silla followed them out.

The large hall that served as the Darklinan kitchen bustled with activity as children came and went. The pair sat and Katya unfurled a map of the city on one end of a long table. "We need to steal weapons," Katya said. "Eadan has the forces split. One group is here on the Vēkarian side, another around the temple, and a smaller force here on the Nējarak side. We'll..."

A young girl ran up to her. "Stilnassa Katya, more troops are here from outside."

"What colours do they bear?"

"Blue and brown with a rearing horse."

"From Nējarak then. How many?"

The child hung her head. "Um, lots. With supply wagons too. They've got like a kitchen on wheels!"

Katya put her hand on the girl's shoulder. "You've done well. Go now and get some food. Silla, make sure the next watch can count," she said. "Larger numbers make things a bit more difficult."

"Do you want to steal their weapons? Out of their camp?"

"Not anymore." Katya's fingers tapped the map. "We've got one more trip to make to those healer's shops."

CHAPTER 33

RADA FINISHED SCRUBBING HERSELF down in the tub as two anxious servants hovered nearby. "I told you I can do this myself. I don't need you."

"Stilniat, our orders are to assist you."

Rada rolled her eyes. "Just stay over there, then. If I need help, I'll ask." She snatched a towel before the maid could get it and dried herself off. All her life servants had waited on Rada, and the journey to Vēkaria had been the first time she'd been forced to be more independent. She liked it.

On the end of the huge timber bed lay a new set of clothes. Servants had measured her after she arrived and disappeared at a run, and within the hour had returned with clothes made of soft fine fabric. She donned a pale-blue shirt of fine linen with a short, upright collar which she topped with a dark brown suede vest embroidered with a snarling lynx. Soft, brown, woollen pants came next, and they had replaced her old boots with tall black ones, like her grandfather's. She surveyed herself.

"Here," said the maid, holding up a small mirror.

Rada squinted and turned about, eyeing her new style and nodded her approval. "Right, I'm done."

"Er, Stilniat, your hair."

"No, it's fine." Rada headed to the door.

The younger woman jumped in front of her. "Not yet, please. Um..." Her words rushed forth on a wave of what Rada thought sounded like relief. "Your grandmother suggested we braid and bead it in traditional warrior style."

"Warrior style?"

"Yes, since you're an honorary guard member."

The other servant beckoned Rada to a chair. "Here, Stilniat, please sit."

"You can do it later. I want to see Mami."

"Your mami thought the hairstyle was a good idea too."

"Really? All right."

Rada slumped on the chair, her legs swinging.

"Get the beads," the older servant ordered the younger. "You forgot them."

The girl rushed from the room.

Rada narrowed her eyes. "She forgot the beads? After you remembered all this stuff? You're trying to trick me. I want to go to Mami!"

The woman pressed down on Rada's shoulders.

Rada knocked her hands aside and jumped out of the chair. "Get your hands off me! I'll make sure you get in trouble."

With a sigh, the servant said, "Your mami is still with the medico and his assistant. They won't let you in yet."

Rada ran to the door, but the woman caught her. "But they came ages ago!"

"Yes."

Rada trembled. "They won't let me in?"

"No, I'm sorry. When he's done, I'm sure you'll be able to go in."

Rada shrugged off the servant's grip. "Do warriors actually have braids?" she demanded.

"Yes, unfortunately. They'll take hours."

Rada sniggered. *Serves you right for not thinking of a better lie.* "You better get started then." She strutted back to the chair and sat with a smug grin.

The other maid returned and as the first braid went in, Rada winced. "Does it have to be so tight?"

"Yes, indeed."

They worked with astonishing speed. "I wish you'd thought of another excuse," the older one grumbled. "This is murder on my hands."

"If you'd just told me the truth straight away, it would have been simpler," Rada said.

"Would you have stayed here?"

"Nope, but I would have waited outside Mami's door, or explored. Now I want the braids."

The younger maid said, "Well, they're going to look amazing. Look at this bead, and this one, it's a little bell."

"You are not sticking a bell in my hair! Cows and goats wear bells and I am not a cow or goat!"

"My apologies, Stilniat." She held out the bowl of beads with shaking hands and they rattled in the metal bowl.

"They're noisy. How many beads are you putting in my hair?"

"Well, the ladies who have this done put a bead in every braid."

"Ladies?" Rada spat the word out. "You mean, la-di-da rich women." *Like Neeren.* "But they'll make too much noise. I'll rattle when I walk. No warrior would wear so many. How can I ever sneak up on someone?" The two women ceased working and stared at her. Rada threw her hands up. "Well, you've never been in a battle, so you don't understand. The beads are not meant to rattle. Don't put them everywhere."

"But that's not fashionable."

"Evika!" Both maids gaped at her profanity. "I don't give a toss about fashion. I bet the warriors didn't have braids that rattled and gave them away and got them killed. Give me a few little braids on either side of my head with the beads and weave it through my usual plait at the back. Done. Make sure they don't rattle about. I will not die because of a hairstyle." She folded her arms.

Once they were done, Rada rose, buckled on her belt and dagger, and swept her blue cloak over her shoulders.

"I wish you'd let us wash that," the older maid said.

"Nope, I like it just the way it is."

Rada turned and bolted for the door. She marched down the corridor towards her mother's room. Two servants passed her, one carrying bloody sheets, another carrying a metal bowl of bloody, gritty water. They blanched, ducked their heads and hurried on at the sight of her. Turning a corner, she saw her grandparents and the medico leave from her mother's room, their backs to her. She slid against the wall, out of sight.

"I've done all I could," the medico said. "The poppy will ease her pain. Light the fire in her room. It may help."

"Surely you can do more?" her grandmother pleaded. "She has given too much, been sent over there to those Talak bastards like a prize heifer, finally returns to..." Her voice hitched "... to die."

"There is too much damage. Her womb, her birth passage, is infected. You saw the splinters in the bowl." He shook his head. "In my experience, most people would have died by now. Stilnassa Jadzia has a will of iron. That is all that is keeping her going. What will happen next is that she will become increasingly cold and pass in her sleep."

Galina turned into Stepan's embrace.

"This is no consolation, I know, but this will be a much more peaceful death than if she'd contracted lockjaw. She will fade into a long sleep."

Rada's heart pounded and she slid to the floor. *Mami! Mami! No, no, no, NO!* The words ricocheted in her mind. She grabbed her knees and rocked herself back and forth, biting her lip to suppress her cries until blood welled in her mouth.

Bubba wailed. The door clicked and Galina emerged jostling the baby. "I'll organise a wet nurse. The poor wee thing is too thin."

"She's a pretty little one. It's a pity her legs are ruined."

"She's a fighter, like her mother and her sister. It's a miracle she's made it this far. We'll get help and make her legs as good as possible."

"Mmm," Grandfather grunted. "We've been down this road before ourselves and caused a child much like this one too much pain. The medico said the child will be in immense pain as she grows and binding will make little difference to the leg."

"We'll try. We have to; she's left them with us. We need to get her named. This is our grandchild. And she's Tikhon's too."

"Can you imagine her life with Sabina as a stepmother? The empress taking in the daughter of her husband's true love? She'd never live down the slight, and the babe would die within a week." He scratched his head. "Fine! If you're... we're going to do this, then she stays here. At least we've got the other one. Rada might be half Talak but she's all Jadzia from the story she told us. She's true to the mould despite her blood." He chuckled. "Shows you that Zaragarian blood will win out every time."

"She may yet have to return to her father."

"Perhaps, but if war breaks out. He'll probably be killed, and good riddance to the supercilious bastard."

Rada's mouth went dry and her stomach dropped. *I never want to go home. Uncle Tikhon is Bubba's father? The empress? Dead in a week?*

The footsteps faded, and Rada heard a soft click. She peeked around the corner to witness a short, thin woman with close cropped hair step out from the room opposite her mother's. The woman looked left and right and silently followed Rada's grandparents.

She was spying on them.

When she was gone, Rada headed to her mother's room. She opened the door and slipped in. The curtains and shutters were open and shafts of bright sunlight reached inside along with the scent of freesias. Her mother lay on the bed, dwarfed by its size, nestled deep within the soft mattress and under a mound of covers. She was grey against the sheets and Rada noticed her breathing from the other side of the room.

Jadzia's eyes opened. "There you are, my brave girl."

Rada ran across the room and jumped onto the other side of the bed. She wriggled close and put an arm about her mother's waist. Jadzia patted her hand. "This is a pretty room," Rada said.

"Mmm."

Rada rolled onto her back and stared at the ceiling. "I heard Granny and Grandpa talking to the medico."

"Ah, I see. What exactly did you hear?"

"That the Talak bastards broke you inside and… and that you're not going to get better."

"I'm sorry, Rada. I wanted this trip to be so much better for you."

Silence.

"Rada?"

"I don't want you to die and I don't want to go back to Talak," Rada blurted.

"You won't be going back there soon. There's going to be a war. You and Bubba will stay here safe."

"I like Granny, but I'm not sure about Grandpa. He looks cross a lot. He thinks I'm like you were even though I'm half Talak."

"Really?" Jadzia's voice was tight.

"He's not happy with Bubba's legs, but I think Granny will help her."

"Rada, before I was born, they had another daughter who suffered like Bubba. They tried to fix her and it ended badly." Jadzia's voice grew soft before it trailed off. "He'll come around."

"But Mami, someone was spying on them!"

"Someone else you mean?" Jadzia murmured.

Rada frowned. "I was just listening. This woman hid in the room across the hall and snuck off after them. And where did they take Bubba?"

Nothing.

Rada turned her head; her mother's eyes were closed. She rose to her hands and knees, heart pounding. "Mami?" she whispered. Reaching out to touch her mother's face, hand shaking, she hesitated and withdrew it as if burned.

There was a loud knock on the door.

Jadzia's eyes opened. "I'm not going to die just yet, sweet one. Tell whoever it is to come in."

"Enter," Rada called.

In walked a tall, broad-shouldered woman carrying a satchel. Behind her, a short, rotund, bald man, also with a bag.

They had had slanted eyes and golden skin. *He's Sennerese.*
"More medics?" Rada asked hopefully.

"No, I believe they are the scribes I asked for. This is Eri and Amida. They have done much work for me in the past, and I trust them."

"Dimashne?"

Amida's brows rose. "Correct, Stilniat. Otherwise, we would not have left the island."

"People don't mind here? You get work?"

"Because they are dimashne, they have a well-deserved reputation as independent from the court and politics. They are honest, precise, and diligent in pursuing their duty to their clients." A long breath left her as she shivered and pulled the covers higher. "Now, Rada, I need to speak with them. Go explore. Check on your sister. It's your mission to see that she is well tended and safe. Can you do that?"

Rada nodded and left, looking askance at the two scribes as she did.

When the door closed, Jadzia said, "I have instructions to send to Stilnassa Katya in Talak, which must be delivered as soon as it is safe. We must prepare my will and protect my assets for my daughters. This must be witnessed and a copy delivered into the office of records by the end of today."

Tikhon's forces had gathered and now marched as one toward Bēdarik. Bashtan and his guards rode surrounded by Mstislavakan led by Dimitri.

"You should be pleased, Bashtan. The emperor has saved you a tiresome journey. Jadzia and Rada are alive. Your daughter is rather remarkable. She'll make a fine Mstislavakan."

"Both her parents would need to be dead for that to happen," Bashtan said. "And even then, she has family."

Dimitri smiled. "Mmm, she can still choose us when she is older. Anyway, her temper could be a problem. I'm not sure she'd follow orders well. Jadzia and the emperor's guard seemed to think it likely she'd stab me." He laughed. "Can you imagine a little girl doing that to me?"

"Only if you called her little," Bashtan muttered. "How is she armed?"

"The emperor gave her a dagger and let her choose from the booty after their battle. Hasn't he told you?"

"No."

"Oh! Well, let me enlighten you."

As Dimitri spun the tale of Rada's part in the battle, Bashtan paled.

"He would've killed her?" Bashtan asked.

"Yes, of course," Dimitri said. "Did you think Rodan would spare a Zaragarian child even if she's half Talak? You truly are a fool."

"Perhaps, I have been. I can't believe my Rada could do all this. She's only a child."

"I don't think she's *your* Rada any longer. Probably never was with a mother like my sister. You should be proud. I mean, the sight of that speck of a girl on Rodan's old warhorse is marvellous! Her feet barely come past the saddle flaps. Even I doubted my sister's sanity over allowing that, but the damn horse seems to like her." He laughed again. "I never would have believed it. Then again, I'd never believe a child could kill my men. One of them had his skull cracked by that sling of hers. I was furious, of course, and let Jadzia know, but in hindsight, what a magnificent child. I wish I had ten like her!"

"Will I see her again?" Bashtan asked.

"I suppose that depends on what we find in Bēdarik."

Bashtan rode in silence, slumped, mulling over all he learned. Could any of this be true? How could Rada kill? *Jadzia, what did you teach her? She was doomed from the moment she was born.*

The column halted on a small plain amid the undulating hills. Tikhon's troops dispersed to bivouac. A day's ride to their east, beyond the swaying hills of golden summer grass, lay

Bēdarik. Dimitri directed their troupe to set up near Tikhon and his officers. Bashtan and his men were hog-tied and left.

Dimitri proceeded to Tikhon and Darcov, who helped set up camp, and bowed. "What are your orders, My Emperor?"

"How is our friend?" Tikhon asked.

"Morose, surly, dismayed," Dimitri said.

"So, normal then," Darcov quipped.

"I've been torturing him with stories of Rada's exploits," Dimitri said.

Darcov grinned. "Clever strategy. That'll make him more miserable. He hates independent women."

"Dimitri," Tikhon said, "I'm still not going to punish her for the death of your men."

Dimitri held up his hands. "I've had time to cool down, and you were, of course, correct. In retrospect, I rather admire the girl. I look forward to shaping her future."

Tikhon stared at him coldly. "I think Jadzia will have a say in that."

Dimitri canted his head, frowning. "Tikhon, when did you last see Jadzia?"

"Right after the attack, then she left." Tikhon paused in his work. "Why?"

"May we speak privately?" Dimitri said.

They moved away from the troops. "Speak," Tikhon said, arms folded.

Dimitri hesitated and cleared his throat. "Jadzia was clearly ill the last time I saw her."

"They injured her gravely."

"Yes, I know."

"You don't understand! I was there. What they did to her... It will take time to recover."

"My Emperor, she is the strongest woman alive, but I suspect will power is the only thing holding her together." He sighed. "My sister and I disagree almost every time I see her, but she is still my sister, and it brings me no joy to tell you that..." He shook his head. "That she looked like death."

Tikhon turned his back on him as a tremor ran through his body. He hung his head momentarily before turning back. "Evikan Talaks. I pray you are wrong."

Two scouts approached. "Report!" Tikhon snapped.

"Your Majesty, the Nējaraks sent troops. They were stationed on the far side of the city but met with Talak lords and shifted to this side."

"That means they're not concerned about the Order members who went looking for Cēdar, so they must be dead. How many?"

"Approximately four cohorts of cavalry."

"Trying to shore up the Talaks quickly. They'll likely have more troops coming."

"Much of the upper city is bedecked in the gold of the old king."

Tikhon laughed. "So much for Bashtan's word on there being no chance of a revolt. Dimitri, for now, keep him alive and as miserable as possible." To the scouts, he said, "Meet me at my tent. I would spend a moment alone."

Tikhon moved to the shade of a large oak tree and knelt. "Mstislav, guide me. I will face ten thousand foes for you but stop up this ache in my heart. Save her. She has ever been your faithful servant as am I. Do not take her from me. I've never quailed before an enemy, but this..." His face contorted, a tear ran down his cheek and he buried his head in his hands. "This will unmake me."

A twig cracked behind him. Tikhon stiffened and finished his prayer. "Mstislav, make my courage never waver, make my sword arm strong and my steel never dull, so I may kill my enemies." He wiped his eyes before rising.

Darcov stood behind him, a broken stick in his hand, smiling sadly.

"How much did you hear?"

"Enough to know that evikan bastard Dimitri gave you bad news."

"He fears Jadzia is dying."

Darcov embraced him. "She may not. She will be in Dēbar now and we have magnificent healers. Her parents will do all to help her. She is too tough to go like this. We must believe it."

Tikhon stepped back from him. "I prayed for it." With a wry grin, he added, "How do I look?"

Darcov shrugged. "Sneeze a bit and they'll think your hayfever is playing up." He clapped him on the back. "Come on, they're waiting."

They walked back to Tikhon's officers and the scouts at his campsite.

"I want to see the lay of things myself," Tikhon said to the scouts. "Escort me in. Darcov, come with us. The rest wait here." His guard stepped forward. "No. Darcov will suffice. Too many and they'll spot us."

They followed the scouts across the valley and forded the Spinner's Run that flowed past Bēdarik. Slinking through giant clumps of pampas that bordered the river, they made their way to the tree line.

The scouts stopped beside a tall pine. "Up there, Your Majesty. You'll need to remove your helmet and anything else shiny."

Tikhon shed his helmet, mail and armour. He smeared dirt on his face before climbing the tree. The branches spiralled around the trunk like a staircase, and he stopped when he could see the entire city and farms beyond. A broad stone wall built upon a rammed earth base encircled Bēdarik; though vast, it was not high — his father had forbidden work on improving the city defences. A broad ditch encompassed the fortification and acted as a partial moat until the river flooded in winter, yet this did not abut Bēdarik's walls, allowing for a section of grassland between it and the stonework.

Eadan and Cedar's combined forces were embedding wooden spikes in the moat walls and, where the moat was dry, into its bed. Further spikes were being rammed along the top of the moat and into the earthen base of the city's walls. Originally, the city precincts included fields and orchards, but the town had grown and the upper city now occupied the slopes that had been pasture. From his perch in the tree, Tikhon saw almost all the houses of the rich bedecked in gold cloth and on a hillside, out of the city walls, sat Bashtan's villa, gold cloth streaming from every window.

A fury lit within him and its slow burn banked his hatred, his disgust. So much lost to this pathetic strategy of his father, Aitor II, all because he couldn't bestir himself to conquer these fools properly. As long as the trade and revenue rolled in, he was happy. Jadzia sacrificed to a worthless coward like Bashtan – a man all ego and no substance. A man who had raped her! A man Rada feared! Without Jadzia, her money and position, he would have stayed some overlooked backwater failure of a lord and now he had the gall to lie and spit on the hands that raised him out of the mire. Fighting to control his features, he climbed back down to Darcov and the others. One scout was missing.

"Where is your friend?"

"Across the river," the remaining scout said.

Darcov assisted Tikhon to don his mail, armour and helmet, saying, "We've company. There was movement in the grasses across the river."

Tikhon gave no sign he'd heard, but said, "They're digging in. We need to return regardless."

Halfway across the river, they froze at the sound of a scuffle and from under a large clump of pampas rolled the other scout and a boy covered in grime. The scout wrinkled his nose and held him by the scruff of the neck.

Once on the riverbank, Tikhon said, "Who are you? What doing here?"

The boy narrowed his gaze, scanning Tikhon from head to toe.

The scout shoved him. "Answer your emperor."

"Stilnassa Katya sent here me to scout what that lot in front of the city are doing, and report back."

"Let him go," Tikhon said. "Katya sent you?"

"I said that. You a bit deaf?"

The scout cuffed the back of the boy's head, making him stagger.

"Enough of your cheek. You are one of Jadzia's Darklinan?"

"Yes."

The scout shook him. "Yes, Your Majesty."

The boy rolled his eyes. "Sorry. I don't get to see the likes of him very often. How am I meant to know?" He bobbed his head. "Your Majesty, is our Lady... Stilnassa Jadzia alive? Is Rada alive? Is Bubba? And Tav?" The boy held himself, hands tucked under his armpits, his toe scuffed the ground and he could not look at Tikhon.

"Yes, though Rodan gravely injured Jadzia. Rada is well and so is the baby. Tav does all the Darklinan honour. He helped save Rada and the baby."

The child's whole body sagged. "Thank the gods. Stilnassa Jadzia is good to us, and Rada is one of us."

"Now, tell me, how are things within the city?"

"They're rounding up any Zaragarians. All the wives and their kids. Master Pavel, at the Order, got beat to death by a mob in the market. It's all gone to shit. We've been keeping track of who's doing what, flyin' the old colours 'n stuff and we tell the Stilnassa and she writes it all down. And we've been nicking their stuff. Got a ton of medico supplies and food. We've even nicked some weapons."

"How did you get out?"

"The drains." He looked them up and down. "But you lot won't fit... er... Your Majesty."

"No, but I'm sure Jadzia's Darklinan are more than capable of getting us in." The boy straightened and nodded proudly. "Come back to camp. I've a couple of packages for you to carry back to Katya and they must be placed where the city will see them."

The group wound its way through the tall grasses and back to camp. Boggle eyed, the boy turned his head to and fro, taking in all the men and women readying for war. They passed a wagon full of long ladders and several teams assembling catapults.

Tikhon beckoned one of his generals over. "Tell Dimitri to bring Bashtan and his men here."

Shortly, Dimitri and his men hauled Bashtan and his troops before Tikhon and forced them to their knees.

"He's Rada's pa," the boy said. "He's an evikan bully! I'm glad you're in trouble. The emperor will sort you out!"

Dimitri laughed. "How does Jadzia pick them? Marvellous!"

The sight of Bashtan enraged Tikhon. Every resentment simmered, waiting for release. "Bashtan, I've seen the city. It is emblazoned in gold. Not what you led me to believe."

"Your Majesty, I had no idea! They would not tell me of their plans, particularly with my connection to the empire through Jadzia. How could I have known? They are fools! I would never rebel against you. The empire has been good to me. I would *never*."

"Bashtan, every window in your house, every balcony is bedecked in gold! You lied. Were you hoping I would walk into a trap?"

Bashtan raised his hands in supplication as his words rushed out. "No! I would never! Neeren! Yes, Neeren would do it. I ordered her not to!"

Tikhon belted him across the face and spat on his prostrate form. "You ordered her not to! So, you knew all along this would occur. What were you hoping to achieve? Were you trying to play both sides before you chose the safest bet?"

"Yes!"

"Coward! You have a chance right now to save yourself a great deal of pain."

Behind him, both Darcov and Dimitri drew their swords.

Darcov shook his head. "Not this one, Dimitri. He is mine."

Bashtan quivered and wet himself.

"This is your chance, Bashtan. Who is the ringleader?"

"Lord Eadan and Cēdar. Apparently, Cēdar is in the city." Hope lit in Bashtan's eyes. "Please, My Emperor. I know my place."

"You know your place? Know your *place!* You snivelling rat! Bashtan, you have no place. You have harmed my daughters – bullied one and would've killed the other! It was only the courage of her mother and sister that saved the babe."

Some glimmer of fatherly possession reared its head within Bashtan and, heedless, he said, "Rada is not your daughter."

"Yes, she is."

Tikhon nodded to Darcov, whose sword sliced down, severing Bashtan's head. Dimitri and Darcov forced each of Bashtan's men to their knees and beheaded them.

They bundled Bashtan's head into a sack and gave it to the young Darklinan, along with the head of General Rodan.

"Take these to Stilnassa Katya. She must place them where all will see. The city will understand it is Rodan who is dead, not I. Tell her we will attack tomorrow morning and I need every aid she and Stilnassa Jadzia's Darklinan can give us." He put his hand on the boy's shoulder. "I am relying on you. This is the Darklinan's chance to make Stilnassa Jadzia proud."

CHAPTER 34

THE DARKLINAN WERE SMILING and playing and talking about Tav's adventures since the boy had delivered the news Jadzia and her children were alive and that the emperor wanted their help. Demenka had struggled to get the small ones to go to bed, but finally it was quiet.

"Gods love the little buggers, but I thought I'd never get them to sleep. I'm off to my family. Tomorrow I—"

"Tomorrow will change everything one way or another, Demenka. Take care of your family," Katya said, but Demenka hesitated. "Go. The little ones will be as safe here as anywhere. Look after your own. We will be fine."

Alone, Katya sat cross-legged on the dirt in the courtyard and stared up at the stars. *Jadzia, may Bethsinidar weave you a path to health, peace and happiness.* Like a living shadow, Katya was clad in black, her head concealed by a secured turban that left only her kohl-darkened eyes visible.

She sat like that until Silla tapped her shoulder hours later. Katya broke from her reverie and turned to face two groups of teenagers; some similarly black clad and the others dressed as well-to-do Talaks. All were armed and one carried a short, iron pry-bar while another carried a bucket of black paint and a brush.

Katya surveyed the teens before her. "This is critical. When you succeed, you will have cemented your place in history. No one will ever doubt the worth of the Darklinan again." To those disguised as prosperous citizens, she said, "You know when to move out. Good luck."

Addressing the black-clad squad, Katya asked, "Is everyone ready? Good. We've much work before dawn." She hefted a backpack onto her shoulders. "Move out."

The moon cast the deserted streets in blue-grey light and the shadows from the alleys reached to snare them. The Darklinan cast worried glances over their shoulders. Nothing moved in a street that always held some form of scavenging life; no stray dogs or cats, not even the rats that infested the nighttime. They rounded a bend and saw other Darklinan working, improving the barricades into The Bone Yard; further protecting their home.

The houses and shops in the poor quarter were shuttered and the owners had nailed boards over them. As they neared the main shopping street that heralded the entrance to this quarter, they halted, entered an alley, opened a gate into the rear yard of a shop, and clambered up some stacked crates onto the roof. They traversed ridge lines and gables with such ease and grace they may as well have been flat. At the head of the shopping strip, Katya snuck forward and hugged a chimney in order to peer down at the street. The Darklinan had reported building works here, and the shopkeepers had erected two solid timber gates across the thoroughfare, and a thick beam held them locked. The tang of pipe smoke wafted up to her and in the shadows next to the gate, men murmured.

"Bugger the rich bastards."

"Keep their war with the empire to themselves."

"I got no complaints with the Zaragarians. I reckon we were worse off with the old guard."

"The likes of Lady Jadzia 'ave been good to us."

Katya's eyes welled with tears. *My friend, I hope you are mending. Tikhon owes you a debt he can never repay.* She edged away and joined the others. They travelled across the rooftops all the way to the edge of the plaza. The stallholders had packed up most of their sites, leaving only a few carts and wagons, their awnings folded and sides locked up. This left a majority of the plaza empty and gave a clear field of view across it.

"It looks clear," a Darklinan said.

"Most of the troops should be with the main force, but the city watch might be out."

Katya and two others slunk across the rooftops to the nearest street before lowering themselves into the shadows and dispersing – the two Darklinan scouting the surrounding streets. A mere shadow, Katya crept through the thoroughfare. Ducking into doorways, listening, scrying the darkness before moving on. She reached the opening to the square and whistled a faint signal. Those from the roof top joined her. The two scouts did not return. They waited, barely breathing, straining to hear.

"Something's gone wrong," a girl said.

Katya put a finger to her lips and gave the girl's hand a squeeze. A whisper of sand grinding under a boot on cobblestones reached them. They pressed themselves against the wall. Katya drew her dagger. An owl hooted.

"That's them," Katya whispered, and the band relaxed as the scouts joined the group.

"A lone watchman dealt with," a scout said.

They walked to the centre of the main square and the lass with the bucket of paint set to work. She drew a large black circle, turning it into the Zaragarian serpent. Inside this, she drew a lynx.

"Jadzia would be proud," Katya said, putting her hand on the girl's shoulder. "She would love this."

Within the circle, they placed the severed heads of Bashtan and Rodan.

The group ran towards the upper city and the rich merchants' shops. Each store had a broad covered front porch, so they sheltered the entire walkway along the street. They saw no patrolmen until they neared the apothecary the Darklinan had robbed. Two guards stood on the edge of the walkway outside the storefront, halfway down the street.

She drew a garrotte, as did one of her companions, and they inched their way along the walls.

"What a waste of time. Whoever hit the place isn't coming back," a watchman said.

"Yeah, I could be at home with my wife and kids."

Too busy complaining, they didn't notice Katya and the Darklinan move behind them.

One of them tapped a pipe against the porch post as he cleared old tobacco out of it. "How is your youngest? She was learning the flute last I heard."

The other laughed. "She's still bursting our ears...."

Katya looped the garrotte around his neck and hauled him back. As she did so, a Darklinan drove her dagger into the man's throat, flicking it sideways and severing an artery. His companion started forward then lurched back as a Darklinan snared him, but the man got his fingers under the wire. He opened his mouth to cry out, and the rest of the band fell upon him, stabbing him until he ceased moving. They dragged the bodies against the wall. Katya boosted a boy onto the walkway roof and passed the short iron bar to him before he disappeared to the rear of the premises.

The girl with the paint stepped out on the street and set to work on the cobblestones. The others waited, leaning against the shop wall. A scraping against the inside of the double front doors signalled the raising of the locking bar and the boy let them in.

"You were right. They'd shut the windows, but I pried one open," he whispered. "I found this." He held up a lamp, flint and steel. They entered and shut the doors, enclosing them in total darkness until the lamp was lit. In the meagre light, Katya inspected the shelves and opened countless small draws containing dried herbs.

"Evika! It's not here," she said.

Meanwhile, the Darklinan entered the preparation room at the back of the shop and came out with two kegs.

"We found some, Stilnassa. They smell like orange blossom, just as you said."

"Excellent," Katya said, still staring at the shelves. "Where would they put it?" A smile lit her face. "Idiot. They wouldn't want to advertise they had it." She got down on her hands and knees crawled behind the counter. At the back of a shelf, she saw a wooden box with a silver lily inlaid into its sides and top.

"Got it," she murmured, and rose to sit the box on the counter. "Come, this is what we need to find in the other healer's shop. It will probably be in a box like this. The powder inside is purple. Do not get any of it on your skin."

"What is it?"

"Love's Lament. It's poison. Which of you is staying?" A tall boy stepped forward. "One keg should be enough. We'll take the other just in case we don't find any at the next place. You'll see our signal. I'll make sure you've enough darkness left to escape."

➤——————➤

Katya and her band left the second apothecary's shop, leaving behind one member and another two dead watchmen.

They headed back towards the plaza, crossing paths with only fat, stray cats. At the head of the street sat a huge double-storey timber building, which occupied the space of about four other shops and whose adjoining yard spread from the back of the building to the next street. As they walked, their whispered conversation barely broke the air.

"Manuzi was one of the first to display the gold. He's not even Talak."

"It profits him to do so," Katya whispered. "He'll probably swap his colours to the emperor's if Eadan and Cēdar look like losing. You say he lives above the shop?"

"Yes."

"Guards?"

"No, stable boy. That's it."

They stopped at the heavy timber double gates that barred the entrance into the rear yard. One of the Darklinan joined his hands and boosted Katya up the gate. She gripped the top, peeking into the yard. Seeing no sentries, she hauled herself up and over the gate. Six large wine barrels sat on a wagon bed, awaiting delivery. Katya moved to the cover of the wagon. She strained to hear, but the only sound of life was the soft wicker of the draught horse from the stable to her right.

A Darklinan girl scaled the gates and joined her. The barrels all sat on their ends with their stoppers facing up. The girl removed the bungs sealing the barrels and Katya donned gloves. Katya painstakingly spooned Love's Lament into each of the large barrels, emptying both boxes they'd stolen into the wine, and the girl pushed the bungs back into their holes.

Each of the barrels was stamped with a large, ornate 'M' and Katya put a slight scratch into the tail of each letter then returned to the squad.

Outside, Katya studied the sky, noting the pre-dawn light creeping forward. "We have to hurry."

They ran across the empty plaza, reaching for the safety of the rooftops. Two flickering glows blossomed in the distance, and the slight tang of smoke tainted the breeze. An explosion rocketed through the air and the burgeoning fires swelled. Flames kissed the sky and spread. Distant screams and cries echoed throughout the city as people awoke to the alarum of "Fire!"

The wine-seller's store burst into life.

The fat merchant ran about tying his pants and donning a shirt, yelling, "Hitch that horse and get that wine out of here! It's paid for! They'll be waiting for it at the kitchens! Get buckets of water! Wet down the walls! Hurry! Hurry! Have them readied if the fire spreads to here."

Katya and the others grinned as the slaves drove the loaded wagon towards the city gates and the field kitchen.

"Now we wait for the poison to take effect. Then we launch phase two."

>———————▶

Tikhon's forces had rested, but upon receiving word from Katya, they had ridden through the night and a large section of them waited, hidden by the last rise before Bēdarik. From his vantage point, Tikhon and his commanders watched the sky, smiling as the orange glow rioted through part of the city.

The enemy forces working on shoring up Bēdarik's external defence rotated in shifts to get food and drink from the field kitchen within the city's walls.

A scout cantered up to him. "Some troops left the wall to put out the fires."

"Good. We'll stay hidden while they enjoy their breakfast."

"Everything depends on Katya and Jadzia's Darklinan. Do you really think a bunch of urchins can save the day?"

"Yes. Being urchins has nothing to do with it. Jadzia trained them; their love of her and their hatred for the Talak nobles are powerful motivation. Do all the troops know to leave the old city and the poorer quarter untouched?"

The officers nodded.

Another scout returned. "The last shift has returned from breaking their fast."

"Move out," Tikhon commanded, and his generals dispersed.

Tikhon, surrounded by his imperial guard and Darcov, moved into position with the forces.

As one, the Zaragarian army crested the rise and moved to meet their Talak foes.

The defenders of Bēdarik, working on the construction parties, ran into Bēdarik. Zaragarian infantry pushed a series of large timber mantlets forward toward the city; behind them rolled catapults. Once the mantlets were in position, archers sheltered behind them and aimed their arrow flight to assail those upon the wall while Tikhon's infantry rushed out, shields before them, to remove blockades across the bridge spanning the moat. Despite the thickening smoke, the archers on the wall targeted them and soldiers fell into the moat pierced by arrows and impaled by the stakes in the moat bed. Zaragarian cavalry galloped along the moat line, shrieking battle cries, drawing fire away from the infantry on the bridge, loosing arrows as they flew past, picking off the Talaks on the wall. Slowly the foot-soldiers pushed the crossed timber barricades off the bridge.

The catapults and their supply wagons took up positions behind their own mantlets. Waves of large rocks bombarded Bēdarik's walls, chipping away at their surface. Several catapults fired clay pots – which exploded into flames on impact – over the walls and into the city.

Infantry units moved long ladders toward the fortifications but remained out of arrow range.

On the west side of Bēdarik, another section of Tikhon's army began an assault on the city.

CHAPTER 35

KATYA WATCHED THE DARKLINAN team leave their compound.

"You can't go with them," Silla said. "You stand out."

"I know, but I don't like asking others to do this work while I stay safe."

Silla laughed. "You're hardly going to be safe."

Katya wore the clothes she had stolen from Jadzia's room and also carried her bow. A full quiver of arrows graced her back, and she carried another full quiver. She left the old temple and headed through the streets of The Bone Yard. She greeted the Darklinan sentries at their barricades and then climbed up to the rooftops, avoiding the small shopping strip of the poorer quarter.

She angled her way across the city, aiming for the west side of Bēdarik and the section of wall where Tikhon said the army would attack. In the old part of the city and the poorer quarter, the houses were crammed together which made travelling between the buildings relatively easy, though a zig-zag route was necessary to avoid the houses whose roofs were still thatch. Katya reached the end of the poorer quarter and the gaps between buildings grew. She moved a plank across the first gap and crossed along it. She bent to pull it back, but hesitated. The city was in chaos. The two fires in the upper section had almost merged into one and the sound of axes rebounded through the streets between the blasts from the catapults' assault on the eastern wall. Crowds of Talaks stood in the plaza gazing in devastated awe as the city burned.

The long tail of a bucket brigade snaked from a well toward the fire. Smaller fires were springing up in the east from the incendiaries Tikhon catapulted in. *No one will notice*. She left the board in place. Planks awaited her at every large break in the roof line; the Darklinan had been busy overnight. She left them all in place and continued on until she was in sight of the wall's western section and the other main gate to Bēdarik. The smoke hung like a sheet in air and visibility was poor. She lowered herself to the streets and stalked forward, cloaked, hood drawn close about her face as if to ward off the pungent fumes. Few people were about as she drew nearer the wall. A section of cleared area held the other field kitchen, but only a couple of bodies lay near the wine cart.

Not enough dead. They must have figured it out.

Along the wall, Talak and Nējarak archers targeted the approaching Zaragarians. The tip of a ladder appeared at the edge of the wall and the Talak archers pushed it away. Screams rent the air as Zaragarian troops fell to their death.

On the edge of Bēdarik's upper city sat an old villa; the sole dwelling not flying the old king's colours. Billowing clouds of smoke roiled down the streets as another shop in the upper merchant precinct burst into flames. Katya darted from her hiding place, covered by the pall, and ran up the hill. She slid to a halt in dismay. The front door of the villa had been bordered up since the Darklinan had scouted the place. She ran to the rear garden. The kitchen door had two boards nailed across it. She picked up a large rock and slammed it against the boards until they gave way and picked the lock.

Exiting the kitchen, she encountered rooms in a state of complete disarray. The Darklinan had reported the owners fled the city before the conflict; so the good citizens of Bēdarik had ransacked it.

Racing up the staircase to the third floor, she slammed open doors, entered each room and threw open windows, looking for the right vantage point. At the last room, she found the angle she needed.

Along the wall, archers fired upon the second Zaragarian force. Two of them reach out to push a ladder off the wall. Katya drew her bow and loosed a series of arrows. The Talaks, attempting to push the ladder, fell, arrows sticking from their backs.

The first of the Zaragarians made it into the city.

Katya kept up a steady stream of arrows, targeting the enemy along the wall until Tikhon's forces overwhelmed them.

———➤

Dressed in clothes befitting respectable citizens of Bēdarik, the second squad of Darklinan headed toward the main city gates. The group strolled through the lanes as if they owned them. A perfect blend of cockiness and care developed from years on the streets fending for themselves.

Talaks rushed to the upper shopping area, buckets and axes and long fire hooks in hand to stop the spreading fire.

"We did a good job. They're going to try to fell buildings to stop the fire."

The sun burned orange through the pall of smoke, creating a murky dusk in the streets. At the sound of heavy footfalls marching down the cobblestones ahead, they darted down a narrow gap between two buildings.

A squad of the city watch strode past. "Oi, you lot!" The Darklinan froze in the dark, rank alcove, waiting. There was no way out. No boxes or crates, and the smooth wall prevented climbing. Surely, they couldn't be seen.

"You! Grab them." Scuffles broke out farther down the street and the muted protests reached them. "Shut ya mouths! They need all hands to fight the fires. Ya coming with us! Stop bloody whinging! The whole city could burn, an' it'll be your problem then."

Watchmen dragged a group of Talaks away to fight the fire.

Jadzia's Darklinan emerged cautiously and continued. The boom from the catapulted rocks striking the wall became a strident thunder and the ground beneath them trembled.

They hid at the corner of a street, peering toward the portcullis and timber gates. A massive rock hit the building next to them, sending dust and debris raining upon the street. The group pressed against the wall, cringing.

"It's not worth it. Nothing is. I'm leaving," a boy said.

The others stopped him. "No! We do this for Lady Jadzia. She helped us when no one would."

The boy hung his head, guilt written across his features. Finally, he nodded.

"It won't be long now," the eldest said. "Look."

At the field kitchen, the cook hunched, grabbing his stomach before slumping over his stew pot, dead. Soldiers along the wall slid down against it, some convulsing as they gripped their abdomens. Others swayed and leaned against the wall before collapsing. A soldier ran to his friend, bent over him, and checked to see if he was alive. He reared back at the sight of purple foam on the man's mouth. "Poison!" he yelled. The cook's assistants lay sprawled next to the field kitchen and the wine wagon. Slowly, each man on this section of the wall succumbed to the toxic drink.

The Darklinan emerged from their hiding place and approached the gatehouse tower. No one stopped them. A hand reached out, gripping the ankle of a Darklinan. She lashed out, kicking the dying man in the face. They pushed the door open and entered the large room that held the windlass for raising the portcullis. Two men lay inside. A third, ashen faced, confronted them, sword raised.

He swayed where he stood. "Get out!"

The Darklinan closed the door, forming a semi-circle around him.

The tip of his sword dipped, and he fought for control of his limbs. "No, you evikan bastard traitors. No." He lunged at them.

The eldest boy sidestepped, dropped to one knee and sliced with his dagger, severing the man's hamstring. The Talak collapsed, and the Darklinan girl finished him.

Two of them worked the windlass and raised the portcullis at the far side of the broad wall.

The others opened the wooden gates into the city.

➤——————➤

The resistance along the wall had dwindled to nothing, and Tikhon gave the signal to advance as the portcullis rose. His forces poured into Bēdarik.

Tikhon rode through the main gates, flanked by Darcov and the imperial guard. The Darklinan were nowhere to be seen, but bodies lay everywhere, soldiers and citizens of Bēdarik. His army slaughtered any who resisted as they cleared the area house by house.

"Get that wagon of wine out of here and dispose of it," he ordered.

Darcov caught sight of movement from a window above them, thrust out his shield to cover Tikhon and an arrow slammed into it.

"Kill them all," Tikhon said. A squad of soldiers entered the building. A woman's screams followed, the cry of a child ceased abruptly, and the body of a man fell from the window.

Tikhon addressed the surrounding soldiers. "Spread these orders. Kill anyone in a uniform: soldiers and the city watch. Kill anyone bearing weapons. If they have weapons hidden in their houses, kill them. If they fly the colours of the old king, kill every single member of their family. Do not kill the slaves if they make no move against you. Do not enter the old city. Rape is forbidden. The soldiers can take what they want from the homes of the dead for forty-eight hours. Darcov, see that the fires are extinguished. I will reward citizens who aid in this."

Darcov and an imperial guard departed, along with a band of soldiers.

A general cantered up to Tikhon. "This section through to the plaza is clear, My Emperor. Our other force has fought through and the Order members have joined us. They..."

"They what?"

"The slaying of Master Pavel has made them savage. I swear I saw one tear a man apart. They fight with no care."

"Perhaps Mstislav has joined them and fuels their fury. This city deserves no mercy. But see to it they know my orders regarding the old city."

Tikhon rode through the streets, surveying the damage done to his city as he made his way to the Temple of Mstislav. His troops held the centre of Bēdarik under total control. Currently they roamed the streets, rounding up resistance.

Inside the temple, he went to the grand statue of Mstislav, put his hand upon it and said, "For victory, I thank you."

The body of Master Pavel lay at the feet of the statue. Tikhon barely recognised the old man. A twinge of resigned sadness plagued him. "You should not have left the temple."

Tikhon strode through the upper levels to survey the city from the temple's tower. Two of his guard remained with him while the others blocked the stairs. The fires had destroyed much of the upper merchant area, but stopped when it hit the long, thin, green strip of park that separated the upper city from those beneath them. The sound of axes still resonated, and multiple bucket lines snaked from the city's wells and the main fountain that heralded the entrance to the upper city. At the edge of the fire, an unburnt building collapsed, and a cheer rose from the fighters. Only one side of the fire burnt uncontrolled and the firefighting effort moved to that area.

"My Emperor," his guard called out. "Master Dimitri wishes to see you."

"Let him come." Tikhon turned to face him. "Well, Dimitri, are your Mstislavakan sated?"

"There are still more to be rooted out and cleansed."

"Of course, and to that end, you can concentrate on the names on this list." He handed over the paper scroll. "Do what you will with them but have them dig their own graves beforehand. My troops have enough to do without wasting time to bury the likes of them."

Dimitri bowed, grinning. "With pleasure, Your Majesty."

"Just remember, Dimitri, no rape."

"Who would risk a mongrel child?"

"Dimitri, you would do well to remember your niece is half Talak."

"Of course," Dimitri said smoothly, "but her case is different. Jadzia has ensured she upholds our best traditions." Tikhon glared at him, until Dimitri bowed, saying quickly. "I didn't think, my apologies."

"Find the Zaragarian women and their children. Ensure they reach the safety of the temple."

Throughout the day runners delivered messages to Tikhon, declaring more districts of the city safe.

"Your Majesty, they have Cēdar and Eadan downstairs."

Tikhon descended to the main hall of the temple to find Eadan and Cēdar, battered and bloody, on their knees before the statue of Mstislav.

"Master Dimitri said to bring these two to you. We found them hiding in a cellar," a Mstislavakan said.

"I'd expected no less." Tikhon glanced around the large hall and saw no women or children. "Where are the Zaragarian brides and their children?"

"We've not found them, Your Majesty."

Cēdar chuckled, wincing in pain from his swollen face. "And you won't. They're long gone. Well over the border in Nējarak, on their way to the Rēsphian slave markets."

"Slave markets!" Tikhon roared. "Zaragarians as slaves!" Tikhon kicked Cēdar in the face, fracturing his already damaged jaw and snapping his neck. He stood before Eadan, drew his sword and drove it through the traitor's neck. "Take their heads and mount them on the temple gates."

Tikhon stormed from the building with his guard and mounted his horse. He cantered to the western gate, noting the wine wagon still sitting at the field kitchen. "Get rid of that!"

He halted outside the city where Dimitri had the prisoners surrounded by his Mstislavakan. Hundreds of men, women and children sat bound, while another group completed a huge, long pit.

"You've worked fast," Tikhon said to Dimitri.

"Yes, Your Majesty, the ground here was softest, and I promised I'd spare the children of those who worked well."

"Begin, Dimitri."

"This will take some time. Do you...?"

"I ordered it. I will watch it," Tikhon said, his face like stone.

The Mstislavakan lined the Talak men along the pit and executed them. The women followed. They hauled bawling children to the feet; a baby was tossed into the grave. Some of Tikhon's guards averted their eyes.

"Wait!" Tikhon ordered. He murmured to one of his blue-robed bodyguard who galloped off toward the gate. The children huddled together, some pleaded and begged, others curled in upon themselves and wept. The wine wagon rumbled up the hill and stopped near the children.

"Give them all something to drink," Tikhon said.

The children twisted and turned to avoid the drink. A Mstislavakan slapped a child across the face. The small girl was dressed in expensive colourful silks and clutching a porcelain doll.

"Stop!" Tikhon yelled. He dismounted and approached the child. Kneeling before her, he said. "I know you, don't I?" Eyes wide, tears rolling down her face, she stared at him. "I do. You're Anfisa; Lord Bashtan's daughter. Aren't you?" She nodded. He wiped away her tears. "You know Rada."

"She's my friend," Anfisa whispered. "She likes my dolls."

"I thought so," Tikhon said. "You know who I am?"

She nodded. "You're the emperor. Rada's Uncle Tikhon."

A bitter taste filled Tikhon's mouth, an iron fist twisting his insides. "Yes. So, I make the rules." The other children listened intently, exchanging glances. Hope crept into their eyes. "You have nothing to fear. He should *not* have done that to the baby. It was cruel. *That* will not happen to any of you." He smiled, taking her hand. "This will make you feel better. You've all been through so much, you're tired and thirsty." He passed her the mug. "Here, you'll feel better and be able to rest."

Anfisa took the mug and drank. "Good girl." He scooped her up and continued to hold her while the Mstislavakan handed out more wine and all the children drank.

"My tummy hurts," Anfisa said.

"I know, but not for long." Tikhon rubbed her back. Her head lowered to his shoulder and, along with all the others, she succumbed to the poison.

Tikhon tossed her into the pit with others.

CHAPTER 36

RADA SLID TO A stop outside a large, colourful room. Her grandmother sat in a rocking chair, cradling the baby, who rioted within her arms. Light from two large windows and the open balcony doors bathed them in sunlight.

Confused, Rada spun around, looking back along the corridor. "Where did she go?"

"Who?"

Rada gasped and entered the room, searching behind curtains, under the single bed and in wardrobes. "I don't understand. She was there, but now she's gone. Poof! Just gone!"

"Rada, who is gone?"

"The skinny woman with the short hair. She hid in a room the other day, listening to you and Grandpa. I saw her today and followed her, but I lost her. One moment she was there, then I went around a bend and..." Rada waved her arms about. "She's gone!"

"A woman spying on us?"

"Yep. I was going to get her too!"

"Rada, tell me exactly what she looked like," her grandmother said.

"I told Mami, didn't she say?"

"No, but your mother has been tired and probably forgot," Galina said. "So, you must tell me."

"Really skinny, but not like skinny because she was sick. I think she was fit, because I saw the muscles on her forearm and, you know, you can't always see that. Only people who train hard or work hard have them. Um... not tall, short hair and dressed like a slave, skin like your colour." Rada paced, her hand resting on her dagger. "Do you think the empress sent her to hurt Bubba?"

"Possibly but leave it to me and your grandpa to worry about."

"I've got my dagger."

"Good. Keep it with you."

A maid knocked on the door, Rada whirled to face her dagger drawn.

"Um, Stilnassa Galina, I have the milk," the woman stammered.

Galina beckoned her in. "Leave it," she said, taking the small pottery jug from the maid. "And fetch my sword and dagger."

"Shh, little one," her grandmother crooned. She put the spout in the baby's mouth and attempted to feed her. The babe took several swallows, then screwed up her face, fisted her small hands and reddened as if she would explode. "She doesn't like goat's milk at all."

"She'll probably yell soon and she can yell, really, really loud for such a small body. Akim thought we could use her as a weapon," Rada said.

"Akim?"

"The captain of our guard. He's nice." Rada took in the furniture in the bright room. "Is this a nursery?"

"Yes, we kept it for grandchildren. You were in here last time you visited. Although you won't remember that."

Rada ran her hands over the beautifully carved rocking horse. "This is big enough for me."

"I suppose, but you've got that huge monster of a horse. What do you call him?"

"BC," Rada said, playing with the horse-hair mane on the toy. "It's short for Bone Crusher."

"That makes sense. He's had to be put in a yard on his own and he's bitten several of the grooms."

"Evika!" Rada said. Her grandmother's brows rose. "Oh, oops! Um, I forgot about him. I should look after him. Akim said that's my job. He's my horse and a good recruit always looks after their mount because our lives depend on it."

Her grandmother gaped. "You've been looking after him on your own?"

Rada nodded. "He was cranky at first, but Akim says that I'm like a fly BC just can't get rid of, so he's given up trying. Now he's a good boy for me, mostly."

Galina smiled sadly and her eyes grew moist. "Well, then I suppose you should keep looking after him. But don't get hurt."

The baby squalled loud enough to shake the rafters.

"I think I must be out of practise. She's not settling."

"It's usually either food, wind, or poop," Rada said. "I can't smell her, so I guess it's not that."

"We will find a wet nurse," Galina said, "and hopefully soon."

Rada held out her arms. "I'll try."

"Once she gets too heavy, tell me. I don't want you to drop her."

"I won't," Rada said. "I'm strong." The baby quietened immediately. "I've been carrying her a lot. Well, me and Tav." Rada's face twisted, and she fought back tears. "I'm going to take her for a walk. I won't go far. But you can have a rest. All right?"

She turned her back on her grandmother without waiting for an answer and marched out. With a shake of her head, Galina rose and caught up with her.

"I'm not going to drop her!" Rada reddened. "I'm not some weak little girl."

"Of course not." Galina's lips twitched.

Rada spun, glaring, but faced only her grandmother's placid expression and no trace of mockery.

The maid returned bearing a sword and dagger, which her grandmother buckled to her side. "Where are we going?"

"Exploring. We'll show Bubba everything. First to the stables. I need something from the carriage, and I'll let you hold her while I talk to BC."

"The stables are a good choice, Rada. The guards are there." She rested her hand on Rada's shoulder. "If you see this woman, or anyone you're sure doesn't belong here, you find me or your grandpa. We'll increase the estate patrols and be on the lookout for her."

They strolled through the vast vegetable gardens and past the tribe of servants and slaves who tended them before reaching the stables. The stable master greeted them, bowing.

"Where is Stilniat Rada's horse?"

A high-pitched squeal, followed by a shout and laughter, came from the back of the stable block.

"Found him," Rada said, and strode through the breezeway.

At the rear, BC, in his own large yard, cantered around with a piece of cloth in his mouth and a groom vaulted the fence. The groom rubbed his shoulder, inspecting the massive hole in his shirt. Akim, Adana and Regansh stood nearby, exchanging coins.

Galina's lips formed a thin line of disapproval.

"Who won?" Rada said cheerfully.

"Regansh," Akim said. "About time you showed up to do your duty."

She passed Bubba to her grandmother, and the infant immediately screamed. Galina slumped.

"Here, Stilnassa, you look done in." Adana took the baby. "Shh you little grot bucket. Everyone knows you're here." The child subsided to a low, rolling grizzle.

Adana said, "You're looking very fine, Rada. And proper warrior braids!"

Her grandmother bristled at their informal address of Rada.

"Stilnassa," Akim said, "forgive us. Rada is one of us now and we don't use titles amongst ourselves. Now, Rada, get in there. He needs a proper brush and you need to clean your gear."

Rada picked up the brush dropped by the groom and climbed the fence. "BC!" she yelled. He did a victory lap past her as she sat on the top rail. "BC! Right now!" The horse trotted up, nuzzled her and knocked her off the fence backwards. Galina gasped. Akim caught Rada and put her back on the rail. "Bad BC!" The horse let out a snort and sidled up to the fence. Rada scratched behind his ear and groomed his face. His eyes closed, and she sidled along the rail to brush his back.

Regansh brought her a bucket. "Here, stand on this to do his sides." She was also holding the baby carrier.

"That's what I wanted from the carriage, thanks. Then I can take Bubba exploring. We need to know where everything is."

"Move him away from us, Rada," Galina said. "You're sending hair flying everywhere."

The Stilnassa watched her granddaughter, happily working away and getting dirtier by the second, first brushing BC then cleaning her gear under the watchful eye of three imposing imperial guards.

"We need to get her more clothes," Galina said.

"You'll never keep her clean," Akim said. "Or out of trouble." Glancing down at her weapons, he whispered, "Stilnassa, why are you armed?"

"Rada observed someone spying on Stepan and I," she murmured. "It happened the other day, but I've only just found out. We'll be stepping up security on the estate and house."

"Have you enough household guards?"

"Yes. We will deal with this, so do not fear for the children," she whispered.

"Stilnassa, we have our orders to leave. Perhaps I can speak to my superiors."

"Akim, I thank you, but I suspect that without direct intervention by the emperor, the empress would derail any attempt for you to stay."

He frowned, whispering, "These children do not deserve this."

"No, they do not," Galina replied. "But we will handle it, never fear. Let's speak no more of this. Rada is returning with that horse."

"As you wish." Akim straightened, wiped the concern from his face and said, "We thank you for your hospitality, but they have recalled us to barracks and we may be on the road again soon."

Rada stopped before them, crestfallen. "You're leaving? But..."

He knelt before her. "We have our duty and the emperor needs us. We must protect him."

"I know, but..." She leapt forward and hugged him. "I'll miss you."

"We'll miss you too," he said, returning the hug.

Adana returned the baby to her grandmother, and she and Regansh knelt before Rada and embraced her.

"We'll be back before long, and then your training starts in earnest," Adana said.

They rose, bowed to the Stilnassa and left.

Rada stared after them. "Everyone is leaving me."

>———>

The great fireplace in Jadzia's room blazed, creating an oppressive heat. The curtains were drawn, and she lay bundled under doonas. Jadzia whimpered in pain as her body spasmed and her rasping breath was the only sound other than the fire's crackle. She looked at the jar of poppy juice on the table near the bed. Her mother had just given her some before leaving. *If only I could reach it.* Cramps wracked her muscles and her belly burned, yet she shivered and the rest of her was like ice. *Evika, this is not what I planned. My children!* At least she'd made them safe.

There was something Rada told her. Something important she should have told her mother. *It's so hard to think. What was it? Gods, if only I could remember!* It hovered on the edge of her thoughts. *Someone watching?* It slipped from her grasp on the wave of poppy. Her head spun, and she tried to focus on the table, but it swirled. She curled into a ball.

Beside her, the shadows shifted and Bethsinidar stepped into view. She lay her hand upon Jadzia's brow and kissed her forehead. Jadzia's mind cleared, but the memory she sought vanished.

"Daughter, rest easy now," Bethsinidar said.

"You? You look the same as when I was little."

Bethsinidar smiled. "Of course. You kept that secret well, didn't you?"

"I wasn't sure I saw you."

"You were scared, and they had sent your grandmother away for her beliefs. You took the practical path, as is your way, and shall suffer no blame for it."

"My baby needs a name."

"Of course."

"I've told my mother my choices."

"Yes, I have seen it. Are you sure?"

"Yes! Why are you here? You put that Sennerese in Rada's path, didn't you?"

"I've always been here and never stopped watching you. Even when you visited that abomination of a temple in the name of Mstislav. You made the choices you needed to in this world. Know this, once you received your true name in my temple, you remained my daughter, regardless of anything else. You knew that in your heart. Jadzia, you've never betrayed one of our faith. You kept Katya by your side. You'd never inform on the young healer Bree and your grandmother lives in your memory like a fire."

Jadzia panted. "Give me the poppy!" Her hands spasmed and her whole body grew rigid. Veins stood out on her neck and a rictus of pain contorted her face. "Evika!" Jadzia screamed.

Bethsinidar's form dissipated. Feet thundered down the corridor, and the door flew open as Rada and her grandparents burst in.

"Mami!" Rada ran to the bed and scrambled onto it. Rada lay alongside her and hugged her through the quilt. Jadzia's lips were blue; sweat plastered her hair to her skin. Galina sat, red-eyed, on the bed next to Rada and Jadzia; one hand resting on each of them.

Her lips moved in prayer. "Hokati, give me strength."

Stepan wept and took his daughter's hand. She gripped it with all her remaining might. "Give me the poppy," she ground out.

A look of resignation passed between her parents. Her mother nodded. Stilnaat Maklova snatched up the bottle and eyed it like a viper. He shook his head.

"Do it, please, Papi," Jadzia begged.

He slumped and moved to her bedside. Easily lifting her shoulders, he poured the entire bottle of poppy juice down her throat.

Another scream tore from Jadzia. Her legs cramped and pain built in her head.

Her breathing slowed. With slurred words, she said, "Make sure she is named."

She stared at the shadows in the room's corner, seeing none of them, but then shifted her gaze to Rada and smiled.

A fire sparked in her skull. Her vision wavered and the last breath of life left her.

⇒——————➤

Jadzia's body lay atop an enormous pyre in a field of the estate. Flowers surrounded it and they had dressed her in black boots and a fine long coat embroidered with horses and the lynx of their family crest nestled within the Zaragarian viper. In her hands rested an ornate sword, and a bow lay by her side.

Mourners had come from all the surrounding estates and from within the city. From lords and ladies to merchants and slaves, a procession passed through the estate all day to visit the site. Each bore tokens which were laid upon the pyre. The household guards held vigil along with either Galina or Stepan.

Rada, carrying her sister, stood beside her grandparents, awaiting darkness.

"You don't have to stay all night," Stepan said to Rada. "Whenever you wish to go in, Granny will take you. She and I will hold vigil till dawn."

"I'll go in when Bubba has to," Rada said, solemn. "I don't really want to watch."

"You just have to stay for the beginning, until the visitors have left," Galina said. "Tomorrow, just us, we'll put Mami's ashes to rest in the spot you chose."

"And we'll put that pretty coloured stone with her name there too?"

"Yes. You chose both with great care. We're proud, Rada," Stepan said.

The setting sun cast the sky in defiant rays of amber and smoky purple. The raucous chorus of birds dwindled as they settled in against the terror of night. Stepan walked forward, carrying the torch to light the pyre, according to tradition, as the first fingers of night touched it. He lowered the torch and in the silence the rumble of a carriage and the hoofbeats of many soldier's mounts carried like the tolling of a bell.

A slave rushed to Stepan, stopping him. He scowled before turning with a placid smile and joining Galina.

The chink of mail and marching, heavily-booted feet tore away the calm respect that blanketed the crowd, replacing it with a ripple of murmurs and an anxious hum of voices. A column of soldiers parted the gathering. Each carried a torch and bore the insignia of the emperor on ghostly blue uniforms. At their centre strode the most beautiful woman Rada had ever seen, followed by two richly dressed women. She bore a fine golden crown inset with sapphires, and wore a gown of shimmering silks. As she walked, the over-skirt revealed the same pale blue of her guards and an underskirt flashed the darker imperial blue. The bodice of her gown was tight and embroidered with gold. She wore an impractical, short-sleeved vest, which ended just below her breasts, and was held closed with a glittering serpent broach.

"Is that the empress?" Rada whispered.

"Yes," said Stepan. "Now be quiet."

Rada stepped back, wrapped her arms around her sister and glowered at the approaching woman.

The procession stopped before Galina and Stepan, who bowed deeply. Rada took the cue and, unable to bow whilst the carrier held Bubba, dipped her head before raising it and staring defiantly at Empress Sabina.

The empress waved her hands, and her guard surrounded the pyre.

"Your Majesty, you honour us with your presence," Stepan said.

"If my husband were in the capital, then I know he would certainly be here to honour Stilnassa Jadzia, with whom..." her mouth twisted in a small moue, "... he has always been so close. Your family serves the empire well, and I'm sure that we can count on your continued loyalty and discretion." Her eyes strayed to Rada, who stepped back and curled her lip. The empress gave a brittle laugh and bent to look Rada in the eyes. "Such fire." She grabbed her chin, turning her head and inspecting her features before letting go. "Well," she whispered. "At least I don't have to worry about you, little girl. I can see the Talak in you." She flicked her fingers and a lady-in-waiting passed her a handkerchief to wipe her hands on.

Rada bristled. "I'm not little," she ground out.

Galina squeezed her shoulder, quelling her.

Sabina reached out to touch the baby and Rada growled. The empress's hand hovered over the baby's head and she smiled predatorily.

"Forgive her, Your Imperial Majesty," Stepan said. "She has suffered a great loss – we all have. And now, on this occasion, it overwhelms her."

Sabina withdrew her hand and stood, suddenly mindful of her surroundings and the crowd. Her mask of sympathy slid into place. "Of course. This is understandable and commendable in young Rada to be protective." She glanced at the sky. "What a pity, my apologies. We missed the first hand of darkness. Oh dear! May I say some words?"

"Of course," Stepan said, expressionless. Though in the torch light Rada thought she could see a vein throb in his temple.

Empress Sabina faced the gathering, her expression at once demure, serious and sorrowful. "The great Zaragarian Empire has suffered a devastating loss. Stilnassa Jadzia served the empire diligently and with honour, as her family has done for generations. Her decades of service will never be forgotten by me... or anyone within our world. She will be written into our annals with the highest honours." The tight lines around her eyes belied her sad smile. "This night we bid her farewell on her final journey to rest in peace in Eviendyti. Her family are in our prayers to Hokati and may Mstislav keep their blades sharp and grant them many victories in the battles to come." She nodded to Stepan, who moved forward and lit the bonfire. Each of her guards stepped forward and ignited the timber on all sides.

Sabina watched the flames begin to consume their prize before turning to leave. Her guard formed up around her, forcing Rada and her grandparents to step back. The last guard fell in, and Rada gasped. She clamped her hand over her mouth as the group left. One by one, people filed past the family, expressing their condolences. Rada gripped her grandmother's hand tightly.

When only the servants and slaves remained, Rada burst out, "I saw her! The spy! She was one of the empress's guards."

CHAPTER 37

"Tikhon, the Mstislavakan cannot be the city watch," Darcov said.

"It's temporary. They're thorough and it keeps Dimitri busy. They'll deal with the initial trouble and then when everyone hates them, I'll bring the regulars in, whom they'll love."

"You hope."

"It will work. How is the clean-up going?"

"Fine. The fire is all but out," Darcov said. "It took out most of the upper merchants. I've got squads rotating shifts to assist with the removal of bodies and debris. People are terrified, but we're spreading the word we've no problem with those who didn't rebel. However, poor quarter and the old city remain locked down."

"Sensible. Come, we'll talk to them. We walk." Tikhon's guard formed up around him. "Darcov, beside me. The rest of you spread out a bit. I do not want to appear as if I'm terrified of an attack."

Darcov picked up his shield and fell in step beside his friend.

Blackened, exhausted faces, hollow-eyed, bowed at the emperor as he passed; some even prostrated themselves. No one spoke. Not a child could be seen and other than the noise of distant hammering, no other sound.

Cart loads of bodies rolled through the streets. Other carts carried burned debris – the wreckage of lifetimes. The tang of ash and smoke tainted the living – their skin, hair and clothes.

"Ensure that all those of our troops who assist in the clean-up know I will pay them extra for this service. Keep note of the citizenry who willingly assist us."

Tikhon stopped outside the new broad gates, which now barred entrance to the poorer quarter merchant streets and the old city.

"Are you sure this is a good idea?" Darcov said.

"Not really, but they didn't fight, so that's something." Tikhon nodded to a guard and flicked his hand at the gates.

The guard marched over and pounded upon them. "Open in the name of his Imperial Majesty Tikhon I."

"I'm not sure I'm going to get used to that," Tikhon muttered.

"You already are," Darcov chided.

Tikhon's brows rose, but before he could retort, a flutter of movement on the rooftop caught his eye. "I think our Darklinan benefactors are watching us."

The guard returned. "My Emperor, what do you want done?"

"Wait."

Darklinan rose from behind the roof ridge lines nearest the gate. A taller figure, armed with a bow, bowed. Tikhon returned the greeting with a flourish. "Stilnassa Katya, greetings to you and the Darklinan. They've our gratitude and all that comes with that."

"It is the emperor," Katya called out to those behind the gate. She slid down the gable, and her extended foot hit the top of the gate, halting her. Still with bow and an arrow in hand, she sat on the edge of the roof, speaking to those below.

Tikhon strode forward. "I am Tikhon, your emperor. I have no quarrel with the people of the old city. Those that did not taken up arms against me are free to roam without repercussions. In fact, I will reward you. I grant you free rein for the next twenty-four hours to take what you like from the unoccupied homes in the upper city."

Katya cast him a quick grin and climbed down the inside of the gate. There was a great deal of murmuring and a metallic clatter. The imperial guard moved into position, hands on weapons. The gates swung open. Standing before Tikhon were the old city merchants. None were armed. They all prostrated themselves before him.

"Rise. I ask for only two things. Do not destroy or burn. Wear blue armbands to signal to my army that you are loyal."

The merchants huddled together, muttering. "We accept."

Tikhon suppressed a smile.

"Accept?" Darcov whispered. "What else were they going to do?"

"Excellent, then send a runner to all your people to let them know."

The merchants dispersed, bickering amongst themselves.

"Get sacks."

"No! Get a cart! We'll take as much from those rich bastards as we can."

"Are Jadzia and Rada alive?" Katya asked, joining Tikhon, her face lined with worry.

"Yes, though Jadzia was injured and Stilnaat Dimitri tells me she may be gravely ill."

Katya blanched; her hands clenched. "We can blame her fate on Neeren. I've killed her."

"Yes, and we've cleansed this place of the rest." Tikhon sighed and rubbed his temple. "Katya, what do the Darklinan need?"

"For the moment, nothing. Though the money Stilnassa Jadzia left will run out soon, and we will need more to buy supplies."

"Done. Katya, the Darklinan are out of the shadows now. I would meet with them at a later date to thank them and talk to you about their future. For now, take care of them and see to Jadzia's villas. Though they lie outside the city, I placed a squad of guards at both to ensure they are not looted. Keep the servants and slaves you deem trustworthy. We will put the rest in work gangs."

"As you wish, My Emperor," Katya said before leaving.

"The poor will strip those other houses bare," Darcov said.

"I've no idea how much there is to strip since the soldiers went through." Tikhon laughed. "You three," he said to his guard. "Tell my commanders and spread my orders to all the soldiers you see regarding those of the old city." Smiling, he clapped Darcov on the back. "Come, Darcov, back to the temple. I need food and drink. Things worked out well."

When they entered the great hall in the temple, an exhausted looking woman in a fine grey uniform was standing head bowed, talking to a member of the Order. The priest touched her shoulder, pointing to Tikhon. Her shoulders slumped, yet she walked toward him and bowed, reluctant to meet his eyes.

Tikhon took one look at the lynx insignia on her shirt and stepped back with a harsh intake of breath. His elation at his victory plummeted and his hands shook. "Speak," he snapped.

"Your Imperial Majesty, I bring word from Stilnaat Stepan Maklova. I..." The woman fell to her knees, tears in her eyes. "I am sorry, My Emperor, Stilnassa Jadzia has passed from this world."

Tikhon stared at her, speechless. His heart pounded, bile rose in his throat and sweat broke out on his brow.

The courier, hands shaking, held out a scroll sealed in a leather tube. "Stilnassa Galina Maklova bade me give you this letter."

Tikhon paled and turned from the sight of it. Darcov snatched the scroll. "Our sympathy and thanks to you in this trying time. Dismissed." Worry creasing his brow, put he a hand upon Tikhon's shoulder to steady him. "Tikhon?"

"Those evikan bastards." Tikhon's face twisted as he raged. "This is their fault! If my father had got off his arse and conquered this place properly, none of this disaster would have happened. The woman I love wouldn't have married that poor excuse of man and she wouldn't be dead. The rebels are lucky they're dead. Right now, I could burn the whole world. This empire will expand and I will do it in the ways of old. There will be no negotiations. No political machinations for quiet takeovers. They will fall and be cleansed. Done!"

"Agreed," Darcov said, handing him the letter.

Tikhon broke the seal and held it so both he and Darcov could read it:

My Emperor, our hearts bleed for the loss of Jadzia. She blessed our lives and the empire with her grace and wisdom. We had the best medicos available tend to her and all agreed that nothing could be done. The damage caused by those Talaks was simply too great. I know you will make them pay.

Rada is a shadow of grief, and she visits the grave daily. One of the few things to make her smile are her horse and her sister, who is thriving in the care of her wet nurse. Stepan grumbles daily about Rada and her horse, but she has crept into all our hearts. Rada dreads returning to Bēdarik and her father. It is plain to me she fears him and we will not return her to that man. For all that Jadzia sacrificed, I hope you will grant her child this, that she may remain with us.

The burdens of an emperor are great and I shall add to them. It is clear the babe is yours and Jadzia's. Is there a name you wish for her? I believe the empress suspects she is your daughter. Rada caught sight of a spy in the house, listening to Stepan and me discuss the child. We searched but could find no sign of her. It is easily within the empress's power to send spies, or worse. My Emperor, she could not hurt Jadzia in life, but with her death, she has the means to do great harm to us all through the babe. We have placed extra guards for your daughter's protection.

I hoped never to witness the death of my beloved daughter and I wish the same for you.

May Mstislav strengthen your hand and sharpen your blade to keep you safe.

My life is yours,
Stilnassa Galina Maklova.

Tikhon tossed the letter into the altar fire in the great hall.

The messenger lingered at their backs. Darcov spun to face her. "I said you were dismissed! Leave us."

"There is one more message, Stilnaat Darcov. The Stilnassa has dispatched riders and a series of horses at way points between here and Vēkaria, should you wish to use them. There will be enough for two of your guard to accompany you." The courier bowed and backed away.

Tikhon let out a desperate, crazed laugh. "Clever old woman."

"What are you going to do?" Darcov asked.

"Well, for one, I'm making you governor of this city."

Darcov groaned. "I'm not cut out for that. I'd rather fight or fuck, not run a bloody city."

"You're the only one I trust completely. Get it in shape and get to work on improving the city's defences. I don't want the Nējaraks to think they can come back. We'll be settling our own people here and we'll bring Talak in line with the rest of the empire."

"What else?"

"I'm heading back to Vēkaria to chat with my empress. I'll ride all day and into the nights if I must."

"She wouldn't dare hurt them, and Galina and Stepan will keep them safe."

"Galina would not send this and name the empress unless she thought the situation was dire. As powerful as they are, they cannot directly take on Sabina. And did you note that my daughter is not yet named? I'll bet my last coin, that's thanks to Sabina. She can take vengeance to a whole new level. By the time I'm done, she won't dare harm a hair on either of my girls."

>———>

Scowling, Galina marched into the building. Her footsteps echoed on the stone floor as she made her way to her husband's study. He sat morosely in his favourite chair, a glass of wine in hand.

"No one will name the child," she said.

"What? How is that possible?" Stepan said, slurring his words slightly.

"Sabina. It seems the empress wants one last act of revenge upon Jadzia."

"Damn her. If Tikhon were here, he'd make this happen."

"He's not, and the child needs a name."

"We can name her. We know she wanted to name her Nadya. She doesn't need it done in a temple." He snorted, shaking his head. "Nadya. A name that means 'hope'. She'll need more than that. It's not like the child's future will be bright."

"Jadzia wanted her named properly. She died for this," Galina said.

"I'm not going to war with Sabina over a bastard child whose future is uncertain at best. We'll name her ourselves."

"That's not the same," Rada said from the doorway. "I bet you haven't tried everywhere. What about Bethsinidar? The Weaver will name her."

Her grandparents gaped and Galina hauled her into the room and slammed the door. "Never say that again. Never!" She shook her. "Do you hear me?"

Rada pouted and wriggled, trying to break her grandmother's hold. "Names are really important! Without a proper name, she'll stay in the Shadow Lands forever if she dies!"

"Rada, she is getting stronger every day. She will not die," Stepan said.

"She will. The window keeps getting left open at night. That nurse was sound asleep, and the window was open with cold air coming in! And Bubba was uncovered!"

"What are you talking about? When did this happen?" Galina asked.

"It's happened twice!" Rada stamped her foot. "Last night and the week before. I don't like the nurse. She seems nice, but how can she sleep so sound? I could have dropped a pot on her head and she wouldn't have woken up! It's a good thing I check!"

Galina looked to Stepan, who said, "Sounds like something you should deal with, not me."

"Rada, no more talk of the Senner Isles or The Weaver. Go to your sister, take her on her morning walk, and I'll join you shortly."

Rada scowled, spun on her heel, and left.

"Stepan, get your head out of that wine bottle! It's been well over a week! Jadzia is gone, and this is not helping. We have two granddaughters to protect and, if Rada is correct, the empress's spy may be still gaining entrance to our home. I'm going to talk to the nurse and then I'm going to increase the guards."

"They're already doing their best. The estate is vast and half of them went with Tikhon." He sighed, rubbing his hand over his face. "Ah! The bottle's done anyway."

"Tomorrow, I think you should take Rada with you on your rounds." He opened his mouth to speak, but she ploughed on. "She needs to see the city and learn about life here. All she does is either train with the guard or endlessly carry the baby with her because she is frightened of losing her. She needs to learn she can trust us to care for them and she needs distraction." He tried to speak, and she held up her hand, forestalling him. "No objections! Your granddaughter needs you and..." Her face crumpled.

He reached her side and held her. "I was going to say yes. You didn't need to go all bossy warrior woman on me."

Galina hugged him back, sobbing. With a faint smile, she punched his shoulder then left the room, heading toward the nursery.

The nurse was standing in one corner of the room, arms folded while Rada glowered at her and wrapped her sister up before bundling her into the carrier.

"Stilnassa!" the nurse cried. "I tried to stop her. She's taking the babe out again. It can't be good for her. She's not learning to settle in her crib. Each night she's harder to get down to sleep and is so restless."

"Really?" Galina said. "Rada here has been taking the baby every night to her room and you've been sleeping through it! So how you'd notice the child being restless is beyond me. And no more open windows at night!"

The wet nurse paled. "Open windows? Stilnassa?"

"I will place a guard on this door at night and one outside the balcony. Come, Rada, let's go on our walk."

Rada's eyes brimmed with tears and she sniffed. "You sound like Mami."

Galina kissed the top of her head. "Mami was like me, yes. Let's visit her later. You picked a pretty spot and the tulip tree there is about to bloom."

"I know. I go really early in the morning, or when I can't sleep. When the sun comes up, it kisses the stone with her name first and then lights up everything else. I know she's not really there, but I like to talk to her."

"Why do you think she's not there?"

"It's just her ashes under the stone. Not her," Rada said forlornly.

"She is in the afterlife. I'm sure she is in Eviendyti, resting where she has everything she needs and can hear you."

"What if she chose rebirth?" Rada asked. "Then she's not going to hear me. She's just a baby with no clue..." Rada's breath hitched. "Or just the thought of a baby."

Galina knelt before her. "Shh, Rada. Your mami will not have chosen rebirth. She will have chosen to be where she can still keep an eye on you both. The link between you was strong. It will not easily be severed. Believe she can hear you, and she will."

They continued on to the stable complex, walking through the vast vegetable gardens. Rada waved to the head gardener. "Hello, Tamat. Can we come and help later?"

"Of course, Stilniat Rada!" he called back.

"How do you know Tamat?"

"He caught me pulling up flowers in the garden," Rada said sheepishly. "I was trying to plant them around Mami's stone. He was a bit cross about the holes. He said he thought a dog had got in, but when he knew what I was doing, he helped. We've planted bulbs around her stone. Some will come up in spring, some in summer and we put in a winter rose."

"What about autumn?" Galina asked, her voice thick with emotion.

"Tamat said the tulip tree will have lovely golden leaves. So, she will have colour all year."

Galina sobbed. Rada stopped and took her hand. "It's all right, Granny. I'm here. You're here. Maybe you should come with me tomorrow for sunrise?"

Galina kissed the top of her head. "I will."

CHAPTER 38

Rada rode beside her grandfather. They left their property and travelled the wide road, passing ornate entrances to other wealthy estates.

"Where are we going?" she asked.

"First to the docks, to my office there. Then," he shrugged, "we'll see."

Instead of crossing the bridge into the city, they followed a road that ran alongside the river. A wagon loaded with open barrels of water passed them. The surface of the water rippled, and a fin protruded, then vanished.

"Grandpa, was that fish?"

"Yes. We deliver the fish caught on the coast to the markets in barrels of water. That way they stay fresh for sale. Some barrels will have lobster in them."

"So, what do you do at your office?"

"Our family has control of all fishing along the coast. Our trading licence came from the first emperor. Many looked on it as a token reward and a slap in the face for our service to him. But we made our fortune trading. We also have vineyards at our farm on the border with Zaragaria, and we breed some of the finest horses you can find in Vēkaria. Up in the hills, we have goats. From them we get milk, cheese and meat, mainly for our own consumption. The estate here houses orchards and you've seen vegetable gardens, so we remain fairly self-sufficient, and once our stores are full, we sell any excess. I also have interests in other people's businesses."

"So, you made that reward into something huge," Rada said.

Stepan swelled with pride. "Yes, our family did."

A barge floated past them, bearing more barrels and a pen containing goats.

"Those barrels contain wine from our vineyards, and those goats are for the estate here. To top off our numbers."

The manicured gardens of the wealthy district disappeared to be replaced by smaller shacks perched on the riverbank. Finally, they reached an area of warehouses at a long dock by the river. Many barges were being unloaded and their goods carted to the warehouse. Corrals held draught horses waiting to be hitched to the next empty barge to tow them back up the river.

Noticing Rada staring at this, Stepan said, "From the barge they go inside where we record and sort them before taking them into market or direct to merchants. We control this whole dock." There was a backlog of wagons waiting. "There shouldn't be so many carts still here. Something has gone wrong."

They dismounted, a worker took the horses. BC tried to bite him, so Rada took charge of him herself, tying him alone to a railing.

Stepan stormed inside with Rada following. They strode upstairs to a central office that overlooked both halves of the warehouse. The room was spartan. A map of Penīdīen graced one wall and a detailed map of Vēkaria lay on a slanted work board with many notes scrawled on paper next to it. The clerk stood and bowed to Stepan.

"Stilnaat Maklova, there are papers to sign for the for the Bureau of Weights and Measures and for the Revenue Office. They have queried the sales figures of our last three shipments."

"What? They've never done this before. We've always been trusted to submit accurate figures and always do."

"I know, Stilnaat, and no errors occurred. The inspectors were here earlier, opening all the barrels, checking goods, making sure we had what we said we did," the clerk said. "They seemed mystified when they finished. I believe someone gave them specific information about us."

Stepan shook his head. "I suppose that's why there's a line of wagons?"

"Yes, Stilniat. The staff are working as fast as they can."

"Come with me and we'll lend a hand. You shouldn't be sitting up here on your arse, but down there helping. Rada, occupy yourself, but stay out of the way."

Rada perused the map of Vēkaria. It was far more intricate than any map she'd seen. It marked the warehouse and the estate along with routes to the coast, to a village of Garzan, and with the Senner Isles lying just a short distance across the ocean. She looked at the papers on the tables then leaned over the railing to watch the activity below. With her grandfather on the lower floor, the pace of activity picked up, and the staff loaded and dispatched wagons faster. A soldier clad in pale blue entered and approached Stepan.

Rada narrowed her eyes, and her mouth went dry. The spy!

Stepan stopped work, and they left, moving around the outside of the building. Rada descended the stairs and chased them. Outside, she wandered along, trying to appear casual but struggling to suppress the desire to run. She paused at the corner of the wall, listening intently. Nothing. Rada edged closer. Nothing. She peeked around the building. No one was there, so she continued to the far side. Still nothing.

She scratched her head. "I wasn't that slow."

Rada walked from the back of the warehouse toward a group of enormous weeping willows whose fronds touched the ground. As she drew near, she heard faint voices. She slid down the riverbank and hugged its craggy edges, tracking the voices. The words remained indecipherable, but her grandfather was angry.

I need to get closer

Rada shimmied up a gnarled, thick root and sat perched on it near the top of the embankment.

"She has the power to make this happen every day if necessary."

"They'll find nothing since we've never defrauded the empire! It's a complete waste of time."

"Yes, of course, but that's part of the point. I can see how much she slowed you down today. If this happened every day, how long do you think your customers will stick around?"

"So, she'll drive me out of business because of the baby?"

"Only if you don't give her what she wants, then she will take everything your family has built from you and ensure your line ends in disgrace. Stilnaat, you are a reasonable man who has seen much of life. You know the baby will have a miserable existence. Even if I wanted, I cannot refuse this task. You don't even have to do anything. Many children die in infancy of natural causes. A window left open, a sudden chill. Anything could kill the girl and no one would ever know. If you give me access one night, then I can make it seem natural and your life will go back to being uncomplicated and you can enjoy the other one."

"Rada will be safe?"

"Of course. The Talak girl isn't of any concern to the empress."

"Fine."

Rada's limbs shook, and she struggled to hold the root as she climbed down and headed back to BC. She drew deep breaths and wiped her eyes. *Grandpa is going to let Bubba die! Stay calm. Look normal. Don't let on that you know. Be brave. Oh! Gods! Hokati help! Bethsinidar help!*

She ran to BC and hugged his head when he lowered it to her. "Help, BC. We have to do something."

Stepan joined her. "That was good timing. How did you know I was ready to go?" he said, far too brightly.

"I... ah... didn't see you in the warehouse," Rada said, sniffling in a thick voice. "So, I guessed and thought I'd just ride BC about and wait."

He stared at her. "Have you been crying? And you're covered in dirt, again."

"Yes, I'm sorry. I was thinking of Mami. And I fell exploring a bit."

"Ah." He sighed. "It's very hard, isn't it? There'll come a time when we can think of the wonderful things about Jadzia without such a gaping hole in our hearts, but not yet. How about we just go for a long ride?" She nodded. "Where would you like to go?"

Rada's mind whirled, and she struggled for an answer.

He'll let Bubba die. Just like Papi.

"Rada?"

"Um. I looked at the map in the warehouse. Can we go to Garzan? I've never seen the ocean."

"Of course," Stepan said.

They left the warehouse, passing through farmland dotted with sheep and cattle. The path followed the river and then divided. The lower, narrower track continued to follow the river and Rada saw the rump of a horse disappear around a bend as it pulled a barge upstream. Their trail climbed the lower slopes of the tip of the Snake's Tail mountain range. Spruce, fir and pine trees replaced the oak and elm of the lower county and lined the road. Rada gazed back over the organised sprawl of Dēbar and beyond. Orchards dotted the farmland on the other side of the river and the distant white specs of sheep and the darker brown of cattle peppered the fields between the waves of tall, ripening crops.

Stepan reined his horse in. "The road should be fairly clear now. Are you game for a bit of speed?"

"Yes!"

"Have you gone fast before? Will you be able to pull him up?"

"Um, I've not gone really fast, but I'm game."

Stepan laughed. "You're definitely my granddaughter!" His horse trotted off and, seeing Rada grinning, he urged his horse into a canter. BC leaped to follow. Rada squealed with glee and her horse surged forward, passing Stepan. BC broke into a gallop and the scenery raced by. Rada pulled on the reins to no avail.

"Slow down, BC!" She pulled with all her might. "Evika! Just a bit!" He slowed a little. "Good boy, BC!" She relaxed and loosened the reins. Stepan drew closer. BC pig rooted and took off. Rada gripped the saddle until her knuckles shone white. When she didn't fall, she grinned and whooped in joy, not bothering to stop him.

Panic filled her as the road ahead disappeared from sight and angled down the side of the hill. "Evvviiikaaa!" she cried, leaning back, hauling on the reins. Nothing. What did Akim say? Her mind raced. "OH!" She shifted her hands down the reins, clenched one around the leather, and braced it on his neck. *Please work!* She hauled on one rein, and he slowed, shaking his head against her command. "Turn. Turn. TURN!" Rada applied more pressure and BC's head and body flexed. He turned, almost colliding with her grandfather.

They stared at each other, pale and shaking. "By the gods, girl! You can ride! I thought I'd lost you!"

"N- no," Rada stammered through chattering teeth. "I... I... I'm good."

"How about we stretch our legs?" Stepan said, dismounting. He held out his arms, catching her as she swung off. "Sweet one, you're shaking like a leaf."

"I... I... don't know why."

"We'll just walk for a bit. Then we'll get back on. Do you want to get back on?"

BC walked beside her, his chin resting near her shoulder. "Yes, once my legs stop shaking."

They wandered in silence. Conifer forests towered over them on either side of the road and formed a thick, dark green blanket to the base of the mountain, halting at a narrow strip of grassland along the coast.

Rada gaped. "That's the ocean?" Stepan nodded. "It's huge! Look at all the tiny boats! Can we go on a boat?"

Stepan laughed. "Where would you go?"

"What about that island?"

The smile fell from her grandfather's face. "No. We can't go there. That's the Senner Isles."

"Oh! I thought it would be farther away. It looked farther on the map in your office."

"From up here, things always appear different, but I tell you what. One day, we'll ride a barge up and back. How would you like that?"

"Great! Which way is quicker? Here or along the river?" Rada asked.

"The river, but the trail is narrow and the barge horses will slow us down."

"So that's Garzan," Rada said, wrinkling her nose. "It's not very big."

"It's a fishing village, mostly. Although to the east is a stand of maples that produce the best syrup in the land?"

"On your map, the city on the Senner Isles is called Penīdā. And this land is Penīdīen."

"Don't they teach you history in Talak?" he asked.

"Not this place. No one ever talks about it."

"I suppose that's true since we banished them. The Sennerese used to live all across the country. They followed Bethsinidar – The Weaver. They were probably the first people here, but they and other followers of that goddess fought the emperor and disavowed Mstislav. Thousands of them fought, died, and lost. They retreated to the isle. Aitor I ordered they stay there and was happy to leave them be as long as they didn't interfere with him. You'll see very few of them and, yes, no one talks about them or the goddess."

They crossed a sturdy wooden bridge. Downstream a long wharf sat empty, but a horseman moved a group of the heavy, shaggy-legged draught horses towards them.

"Where are they going?"

"Back to the warehouse. We've enough that they can rest between each journey. Your mother used to travel down on a barge just so she could ride one of them back." He fell silent, staring into the distance, a look of utter hopelessness on his face.

"Grandpa?"

"Mmm?"

"Are you all right?" she whispered.

"What?" He returned to her. "Yes, just a little lost in memories. They're a nice place to be, even if they make your heart ache. Come, let's get something to eat at the inn. Annata makes the best griddle cakes and we might get some maple syrup."

The inn lay at the far edge of the prosperous village. Every house had a slate roof rather than thatch, and good-sized vegetable gardens while chickens and geese wandered the street.

"The villages in Talak aren't like this. Most of them have thatch roofs, not slate. And these houses are bigger."

"The people of Garzan have done well from the empire."

The inn sat not far from the shore. They tied the horses up, and Rada ran to the sandy beach. She danced back and forward with the waves that lapped the shore while her grandfather disappeared into the inn. Rada strolled to the beached fishing boats, their lateen sails neatly furled while nearby men and women worked on repairing nets.

"Is all the fishing done for the day?" she asked.

"Yes, Stilniat. We go out very early in the morning, then we ship the fish down to Dēbar."

"What do you do the rest of the day?"

One woman laughed. "Fix things or tend our land. There's always something to do, Stilniat."

"Oh, um, of course," Rada said, embarrassed. Head lowered, she kept walking, spying a boat and fisherman sitting alone further along the shore. Noticing the golden hue of his skin, her footsteps faltered, but he looked up, an impish smile plastered across his face.

"You're brave, aren't you?" he said. "To come and talk to the evil Sennerese!"

"Evil?"

"That's how most of your kind act. Like we boil up children for breakfast!" He laughed, his teeth flashing white from within his curly, grey-streaked beard.

Rada's eyebrows rose. *He's crazy.* "I'm not scared. I can take care of myself."

"Can you now? Good to know," he said without mockery.

"Why are you here?" she asked. "Are you dimashne?"

"Oh, so you know a little about us? No, I'm not dimashne. I'm a fisherman waiting for my pay. As soon as I get it, I'll head back home," he said, gesturing at the island. "There's a purple lobster that grows on the island. We harvest them and sell them to the houses of rich Zaragarians," He looked her up and down. "Like yours, I'd say."

Rada took in her appearance, frowned. "You act like having money is bad. It's not. You like it enough 'cause you're waiting to get paid. Why do you need it, anyway? If you stay on the island all the time, why do you need our money?"

His eyes narrowed. "There are still things we need that we can't make, so we must buy them and for that we need your money. Your kind hate us, but they're happy to profit from us."

"I don't hate you. There are better things to hate than you."

"Are there? That's refreshing. What's your name, child?"

"Rada," she said, arms folded. "What's yours?"

"Masaru."

She turned, looking at the Senner Isles and their grey peaks that cut the skyline. "Masaru, is it all mountains? On the map, the mountains take up everything?"

"Not all mountains, no. But they cover a lot. There's plenty of fertile, flatter land along the coast, and those mountains have towering fir and cedar trees on their lower slopes. We made the temple of cedar and when you walk in the door, you can smell the wood." He smiled in remembrance. "At night, you can see the pathways to the temple lit up by torches, even from the ocean. They guide us home."

An idea took root in her mind.

"Masaru, does it take long to get to the islands?"

"A few hours. If the wind is right, less."

"How does the sail go up?"

"I pull this rope, but it's not that simple. It takes time and skill to sail."

"If the wind isn't right, do you row?" she asked.

"That's what the oars are for."

"Rada!" Her grandfather's call interrupted them. "What are you doing all the way over here?" He cast a disparaging glance at Masaru, who ignored him and looked out to sea. "Come on, Rada, I've ordered food. Let's head back to the inn."

She held her grandfather's proffered hand as they headed back, but she turned, taking one last, long look at the boat.

CHAPTER 39

RADA SAT CROSSED LEGGED by her mother's grave. The sun blazed its farewell across the sky, casting the city into a dark silhouette.

"I don't understand, Mami. I had a nice day with Grandpa, but... I don't think he's good. He thinks Bubba is a bastard... That can't be good. You used to call Papi a bastard. I don't think it's the same thing, but I'm not sure, but I *know* it's wrong. How can Bubba be bad? She's tiny! And she's *my* sister! Granny is nice, but the priests are as stupid here as back home and no one will name her. And that's the empress's fault! Now she must be really bad. Mami, it's all a mess! A *big* mess!"

She lay on the soft grass, curled into a ball, and cried. "I wish you were here," she whispered. "You'd be so cross. You'd stop them and you'd get Bubba named properly." She sat up and slammed her palm down on the ground. "What kind of name is Nadya? It's wimpy. She's a fighter, not a wimp!" Rada said. "We've done heaps of scary stuff together. We escaped on the horse! There were the spidies! She did it all and she's still here! She's tough and I love her." Rada drew shuddering breaths, her stomach clenched and she felt hot and queasy. "He's going to let the empress kill Bubba. He will, I know it. I bet that's why the windows were open and I stopped her catching a chill and getting sick. I'll stop them again. I love you, Mami. I'll make you proud. I'll get her named and we'll be back before anyone knows we've gone."

She rose and headed into the villa. In the kitchen, she grabbed some apple cakes, still warm from the oven.

"They're for tomorrow, Stilniat Rada," the cook told her.

"There'll still be some left because you made extra, for *me*," Rada said in a singsong voice. "Thank you!"

"Don't burn yourself, you little imp," the cook called as Rada ran from the kitchen.

"BC will love this!"

"Don't you dare feed my apple cakes to that damn horse!"

Rada's laughter rang back to her.

At the stables, Rada walked into the tack room to see the stable boy polishing leather. "Here, Fabian, have an apple cake. They're still warm."

Fabian dropped what he was doing and they sat bedside each other on the floor of the room. "This is good!" he said.

"Apple cakes are the best. I once held up the slaves back home and robbed them of their pastries."

"You robbed them? Weren't they *your* servants?"

"Yes," Rada said, "but I was only little then and I was pretending to be a bandit. They were scared of my sling, so it was fun."

"I don't blame them. I've seen you shoot. You could shoot the eye out of someone's head with that thing."

Rada grimaced; a sick twisting gripped her gut. She avoided his gaze and looked down at the cake in her lap.

"Aren't you going to eat that?" Fabian asked.

"It's for BC."

"It's not good for him."

"I'll eat half then," Rada said, smiling. "How is he? It was a big ride today. Is he tired?"

Fabian snorted. "Tired? Him? That horse could to it all again. Those warhorses are used to much harder rides than you gave him."

Rada smiled. "That's good. Fabian, can you move my tack down a peg so I can get it without having to ask you all the time?"

He laughed. "No problem." Fabian rose, wiping his hands on his pants. He rearranged the saddles hanging on the wall and moved BC's gear to a lower rack. "You know you didn't need to give me an apple cake to get me to do this."

"I was bringing you the cake anyway," Rada said, looking offended. "I like talking to you." She murmured, "You remind me of a friend I used to have."

Fabian paused in his work, looking carefully at her as she stared, head bowed, at the half cake in her lap. He put his hand on her shoulder. "Things will get better now you're here." She nodded but refused to look up. "Are you *really* going to feed that to BC?" he asked plaintively.

Rada sobbed a short laugh and raised her teary face. "Here," she said. "You have it. I'll get him an actual apple. It'll probably be better for him anyway."

Fabian snatched the cake and gobbled it down. "You're right, definitely," he said around the last mouthful. "Apple will be much better for him." He held out his hand and hauled her to her feet.

"Thanks," she said, leaving. She headed back to the villa. "Get better? I'll make it get better."

■——————▶

Rada lay awake listening to the noises in the house fade to nothing. Only the crickets outside her window keeping her company. She counted to herself and pinched her skin to stay awake. Finally, she rose and padded her way to the nursery. A guard stood in front of the door.

Rada's stomach tied itself in knots, but she walked on. "I'm going to get my sister," Rada whispered.

"I know," the guard said. "The Stilnassa said you might come. In you go."

In the room, the wet-nurse was sleeping on her back, snoring loud enough to raise the roof.

The window was closed. *Granny's guards must be working.* Rada picked up her sleeping sister and held her against her chest. The baby stirred but settled into Rada's arms. Outside the room, the guard followed her down the corridor.

She turned and looked at him. "She's safe with me."

"I know, Stilniat, but my orders are to guard your door when you take the baby."

"All right. Come on then."

Reaching her room, he opened the door for her.

"So, you'll be outside the door all night?"

"Yes."

"You won't move at all?"

"No."

"I'll feel very safe then," Rada said as the door clicked closed. "Evika!" she whispered. "How are we getting out?"

She dressed in her boots, pants and jacket, grabbed her small backpack and loaded the baby into her carrier across her chest. Rada eased open the door to her narrow balcony. She peered down. *There's no guard.* Gingerly, she swung the door wider. She froze. Waiting to see if the guard outside her door heard. Nothing. She closed the door and moved to the edge of the railing. An ancient ivy clung to the side of the building. The quarter moon's weak light was just enough to discern vague shapes. Rada leaned out, feeling the ivy. Her hand settled around a vine the size of her wrist. She tugged it. It held fast. Beneath the vine was a thick bed of agapanthus. Her heart did a back flip. "Bubba, do you think they look soft?"

She straddled the railing. Her backpack slipped and she slid towards the ground. Gritting her teeth, gripping the timber rail, she righted her balance.

"Hold tight, Bubba," she whispered.

Clinging with her knees, hands shaking, she let go and tightened the straps of her pack. She wobbled again and clung to the rail. Rada swung her legs over the balcony and only her toes fit on its narrow lip. Rada inched her way toward the ivy. She twisted and peered at the ivy. She wrapped one hand around the thick vine, braced herself against it and leaned forward, looking for a second handhold. Her fingertips touched another sturdy runner. Stretching, she couldn't reach it. Rada bowed her head, thinking, one hand on the ivy and the other clinging to the rail.

"I'm sorry, Bubba, but we have to do this. You hold tight and bury your face in me so you don't get prickled. Just be brave, Bubba."

The baby slept on, content with the companion who'd carried her for most of her short life.

Rada grabbed the thick ivy in her left hand, the stone wall scraped on her fingertips. She drew a deep breath and launched herself from the balcony, aiming for the second vine. She missed. Her fingers scrabbled in the foliage. She face-planted into the leafy wall, clinging with one hand, and slid down the vine. Bubba woke, grumbling. "Shh. Shh. Please," she whispered. Panicking, she seized the leaves in front of her and found another thinner vine halting her descent. She pushed her toes against the wall, desperate for purchase, and her boots hit a vee in the branches.

"See? Easy."

Rada inched her left hand down, no longer feeling the scratch of the stone. "Huh?" The vine loosened its age-old grip on the mortar and slowly peeled away, taking Rada with it.

"Oh, evika..."

Her centre of gravity shifted. She lost her footholds as the vine buckled under her weight. Rada dangled in the air, a foot away from the wall, clinging to the vine that now formed a leafy roof overhead.

The baby grizzled. Heart racing, Rada hummed a halting lullaby. *Gods, please. Bethsinidar, help.*

A frisson in the air breathed upon her. A spider crawled across Rada's hand.

"Not the spidies again, please?" she begged.

They gave a small downward lurch as more of the vine tore from the stonework. Rada, eyes closed, gritted her teeth and hung like a fish on a hook as the whole plant pared from the villa and lowered her with a jolt to the ground. Stunned at the solid footing, she opened her eyes, looked about, and grinned.

She kissed Bubba's head. "I knew it'd work."

A dark shape loomed over her and she darted back as the last tendrils of ivy gave up their hold and the plant collapsed at her feet.

"It worked better in my head." She took in the huge mess. "We better be quick. I think they'll notice this in the morning."

Rada glanced around, searching for shapes that might be guards, and saw none. "We know one is outside your window, Bubba," she whispered. "Maybe they're patrolling." She kept to the deep shadow of the house. Rada poked her head around a corner and saw two guards stationed at the rear door of the kitchen. They were whispering. One wandered off a short distance and relieved himself, and the other had his back to her. She dashed into the tall herb garden and hid behind a huge lavender bush.

Rada waited until they talked again and then snuck through the herbs and into the main vegetable garden, hiding by the grapevine-covered fence that surrounded it. With the grapevine as cover, she ran straight toward the stables, stopping when she reached the edge of the garden. Across the drive sat the long, double-storey stable complex. The stable master, grooms and stable boys, slept upstairs above the horses. No lamps shone from the building. Rada grinned and walked to the rear of the stable.

The great double doors at one end sat open and she slipped in. Horses shuffled and nickered to her, and the smell of hay tickled her nostrils. She gripped the tack room latch and lifted it, inching the door open. Its creak exploded in the still night air. A horse whinnied and stomped, a man mumbled upstairs and floorboards groaned under his weight as he rose. Abandoning caution, Rada rushed in, grabbed BC's tack and dumped it around the side of the building, before dashing back and closing the door.

She stood shaking, plastered against the wall as the footsteps inside drew near. The baby squirmed and settled. The faint light of a lamp shone through the enormous doorway as a groom checked on the horses. Rada held her breath. The footsteps moved up and down the building. Finally, she heard a door snick and the boards creak again as he returned to bed. She gathered the bridle, girth and saddle blanket, ran to BC's paddock, before returning for the small saddle. She hefted the saddle and other gear onto the top rail of the fence.

"BC," she whispered. "BC, treatie time."

BC trotted up to the fence and took the proffered piece of carrot.

"Now, listen," Rada ordered, climbing the railing. She shook her finger at him. "You need to be really good and really quiet. Both of you," she added, patting the baby's cheek. The big brown horse sidled up to the railing and she tossed on his blanket, saddle and bridle. Climbing down, she did the girth up, but had to climb the fence in instalments, stopping at each rail to tighten it some more with the aid of each height increase.

She led him out of the field and closed the gate, before climbing the fence and hopping onto his back.

Her sister quietly grumbled and Rada, popped her finger in the baby's mouth, quelling her.

"There'll be guards out the front."

They stuck to the grass, which muted BC's hooves, and reached the rear orchard. Riding through the avenue of apple trees, moonlight streaked between the branches, casting milky fingers. Rada squinted, searching for signs of guards. Nothing. They moved on. The edge of the orchard was ahead and from there the cart track met the main road. BC stepped hesitantly forward. He halted, refusing to go on. The soft chink of mail alerted Rada to four guards meeting upon their patrol, muted voices soughed through the leaves. Rada held her breath. Unbidden, BC turned, left the aisle and moved under trees, Rada ducked, one hand cradling her sister's head. BC wove through the trees, until the orchard gate lay in sight. Beyond it was the road along the river to the docks. One guard leaned against the closed gate. Rada drew her sling and fired a pebble over the wall into a tree some distance from his post. It rustled the leaves, missing the tree, but landing with a meaty *thunk* on something lower.

The guard, turned, opened the gate and called. "Who's there?" He walked farther away from the gate. "Hey!" He broke into a run. "Show yourself!"

Rada listened, transfixed, but at the sound of the other guards returning, BC trotted out from hiding, through the gate, and disappeared into the darkness toward the docks.

>——————→

Sitting in the tree, the black clad assassin watched as her compatriot fell forward, breaking cover, clutching his face. He rose and raced down the street, drawing the guard along with him. Her mind raced. What happened? Who shot at him?

Her brows rose as an enormous horse with a small rider exited the orchard and vanished into the night.

"The girl. So, the tales are true, but where on earth is she going?"

The other guards arrived at the gate.

She climbed down, slipped between the shrubs, slid into the water and swam across the river to her waiting horse.

"There's no getting in tonight," she whispered, as she mounted. Still, where was the child going? Curious, she urged her horse onward, fording the river upstream and following Rada's path.

>——————→

The dark was not friendly. Rada knew it like she knew her own name. BC marched down the road, alternating with trotting until Rada's legs grew tired. His footfalls echoed on the hard surface, and it seemed to her as if she could hear a ghost horse behind them. The hairs on the back of her neck rose, and a shiver ran down her spine. She couldn't shake the feeling she was being watched. Rada reined in BC and listened. Nothing.

She waited, intent, hearing only her rapid breaths. Hands vice-like around the reins, she urged her horse on.

They reached the wharf and warehouses, and she shuddered at the jet-black monoliths as if each would swallow them whole. Rada hunched over her sister protectively, wrapping an arm about her. The baby grizzled and squirmed. BC's hoof beats reverberated on the timber dock and as they moved between the buildings. She directed BC to the riverside trail the draught horses travelled.

The gurgle of the water and the dull rhythmic thuds of BC's feet on the dirt track lulled her and, no longer hearing phantoms behind her, she relaxed. "We're going to make it, Bubba. The goddess will pick your name and it will be something powerful. We're going to try trotting again, Bubba. So, get ready." She wrapped an arm around the carrier, supporting her sister's head. "Ready? All right. Be good, BC." The horse launched into a smooth trot. "Good girl, Bubba. We're getting better at it!" The moment Rada bounced in the saddle, BC slowed to a walk. Rada gently pressed his sides, making him lengthen his stride and quicken his pace.

Rada's eyes grew heavy and her head drooped. A low hanging branch smacked her in the face. "Ow!"

She blinked furiously, rubbing her eyes. "Bubba, I don't even know how far we've come."

"Far enough," an amused voice answered. A horse launched out of the dark at her. The black clad nightmare on it reached for Rada. There was no face, just eyes and teeth amid pitch.

Rada squealed and BC pig-rooted, belting the other horse with both back feet. It reared sideways, swiping its rider into the bushes. Rada rocked forward, pushing her hand on BC's neck to right herself as he galloped away. She gripped the saddle and reins with one hand and braced the baby carrier with the other. Bubba wailed at the top of her lungs. The rider drew closer and Rada kicked BC, but he slowed.

Slide off, my warrior.

"Bethsinidar?"

Yes. Get off, now!

Rada kicked her feet out of the stirrups and propelled herself from the horse, landing on her feet. The baby screamed. Rada ran into the bushes and scrambled halfway up the slope to the road.

"Shh, Bubba, please." Wide-eyed, she stroked her sister's cheek and put her finger in the baby's mouth to pacify Bubba, but the baby wailed.

Invisible arms settled around them, and the infant stilled. *Watch.*

BC charged the oncoming rider, teeth bared. He reared, striking the horse and the assassin's leg. She howled in pain and the blow knocked her askew in the saddle. The steed reared and struck at BC, who danced away, before ploughing forward to tear a fist sized chunk from the animal's neck. BC spun and belted the horse's loin with both back feet. It staggered and slipped but stayed upright.

Rada gasped, her stomach twisted in lead knots.

Breathe. Remember, lock the fear away. Just breathe. In, nice and slow, now out.

Rada exhaled. She opened the door in her mind, shoved her terrors inside then slammed the door shut.

The assassin drew a sword. BC shook his head and snaked his neck, teeth bared.

Horror bled through Rada.

Breathe. An iron will gripped her.

Rada fought down the panic. Loaded her sling.

The assassin urged her horse forward. It refused. BC reared, pawing the air, shaking his head.

The assassin raised her sword.

BC prepared to charge.

Rada fired. The stone flew as her great dark horse surged to attack. It whistled past BC's head and smacked into the brow of the assassin. She reeled and toppled from the saddle. Her horse bolted, leaving her sprawled in the dirt as BC brought his hooves down on her head.

CHAPTER 40

THE VILLAGE OF GARZAN lay quiet, lulled by the soft waves into peaceful slumber. Rada sat on BC on the sandy beach and stared across the ocean. Distant lights, like orange stars, winked in the black.

"That's the temple, Bubba."

Rada sidled BC up to a sandbank and jumped off. She walked to a fishing boat resting on the sand and looked dubiously at it. "Bubba, it's bigger than it was the other day." Peering inside it, she shook her head. "Evika! I think we can't work this one." Rada hunted about and spied a small rowboat beached up near the dunes. She ran over and scrutinised it. "Looks all right, Bubba. What do you think?"

The baby slept. Rada poked her cheek, a twinge of doubt niggling at her. "You've slept like a log since the fight. The goddess did something, mmn?" Rada stroked the baby's cheek. "But she wouldn't hurt you, would she? She's helped more than anyone else... apart from Mami." Her voice hitched. "I'm going to tell you all about Mami, I promise."

She unslung the baby carrier, kissed her sleeping sister on the forehead, and laid the carrier in the boat's bottom along with her backpack. Rada pushed on the prow of the boat. It didn't budge.

"Evika! Come on, Rada! You wimp!"

She heaved again, her feet digging into the sand as she strove to move the vessel. Nothing.

"Maybe it's easier the other way?" She grabbed the anchor rope tied to the prow and tried to drag the craft around. It tilted and moved an inch but refused to budge. Rada kicked sand into the sky in fury. She stomped about, head down, thinking. Abruptly, she halted and stared at BC grazing nearby. "BC," she called. "Treatie time."

He trotted over, looking for his treat. "You've got a job first," she said. "There's only one bit of carrot left. You went through five bits while I tried to get back on." He shoved her with his nose. "Job first, treat second."

She hauled some more of the anchor rope out, cut it, and tied it to her stirrup. She led BC toward the water. The rope drew taut and the stirrup leather groaned. BC halted and kicked the sand up irritably. "Come on, BC!" Rada showed him the carrot and walked to the end of the reins. He stretched his neck out and tried to snatch it. Snorting, he dragged the boat to the beach. Rada waded into the cold water. "Just a bit more." He flicked the water and curled his lip but dragged the prow into the ocean. The boat sat gently rocking with each wave.

"Good boy!" She gave him the carrot and untied the rope from the stirrup. Rada led him to the sandbank and, from its height, removed his gear. She lay her head on his shoulder. "You were the best boy ever, BC!"

Turning for the boat, she let out a little squeal. The waves had rocked it off the shore.

"Oh! Evika! Bubba!" She raced to the shoreline and waded through the water until she gripped the side of the boat. "Evika!" She grunted as she hooked her arms over the side, clinging and wriggling until she slid into it.

Breathless, she sat on the seat and gripped the oars. "Come on, Bubba. We can do this."

"Which way?" Rada looked over her shoulder seeking the distant temple lights. "Got them." She hauled on the oars, saying. "Well, Bubba, Mami wouldn't be cross with us... I don't think. She'd be really, really cross with just about everyone else."

Red faced, sweaty, hungry, thirsty and exhausted, Rada leaned on the oars. The lights were still there, but they didn't seem to get any bigger, yet she could make out the hulking shape of mountains through the absence of stars. Her shoulders burned and her lower back ached. "Come on, Bubba. Come on!"

She pushed on.

Oars in.

Oars out.

Oars in.

Oars...

Her blistered hands slipped.

"Bubba, I just need a little rest. Just for a minute."

Rada's head drooped and her eyes closed.

The boat bumped into something, and she woke with a jolt.

"The high priest told me to go fishing tonight," Masaru said. "I didn't think I'd catch you."

Rada blinked owlishly at the fishermen in the boat beside her. "Where'd you come from? Oh! Evika! How long have I been asleep?" She gripped the oars and winced, dropping them and blowing on her hands.

"I take it you want to get to the Isles," Masaru said.

"Yes."

At that moment, the baby woke and wailed.

"A baby? You've brought a baby with you!"

"My sister. She needs a name and no one will name her."

"Where are your parents?"

"I ran away from Papi, he's..." her face twisted, "not nice. Mami is..." she looked out to sea and groaned. "Mami is dead. She wanted Bubba named. Bethsinidar will name her."

"I see." He murmured something in Sennerese to the other men and they used a boat hook to draw the little rowboat closer. Masaru jumped in with Rada. "Come with us. We'll get you there more quickly."

Rada moved to her sister. "I can't pick her up," she said plaintively, holding out her bloody hands.

Masaru gathered the baby and passed her carefully to a sailor. "Ready?" he asked. Rada nodded and he lifted her up, where muscular arms took her and transferred her across. Masaru tossed the remains of the anchor rope across, and they tethered the rowboat to the larger vessel.

As the men worked the oars, Rada asked, "Did I get very far?"

"Halfway," Masaru said, rocking the baby. He transferred her to his shoulder and rubbed her back.

"Only halfway! But I rowed and rowed."

"Halfway on your own is extremely good. You're not as strong as us and you've no sail."

A sailor put a bucket of water in front of Rada. "Sea water. Put your hands in that," Masaru ordered. "It will hurt, but it will help."

She grimaced, closed her eyes and immersed her hands. The slightest movement of her fingers sent lightning through her. Rada bit her lip to keep from crying out.

Masaru studied her, a knowing look in his eyes. "Just a bit longer. All right, take them out."

Rada whisked her hands out and blew on them. "Evika!"

The sailors laughed. "Not a proper Talak lady, this one."

She scowled. "I never want to be a proper Talak lady. I want to be like my mother, a true Zaragarian!"

Every sailor stopped their work and turned to stare at her. Rada stiffened, eyeing them warily. Masaru continued rubbing the baby's back while she grumbled vociferously about the latest indignity forced upon her. He spoke to the men in Sennerese and they went back to work.

"Watch your tongue, girl. The Zaragarians exterminated most of our people and drove us back to this isle. I don't think you know what it means to be a *true* Zaragarian, but everyone on this boat does. We all lost ancestors to the war true Zaragarians and their imposter god started. You're lucky we have a rule that all who seek the goddess's blessing must be assisted, otherwise they'd have tossed you overboard for those words."

Rada quailed, wriggled on the seat and wouldn't meet his gaze.

"Why is he an imposter god? Mstislav is the god of war. He protects all the other gods and his people."

"Except Bethsinidar, whom some of your kind would say is his mother. He has not treated his mother well."

Rada frowned. "Um... I don't... I don't think she needs protecting," she whispered.

Masaru leaned closer to her. "Why is that?"

Rada clamped her mouth shut and stared out at the sea. "What is your full name, Rada?"

"Rada Lujza Ortakli. Daughter of Lord Bashtan Ortakli and Lady Jadzia Zora Maklova of the First Circle."

Masaru's brows rose and again the sailors stared at her, murmuring to each other. "Damn the gods and all their schemes!" Masaru spat. "A Maklova. Do you know your great-grandmother is buried on the island?"

Rada gawped at him. "Great? Buried?"

"Your mother's grandmother."

Her mind whirled. "Oh! Mami, said she showed her some of Bethsinidar's temples and they walked the... Pilgrims' Trail. But I didn't know she was here."

"Your family kicked her out when she refused to stop following The Weaver. That's what *true* Zaragarians do, even to their own families."

Rada looked at her sister, now quiet in his arms. For a long while she said nothing, dwelling on his words and all that had befallen them.

"My grandpa would have let the empress kill Bubba."

"The empress! Child, what have brought to our door?"

➤⟶

Rada lay curled at Masaru's feet, clutching her backpack out of which stuck the head of a ragged looking bear. He shook her awake and she sat beside him, rubbing her eyes. The pilot steered the boat around the jagged, barren rocky islet that protected the coast and created a bay. They glided alongside the wharf, and the sailors moored the boat. The angry red glow of sunrise cut through the retreating night and the small city of Penīdā revealed itself. Stone buildings with thick, high-gabled thatch roofs; streets that curled from the shore around the mountain sides. Above it all towered the multi-tiered pagoda of the Temple of Bethsinidar. Woven around it were smaller buildings with tiled gables whose edges curved gracefully up.

"It's a pattern," Rada said. "The temple and the buildings they form a kind of web."

"Yes. Remember, she is a weaver. Your naming starts your thread in the great pattern of life. This honours that notion," Masaru replied.

Rada gathered her backpack, wincing at the pain in her hands, gently pushing Grokky's head inside it. She saw Masaru watching her, brow raised. "It's... um... I'm looking after him for Bubba," she said, embarrassed. "He's not mine anymore. I'm too big for a bear." She slung the pack over her shoulders and tried to don the baby carrier, but her fingers fumbled on the ties. "Please, can you do this up?"

"I can carry her for you," Masaru said.

"No... thanks. She's my sister and I should look after her."

"Very well." Masaru tied the carrier to her and put the infant inside it. He lifted them both onto the wharf and joined them. "Straight to the temple, yes?"

"Yes." They took a street that climbed the slopes of the mountain. Rada paused, catching her breath, and took in the towering, jagged peaks that dominated the centre of the island. "There's still snow on them."

"Yes, all year."

Her stomach rumbled, and Masaru laughed. "They'll feed you at the temple. Come on."

Rada lowered her head and marched. "Almost there, Bubba. I wonder what name Bethsinidar will choose for you. As long as it's not Nadya." She pulled a face. "Yuck!" She focused on her feet.

Left.

Right.
Left.
Right.
Left.
Her shoulders burned, and her back ached from top to tail.
Right.
Left.
"We're here," Masaru said.

Rada looked up. Before them lay broad stone steps that led to the main temple. Intricate carvings ornamented the gables – webs, dotted with spiders, all climbing toward the peak. At the top of the stairs waited an elderly man and several grey-robed acolytes. Rada's mouth grew dry, a tremble ran through her. She hugged her sister. The baby fidgeted and twisted her head about.

"That is Akihiro. He is the abbot at this temple." Masaru prodded her up the stairs.

Rada took the steps slowly, stopping halfway to turn and gaze back toward the mainland. A shiver ran through her and her stomach back flipped. *It's so far.* She bowed her head. *Breathe.* Her mother's words returned to her: *Remember who you are.* Rada straightened and made her way to stand before the abbot. "I am Rada Lujza Ortakli. Daughter of Lady Jadzia Zora Maklova. Sir, please, my sister needs a name."

"I know, child, but first you both need to be fed, cleaned, and your hands need tending."

An acolyte stepped forward to take the baby from Rada; she stepped back scowling.

The abbot knelt beside her. "Rada, you've come a long way and endured many trials." He smiled at her and in the depths of his eyes, she saw flickers of vibrant blue. "Do you think the goddess aided in bringing you all this way just to hurt the baby?"

"No, but I want to stay with her."

"Of course. She will not leave your sight, but I know you are tired and my acolytes will take great care of you."

Akihiro lifted the baby from the carrier, cradling her as he examined her face.

"She's been too quiet since Bethsinidar helped us. That's not right... I'm a bit... scared."

"She's dehydrated and needs to feed and she..." He raised his eyebrows. "She stinks."

Rada shrugged. "All she does is eat and poop. Oh, and sleep... and scream."

Rada followed the acolytes between the buildings and along a narrow path to the cave. Flickering torchlight revealed steam gently rising from hot springs. A small bath already awaited the baby. Clean clothes for Rada sat nearby.

Rada stripped and prepared to get into the spring.

"No. Stand in that empty tub." A bucket of spring water, a cloth, and soap were placed in the tub. "Soap yourself up here, scrub, and rinse off. Then you can get in the spring. You smell almost as bad as your sister."

>———>

Galina woke to pounding on the bedroom door. She sat up, wrapped a shawl about her, and opened it.

"What!"

The wet-nurse stood in the hall, wringing her hands. The anger on Galina's face evaporated, replaced by concern. "What is it? Is the baby all right?"

"The baby is gone!"

"She'll be with Rada," Galina said.

"Rada is not in her room and I can't find her. She always brings the baby back to me for feeding and this morning she hasn't."

Galina's lips drew into a tight line, and she shook her head. "Go get yourself some food and return to the nursery and wait. I'll find them."

She shut the door and dressed.

Stepan rolled over. "What's the problem this time?"

"That damn nurse is in a panic because Rada hasn't brought the baby to her."

"Not like her, but it's probably nothing. We've had guards everywhere." Stepan rolled back over. "Wake me up, if there's really trouble."

"Certainly, then you can come to the rescue." She slammed the door on her way out.

Galina walked to Rada's room. The bed covers were tossed back and the sheets rumpled.

"Well, then she did actually sleep in here. The stables... she must be there."

At the stables, the hands were preparing feed rations for horses and mucking out stalls.

She waylaid one of them. "Fabian, have you seen Rada?"

"No, Stilnassa, not since last night."

"Last night?" she said, razor sharp.

He bowed. "Stilnassa, she stopped by with apple cakes and asked me to move her saddle, so she could get to it more easily. I did as she asked; she is only small, so..."

"So she could get to it more easily," Galina said, a knot forming in her gut. She strode to BC's field to find it empty. "Rada, what in the name of all the gods? Where are you?"

She ran to the house and yelled at the soldier on the main door. "Get me the captain of the guard, now! Move it!" To a passing servant, she said, "Rouse your master!"

The guard captain ran toward her. "Stilnassa?"

"Report on last night," she snapped.

"All was quiet except for one incident at the orchard gate. The men spotted someone spying on the property. They chased him off. No one entered."

"The guard on the baby? What did he report?"

"Nothing untoward. Stilniat Rada took the child back to her room and they never left."

"Rada and the baby are missing. So is that damn horse. Search the grounds!"

The chatelaine stopped before Galina. "Stilnassa Galina, what's happened?"

"Rada and the baby are gone. Have all the servants search the house from top to bottom," she said before striding back to Rada's room.

Once there, she threw open the balcony doors to let in more light. Her hands flew to her mouth as she took in the wreckage in the garden below. The hundred-year-old ivy covered the grass like a blanket. Galina leaned on the railing and stared at the marks on the wall where the plant had taken root; she could see clear outlines of its thick vines. She leaned out, easily able to reach them. Her hands shook. In the distance, she saw the guards assembling.

"Come!" she cried. "Shift this ivy." The men and women ran over and set to work. "Be careful! They... Their bodies may be under there."

"No sign I take it," Stepan said, entering the room. He joined her on the balcony, agape at the sight below. "Evika!" he said, embracing his sobbing wife.

"Stepan, we can't lose them too!"

"They might not be under there."

"I know, but we have to check. The horse is gone too. Stepan, if they are not under there, then where in the world are they? An empress's assassin would not take the horse."

"She might; to make it look like Rada ran off," he said. "But I doubt they could take the horse, no matter how hard they tried."

"Where would she go?" Galina said. "She doesn't know this land."

Stepan grimaced. "She knows one place, and it was her idea we go there."

"Garzan? Why would she go there?" Galina paled. "Oh, Stepan, no."

"She's as stubborn as Jadzia was, and you know how hard it was to stop her from doing something once she put her mind to it. We'll search. Hopefully we'll find them here," he said.

"If they're here, Stepan, most likely an assassin will have killed them."

CHAPTER 41

Tikhon and the two guards, covered in dust from the trail, reached the outskirts of Bēdarik.

"Make way!" the guards bellowed, and the crowd at the city gates parted before them.

They slowed their exhausted horses to a walk.

"First to the Maklova's estate," Tikhon said.

The citizens of Bēdarik bowed to him as proceeded, but their emperor's appearance provoked a wave of murmurs in their wake.

Tikhon halted his horse. "My people! The Talak rebels have been crushed! They have paid for their crimes. There will be many opportunities for our people who wish to travel and settle there as part of the new order. But you will hear more on that soon." The ripple of worry that followed him turned to joy as the crowd cheered and raised their fists in salute.

Proceeding, he waved and acknowledged their praise and greetings. Once they left the main trading strip, they urged their horses onward, slowing only when the estate gates were in sight. The estate was a hive of activity. Guards roved the grounds, clearly searching for someone. They halted in their work to bow to him as he passed. Tikhon dismounted at the main double doors and strode into the villa.

"Where are the Stilnassa and Stilnaat?" he asked a passing servant.

"They are in the Stilnaat's study, My Emperor," the man said, bowing. "This way, please."

They stopped outside a door and the servant reached to knock, but Tikhon forestalled him, listening to raised voices within.

"If she is there, you have to bring her back!"

"Do you know what it will do to this family if she has gone there? You won't have to worry about Sabina anymore, you'll have to worry about the Order! Galina, they won't keep her, they can't afford to. They'll send her back and for the rest of the world, it will be like she had an adventure."

Tikhon dismissed the servant and pushed open the door. Galina, arms folded, stood on the opposite side of the room to Stepan.

"My Emperor!" Stepan exclaimed, bowing. "Why are you here? Has something gone wrong?"

"Perhaps you can tell me that? Where are the girls?"

Galina bowed to him. "Your Majesty, thank you for heeding my missive."

"You wrote to him!" Stepan said.

"Of course! He is in the perfect position to deal with Sabina. We cannot. Apparently, we cannot even get on a horse and ride to Garzan to see if she went there!"

"I've been on the road for days! I am tired and getting angrier by the second. One of you tell me what has happened, now!"

"You may as well tell him, Galina. You're off to a good start," Stepan said.

"Rada and the baby are missing. BC is gone as well. It looks like someone climbed on the old ivy near Rada's room, but we don't know if it was her leaving, or the assassin coming in. We've searched high and low but we can't find them. We don't know if the assassin got them."

"But," Stepan said. "Rada was angry that the babe hadn't been named. She suggested going to the Temple of Bethsinidar."

"What!"

Stepan held up his hand. "We said no, of course! But she asked to visit Garzan the other day and I took her. Rada is much like Jadzia was. I fear she hasn't let this go."

"And you are too scared to go and find out." Tikhon shook his head in disgust. "Galina, walk with me, show me Jadzia's resting place. Then I'll deal with the empress."

Galina led him through the villa to the rear gardens and the stand of poplar trees. A colourful hammock hung between the trees.

"I put it there as a surprise for Rada. She was coming out here in the small hours of the morning and sleeping beside her mother. She hasn't seen it yet."

Tikhon nodded, though the granite headstone held his attention. His vision blurred and he sucked in a shuddering breath.

Galina bowed and retreated, leaving him to his grief.

He knelt beside the grave. "You should still be here, my love." His voice thickened with emotion. "I took a chance and I failed you. You were rightfully angry." His voice broke and a sob escaped him. "But I was going to spend years making it up to you..." His voice trailed off and he shrank to the ground, head bowed, shoulders shaking. He sniffed, wiping at face and said, "Bashtan is gone, you'll be pleased at that. And that snake Neeren. Your Darklinan saved the day. You told me they would prove their worth... You were always right." He shook his head. "What am I going to do without you?" Tikhon sat there, staring into space, lost in remembrance. He hung his head, rested his hand upon her name. "I promise you this, on my life, if your daughters live, I will keep them safe."

Tikhon rose and walked to Galina.

"I'm going to ride to Garzan regardless of Stepan," she said angrily.

"I know but let me deal with Sabina first. She had no reason to hurt Rada."

"Rada would have done everything in her power to save her sister. Sabina wouldn't think twice about killing her."

"Just wait. I'll discover what she's done. It won't take me long, then I'll return and tell you. If the girls are alive, then I'm coming with you."

⇒

Tikhon's deep blue imperial robe rippled as he swept into the throne room and the golden serpent embroidered on its back writhed as if alive. Grim faced, he ascended the dais and sat, fingers drumming on the arm of the throne. He hated the performance – the crown, the robes, none of it counted. Might. The power to wrangle factions and command genuine loyalty, *that* mattered. This was merely costuming, staging, and it was something that held weight with Sabina. He knew better. A man could dress the part all he wanted but without grit and the skills of an able commander, even a king was doomed. His father had been, he'd made sure of it. He glared at the empty, smaller throne beside him and felt a tightness in his chest. Jadzia should have been there. She had been his right hand all his life.

Sabina entered, bejewelled and wearing a travesty of a traditional Zaragarian outfit; pants of bright red silk, a fine white high-collared shirt ornately embroidered with the gold falcons of her family crest and a full length flowing red jacket which formed a ridiculous train behind her bearing the Zaragarian serpent.

She put her foot on the dais to join him.

"No."

Guards blocked her path.

"My Emperor?"

"You've disgraced yourself. You sent an assassin after my daughter! A mere babe! A babe with no name because you pressured the temples to refuse Galina's request."

"I—"

"Don't even think to deny it, Sabina! You have always been jealous of Jadzia. Now you take this out on a child for petty revenge!"

"I was thinking only of you, of this family. The girl is an abomination! She will never live up to our standards or make any kind of fighter. Her imperfection brings disgrace to you and the royal family."

"I believe you've forgotten my grandmother, who, despite her difficulties, would've carved you up in an instant," he said. "Where are my girls?"

"Girls? I only sent them for the babe, not the other one."

"Tell me what has befallen them! Now!"

"I don't know!"

He nodded to the guards, who seized her. "I find that hard to believe." Tikhon gripped the arms of his throne and fought for control. His head ached and a sea of red tinged his vision. His words fell like icy razors upon her. "I'm offering you this brief window of opportunity to save yourself from a substantial amount of pain," Tikhon said. "Tell me everything."

Sabina struggled against the guards. "You can't do this! I'm Empress."

Tikhon flew down the steps and grabbed her by the neck. "Speak what you know, now!" he roared.

She quailed, stunned. "Tikhon, I swear. I don't know where they are. I sent two of my guard; only one came back. He said there were too many guards. They never made it onto the estate."

"The second one hasn't returned?" Tikhon demanded.

"No!"

"Sabina, your fate is linked to these girls. If harm has befallen them due to you, you will be beheaded for treason. If they survive, I will dethrone you and appoint Varvara empress in your stead."

Sabina sagged. "She is only second wife!"

"She has not tried to murder members of the royal family! She has never lied to me. She has never sought to hurt me or those I love. *Never!* You never had the qualities it takes to be a truly great empress. You are narcissistic, vain, malicious and spiteful. It should never have been you sitting beside me up there. You are not worthy! And the one woman who was, is gone and you sought to kill our child!" He shook his head. "No! I've decided. You will never sit on this throne again." He sighed and rubbed his eyes, exhaustion and grief a lead mantle upon his shoulders. To the guards he said, "Blindfold her. Take her to the cells, via the hidden ways. She is allowed no visitors. Then kill every last member of her personal guard."

Dressed in the robes of an acolyte, Rada stood beside Akihiro in the Temple of Bethsinidar. Each floor of the building left a central gap of decreasing size, so from the ground a visitor could stare through the structure to the topmost roof.

Rada gazed in rapture at the design. The rich red-brown cedar walls and bannisters twisted in intricate webs that trapped trees and flowers in their carvings. Rada noticed deer, horses, hounds and birds – even men embraced in the carved web. She lost count of the animals depicted and, running to the stairs, saw that the webs from the gables outside flowed in here, interlinking the entire pattern with the staircase and interior beams, carrying it up, connecting it across levels.

"It connects again at the top, doesn't it?" she asked excitedly.

"Yes."

Tentatively she touched the pattern, warmth and a faint vibration meeting her hand. Her jaw dropped and she spun to face the abbot, who laughed. She ran to the middle of the building and stared through the levels. "I feel like it could go on forever."

"Yes, that is the point. It represents Bethsinidar's Great Web. Her tapestry for this world and her hand in all our futures."

Rada spun around. "It's beautiful. I wish... I wish Mami could see this."

"Your Mami witnessed this when she was a child. Her grandmother brought her here for her naming."

"When she was a baby?"

"No, she was older. Old enough to choose to receive a true name from the goddess."

Rada gaped. "Mami did? She never said! But she went to the Temple of Mstislav!"

"I know. You go there too, but you may have a true name here if you choose."

"Me?"

"Rada, how do you feel?" the abbot asked.

"Great!" she said, bouncing on her toes.

"And before you came inside?"

Rada stilled. "Um... tired. I was really tired."

"Do you feel different when you walk into Mstislav's temple?"

"I like to visit Master Pavel, but... I don't feel any different inside me."

"What do you see in his temple?"

Rada frowned. "His statue and... blood."

"And here?"

"Life. I think it's alive."

"Yes, Bethsinidar is life and hope. Think on this. She will offer you a choice."

"I'll meet her?" Rada gulped.

Akihiro didn't answer. He placed the baby on the floor in the centre of the room. The acolytes surrounded them. A follower moved Rada out of the circle, but Akihiro's voice — somehow his and yet higher, more feminine, said, "No, Rada may stay in the circle."

They carried in a large metal drum and set it in line with Bubba's head. An adherent stood opposite the infant's feet, holding a flute. The abbot unwrapped the blankets around the child and removed her clothes. She squirmed, so he sang a lullaby to her as another follower passed him a henna pot and fine brush.

"That's what Mami used to sing."

"Yes, I thought she might like it. It would help if you sang along too," he said. Rada sang with him. One of the followers picked up the tune on his flute and accompanied them. The music slid into Rada's soul, soothing and lulling her like a mother's embrace. The babe stilled, closed her eyes and slept. Rada yawned, and her eyes drooped.

"Just the babe, if you please. Not the girl," the abbot said.

The soft touch of the melody left her, circled around, and flitted away. On its last, long note of farewell, Akihiro started painting and a new tune began with the long, deep, bass beat of the drum interspersed with low notes of the flute – sombre, slow, drawing power from the earth and the rocks. The stone floor beneath Rada's feet grew warm and the hairs on her arms rose. She held her breath as the world around her froze.

Hands materialised on her shoulders. "Breathe, Rada," said Bethsinidar.

Rada turned. "It's you. Really?"

Bethsinidar smiled. "Of course, this is my temple."

Her long black hair billowed and floated as if in the wind.

"You look like the picture at the old temple with the Darklinan." Rada could still hear the music, but it was muted and no one around her moved. "What's happening?"

"You are both safe. Everything is still happening around us, but for a little while I'm going to allow you to observe what I and the others can see. Would you like that?"

"Um... all right."

Bethsinidar kissed her on the forehead and the music swelled through Rada. The abbot had drawn more webs around her sister's face and up over her scalp. The drum beat quickened and the flute notes waltzed throughout the room – gay, bright, spritely. Blue sparks crackled in the air and formed a mist that swayed and gambolled through the building. It swirled around the circle like a mini-tornado, reaching to the towering peaks of the temple where it flowed into the carvings throughout the edifice. Each frenzied beat of the drum and rising carillon of the flute drove it on until every carving glowed blue and the animals seemed to writhe in the web.

The crescendo exploded with one drum boom that reverberated through Rada and quietened on a long, high trill from the flute that faded to the depths of the earth. The drum beat like a slow heart, and the carvings pulsed in sync with it. Rada's hair floated around her head. The abbot stood within the circle of followers, and the goddess knelt by the baby's head. Bethsinidar held out her fingers and the babe, now awake, gripped them. A beatific smile graced the goddess's face, and she placed her hands around the child's skull. The babe waved her hands as if to drag the goddess back to her. Bethsinidar looked at the temple's peak and a glowing blue eye formed on her forehead. The drum beat quickened, a heart racing.

Boom.

The world slowed, suspended between heartbeats.

Bethsinidar lowered her head, bathing the infant in the glow of her blue eye.

Zaklina, a whisper on her breath, gathering strength as it rolled from the mouths of her followers.

"Zaklina Nadezhda," the goddess cried. She whispered a final name into Zaklina's ear – her true name.

The floor under Rada's feet shook. Bethsinidar's glowing eye pulsed and blue mist poured from the timber, swirling around the room, darting between those in the circle, caressing Rada's skin and channelling through the goddess into Zaklina. The pattern the abbot had painted spread, and a glowing blue web crawled across the baby's body, pulsing in time with her heartbeat before vanishing.

"Zaklina's thread is anchored," Bethsinidar said.

The abbot took Rada's hand and drew her toward the goddess. He gathered the babe with great care and placed her where Rada had been standing.

"Sit, Rada," Bethsinidar urged. "You have been through many trials and will face more, of that I am certain. Rada, you are brave and resolute. Do you want my blessing? Do you want a true name?"

"I already have a name. How is a true name different?" Worry creased her brow. "Aren't I already in the great tapestry?"

"You are. Everything born of this world is. Your true name is one only you and I know. It reflects who you are in your spirit and it can shape your thread. The blue mist is The

Flumenàniat, some will come to call it The Wild. It flows like an invisible river through this world and every living thing; some, when they die, become part of it. In the past, people known as Alitariya—"

"Sorcerers!"

"Yes, of a sort. They tried to control it. It is not tame or without... purpose and we seek to maintain balance. In the ceremony here, it will touch you." She pointed a finger at Rada's heart. "Here. It will discover your truth and we will find a true name for you. It will know you."

Rada looked at her sister. "Please..."

"Rada, there is more. Do you swear an oath to me and to protect your sister? You will never be able to speak about any of this."

"I swear. Bethsinidar, I'd like your blessing and a true name."

Bethsinidar picked up the paintbrush. "Remove your shoes." On the inside of Rada's little toe, Bethsinidar painted a tiny web.

"That's not very big. Bubba's—"

"Zaklina's," Bethsinidar said, "serves another purpose. Yours must be hidden. There, done."

Bethsinidar took her hands and the drum began a beat that thrummed in Rada's chest. The goddess entered her mind and the drum altered, matching her heartbeat. Her journey unravelled from the safe recesses of her mind and replayed itself. The sound capered through the air as the flute evoked a tune that spoke of love, joy, and she saw her mother. The blue mist of the Flumenàniat crept into the room, circling the baby and reaching out tentatively to Rada, like a wild colt. It wrapped around her hands and ran along her arms. The steady heartbeat of the drum filled her and anchored her as the music became laced with foreboding and they rode through the forest; Tav was there and her uncle. The mist grew, taking on shapes of her memories. The melody soared to giddy heights and dived on a plaintive trill, shifting to a bittersweet refrain full of pain and grief that brought tears to her eyes. She tried to pull her hands away, but Bethsinidar held her in a vice like grip. The goddess's eyes were obsidian and rainbow lightning danced across them; before being mirrored in her followers. Rada looked at her sister lying on the floor. Love and fear for Zaklina overwhelmed her. She let out a soul deep sob that the music cradled.

The mist raced into the building, every particle caressing both the girls, before launching into the temple carvings. Rada watched it throbbing in time with the drum.

The beat slowed.

Her heart slowed.

Her eyes drooped.

The drum stopped.

She hung poised between one life and the next.

The Flumenàniat raced from the carvings into Bethsinidar, then through Rada before dissipating. Pain stabbed her mind and her toe burned.

"I see you, Rada Lujza, known to me as Erisna. I give you this gift – you and your sister are bound together. Come what may – you will always know each other."

CHAPTER 42

TIKHON RODE ALONGSIDE GALINA as they reached the riverside wharfs; a small contingent of imperial guards followed, including Akim, Regansh and Adana.

The wharf was bustling, a backlog of barges sat waiting to return upriver and a crowd had gathered around one warehouse.

"No! Please, no," Galina whispered. "They've found her?"

"You don't know that," Tikhon snapped.

They drew their horses in at the edge of the crowd.

"What's happened?" Galina asked.

"A body. The first barge back upriver found a body on the trail. They've brought her back," a bystander said.

"Her?" Galina gasped.

Tikhon pushed his horse into the crowd.

"Make way for the emperor!" Akim commanded. Shocked faces turned towards them as the crowd parted. The guards flanked Tikhon and Galina as they pressed forward. At the warehouse doors, Tikhon leapt from his mount and strode inside. Galina ran to catch up.

On a table in the centre of the room lay a body covered with a blanket. They froze at the sight. The warehouse foreman rushed to Tikhon, bowing.

"Your Imperial Majesty! Such an honour!"

Tikhon, rigid, fixated on the body and ignored him. A guard blocked the foreman from approaching further and shook his head when the man attempted to speak. Tikhon stared at the shape. *It's thin enough to be a child, but... It's too long. Too tall.* The unfamiliar knot of fear inside him unravelled a little. Galina clenched her jaw and took Tikhon's hand.

He gave her shaking hand a squeeze, and turned to her with a relieved smile. "Galina, it's not her. It's too big."

"What?" she asked shakily. She blinked, shook her head. "Not her!" Her jaw dropped. "You're right! How can it be?" A sharp, near hysterical laugh escaped her.

Together, they moved to the corpse. He drew back the blanket and revealed the crushed skull and broken body of a black-clad adult.

"Well, there's the assassin."

"What did this?" Galina said, horrified. "Are any bones left whole?"

Tikhon grimaced. "It doesn't look like it. As to what did it, my guess is the old war horse I gave her. She called him BC for a reason." To the foreman, Tikhon said, "Was anything else found?"

"No, Your Majesty. The boat returned with only this one, but I know they searched the immediate area and found no others."

"I want someone from the boat to show us where the body was found."

"Your Majesty, you'll not miss the place. The ground is covered in blood and bone," the foreman said.

"Akim, Regansh, ride the river trail. Find the spot, search thoroughly, and wait for us." The two left at a jog and the sound of departing hoof beats rang in Tikhon's ears like a knell.

"Foreman, I want that body wrapped and bound tightly. We will collect it on the way back and return it to its mistress." Tikhon placed an arm around Galina. "There's still hope," he said. "We'll comb the area."

"They may be injured or... dying," she said, shuddering.

"Then we'd best get moving." Tikhon marched to his horse and mounted. He willed himself to calm while Galina mounted. Never in all his years had he felt as helpless as he did now. It was too late to do much. They'd had to fight their battle alone, and all he could do was mop up and care for what remained. If they'd survived.

They cantered a long stretch before slowing at the sight of Akim waiting. The soft ground near the river was churned up except for where the body had been crushed. There, the soil lay flatted, depressed and filled with thick, congealed blood and bone fragments.

Galina started to swing off her horse. "No, Galina, let the troops look. Several of them are trackers. They will be better able to discern events than us."

Pale, face creased with worry, Galina nodded.

Twin demons of grief and guilt taunted Tikhon as he watched the guards. He needed to move, to do anything other than think. His hands clenched and unclenched and a vein throbbed at his temple. He burned with the need to scream at them to work more quickly.

"What will you do with the body?" Galina asked. "I would have left it in the woods as carrion."

"I fear my empress will be lonely in her cell, so she shall have the company of her faithful servant."

Galina blanched. "That's... creative."

"And well deserved,"

His troops returned. Tikhon's breath hitched. "My Emperor, we've found where someone hid in the bushes and up ahead near a log there are many hoofprints. Beyond that, one horse's tracks are visible. There was no blood evident."

Tikhon let out a disbelieving chuckle and turned to Galina with a grin. "They survived. My little lioness has done it."

Galina smiled half-heartedly. "They may still be injured."

"Have faith, Galina. Remember, Mstislav loves the brave and Rada is certainly that."

He spurred his horse onward, leaving them to catch up.

Bethsinidar, stood in her temple, smiling sadly as she watched Rada's boat depart. The Flumenàniat flowed around her.

I know. She held out her hand and the The Wild caressed it. *I feel the weight of their names – Zaklina Nadezhda. Zaklina – one who supplants, Nadezhda – hope.*

And Jadzia, my lost one, she chose well. Rada – filled with care, Lujza – a warrior. Already the child's names have borne fruit.

You chose their true names well – Alafia – child of peace; Erisna – child of strife.

The Flumenàniat glowed brighter.

Yet both have only just begun their journeys. These threads will take decades to play out.

If they work together, then the order of this world will be restored.

➤——————➤

Rada rocked on her seat as the boat hit the sand. Garzan, a dot in the distance, lay to the east. Masaru jumped out of the boat and lifted Rada down onto the beach. Another sailor passed him Zaklina.

"You have a bit of a walk, but we couldn't drop you closer. It's best if they don't see you with us," he said, placing Zaklina in the carrier strapped to Rada's chest.

"I know. It's fine. I can see the village, so I won't get lost."

"Remember," Masaru said, bending down to look her in the eyes. "Remember about the flask of milk in your pack for the baby and there's food in there for you too."

She wrapped her arms around his neck. "I *know.* Thank you. I wouldn't have made it across the water if it wasn't for all of you." She waved and made her way along the beach. "Come on, Zaki! It's so good! Zaki! Zaki! Zaki! It's a great name! The best! Let's find BC and tell him." She swung her arms and sang a bright tune as she marched. "You know, Zaki, we might not get into as much trouble as I thought because... well... she looked down at herself... at least our old clothes are clean again. So that's one less thing to yell at us, isn't it?"

By the time she found BC, her arms were no longer swinging and the tune had lost all of its jauntiness. BC stood where she'd left him, grazing the coarse dune grass.

"You're getting fat, BC," she said. "Bubba got a name. Want to hear it?" He kept eating grass. "It's Zaklina! But we're just going to call her Zaki, right?" The horse twisted his neck and snorted at her. She wiped spittle from her face. "Fine!"

Rada walked to where she'd left his gear and returned with his bridle. "Keep your head down." Between his bites at the grass, she tried to slide the bit into his mouth, but her bandaged hands were clumsy. "Just a bit more... nearly..." BC threw his head up and spun, shoving her sideways and letting out an ear-splitting whinny. She fell onto her backside and slid down the face of the dune.

"Rada!" Galina called, her face shifting from relief to fury in a heartbeat.

Rada stood, grinning. "Granny! Uncle!" Seeing Akim and the others, she exclaimed, "You're all here!" Granite faced silence greeted her.

Rada bit her lip. She looked down at her dirty clothes. "Zaki, we're not even clean now." She smiled sweetly at them and gave a small wave. None returned it. "We're in way more trouble than I thought."

Galina ran to her and embraced her. Tears filled Tikhon's eyes. His chest felt like it might burst and a great weight lifted from his shoulders. He wanted to hold her, scold her, praise her all at once, yet the sight of them alive and well overwhelmed him.

"Are you all right? Are either of you hurt?" Galina said.

"No."

"Good!" Galina smacked her hard on the bottom. "Don't you ever run away again! Do you hear me? We've been frantic!"

Rada's bottom lip trembled. "Bubba needed a name! And you wouldn't do it. And Grandpa was going to let her die. I heard him!"

"What?" Tikhon said, his voice strained. He knelt before Rada. He gave her a crooked smile. "Hello, my lioness." He sat in the sand and pulled Rada onto his lap and embraced both the girls. "We thought the assassin had got you both."

"No! BC got her and squashed her! A lot!"

He chuckled. "We saw that. He did a very good job."

"Uncle, the empress sent her to kill Zaki."

"Zaki?"

"Yes, Bubba has a name now. Zaklina! Zaklina Nadezhda."

Galina sat beside them and stared at the trio. "Nadezhda. Nadya," she said, bemused.

"Yep. Like Mami wanted, just not as first name, because really it's an awful first name."

"I understand," Tikhon said, his eyes flicking to Galina. "But, Rada, I think you need to tell me everything that's happened since you've been with your grandparents."

Rada drew a deep breath and began her story. Her voice rose and fell with excitement and fear, and she waved her hands about as she spun her tale. While she talked about rowing across the ocean, Tikhon turned over her bandaged hands and inspected them. He kissed her forehead.

She began to talk about the island, but Tikhon said, "Enough. It's enough that we know she has been named."

Rada bit her lip, eyes darting between him and her now pale grandmother. "So, Grandpa was going to let the assassin do what she wanted. I had to do something."

"I see that, but if you'd waited, I would have been here and I could have made another temple name her, no matter what the empress wanted."

"I didn't know," she said, downcast. He shifted Rada to his side and removed Zaklina from the baby carrier. He laid her along his legs and unwrapped her.

"Rada, what have they done to her leg?" he asked, his brow furrowed.

"They splinted it and bound it up. Akihiro said it would help make it better, but it would take a long time. She screamed a lot at first, but they gave her a special drink to make her sleepy.

That's why she's so quiet. They said it wouldn't hurt so much after a little while and she's got to wear it almost all the time."

"It will help?" Tikhon asked, dubious.

"That's what he said."

"All right," he said, sighing. "I require an oath from all here that none of you will ever reveal what you have just heard."

His guards knelt and held their swords before them. "You have our pledge of silence."

"Rada, you must never talk about this to anyone else. Do you swear this?"

She knelt and held out her dagger, mimicking the guards. "I swear it!"

"Good girl."

She grinned at him. "Am I still in trouble?"

"Yes."

"Will I get another smack?"

"No, I think you've had enough of that in your life." Beside him, Galina stiffened. "But you will be punished. I'll think of something, perhaps cleaning out the imperial stables for a week."

Rada brightened. "That doesn't sound too bad."

"There's over one hundred horses."

Her jaw dropped and she slumped, collapsing on the ground. "No!" she cried to the sky, raising her fist melodramatically.

Tikhon rolled his eyes. "Now go with Akim and catch BC. I'll look after Zaki. Akim, take everyone back to the village and stable all the horses. The day is nearly done and we'll stay here tonight." They departed. "Galina, stay a while. I would speak with you."

Ashen faced and haggard, Galina said, "I'd no idea Stepan would do that. That he'd betray family like that."

Tikhon weighed her words. "I believe you, but Zaki is my daughter. I will formerly acknowledge her and she will live in the palace."

"But Sabina?"

"Sabina will never leave her cell. Varvara will be empress. She has a kind heart; she'll treat Zaki well."

Galina nodded, slowly. "That is your right as her father, but Rada will miss her."

Tikhon drew a long breath. "No. No, she will not. Rada will come with me. I plan to adopt her."

"You can't!" Galina cried. "This is too much, My Emperor, please!"

"Rada will be raised and educated with my boys. She will have the type of education I know Jadzia wanted."

"We can give that to her."

"You could, but I don't think Stepan deserves to have that privilege. You will still see her as often as she wants," he said. "But should any rumours circulate about today, she will be far more protected with me as my daughter. I've always loved her as if she was mine."

Galina wept.

"There's more, Galina. You have been unfailingly honest with me over the years. You are not afraid to stand and say what needs to be said. I want you to be on my advisory council. Will you accept?"

"After this? How could you want me after this?"

"Because you were going to defy Stepan, and I witnessed the horror on your face at what he would have allowed to happen. And for decades of other reasons. Will you accept?" he asked.

"Yes, of course."

"Understand, this is not a token gesture because of Rada. I have much work for you."

"Yes, My Emperor."

"It's getting dark and chilly. We should return to the inn." He wrapped Zaki up and passed her to Galina. "Here, enjoy our little Zaki. If she's anything like her sister, then our peaceful days will be few." He rose and helped her up.

"Thank you, My—"

"Just call me Tikhon when we are alone."

She gave a small bow. "Tikhon, I think I've aged years in this last day."

"You're not the only one."

By the time they reached the inn, darkness veiled the land. The quarter moon lay hidden behind thick banks of cloud.

Rada ran out to of the stables to greet them, followed by Akim. "BC is all on his own again. He can be such a grump! Oh! And the innkeeper's wife is baking apple cakes!"

"Stilnassa Galina, My Emperor, there are only two rooms spare."

"Rest, Akim. I'm sure Rada can show us where they are. Is there enough room for you all in the stables?

"Yes, there and the building on the docks," Akim said.

Tikhon and Galina followed Rada into the inn. It was crowded with people, all of whom rose and bowed. "This must be the entire population of the village," Tikhon said to the innkeeper.

"Yes, Your Majesty. It's not often the emperor visits."

Tikhon smiled. The bags under his eyes showed his exhaustion. "I'm pleased to be in Garzan with Stilnassa Maklova," he said to the crowd. "I'd like to buy everyone a round of drinks!" Cheers rose. "And I will double each of your daily profits if you will leave the inn after that, so my men can bunk down. It's been a long, tiring day and they have served me well these few weeks. We are all exhausted. We've crushed a Talak rebellion and raced here to find our wayward girls!" The cheering grew louder.

"Your Majesty, I'll show you the rooms." The innkeeper's wife directed them upstairs. "May I ask what brings you to Garzan?"

Tikhon laughed. "You may. Young Rada, here, took it upon herself to save her sister from an assassin and fled all the way here on her horse, vanquishing the killer on the way. Her grandmother and I came looking for her." The woman looked amazed and confused. "You see," Tikhon said, a hint of pride in his voice. "Rada's sister is my daughter." He took Zaki from Galina and showed her to the woman.

"Oh!" Her eyes moistened with tears. "Oh my, Stilnassa Jadzia was your mother? Is their mother? Bless you, child," she said to Rada. "The two of you alone? With an assassin after you? It's a miracle you survived." She opened the doors to the rooms, which sat side by side. "I'll bring you up food and drink and I'll tell your men they can sleep downstairs. Rest."

She left them.

"Plausible?" Tikhon asked.

"Very," Galina said.

"Good. We need no wild rumours flying about. They might hit upon the truth."

Rada woke with a scream in the middle of the night. Galina grabbed her shoulders. "Rada?"

Akim thrust open the door to their room as Galina struggled with Rada. The child fought and scratched.

"Ow!" Galina let her go.

Akim wrapped his arms around the girl. "Rada!"

Tikhon ran in, bleary-eyed and clothes askew. "What is it?"

"Nightmares, ever since the battle with Rodan, but usually she wakes immediately."

Rada stilled and burst into tears. Akim let her go and she launched into Tikhon's arms. "Shh. We're all here. You're safe."

The clouds had cleared during the night and Akim opened the timber shutters, letting in moonlight before lighting a lamp.

Zaki wailed in her makeshift crib and Galina went over to her. She reached out to pick her granddaughter up and froze. In the waning moonlight, the baby's skin was alive with tattoos. Nausea rolled through her. "Tikhon," she whispered, horror filled, pleading.

He carried Rada to her and all three stared at the babe. "The pictures. They painted them on her for her naming."

"Gods damn them all to ebatov! May they burn there for eternity. I will end them for this," Tikhon said.

He put Rada down and picked up his wailing daughter. "Shh, little one, all is well. Shh." The moment he stepped out of the moonlight, the patterns faded and Zaki's skin was unblemished.

Galina sank down upon the edge of the bed.

The innkeeper's wife scuttled down the hall to their room and said, "Can I help? Is there anything you need, Your Majesty?"

Tikhon looked at Galina, his eyes desperate.

"No, it's fine," Galina said quickly. "Rada had a nightmare and woke the baby." She rose and felt Zaki's brow. "Though some willow bark tea might be good, I think the babe may have a slight fever."

"Well, I'm not surprised on either count with all those poor lambs have been through. I'll make some and bring it right back up."

"Fever?" Tikhon hissed at her.

"You know the truth," Galina said through tears. "We cannot hide this. This will get her killed and Rada with her."

Rada stood between her grandmother and Tikhon. "Wait, what? What's happening?"

Tikhon sat on the bed and drew her beside him. "Those pictures mark her as a follower of Bethsinidar, but not just any follower. They have marked her to be a high priestess. Anytime the moon is out, they will be visible."

"On the full moon, I've heard that they will glow," Galina said miserably. "Everyone will find out eventually and they'll know Rada brought her to them."

Rada shook. "But I just wanted a name for her!"

"Shh! Keep your voice down," Tikhon whispered.

The heavy footsteps of the innkeeper's wife sounded coming up the stairs. "Here it is, Stilnassa. The spoon's there so you can ladle it into her a bit at a time."

"My thanks." Galina took it from her and ushered her out. "You've had a long day too. We'll be fine now." She closed the door.

"I only wanted a name. They never said this would happen. I'm sorry! I wanted to fix everything and I messed it all up," Rada said, panicked.

Galina sat with them. "We have to protect you both."

Tikhon rocked his daughter, his finger held in her hands. "You beautiful, beautiful girl. They have stolen your future." He walked to the shutters, opened them and stood gazing at the artwork on Zaki's body. He undid her little wrap around jacket and stared, shaking his head, as the intricate web pattern laced around her entire frame. "Galina?" he asked.

She shook her head. "I cannot bear to see it. They've desecrated her body. They have robbed us."

Rada walked to him. "Let me look, please?" She gazed in wonder at the patterns. "It's pretty."

"Yes, I suppose it is, Rada," Tikhon whispered. "But you never say that again. Keep such thoughts in your heart."

A shape stepped out of the shadow of the stable. "Uncle, look. That's Masaru. He found me and brought us back."

Tikhon narrowed his eyes. He clenched his jaw, and he wrapped Zaki's back up in her blankets. He tried to hand her Galina.

"No! I cannot," she said, turning from Zaki.

"Granny! You love Zaki. I know you do!"

"That is no longer your sister. She is an instrument of a manipulative goddess. Mstislav, save us."

Tikhon scowled at Galina and put Zaki in her bed. "Keep watch over Zaki, Rada."

He gathered his sword and left the room; Akim followed him. "Only you, Akim; no others."

They walked stealthily down the stairs. Adana stirred, but Akim said, "Stay put. Nothing is wrong. Just a restless night." Outside, the guards on duty moved to follow them and Akim shook his head. "We'll not be far, just near the stables. The emperor needs to clear his head."

Tikhon barely noticed his surroundings. His thoughts whirled and his heart pounded as he neared the stable. Akim caught his arm and Tikhon shrugged him off. "Think, My Emperor! Don't plunge into the dark. You've not even drawn your sword."

"Greetings, Emperor of the Zaragarians, I have no wish to fight you," Masaru said, stepping out of the shadows, yet out of sight of the inn.

Tikhon charged.

Masaru pivoted and used Tikhon's momentum against him, flinging him over his shoulder and onto the ground. Akim lunged forward, sword drawn. Masaru darted back, hands raised. "I only defended myself. I am here to talk," Masaru said.

"Wait, Akim," Tikhon said, getting up. "You slippery, evikan bastard."

Masaru inclined his head. "Sadly, you are not the first to say that."

"You have some nerve to show yourself! How dare you do this to *my* daughter! Why are you here?"

"You know why."

"You cannot have her," Tikhon said. "I would rather she were..."

"What? Dead? I don't believe that. You are furious because you love her – love them. We never turn someone away who seeks our goddess's help. Rada came to us and asked for her sister to be named."

"Semantics! You lot plot and plan and twist. I'll bet the spider's been sitting on this for quite a while," Tikhon spat.

"I have no answer for that, other than to say, the outcome of the ritual is never certain."

"If that was the case, you wouldn't be here waiting in the shadows."

Masaru shrugged. "I was told to follow you, watch and wait. That could have been a day or a year, but when I saw you at the window, I realised her markings cannot be hidden. I understand your pain. I've lost children of my own, but she will be well cared for and taken somewhere very safe. Can you say that if she stays with you?"

Tikhon paced, his hands clenching as he walked. He cast venomous glances at Masaru, and his shoulders shook. Rage burned white hot within him. There was no scenario for success. *If she stays with me, she will die as certainly as I stand here.*

He stepped out of the shadows and looked back at the inn to see Rada at the window, her sister in her arms; his heart ached. *Even in this light, I can see a faint glow.*

"I'll never see her again, will I?"

"I do not know."

Tikhon snorted in disbelief and stalked back to the inn. Once upstairs, he leaned his head against the door to their room and drew a shuddering breath. He looked at Akim. "I have no evikan choice."

Akim, sombre, shook his head.

They entered the room.

"What happened, Uncle?" Rada asked.

Tikhon took Zaki from her. "He wants to take her, Rada."

"No! They tricked me!"

"Yes. I don't like it one little bit. I want you both with me, but these markings... I can't keep her safe. I hate them, but they will keep her far safer than she will be in Vēkaria. It's not much, Rada, but it's a chance."

Rada wept. "Granny." Galina lay curled on the bed, staring at the wall. Rada shook her. "Granny, please."

Galina rolled toward her, face tear streaked, sat up and embraced her. "I know, my sweet. I know." She looked at Tikhon. "How will you explain the baby's absence?"

"You set that up yourself," Tikhon said bitterly. "Fever, wasn't that what you had planned?"

She looked away.

"Rada, do you want to come with me?" Tikhon asked.

"Yes." She let go of Galina and took his hand.

"Pray little Zaki stays quiet," he said, covering the baby's face and walking solemnly out.

"Stay put," Akim said to the now awake squad downstairs. The sight of the grief-stricken emperor and Rada crying quietly, stunned them and they bowed their heads. The procession passed by the outer guards and headed toward the woods that lay a short distance from Garzan.

Please, by all the gods, stay quiet, little one. Just stay quiet. Or this will never work.

He could hear Rada murmuring prayers. "Good girl, Rada, it's working."

They waited deep in the tree line.

Rada stood beside Tikhon. "Will he find us?" Rada asked, fidgeting with something in her pocket.

"I'm sure he will," Akim said.

Rada's breath misted in the cool air and she wrapped her arms about herself. "Zaki will freeze before he gets here."

"No, she won't," Masaru said from off to their right.

Rada whirled and shot a pellet toward the sound of his voice. It clanked against a trunk. "I hate you! You tricked me and you lied." She loaded another pellet. Tikhon and Akim did nothing.

"We never lied to you." She loosed another pellet. Missed. "We did as you asked." Rada fired again. Missed.

"Evika!" she said. "I'm out."

"Thank goodness," Masaru said from right behind her. "I nearly ran into a tree dodging them."

Rada drew her dagger.

"Enough, Rada," Tikhon said. Akim took the blade from her.

"This is not fair!"

"No, it's not." Tikhon knelt beside her and drew her closer. "Let's say goodbye and give your sister a kiss."

Rada refused to look at him, but she put her forehead against Zaki's. "I will always love you, Zaki. Always." She kissed her cheek and stood beside Akim, clutching his hand.

Tikhon rose, drawing Zaki to his face. He kissed her forehead and ran a finger along her downy cheek. "You're not taking her to the island, are you?"

Masaru held out his arms for the baby.

Tikhon rocked her, making no move to hand her over. "You'll have to answer me if you want her."

"She is not going to the island."

Tikhon passed his daughter to Masaru; his shaking hand lingered on her small blanket. "We will say that she died of fever during the night," Tikhon said, bluntly. "And that we have buried her here in the woods."

They watched Masaru's retreating form until it merged into the shadows and vanished. Tikhon sank to his knees and doubled over weeping. His hands dug into the earth and he roared in pain and frustration. His fist pounded the ground and Rada jumped back. Shocked, trembling, she choked back her sobs, tightened her grip on Akim's hand and leaned against his leg, staring at her brave uncle undone by sorrow. Tikhon punched the ground one last time and rose, sniffing and wiping his eyes.

He turned his desolate eyes to Rada and his face crumpled. He held out his hand. She shrank back. "It's all right. I'm not angry. Just sad, like you. I'm sorry, sweet one. I didn't mean to scare you."

"It's all right," she whispered, her voice thick.

He smiled faintly and shook his head. "It's all an evikan big mess, isn't it?"

She nodded and ran into his arms. "We needed BC," she said between sobs. "He could have smashed him to bits and then we could have ridden off and hid somewhere nice with Zaki."

"*That* would have been perfect. I think you can plan all my battles." Shuddering, she punched him on the shoulder, once, twice then rained blows upon him. He held her, saying only, "Shh, shh" until she ceased and buried her head against his chest.

By the time they reached the inn, Rada was asleep.

"Akim, we're going to come back here and burn that damn temple to the ground with all of them in it."

COMING SOON

Welcome back to the world of Altaica.

War between the clans rages across Altaica. Pio along with his mother, Lucia, and best friend, Kiriz, travel the Bear's Teeth mountain range with an Asena escort to reach a safe haven.

Pio is a boy who can't seem to stay out of trouble and soon he discovers that, even with the Asena, they are not safe.

Foretold to be the next bard kenati, the first in generations, he is untrained and unaware of his full capabilities. Yet if Pio has any hope of saving those he loves, he must attempt his magic and grapple with the Wild—a powerful presence that thrives in Altaica.

Armed only with his flute, he must bend the Wild to his will to prevent tragedy.

MORE FROM
TRACY M. JOYCE

PRAISE FOR THE SERIES

"Dang it's good...This is one of those times. This is a series that will keep you wanting more." Jelilat, Goodreads

"Altaica left me speechless. It is a brilliant YA epic fantasy, definitely among the best I've read." Victoria, Goodreads

"Badass from start to finish." Jenna, Goodreads.

"What can I say about Asena Blessed? Altaica (the first book in the series) was a great read, but Asena Blessed is a triumph." Brendan, Goodreads

"After reading Asena Blessed, I realize that Altaica is just a tease, the tip of the iceberg... I read it in one sitting and I felt like I lost a friend once I finished Asena." Arec, Goodreads

ABOUT THE AUTHOR

Tracy M Joyce is an Australian author of speculative fiction.

Tracy writes epic fantasy for teens through to adults. Her stories are gritty, a little dark and morality is like quicksand. You won't find any unicorns or fairies here...

Although her stories include romantic elements, they are not romance driven novels. Do not buy these books if you're after a fairytale....

Consider this a warning: Expect kickass heroines, battles (big ones, small ones – let's face it, if she'd put gunpowder in this world then there'd be explosions too!), gore, political scheming, horses, archery and a touch of magic, but NO fairies, elves, pixies, orcs and definitely NO unicorns. (Unless, of course, its a combat trained unicorn with stealth capabilities .... then...maybe...)

www.tracymjoyce.com

www.ingramcontent.com/pod-product-compliance
Lightning Source LLC
Chambersburg PA
CBHW031927110726
47902CB00001B/71